SELF RESCUE

OTHER BOOKS IN THE
DANIEL BYRD ADVENTURE SERIES

MOUNTAIN JUSTICE

A LITTLE BIT KIN

A DANIEL BYRD ADVENTURE

SELF RESCUE

PHILLIP W. PRICE

LANIER
PRESS

LANIER PRESS *a Division of BookLogix*

Alpharetta, Georgia

ISBN: 978-1-6653-0648-5 - Paperback
eISBN: 978-1-6653-0649-2 - eBook

Library of Congress Control Number: 2023917327

⊛This paper meets the requirements of ANSI/NISO Z39.48-1992 (Permanence of Paper)

0 9 2 2 2 3

AUTHOR'S NOTE

I was employed by the Georgia Bureau of Investigation for thirty years. About half of that time involved investigations of the drug trade.

In my career, there were no pirates, but those who thought they were smuggled drugs into the US from South America. I was heavily involved in the interdiction of airplanes and boats loaded with marijuana and then later, cocaine. This tale comes from some of those adventures, but is consistent with the drug business as it existed in the early 2000s.

I want to give a big "thanks" to a small group of smugglers from central Florida who tried their best to shoot me—and failed. For someone who has always been a poor shot, I won that gunfight.

No law enforcement officer enacted a single law against a single drug or substance. But each of them was tasked with the insurmountable job of holding the line the politicians drew in the sand. This book is dedicated to the small band of drug warriors who tried to stem the tide.

The characters in this novel are composites of individuals whom I have known and worked with throughout my career and beyond. All the individuals who inhabit this work, both the good guys and the bad, are taken from a variety of people, locales, and life events.

PROLOGUE

MAY 26, 2023
DAWSONVILLE, GEORGIA

Daniel Byrd climbed out of his Tahoe and looked at the front door of the funeral home. He dreaded going in and yet he looked forward to seeing so many familiar faces. He checked that his tie was centered, shoes shined, and cuffs were the proper length. He held his head high and strode across the parking lot.

Byrd recognized "Chargin' Charlie" Jenkins, a retired troop captain for the Georgia State Patrol, and Deputy Director Will Carver, of the Georgia Bureau of Investigation, talking in low tones.

Both men stopped and smiled as they saw Byrd walking over. Byrd shook hands with both men. "Good to see you two," Byrd said.

Jenkins nodded. "Sorry to see you under these circumstances."

Byrd nodded. "He had a good run. He was in his nineties."

"He's not in pain anymore," Jenkins offered.

Carver gave Byrd a hug. "I know you two got close after the airplane deal you worked."

Byrd hung his head. "Yep. He was a good man. We would get together occasionally for a cup of coffee, and he'd tell me about the good ol' days."

When he went inside, he had to stand still and let his

eyes adjust. He hated those vulnerable few moments. Once his vision returned, he saw Scott Andrews talking to Tina Blackwell. The two were both Inspectors with the GBI, the agency where Byrd was employed.

Both gave him a hug and a pat on the back. Blackwell leaned toward him. "How are you making it, big guy? You haven't been down to headquarters lately."

"Keeping my head down," Byrd said.

Blackwell sighed. "Don't be a stranger. We still love you at headquarters."

Byrd nodded then wound his way through the crowd of friends. He waved at Jill Leonard and Mario Ortega, old coworkers from his drug enforcement days.

His friend's youngest brother, Ralph, looked mournful and lonely sitting at the foot of the polished wooden box. Byrd went to him, bent down, and whispered, "Sorry for your loss," into the man's ear.

Ralph was hoarse when he replied, "He would have liked that casket you helped me pick out. He would be proud."

Byrd smiled. "He would love all these folks getting together, that's for sure." Byrd sat down beside the brother. The two men were similar in size and build. "How are you doing, Ralph?"

Ralph chuckled. "Hanging in there. I'm the last one left of a family of seven sisters and two brothers."

Byrd nodded. "It all goes pretty fast, doesn't it?"

The man nodded. "The blink of an eye."

Byrd looked around the room and wondered about his life. How would he be remembered?

"He thought you were a damned good agent. Said you'd come by to check on him. His family sure does appreciate you," Ralph said.

Byrd nodded. "I know."

Ralph leaned closer. "He didn't say much good about his job. He seemed to think secrets were best kept close. He spoke highly of you, though."

Byrd suddenly felt very old. "Thanks for telling me that."

Ralph nodded. "I guess that was part of your job, huh?"

Byrd nodded. "In some ways, keeping secrets was the easy part."

"At least you were both part of the good guys," Ralph remarked.

Byrd stood and rubbed his face for a moment. "Good and bad are relative terms. There's a Latin term, *malum in se*—an offense that's wrong from its own nature. Irrespective of any laws."

"Like murder?" Ralph asked.

"Yep," Byrd said. "Then there's *malum prohibitum*. That's an offense prohibited by statute but not inherently wrong. Drug charges fall into that category."

Ralph smiled. "The drug laws keep changing. I guess that makes it tough."

Byrd looked away. "Sometimes you do things the law prohibits, but it's the right thing to do. I'd say I fought evil, even if sometimes I might have bent the law."

Ralph shook his head. "He was never bitter about getting shot. But he always seemed to miss the job. You'll sure get into some wooly situations."

Byrd looked thoughtful. "Back when I started as a state lawman, they told us to look in the mirror every morning before we went on duty."

Ralph nodded. "The State boys always look sharp. That's for sure. I see all these troopers here, looking big and tough."

Byrd smiled good-naturedly. "Well, that's not why

they wanted us to look. They told us when we looked in the mirror, there was a good chance we'd be looking at the only backup we'd have that day."

Ralph looked Byrd over. "I never thought about that. I guess you were on your own a lot."

Byrd glanced away for a moment. "You learn to handle business. You learn if you dig a hole, you better be prepared to pull yourself out of it."

"You boys did what you had to do," Ralph said as he stood and headed for the restroom.

Byrd spoke to his back. "I did, and then some."

Byrd thought back to the first time he crossed the line. Back to 2004. It seemed like only yesterday.

PART 1
SMUGGLER'S BLUES

CHAPTER 1
EVERYBODY HAS A ROUTINE

FRIDAY, NOVEMBER 12, 2004
11:45 A.M.
FORSYTH, GEORGIA

Georgia Bureau of Investigation Special Agent Daniel Byrd looked behind him. He was doing his best to control his breathing. He was decked out in tactical clothing and a heavy vest. The vest had panels on the front and rear proclaiming "GBI" in bright gold letters. The helmet he wore was heavy and restricted his peripheral vision. Byrd assumed the State had bought the helmet and vest from the lowest bidder and wondered if they would stop anything.

At six feet, two inches tall, and around two hundred pounds, Byrd knew he would make a big target. He brushed his brown hair back and took the measure of the door in front of him. He was happy that, for November, the weather was pleasant.

The other GBI agents were lined up, everyone dressed in tactical armor and ballistic helmets as well. There were four more agents in all—a couple Byrd knew and a couple he did not. They had exchanged pleasantries at the briefing, but Byrd wasn't comfortable with how much experience he would have behind him when they entered the house.

The briefing had been short and to the point: A murder suspect was located in the house. The most current intelligence was that the suspect was alone, but he was armed. Because of houses in the immediate vicinity, agents were to only carry handguns. Byrd preferred his riot shotgun when going into a dark house. The sun had come up behind him, but he knew it wouldn't penetrate the covered windows. He had hung a small flashlight from a lanyard, now bouncing off his chest, for that reason.

Byrd had his issued Glock extended as he crept toward the front door of the little house. Byrd took a deep breath and stepped up on the concrete steps leading to the wooden door. He pounded the door with his left hand and shouted, "State Police with a warrant! Come to the door, NOW!"

Byrd listened intently but heard no sound from inside the house. He stepped back, nodded at the agent behind him, and kicked the door open. The wood was old and flimsy and gave with the first try.

When the door crashed open, Byrd clicked his flashlight on with his left hand and checked the living room, then he turned off the light and stepped into the house. He found a wall and let the other agents funnel in.

The five agents stood in the living room and evaluated the situation. Without speaking, Byrd, as the team leader, motioned for three of the agents to follow him down the main hall leading to the bedrooms. In the briefing, Byrd had designated an agent to wait in the main room and cover their backs. At least the floorplan he had seen in the briefing was accurate, so far.

Byrd put his foot down carefully, aware of every small sound they were making. With his back close to the wall, Byrd moved forward, keeping his pistol trained down the hall, or "fatal funnel." As Byrd looked down the dark hall for signs of their target, he understood the meaning of the term. If anyone popped out of one of the rooms in the hall, he and the team would have limited options.

He was less than a yard into the hall when the man stepped out and fired. The first shot hit Byrd in the chest, dead center in the tactical vest, and the second hit his right hand. His hand stung with pain, but he fought it off to fire back. He fired four shots at the retreating shadow as the team moved back.

Byrd heard movement ahead and dove to the floor, arms extended in front of him. The target stuck his head around the corner and Byrd pulled the trigger. He saw the first shot hit the man in the face, and the second hit the man in the neck.

The target grabbed his neck and shouted, "Fuck! That hurts."

The lights came on in the room and Byrd got to his feet. "Sorry, I was trying to hit you in the face both times."

The "bad guy's" face mask was marked with a red streak and his neck was blotched where the training round had hit. He tossed the mask on the floor.

A man in the red shirt and red hat of a firearms instructor stepped into the room. "Damn it, Byrd. We train to shoot center of mass. What the hell is wrong with you?"

Byrd pushed up from the floor and dropped the magazine from his gun. He caught it with his left hand and then ejected the live round. "I acted on instinct. And I hit the target, didn't I?"

Lamont "Monty" Davis was having none of it. "That's not how we train. We train to put two in the chest and one in the head."

Byrd didn't buy it. "The neck is part of the head. And for that matter, so is the face."

Davis frowned as he took out a clipboard and made notes. "But your first four rounds missed completely."

Byrd holstered his gun. "That's why we don't carry four shooters. Those extra rounds are there for a reason."

Davis shook his head. "I know you're kidding, but you can't ever be cavalier about rounds that come out of that barrel. You want to be damned sure they hit the target, and not some innocent kid caught in the crossfire."

Byrd hung his head.

Davis continued, "Let's get lunch, everyone, and then we'll head back to the classroom to watch this mess on video." He looked at Byrd pointedly. "Maybe *someone* can learn from your mistakes."

Byrd grinned. "Maybe so. I don't seem to be able to."

The group, including instructors and "bad guys," headed back to the training room. The man Byrd had shot in the neck didn't smile as he filed past.

Byrd stripped off his tactical equipment and pushed it into a corner. He turned in the pistol and magazines loaded with the wax bullets. As he did, one of the instructors gave him a bandage for his bleeding hand.

Byrd was in his tenth year with the GBI, the premier law enforcement agency in the State of Georgia and recognized worldwide for professionalism. Byrd had served in the Drug Enforcement Section for five years before a transfer to the Gainesville Regional Office. He was one of eight agents tasked with the investigation of major crimes in the fourteen counties his office encompassed.

Monty Davis pointed at Byrd's bloody hand. "We get that pretty often. Officers shoot at the threat they perceive. Often, they lock in on the hand with the gun in it. I guess we're going to have to issue gloves or buy bandages in bulk."

Byrd shook his hand to increase the circulation. "I'm voting for the gloves!"

Byrd was on the final day of the High-Risk Search Warrant Execution class. He had been through four grueling days, mostly outside. The house he was just inside was built in the firearms training section of the Georgia Public Safety Training Center in Forsyth. It seemed to Byrd he spent about a fourth of his time training at the center located sixty miles south of Atlanta. The GBI encouraged training in general topics and specialized matters.

He sought out fellow agent Tim Atkinson in the group of law officers. Atkinson was assigned to the Gainesville GBI office with Byrd.

"Do you want to get off the property and get lunch?" Byrd asked.

Atkinson was a wiry, long-distance runner, who claimed he ran so he could eat anything he wanted.

Atkinson smiled broadly. "Hell yes, Teddy. We've only been here a few days and I'm already tired of the food."

Davis turned toward the two men. "Byrd, what did he just call you?"

Byrd played dumb. "What do you mean?"

Davis raised an eyebrow. "I heard him call you 'Teddy,' didn't I?"

Atkinson laughed. "That's his new nickname."

Davis laughed out loud. Then he said, "I'll have to remember that when we go over Teddy's video this afternoon."

Byrd's face was red. He grunted and turned to leave. Atkinson followed Byrd to the parking lot, chuckling as they walked. "I get the feeling you don't care for the name Doc gave you?"

Byrd shrugged. "I guess I should feel lucky Doc wasn't

in the class. Everybody here would have been calling me Teddy all week."

The two men climbed into Byrd's Crown Victoria after they retrieved loaded guns from their respective trunks. Byrd fired up the unmarked police car and wound his way to the outside. "Would barbeque work for you?" Byrd asked.

"Outstanding," Atkinson said.

FRIDAY, NOVEMBER 12, 2004
8:38 P.M.
CANTON, GEORGIA

Living on the north side of Atlanta had benefits. Driving back home from middle Georgia wasn't one of them. Add Friday night into the mix, with people beginning to shop and seek entertainment in the holiday season, and Byrd's trip had been excruciating. What should have been a two-hour drive ended up doubled.

Byrd plodded up the stairs to his apartment and worked his key into the lock. The moisture in the air had made the wood swell, so he used his left shoulder to shove the door open, then dragged his bag full of mostly dirty clothes into the living room and dropped it. He found a bottle of diet lemonade and poured half a glass after adding ice. He finished the glass off with vodka, and then took a long sip and rolled the glass along his forehead for a moment, cooling himself.

Byrd then took off every piece of clothing he had on. He dropped them, one by one, next to his bag. Naked, but armed with a drink, he padded into the bedroom and found a pair of khaki pants.

He took everything from the dirty clothes and moved them to the clean ones. The right front pocket was reserved for keys only—the keys to his government car needed to be easy to grab on the run. Since the ignition was on the right side of the steering column, the keys would always be in the right front pocket. The rest of his routine needs were in the left front pocket so that reaching for money or a credit card wouldn't tie up his gun hand. Credentials, with the GBI badge on the outside, were always in the left rear pocket or a shirt pocket, again to prevent tying up his gun hand.

With that ritual completed, Byrd laid his service weapon on the kitchen table and disassembled it.

Once the gun was clean, Byrd rose wearily and started a shower. He scrubbed his arms and legs briskly and then rinsed his hair. He stood for a moment in the rushing water, enjoying the feel on his skin. Then he turned the water off and toweled himself dry. After taking another sip of the drink, he found and pulled on a pair of briefs. Byrd had no intentions of chasing a burglar around in the middle of the night with his junk swinging in the breeze.

He stood for a moment in front of the mirror as he brushed his teeth. The blue eyes staring back at him looked tired. He tossed the toothbrush on the cabinet and looked away.

As Byrd stretched out on his bed, he wondered briefly if he had obsessive-compulsive disorder. He dismissed the idea as he clicked off the light and rolled onto his left side. Always the left side.

SUNDAY, NOVEMBER 14, 2004
11:45 A.M.
CANTON, GEORGIA

It was a quiet Sunday morning when a young man came out onto the upstairs porch dragging a mattress. He held it with one hand and beat the side of the mattress with the other. The agents watching him had dubbed him "the mattress beater."

The little house the mattress beater was staying in was just off Main Street in downtown Canton, Georgia, a short walk from the Cherokee County courthouse. Since the ground floor seemed to be rented by a family, the agents were focused on the top floor, which was occupied by an older man who had been seen taking money and sending people up the stairs. The mattress beater hung around outside the rented rooms most of the time. Then there were the girls.

In the time that agents had watched the rental, the female occupants, who were middle-aged, had changed every Sunday. The agents hadn't been able to interest Homeland Security or the FBI, but there was no doubt the women were in servitude. They never left the apartment, except for the occasional smoke break.

The case agent for the investigation was Freddie Torres, an employee of Sheriff Albert Haggin. Torres was assigned by the Cherokee County Sheriff to the Cherokee Multi-Agency Narcotics Squad. As the name implies, the unit is a task force among Cherokee County law enforcement agencies. Torres was concerned that the task force might not exist come the new year, and Torres was a natural drug agent. He wanted to keep his job.

Just over a week ago, Sheriff Albert Haggin had lost his reelection bid. Now Freddie and the other agents of the CMANS were worried they might be back in a polyester uniform working a patrol car soon.

That didn't stop them from doing their job. Torres was convinced, as were most of the agents in the squad, that these women were sex slaves. And they planned to get their boss this morning when he showed up.

"Six-oh-seven to six-twelve," Torres heard his radio bark.

He grabbed the microphone out of his lap. "Six-twelve. Go!"

"We have a minivan with a Hispanic male driver and a female sitting in the back seat. They just turned onto Main Street and are headed your way."

Torres's pulse quickened. He checked his watch. It was five minutes to noon, and the usual time for a pickup. They had done surveillance on the little apartment on two previous occasions, and each time, the driver had been in a different vehicle.

The apartment could only be accessed by turning into an alley created by two old homes that served as lawyers' offices. The lawyers shared the back parking lot that also served as parking for the second-floor apartment.

When he saw the van come into view, noting its Texas plates, he put his Ford truck into gear. As soon as the van rolled past the government pickup, he pulled in behind the little van.

When the van had nosed into a parking space near the steps to the apartment, the driver shut off the engine and looked over his shoulder at his passenger. What he saw was a group of armed men and women rushing toward him.

One of the agents yanked the van door open and pulled the driver out before he could do anything. He was thrown on the ground and handcuffed immediately. As the people checked him for weapons, he saw the badges and the markings on their bulletproof vests. He actually relaxed when he knew the attackers were the police. His fear was they were members of another group.

The other agents pulled the woman from the back of the van. She was not what the agents expected. They had been severely limited in their surveillance options, so the women dropped off had only been seen from a considerable distance. Now they saw that the woman was around fifty years old, dressed in a loose-fitting dress, and carrying a bag of personal belongings.

Torres walked the van driver over to the shade of a tree and sat him down. It would be hard for him to escape while seated on the ground with his hands cuffed behind him. Torres searched the van driver's wallet for identification as the raid team, made up of other CMANS agents, climbed the stairs and made entry into the apartment.

Torres spoke fluent Spanish and was prepared to ask the driver about his day when the driver looked up and smiled. "You boys the local narcotics team?" His English was perfect, though it was influenced by living in the South.

Torres nodded. "What gave it away?"

"I guess you want what's in the van?"

"We sure want to talk to her. Does she speak English as well as you do?"

The driver frowned. "The *abuela*? Hell, I don't know if she can speak English or not. I just drive them around as a side gig."

Torres looked back at the minivan. "What else you got in there?"

"Something that will make your day, and ruin it at the same time."

Torres kept one eye on the driver while he walked around to the back of the van. When he opened the door, he saw ten neatly stacked blue plastic air-tight containers. Each one was full of large chunks of crystallized shards. He hefted one and was shocked that it weighed in the area of two pounds.

Torres froze. His heart was in his throat. He was certain the containers were kilogram sized. And they had in them the most crystal meth he had ever seen.

The mountain home-brew meth, a grainy, tan-colored powder that smelled like cat piss, was readily available anywhere in Georgia. The ingredients to make the old-school powder meth were, between public awareness and legislation, getting harder to procure, and the cook operations were becoming less frequent. Freddie had heard about the new iteration of methamphetamine, which was crystallized. The crystals were frequently hunks the size of your hand, and the high was supposed to be better and cleaner.

The truth was, the two were chemically identical. But the marketing was unstoppable, and the prices for Mexican crystal were getting cheaper each day.

Freddie shook his head in wonder. In a meeting in Atlanta last year, he had been told it was coming their way. Now it was here. As the drug agent stood looking at the boxes, he dreaded the impact of the wave of meth coming from Mexico to his city.

CHAPTER 2
GOING FOR A SPIN

SUNDAY, NOVEMBER 14, 2004
3:45 P.M.
EAST OF EL PASO, TEXAS

Texas State Trooper Montana Worley graduated from the Texas Highway Patrol academy just over a year ago. The tall, willowy brunette was proud to wear the Texas tan-colored uniform and prouder to be riding solo after all these months of apprenticeship. Her issued western hat was on the seat beside her, and her issued black cowboy boots were finally broken in.

It was a crisp, bright day in El Paso, and Worley enjoyed patrolling the interstate highway in the area. I-10 was the primary corridor from the border to the East Coast. She would patrol slowly in either direction, looking for cars or trucks that seemed out of place.

She was working her second month alone on the road and still learning her way around the vast high desert that was West Texas. She was assigned to Region Four (the West Texas Region) in District B (the El Paso District). District B encompassed six counties, reaching over three hundred miles into the Big Bend area.

Trooper Worley was following a service truck as it

traversed I-10. The truck was called a hi-railer, a truck capable of operating on the rails or the highway. The truck was labeled as the property of CSX Railroads and was headed east. The rookie trooper first became curious about the truck when she noticed the Georgia license plate. Before becoming a trooper in Texas, she had been a city police officer in Georgia. And she was pretty sure that the CSX didn't operate west of the Mississippi. She remembered from her training, several people in the Narcotics Service had pointed out that cartels—the Mexican Mafia to investigators—were using disguised commercial vehicles to transport drugs from the border to the East Coast.

Montana called her dispatch center and had the operator run the license plate on the truck to see if it was stolen. When the results were negative, she asked dispatch to check the plate through the El Paso Intelligence Center, the federal clearing house for information on suspected traffickers in drugs and humans.

Montana was staying as far back from the truck as she thought was reasonable, as she waited for her sergeant to catch up and help on the investigative stop she planned. Her Highway Patrol Crown Victoria was pacing the truck without effort. Trooper Worley had crossed out of El Paso County and into Hudspeth County a few miles back.

She brought the radio microphone up to her face. "Forty-four-twenty-nine to El Paso."

The response was immediate. "Forty-four-twenty-nine."

"Can you advise a location for Forty-two-oh-three?"

Montana knew that backup could take a while to catchup in the high desert of West Texas.

Sergeant Helen Camos came on the radio. "Forty-two-oh-three to Forty-two-twenty-nine, I am about ten to fifteen miles behind you. I am coming as fast as I can."

Montana didn't want this truck to get away but as the newest trooper in the district, she wasn't about to do anything impetuous. "Ten-four, Sarge. I'll keep back and wait on you to catch up."

"El Paso to Forty-two-twenty-nine."

Montana frowned. *What now?* she thought. "Go ahead, El Paso."

"I have EPIC on the line. They advise this vehicle is part of a DEA investigation. If you stop them, use extreme caution."

Montana frowned. Her sergeant would kill her if she tried to stop the truck alone now. "Should I drop off, Forty-two-oh-three? I'm without backup, and if I follow them much longer, they are going to notice me back here."

As Montana focused on the car in front of her and waited for an answer from her supervisor, she heard a sound like a small explosion. Suddenly, her patrol car was spinning around to the left and she was fighting the wheel for control. The Highway Patrol car ran out into the sandy median. Disoriented for a moment, Montana focused on keeping the sedan out of the oncoming lane of traffic. She bounced over sharp rocks and pieces of asphalt littering the gap between the east and westbound lanes.

She skidded to a halt, pointing back toward El Paso. *What the hell just happened?* she thought. She jumped out of the patrol vehicle and walked around to the rear. Her right rear tire was flat, punctured by a rock in the median. Then she saw the damage to the rear quarter panel, and she suddenly realized that her car had been PIT-ed. The Pursuit Intervention Technique, or PIT maneuver, was part of basic training for a trooper. It was a fast, safe way to get a fleeing criminal off the road before someone was hurt. The officer would get near the rear axle of the target car, cut in and spin the car out.

Montana had heard that the cartels were training their drivers to execute the PIT when a load was at risk. She sat in the car for a moment as the dispatch center responded to her earlier question. She had only heard the radio operator say something about waiting for more help as she spun into the median.

Trooper Worley grabbed her radio microphone in frustration. She spat into the mic, "Forty-two-oh-three, I'm out of the hunt."

Her sergeant came on the air. She said, "Forty-two-twenty-nine, are you ten-four? I am coming toward you as fast as I can."

"Forty-two-twenty-nine to Forty-two-oh-three. I was just PIT-ed by a secondary vehicle. I went into the median and lost a tire." She kicked the floor of the patrol car for good measure.

The dispatch center interrupted the conversation, "Forty-two-twenty-nine, I'll get a wrecker headed to you." Because the trunk of the car was loaded with equipment, and the potential damage that could have been done in the spin into the center of the highway, it was standard procedure to get a tow truck to respond. That meant that she was done for the day.

The dispatcher continued, "And I'll pass the lookout on the truck to the rest of the state. Did you get a look at the car that hit you?"

Montana hung her head. "I did not see the secondary vehicle, El Paso."

Her Sergeant came back on the radio. "Forty-two-oh-three to Forty-two-twenty-nine, I am about five miles out."

She got out of the black-and-white car and kicked the deflated tire with her boot. It felt good enough that she did it several times. She was about to try to kick the fender when she saw her Sergeant appear around the sweeping curve she was parked in.

The Sergeant pulled her patrol car, another Crown Victoria with the distinctive honeycomb grille, into the median behind Montana's unit and activated her emergency lights. Sergeant Helen Camos got out of her car, placed her issued hat on her head deliberately, and walked up to Trooper Worley. Her royal-blue tie was flapping on her chest as a big truck passed.

Camos glanced at the flat tire but looked Worley over. "You okay, Troop?"

Montana nodded. "Yes, Sarge. Just pissed off. I lost that load because I was stupid. I should have been watching for following cars."

Camos shrugged. "You're still on probation, aren't you?"

Montana was alarmed. "Yes, ma'am."

Camos shrugged again. "Not the only load to get through on this stretch—not even the first one today! You did what we trained you to do. You didn't do anything stupid; you just lack experience. But you're in a damned good place to get it."

Montana relaxed. "Thanks, Sarge. I appreciate it."

"You did good not trying to stop that truck by yourself, Troop. Your patrol car can be fixed, but we need every trooper we have to cover this state."

Both troopers turned and looked as a big pickup truck pulled in behind the DPS Crown Vic. Montana had her hand on her service weapon as she watched the truck stop behind her boss's car. She relaxed when concealed blue and red lights came on in the grille and headliner of the truck.

Sergeant Camos frowned. "We can relax now; the Texas Rangers are here."

The Texas Rangers was the oldest state law enforcement unit in the US, formed in 1823. Even modern rangers were expected to live up to the public expectations of the legendary western law officers who preceded them. Ranger policy dictated that rangers wear a light-colored western hat, western boots, a dress shirt, a conservative tie, a dress jacket, and their issued badge fashioned from a Mexican silver coin when performing their duties.

The driver of the truck walked up to them, holding his white hat to prevent the draft from the traffic snatching it from his head. He was dressed in black pants, a dark jacket, and a white shirt. Montana could see the edge of the famous circle star badge protruding slightly under the jacket lapel.

He shook hands with the sergeant, who seemed to know him, and then extended his hand to Montana. His voice was firm and distinctly West Texan. "Trooper," he said to Montana. "I'm Ranger Clete Petterson. Are you okay? I heard all the traffic on the radio."

Montana nodded. "Ranger. I'm fine, thanks."

Petterson pointed at the tire. "Bad luck. But lucky it was only a damaged tire. The San Antonio District had a trooper flip one of the new Chargers like that. Broke his leg in the crash."

Montana shrugged. "I'm just glad I'm not the only one to get snuck up on. I feel like an idiot."

Petterson shook his head. "You did good. Calling in the tag number has saved the day. We're digging into the truck as we speak. This is a common tactic of the Mexican Mafia. They disguise service trucks to match businesses you see traveling on the interstate. We think these particular trucks are being built in some small town in Georgia."

"I wish I could tell you more. I was staying back on

purpose and didn't make out a lot of details. Dispatch told me it was part of a DEA investigation, but I guess you heard that."

Petterson nodded. "I'm working with a DEA agent on this case. That's why I headed out here. Can we go to my office so that you can show me on the map where you picked the truck up? And I want to call the CSX Railroad Police. They can send us photos of what their legitimate trucks look like."

"Sure," Montana said. Her Sergeant raised an eyebrow but gave her a thumbs-up.

Petterson motioned to his truck. "Sergeant, if you want me to, I can wait with your trooper for the tow truck, then I can drop her off at your offices."

Sergeant Camos nodded and then walked back to her patrol car, tossing her hat into the seat and dropping in behind it, then pulled away.

Montana had only been around one other Texas Ranger, and he had been much older than her. This man was probably ten years her senior, but he had a youthful energy and seemed to smile more than a lot of cops she had met in West Texas.

Once her Crown Victoria was on the back of the wrecker, Petterson pulled back onto the interstate and looped back toward El Paso. Petterson drove with one hand while he used the other to talk. "You said the truck was a hi-railer, but how are you sure? Do you know what a hi-railer is?"

Montana was sure. She said, "My dad worked for the railroad after he got out of the army. He worked in a yard in Cartersville, Georgia, for CSX. I know their logo and the way they mark their trucks. This one didn't look right to me, and I know CSX doesn't have rails east of the Mississippi River."

Petterson was impressed. "You need to be sure to apply for the Criminal Investigations Division when you have enough time. You're one smart rookie."

Montana blushed. "Thanks. But I'm only a rookie here. I had some street experience before I left Georgia."

"When you put on the Texas tan, nothing that came before matters. They didn't tell you that in trooper school?" He laughed.

She shrugged. "Does that mean my first marriage doesn't count?"

Petterson cut his eyes over. "A youthful mistake?"

"For sure a mistake. And I guess I was pretty young. But old enough to know better. He couldn't keep his dick in his pants."

Petterson nodded but kept his mouth shut.

Finally, Montana said, "What about you?"

"If you mean, can I keep my dick in my pants, the answer is yes. If you're asking about my marital status, I am a widower."

Montana stared at the road. "Sorry."

Petterson shook his head. "She was a good woman and a nurse at the hospital here. One day she started falling down when she would turn around. Next thing, she was falling all the time. We got her checked out within a few days of the falling starting, but it was too late—brain cancer, of a particularly aggressive breed. From the time she was diagnosed until the time she died was less than two months."

The truck was suddenly very quiet. Thankfully, Petterson broke the spell. "You had no way of knowing."

Montana mumbled, "Sorry for your loss."

Petterson shrugged. "It was five years ago. But it seems like yesterday that we buried her. We were sweethearts in college. She put up with me moving from Fort Worth to get on with the Highway Patrol. And she pushed me to become a ranger. I got my star three years to the day from when she died."

Montana sat quietly, looking at the road.

Petterson shifted uncomfortably. "I didn't mean to talk about me. Tell me more about growing up in Georgia. What brought you out here?"

"It's a long story."

"Will it last longer than your first marriage?"

Montana's eyebrows shot up. "What the hell does that mean?"

Petterson laughed. "It means I want to lighten the mood. And if the story of your migration to Texas will do that, I'm ready for it."

Montana laughed too. She pulled her hat off and wiped her forehead. They were riding along I-10, parallel to the Mexican border. She looked into the distance, trying to see what Mexico was about. Then she slumped into the seat and said, "I pulled over this murder suspect and he shot me in the chest."

Petterson glanced over at her. "That sounds like a story I need to hear. Should I stop somewhere for popcorn?"

Montana shook her head. "Maybe tissues. It's a sad story."

"Do you die in the end?"

"Nope," she said.

"Then I can handle it." He listened as he drove toward El Paso.

CHAPTER 3
GENERALLY SPEAKING

MONDAY, NOVEMBER 15, 2004
10:11 A.M.
BOWENS MILL, GEORGIA

Around two hundred and fifty miles away from Daniel Byrd, Mitchell Warren strode across the graveled parking lot toward his training building. His shoulders were squared, and his back was ramrod straight. He looked neither left nor right. He was dressed in desert camouflage and tan combat boots and wore the beret of the British Special Air Service, of which he had never been a member. His collar bore three stars on each side.

He popped in a breath mint to hide the smell of the alcohol he had used to replace a heartier breakfast. When he cupped his hand near his mouth and exhaled, he convinced himself the smell was gone. For a moment, his confidence waned as he considered the pedestrian nature of his current assignment. No more days on the battlefield in some foreign country with just enough money to pay him and the team he had assembled. No more high-flying adventures all around the globe. Age and injuries had recently caused his regular employer to put him out to pasture. He snorted and spat on the ground near his rough desert boots.

He came to the door of the block building, glanced around once, and reached for the door. As soon as the door flew open, two dozen students inside stood to attention. Their eyes were locked forward, but each had cracked a salute and stood waiting. Warren took a moment to savor the sight, then made his way to the front of the class. The room was not state of the art but it had everything a budding clandestine tactics class needed. Rows of tables with straight-backed chairs, a dry-erase board in the front, and an overhead projector for the class presentations. The student barracks were equally spartan, but some of the students thought of them as luxury accommodations.

The students were a variety of body types, ethnicities, and cultures. Some were fit; some were fat. Some were dark and some were fair. Almost all of them were in their late twenties. And for the first time, two were women.

The instructor also stood at attention. Warren turned to him, returned his salute, and then turned to the class. Warren announced, "At ease, ladies and gentlemen."

The students relaxed and waited. Each of them was dressed in some kind of military clothing. Several had the same desert camouflage as Warren and their instructor. Others wore jungle fatigues or plain green tops and pants.

Warren noted that the native Spanish speakers were seated in a group. He knew that most of the students had a limited command of the English language but that didn't matter since most of the training would be hands-on.

"I am General Mitchell Oliver Warren. I am the founder of this little school for fighting men and women. You are being afforded some of the most secret, effective, and skilled training available in the world." Warren paused and looked around the room. "I hope you appreciate the people who have sponsored you. This training is not cheap."

He heard one of the Nicaraguans say, "*¡Esa es la puta verdad!*"

Warren kept his face taunt. "The value will be obvious by the time you graduate. Take advantage of the experts I have assembled to train you. This is a deadly business that we are a part of, make no mistake. Everything you learn here can be the difference between life and death."

His voice was raspy from cigarettes and liquor, and he looked like he was hung over. He had stayed up late the night before to brief his instructors on the latest batch of mercenary wannabes. He had spent much of the time drinking Scotch whisky and telling war stories about his time in the Persian Gulf, Iraq and Iran, and an extremely suspect story about a trip into North Korea.

Warren's instructors were mostly retired or fired law enforcement officers from around the area. Only one, the man standing in the classroom now, had any military experience. He had been a member of the Alabama National Guard for a couple of years and had liked the training and the discipline of the military. But he liked to drink and smoke weed more.

Warren croaked, "You men and women will be the vanguard of your home country. You will be the elite few when you leave here. And you will take your place with the military leaders of your country."

Most of the students were beaming with pride. They might not have known what Warren was saying, but they recognized the tone of voice and the demeanor. They had been told awe-inspiring stories about the old soldier who stood in front of them, and now they were hearing from the man himself.

Whack! Warren slapped the riding crop he carried under his arm down onto the table at the front of the room. He turned to the instructor. "Now, Colonel Green will resume your class. Thank you for your attention." The students and the instructor snapped to attention. Warren walked briskly from the room and back toward the building where his office was.

Back in the classroom, Colonel Green, whose name was not Green and who had never held the rank of Colonel, went back to the slide projected on the wall. He was hiding his smile from the students. In this class, he was a Colonel. He knew the General would randomly assign rank to the various instructors as the classes were taught. *It felt good to be promoted*, he thought.

Carl Hollander had been a street cop in the city of Tifton, where he had never been promoted. Carl was the quintessential local bully. When the Police Chief got a complaint about Hollander, he first wrote it off as Carl being an aggressive officer. He was one of the first Black officers to come to the department with a college degree. His reports were the best the chief had ever seen. The chief learned, too late for his own career, that the reports were also mostly fabricated. Black residents who were bullied by Hollander finally applied enough pressure on their council members that the chief was fired. On his way out the door, he fired Hollander.

But during his tenure with the police department, Carl had gotten advanced training, even becoming a certified police instructor. So, when the chief bounced him out the door, Carl bounced into the Counter Insurgency Academy.

He taught self-defense, firearms, and a few other courses to the eager students at the training center. The students seemed to come in a steady stream, and even the jaded Hollander wondered if Warren was the real deal.

Mitchell Warren had founded the Counter Insurgency Academy fully aware of the acronym. In fact, he named the training center with the acronym in mind. He would get a laugh when he ordered embroidered shirts with the large letters "CIA" above his name. Warren told people, employees, and family that he was a former and current covert contractor for the agency with the same initials. He would talk in circles and espouse his deep government connections, and, in some cases, he could back that up.

Warren had been born to a mother who was addicted to heroin and lived mostly on the streets in Jersey City, New Jersey, in 1949. She had lived in sight of the bright lights of New York City but died without ever visiting the place where she thought her dreams could come true. Warren's father wasn't identified on his birth certificate or any place else Warren could find. He had been raised by his only uncle, a Marine Corp captain who saw to it that he got a good education. He joined the Marines in 1973, as an officer candidate, and served with honor in Japan and later in Hawaii, rising to the rank of Captain. But his military career was cut short, suddenly, by a Naval Criminal Investigative Services investigation—which had turned out to be a blessing.

Somewhere along the line, as he was subjected to a variety of psychological and physical tests, he caught the attention of a recruiter for a clandestine agency in the government. Warren never knew for sure the government agency whose staff had taken him under their wing. But he was indebted, at least in his mind, to the men who gave him work, food, and special training.

Warren had served the government, or whoever they were, well. He trained in several friendly countries and was recognized for his growing skill sets. Warren had been a natural leader, and with some college and leadership training, he began to excel.

On his twenty-seventh birthday, he led a merry band of mercenaries into a camp in Jordan where a group with interests contrary to the US needed to be taught a lesson. Warren led the group into the camp after walking for miles across rough terrain to get there. His men attacked at dawn and shot up the camp, without a single casualty on either side. But the message had been sent, and Warren was a problem solver. His payment had been in five-pound bags of opium. He was able to trade his payment in for cash in Marseille, and suddenly he was a very wealthy young man.

Upon his return to the US, he threw a huge party in New York with his paycheck. It was at this party that he first met his future wife, a pilot for a delivery company. She was infatuated with the buccaneer, and he was enthralled with this strong woman.

Between trips to the far reaches of the world, Warren married the young pilot he called "Darlin'." She had family in Fitzgerald, Georgia, and soon the newlyweds were building a house on a six-hundred-acre parcel near the Ocmulgee River. Warren left the details to Darlin' and left home again for almost a year to help with a "problem" in Nicaragua.

When he got home, he was welcomed by Darlin' and a son. Within eight more years, he fathered four more children—daughter, son, daughter, and daughter, in that order. During the same time, he met with executives for a large Atlanta-based company whose top people had been threatened with kidnapping by a particularly violent drug cartel. Warren made a quick trip to the Mexican coast during which he was rumored to have held the cartel leader's son hostage and threatened to mail the son's penis to the man. There were no more threats, and Warren was six million dollars richer.

Warren entered his office and locked the door behind him. Tossing the riding crop on the desk and turning to the bookshelf on the back wall, he walked over and found the worn copy of *The New Centurions* by Joseph Wambaugh. He hooked his finger over the spine and pulled the book out. It pivoted back and the bookcase split in half.

The bookcase opened to reveal a military-grade telephone and a military radio. Each was designed to encrypt the voice conversations from the room. Warren checked his watch, then turned the radio set on the left-hand side of the cabinet on. He waited for the various systems in the radio to stabilize and for the radio to run through its self-check. Once the display indicated that the radio was receiving on the chosen channel, Warren sat down to wait.

While he waited, he checked the monitors above the radios. He scanned each of the closed-circuit cameras located around the compound. The office he was in was the nerve center for the six-hundred-acre complex he liked to call "the farm." As he watched the monitor, he saw the centerpiece of his complex, located near the river on a ridge. He had built a four-thousand-foot runway on the highest part of the property, surrounded by trees on all sides. The runway was as solid as a rock but looked like a long, slim pasture. The grass was kept in check with goats that were herded away when a plane was expected.

Next up was the front of the training center building. He chuckled as he thought how the training center had ended up being a cover for everything he was doing. Contactors had flocked to bid on the construction of the center and the runway. The buildings for the training center and Warren's office had set him back over four hundred thousand dollars. The runway alone cost almost double that.

Then several small cabins had been financed by a certain unnamed agency. Each cabin was suitable for use as a retreat, a hideout, or a prison cell. The walls were thick, the floors were concrete, and each floor had a drain, in case someone happened to be bleeding. The cabins were far enough away from the main house that teams could come and go without the knowledge of the other residents on the property.

The cheapest feature, and one of the most intimidating to visitors, was the fourteen-acre lake and the adjacent swamps. The area was home to a variety of reptiles, the largest being alligators and the smallest being six different types of poisonous snakes.

The sudden, loud beep the radio made when it received encrypted traffic went off. Government-quality encrypted radios couldn't be sold to private individuals by the manufacturer. But the radios, once discarded by the government, were readily available on eBay.

Warren grabbed his radio microphone as he heard, "This is your customer from the south calling. How do you hear me?"

Warren was cautious since the encryption made it harder for him to recognize voices. He pressed the red button on the microphone and called back, "I hear you loud and clear. Is the CEO on this call?"

The reply came back quickly. "He is not available. We are trying out the device you sent. It seems to work well on this end."

Warren nodded to himself. And the encryption module they were using was complex enough that he was confident no one was listening in. Even the NSA would have a hard time monitoring his radio in real-time.

MONDAY, NOVEMBER 15, 2004
10:30 A.M.
CIUDAD JUÁREZ, CHIHUAHUA, MEXICO

El Gordo sat at the radio console and dialed the numbers into the machine. He was rewarded with the beeping sound which indicated a solid connection. He thought the machine was overly complicated and didn't want his boss to think he wasn't up to the task of making the radio link. He couldn't wait for the secure phone to arrive.

The gringos and their secret codes and spy talk frustrated him. But he had to admit that the old "general" could produce what he promised. The single most difficult part of running a drug organization from Mexico was communicating with operatives in the United States.

Most people thought getting drugs across the border was difficult, but it was a game of numbers. An organization might send twenty or thirty pounds of meth or cocaine in a given day. The organization knew that eighty to ninety percent of the drugs would make it to the other side. The mules, or drug couriers, used were as disposable as tissues. It was the coordination of the movements on the US side which presented the greatest challenge. Police agencies literally lined the interstate highways looking for the big cache of drugs or money. Money being the prime mover, since laws enacted in the 1980s allowed the agency catching the cash to seize it for departmental use.

Drug trafficking organizations, DTOs in law enforcement parlance, were concerned about the potential for government wiretaps and were loath to plan operations over a phone line, cellular or otherwise. The leaders of the DTOs were immune from incarceration, as long as they stayed in Mexico, as Joaquín Archivaldo Guzmán, commonly known as "El Chapo," demonstrated during his escape from a Mexican prison in 2001.

El Gordo's boss was one of those leaders.

"The customer wants to talk to you directly. Do you have an estimated time for the special phone to arrive?" El Gordo said into the microphone.

The scratchy, burbly voice came back. "It should arrive Wednesday night. I would be honored for the customer to call me direct on Thursday. Is that soon enough?"

The big man turned to his boss.

Vincente Acosta-Hernandez was one of the most feared men in Mexico. He stood in the small office, dressed in a three-thousand-dollar Italian suit. He was small compared to his minion, standing five feet, eight inches tall. His remaining hair was white as snow, or more aptly, cocaine. He was in his early fifties. But there was no doubt to anyone watching who was in charge of the operation.

Raised in the Mexican State of Guerero, Hernandez joined a group of drug manufacturers and importers at the age of fourteen. In 1983, he was a member of the Guadalajara Cartel and worked for Miguel Ángel Félix Gallardo. After Gallardo's arrest in 1989, Hernandez formed the Coastal Cartel, in direct competition with his old friend, El Chapo. El Chapo ordered hits on Hernandez twice in 1995. By 1996, while the world was watching the Centennial Olympic Games in Atlanta, a 9.3-ton shipment of Hernandez's cocaine, concealed in cans of salsa and destined for the United States, was seized in El Paso, Texas. When El Chapo was arrested in 2001, Hernandez became king of the hill. Hernandez was considered a folk hero in the narcotics world, celebrated by *narcocorridos* extolling his exploits.

Hernandez was known throughout Mexico as *"Rojo."* Some say the name came from the man's ruby-red complexion, an early sign of hypertension. Others said the name was a reference to the color of his hands, from the blood of his many enemies. Rojo spat on the floor. "Tell the gringo I will be calling him first thing on Thursday morning. Tell him he should be by his phone. *¡Mejor que no me chingue!"*

El Gordo nodded. He turned to the microphone and said, "Your customer is ready to talk. If it must be Thursday, then it will be. But you should know that the customer expects to talk to you on that day. And without delay."

El Gordo leaned in, hoping he hadn't lost the connection. The reply came back, "I look forward to talking on Thursday."

Rojo waited for the connection to be broken. "That gringo and his magic boxes are a pain in my ass." Then he turned and left without commenting.

El Gordo let out a long breath.

CHAPTER 4
WHAT HAPPENS IN CHAMBERS STAYS IN CHAMBERS

TUESDAY, NOVEMBER 16, 2004
6:57 A.M.
WOODSTOCK, GEORGIA

Daniel Byrd sat in the office of Anne Kuykendall on a soft green chair. Anne Kuykendall was a professional counselor who specialized in the treatment of post-traumatic stress. The room seemed more like a cozy sitting room than a business office.

They had been talking for fifty-five minutes, and Anne Kuykendall sat on a sofa with one foot tucked under her. "I need to check the calendar, but I think we are at the year-and-a-half mark. How does that make you feel?"

Byrd laughed. "Like I'm screwed up."

Anne shook her head. "You're less screwed up than most people I see. Give me a deeper answer."

Byrd hung his head. "I didn't know there would be a test. I should have studied more."

But Anne wasn't buying it. "Life isn't a joke. Give me a serious answer."

He looked up and met her eyes. "I'm better. The dreams

are gone, mostly. And when I have them, they are less dramatic."

Anne leaned forward. "And the drinking. How is that going?"

He shrugged. "I limit myself to two drinks a night. Absolutely no drinking and driving."

"Was that a problem?" she asked.

Byrd frowned. "When I was working undercover, I drove a few times when I shouldn't have."

"Have you done that outside of work?"

He shook his head. "Nope. It would ruin my career. There is no way I could do that. And if I were working UC nowadays, I wouldn't do that."

"Have you thought about getting help from a group like AA?" Anne asked warily.

"We train in this concept of self-rescue. When you're working alone, a long way from help, you have to apply your own tourniquet and stop the flow of your own blood. State officers train and train again on these skills. I guess I figured I could apply the same principles to my personal life."

"Interesting. I know people who have self-treated heroin addiction and alcohol dependancy. I doubt you are physically dependent on alcohol but have certainly been psychologically dependent."

"I'm going to the gym when I can," he offered.

"That's good. How about rest? Are you sleeping well?"

He smiled. "It's getting better."

"How about your personal life. Or, you might say, your love life?"

He glanced at his watch. "Damn," he said. "I have to be in court in Blue Ridge this morning at ten. Thanks for seeing me early, but I need to get going."

"Answer the question," Anne said, firmly.

"I'm still seeing the assistant district attorney. I guess I like women smarter than I am." He chuckled.

"She's still married?"

Byrd shrugged. "Her husband is a jerk."

Anne shook her head. "This relationship isn't going anywhere."

Byrd nodded. "I know. I get it. This won't last long, I'm not her type."

"What's her type?" she asked Byrd.

"Married men," Byrd admitted.

"Not good," Anne clucked.

Byrd hung his head. Then, after a moment he looked Anne in the eyes. "Am I a sociopath?" Byrd asked.

"Doubtful," she said. "Why?"

"Because I don't feel any remorse for killing Lumpy Cochran. Isn't that something I should feel?"

"If you didn't feel anything, you wouldn't be here. No, that's not my concern for you."

Byrd stood to go. "What is your concern?"

Anne smiled. "That you'll try to punish yourself for what happened."

Byrd thought that over. After several seconds he nodded. "Thanks."

She stood up as well. "How are things with the judge you had trouble with?"

"She still tries her best to make me look bad," Byrd offered.

"That must keep you on your toes. I don't understand why she still has a job."

Byrd grunted. "If it were up to me, she wouldn't have a job." Byrd smiled wryly. "I'm headed to her courtroom this morning." He gave Anne a quick hug and turned to leave. "Wish me luck!"

TUESDAY, NOVEMBER 16, 2004
11:12 A.M.
BLUE RIDGE, GEORGIA

He had been sitting in the hallway outside the court-room of the Fannin County courthouse with Jackson "Doc" Farmer for over an hour. He was a sequestered witness for the government in the case that was to be called today.

Normally, Byrd and Farmer would wait in the district attorney's offices, but Judge Linda Pelfrey had insisted they wait in the hall. Judge Pelfrey was not a fan of Agent Byrd.

Byrd was surprised when the bailiff, a retired deputy, came for him. "Agent Byrd, the judge wants you in the courtroom."

Byrd stood, brushed a hand through his hair, and straightened his tie and jacket as he made his way into the courtroom. Doc gave him a thumbs-up.

The judge, seated behind the bench, wore a black robe which made her blond hair look even more striking. She looked directly at District Attorney Jerry Mason and said, "Mr. Mason, are we ready for the hearing on the case at hand? The defendant, Mr. Fisher, has been sitting in the county jail for several months, and I only recently approved his bond. I understand he has been released, but this case has languished long enough. We have a duty to move it along."

Byrd glanced at the judge. He suspected that the defend-ant, Brandon Fisher, was the judge's meth connection. Byrd had arrested Fisher more than once in connection with the primary drug of choice for the users in the mountainous north of Georgia.

Mason stood up. "Your Honor, the government is ready to move forward on this case. We have the GBI Agents who made the case against Mr. Fisher in the courtroom, but the defendant had not made an appearance."

Fisher's court-appointed attorney stood behind the defense table. "Mr. Fisher is on a vacation with his family."

The judge slammed her pen down on the bench. "Who allowed him out of the court's jurisdiction while his case was pending? Can you answer that question, Mr. DA?"

Mason stood his ground. "Even I know that Mr. Fisher isn't taking his children to the beach. Clearly, his bond should be revoked immediately."

Judge Pelfrey raised an eyebrow. "I'll entertain a motion to revoke his bond, Mr. Mason." She shifted in her seat. "Is counsel for the defense doing anything to locate Mr. Fisher?"

The court-appointed attorney stood again and nodded. "Yes, Your Honor."

"Fine," she spat. At last, she looked the courtroom over and made eye contact with Daniel Byrd. "Agent Byrd, will you please join me in chambers? There is a matter we need to discuss."

Byrd stood uncomfortably. He looked to Mason for a lifeline, who spoke up. "Since Agent Byrd is a witness in the matter before the court, would it be wise to have an ex parte conversation with him, Your Honor?" Mason asked.

She cut her eyes at Mason. "I think I know what I'm doing. And what I want to discuss has nothing to do with this case." She stood and motioned to Byrd. "Come into my chambers, Agent Byrd."

The judge disappeared through the door behind her bench. Byrd strode toward the back door of the courtroom and stepped into the back hallway. He reached into his jacket pocket to turn on his recorder and then knocked on the private entrance to Judge Pelfrey's chambers. He heard a muffled "Come."

Byrd stepped into the office and the judge motioned him to a chair. As Byrd dropped into the hard-backed seat, the judge made her way around the back of her desk, which was covered with legal documents and law books. She unzipped the front of her robe and took it off, using a hanger on the wall for that purpose. Byrd was surprised to see she was wearing only a bra and panties. The items of lingerie were black and seemed to be very high quality, and Byrd could not help noticing how beautiful the judge was and how well she modeled the lingerie.

Byrd stood up uncomfortably, hesitant to further anger the judge but not willing to get in bed with her, literally or figuratively.

She turned to face Byrd as she sat in her high-backed office chair. "Sit back down. I want to ask you a question—but I don't suppose you'll tell me the truth, will you?"

She leaned forward in her chair and propped her arms on a copy of *Georgia Rules of Evidence.* Byrd thought back to the time four years ago when he had seen her partying with two men and using meth. She had been nude, but it had been at some distance. Up close, he had to admit she was a striking woman. Moreover, her skin tone was much healthier than it was a few years ago. Her face and arms were tanned and toned, and the overall impression was pink skin, not the gray that indicated heavy meth use.

Byrd tried to sound calm. "Your Honor, I can't be in here while you are dressed, or undressed, in this manner."

The judge jumped straight to it. "I know what you're doing, you fucking lying son of a bitch!" She pointed at Byrd as she spoke.

Byrd shrugged. "Judge, I can't lie to you. You know that." He was making his way to the door.

She scowled. "That doesn't answer my fucking question. It's simple: Am I the subject of a GBI drug investigation?"

He could give her an honest answer to that question. But it would bring on more talk, and he was under orders not to reveal that the Judicial Qualifications Commission, a state agency created to conduct investigations and hearings with respect to complaints of ethical misconduct by Georgia judges, had an open inquiry on Judge Pelfrey.

Byrd grew even more uncomfortable, not in the least because of the question. She had swung her legs up, crossed them at the ankles, and propped her high heels on the desk. He followed the movement with his eyes.

"I don't work in the drug office anymore, judge. I haven't since I came here in 2001," Byrd said.

She shook her hair out and leaned back. "Agent Byrd, are you a tit man or a leg man?"

Byrd considered the question for a moment, thanking God that he had turned on the recorder. "I like my women to have both."

She smiled. "You know, we could make nice and put the past behind us. I could make things a lot better for you in this circuit."

Byrd looked her legs over again. "Judge, I just think that would be a problem for both of us. You are a very attractive woman—"

She interrupted, "But the do-gooder can't be seen with a woman like me."

"Ma'am, that isn't—"

"Cut the bullshit," She interrupted again as she stood and put her hands on her hips. He got a whiff of her perfume. "You're not going to tell me what I want to know, are you? Hell, I may have made some mistakes in the past, but I'm clean as a whistle now and you'll have to make something up to hang any charges on me."

"Judge, as far as I am concerned, there is no GBI investigation. And I would love for our relationship to be peaceful. I plan to work up here for a long time."

Judge Pelfrey moved to block his exit.

Byrd stood as he continued, "Judge, I have to get out of here. No disrespect, because you *are* a very attractive woman, but I can't be in here right now."

Byrd saw her smile and wondered who had won or lost this meeting as he turned and left the office. As soon as he was out, he turned off the recorder.

His face was red as he made his way back into the courtroom, moving toward Mason. When they were close enough together to talk quietly, Mason said, "She must have taken off her robe. You look like you're about to bust."

Byrd nodded, surprised that Mason knew. "Did she do that to you?"

Mason shook his head. "Nope, but she has done it to some of the other lawyers in town. They say she has one hell of a body."

Byrd nodded again. "She does."

"I have this image that she only wears underwear under her robe all the time. I have a hard time getting it out of my head." Mason smiled.

"I think she gave up meth for pills. Probably benzo."

"To calm herself down?" Mason asked.

"Meth folks use it to make the down less harsh. Some folks eventually use it as a substitute. Do you think the defense attorney will show?" he asked.

Mason shook his head. "Rose just came in to tell me. He had a death in the family and went to South Georgia for the services. He filed a notice with the clerk, but if I tell the judge that right now, she'll just jump my ass."

Byrd paced the area within the bar. He looked back at Mason and asked, "Then do I need to hang out here, or can I go?"

Mason thought about that for a minute. "Why don't you grab some lunch? And Doc can go, I don't plan to use him as a witness. When the judge takes the bench again, I'll tell her the hearing can't go forward and get you dismissed."

Byrd shrugged. "Sounds good."

Byrd found Doc waiting patiently in the hall. "Jerry says you can go. I'm going to have to wait a little while though. Do you want to go to lunch?"

Doc shook his head. "I need to get over to Union County. Why don't you take Jerry's secretary to lunch? Don't you need to mend some bridges?"

Byrd nodded and shook Doc's hand. "Yeah, okay."

He found Rose Mitchell working in a filing cabinet almost as tall as she was. Byrd and Rose had been swept up in an investigation into corruption in Gilmer County, the county just north of Jasper. The case had resulted in Rose's husband going to jail and the sheriff and chief superior court judge—Judge Linda Pelfrey's father—going to the morgue. As primary witnesses in the case, Rose and Dan Byrd had been discouraged from having contact outside the district attorney's office. Things had been strictly business for over a year before they dated on-again, off-again.

When she finished in the file drawer, she slammed it shut then, spotting Byrd, she walked over. Before he could react, she grabbed the back of his head with her left hand and pulled his face to her. She kissed him deeply for a moment then let him go.

"Damn," he said.

Rose sat down at her desk and opened the file she was working on. She propped her chin on her left hand, elbow down on the desk. After she had found the information she needed, she made a note on a legal pad.

She glanced at the file again then shut it with finality.

"Did you come by to buy my lunch?" Rose asked.

Byrd nodded. "Absolutely. First, though, can I use your phone to call my office?"

"Sure. Use the one on Mr. Mason's desk. That way you can have some privacy."

Byrd went into the back office and closed the door. He dialed the office and Machelle Stevens, who ran the GBI regional office, answered on the first ring. "GBI, how may I help you?"

"Hey, Machelle. This is Danny Byrd. I need to speak to Tina."

"She's looking for you," Machelle said. "She wanted to know how things went at the Fannin County courthouse."

"She must have a crystal ball," Byrd said.

"Were you in front of that crazy judge?" Machelle sounded amused.

Byrd dropped his voice when he answered, "You guessed it. And she's still crazy as ever."

Machelle grunted. "Hold on. I'll get Tina on the line."

The wait was short, and Christina "Tina" Blackwell was on the line. "Are you in jail?"

"Nope. Not yet," Byrd responded.

"How did things go with the judge?"

"She tried to hold a hearing on an old assault case. She made me sit in the hall for a couple of hours and then, as it turns out, the defense attorney is out of town."

"Did she try to talk to you directly?"

"I'll do a full report. She called me into chambers and took her clothes off."

"All of them?"

"Down to her bra and panties."

"Did she come on to you?"

"The stripping down to her underwear could be interpreted as coming on. She seemed to be trying to make nice with me, but she's all over the place—she looks like she's sober, but she still acts like she's off her rocker."

Blackwell paused for a moment. "There has been a development with her situation."

Byrd had a bad feeling. "What kind of development?"

Blackwell sighed. "The governor wants to appoint her to the Court of Appeals."

"*What?*"

Blackwell kept her voice even. "Calm down. I know this sounds crazy, but it might solve several problems: she gets out of that circuit and also can't directly impact your cases."

Byrd wasn't convinced. "The governor plans to promote her to a higher position to punish her? Is that how this all works?"

Tina tried to use a soothing voice. "She might be higher up the food chain, but she has less influence in that job. I know it sounds like a win for her, but it's also a win for us."

"What about the Judicial Qualifications Commission? I thought they were looking to get her off the bench."

"That was discussed, but she has enough clout in the capital to keep her protected."

Byrd shook his head. "This is bullshit! She just propositioned me in her chambers."

"You didn't have sex with her, did you?"

"Tina. This isn't funny. That woman is crazy."

"Teddy, at least you won't have to deal with her."

At the use of the nickname, Byrd groaned. "Don't you start calling me that! Doc, must have told everybody in the office."

Blackwell laughed. "He has."

Byrd slumped into a chair. "Great!"

"Come to the office tomorrow or the next day. I'll tell you what I know about this appointment. In the meantime, forget about it. I promise you, this will work better for you. Trust me."

"Right," Byrd said. Then hung up the phone.

He was glum when he came out of the office and Rose noticed his demeanor. "Is everything okay?" she asked.

Byrd nodded. "Just some GBI stuff. Office politics, I guess you could say."

He escorted Rose out into the hall. They skirted around to the courtroom. When he stuck his head in, Jerry Mason was talking to a witness and the judge was nowhere in sight. "Mr. District Attorney, is it okay if I take your staff to lunch?"

Mason looked up and nodded. "Sure, I think the judge went back to Ellijay, so you should be good for the rest of the day."

Byrd tried to be animated during lunch, but his mind kept drifting to Judge Pelfrey. Rose was patient and tried to offer courthouse gossip that usually might have gotten Byrd interested. They walked back to her office and Byrd was preparing to leave when Jerry Mason called out, "Daniel, is that you?"

Byrd acknowledged the shout. Mason continued, "You need to call Inspector Carver in Atlanta."

Carver had been Byrd's SAC until a year ago, when Carver had taken a promotion to the GBI Headquarters. Byrd called Carver's direct line and the familiar voice came on.

"I understand you and your favorite judge are still rubbing each other the wrong way."

Byrd laughed. "Same story, different day. But this time she offered to rub me some other way, at least that was the way it seemed."

Byrd described the meeting to his old boss while Carver listened quietly.

"Well, it sounds like she is sober, like you said," Carver finally noted.

"Her skin looked healthier. And I was able to see a lot of it," Byrd commented wryly.

"It's a shame we don't have some kind of video recorder to send you in with. You know, if you only listen to the recording, there is no way to know that she took anything off. I assume she doesn't mention anything, and neither do you?"

Byrd thought about her words. "I guess you're right. But who would have thought she would have pulled a stunt like that? I sure wasn't expecting it. Now I hear she's going to be on the Court of Appeals."

"I'll brief the Director on her latest antics. In the meantime, just keep your distance from her."

Byrd understood their concern. "Boss, I'll do my best. She comes on to me for a couple of seconds, then she gets angry and cusses me out."

Carver laughed. "You probably deserved it!"

Byrd laughed, too. "You're right."

Carver grunted. "That's what I thought."

"Any idea when she will be promoted?" Byrd wasn't getting his hopes up.

"Judges are appointed," Carver corrected. "And, no, I don't know for sure when the appointment will be announced."

"Well, this ain't my first rodeo. I'll keep my head down until I hear something."

"This ain't my first rodeo either," he said. "If I hear anything out of the state capital, I'll let you know. Stay safe, Teddy!" Carver hung up.

Byrd groaned.

TUESDAY, NOVEMBER 16, 2004
3:44 P.M.
CANTON, GEORGIA

CMANS Agent Freddie Torres was surprised when the office secretary said the United States Attorney's Office was on the phone and had asked for him by name. Torres was beaming with pride when he picked up the call.

"This is Agent Torres. How may I help you?"

"This is Selena Gonzalez, Assistant US Attorney for the Northern District of Georgia."

"Yes, ma'am. What can we do for you, Ms. Gonzalez? "

"Agent, the US Attorney has personally assigned me to take the lead in prosecuting the Mexican man who brought those kilos of meth to Cherokee County."

Torres was shocked. The normal process was for the local District Attorney to approve any federal prosecution. That usually took at least one face-to-face meeting to get the facts of the case out in the open.

"Has our DA's office been involved in this decision? We usually have to get their approval to give a case to the feds."

Gonzalez was unfazed. "We spoke to the DA and to the sheriff. They are in full agreement. This has been approved at the highest levels."

Torres exhaled. "That's a relief. So, what do we need to do?"

"You can expect a visit from the DEA to pick up the evidence and have it processed in Miami for court."

Torres had heard that was the process when the case went into federal court. After the call ended, he wrote down the name of the DEA agent who would be coming and sent an email to his boss.

Within two hours, David Clemente walked into the CMANS office, flashing his DEA credentials for the secretary, who invited him in.

Freddie Torres was already taking the necessary steps to transfer the drug evidence when he met the young DEA man, dressed in cowboy boots, jeans, and a western-style shirt, in the entry hall.

Torres extended a hand and Clemente shook firmly. "Thanks for making the drive up. I guess we could have driven this down to you," Torres said.

Clemente shrugged and laughed. "No problem. I get paid the same whether I'm playing pack mule or working undercover. There is sure less risk with this assignment!"

Torres escorted the DEA man into the office conference room. "Where are you from, Agent Clemente? I'm from Peru, originally."

Clemente laughed again. "East LA, man. I don't speak a word of Spanish. I wish I did."

Torres laughed, too. "That's not uncommon."

Torres had the paperwork prepared to transfer the drug evidence, and with very little fanfare, over twenty-five pounds of meth was handed off. Clemente gave him a business card as he walked out the door. Torres closed the office door, verifying it was locked.

He heard Clemente outside making a phone call. Torres was puzzled. He couldn't make out the words, but it certainly sounded like he was speaking Spanish. Torres shrugged it off, thinking the DEA man might know a few words of the Latin language.

Torres was typing a report on the case transfer when he realized he had failed to write the evidence receipt number in his notes. He figured it would be an easy fix—just call Agent Clemente and have him check it.

His first concern came when he called Clemente's cell phone and found the number was out of service. It was concerning, but he still had the office number for DEA Atlanta on the agent's card.

Torres called the number on the card and got a female voice who responded, "Yeah?"

Torres frowned. "Is this DEA?"

The voice on the phone hesitated. "Yeah."

"I'm looking for Agent Clemente."

He heard a muffled conversation take place on the other end. Then the female came back on the line. "He ain't here. He is out in the fields, working somewhere."

Torres left his name and office number. Then he pulled another card he had for another DEA agent he had met in a drug class a while back. This number was different from Clemente's DEA office. Torres suddenly felt like he was going to be sick.

He dialed the number on the second card and waited. "DEA Atlanta Field Division. How may I route your call?"

Torres didn't like the tone of this call, so much more professional than the one before. "I need to speak to Agent Clemente."

"One moment." Music came on in the background.

"Clemente. Who's calling?"

"This is Agent Torres with CMANS. You were just at our office a little while ago."

"Not me. I've been in the office all day. You must have the name wrong."

"Is this David Clemente with the DEA office in Atlanta?"

"The one and only. How can I help you out?"

"You weren't at the CMANS office in Canton today?"

"No. Was I supposed to be?"

Torres had a very bad feeling. "Do you know an AUSA named Selena Gonzalez? She was assigned a drug case out of Canton."

There was a long pause. "My friend, there is no AUSA named Gonzalez in Atlanta. I know everybody who works in the Drug Prosecution Division. What's going on?"

Torres dropped the phone. He slumped in his chair, trying to figure out what to do. *How do I tell my boss I just gave away all that meth?* he thought.

TUESDAY, NOVEMBER 16, 2004
8:22 P.M.
BOWENS MILL, GEORGIA

The general looked up to see Omar, his oldest son, come into the room at a run. Mitchell Warren assumed his son had heard the gunshot from his office. Omar's eyes were wide; his mouth hung open. At six-foot-one, and more than two hundred pounds, Omar was no longer a boy. He ran his hand through his unruly hair that fell to his shoulders.

Mitch sat at his desk, a sheepish grin on his face and a smoking .45 automatic in his right hand. The smell of gunpowder was strong, and Omar just shook his head.

Mitch stood and walked around the desk. He put his arms around the twenty-year-old and gave him a rare hug. "Sorry, Omar. I guess I sent everyone in the house into orbit with that."

Omar seemed angry. "What did you think you were doing? You could have hurt somebody!" Omar said as he stood with his hands on his hips.

Mitch grinned again. "I was seeing if this gun was empty." He dropped the magazine and worked the slide. "It wasn't, but it is now."

"Not funny, Dad. If anything happens to you, what are we supposed to do? Hell, we can't run the farm without you here."

Mitch mulled that over. He sat on the big couch he had installed for his naps. He patted a spot beside him and Omar sat down reluctantly.

"Son, your mom knows where there is enough money for y'all to live on. I'm sorry we don't have the kind of relationship where I can take you with me to work or talk to you about what goes on at the office. I took a different path, that's all." He tried to sound upbeat.

Omar leaned away but kept his seat. "You've been gone almost my whole childhood. Now, you come home and build this 'school.' My friends say you train terrorists like the ones who attacked our country. And I'm stuck trying to defend you with no ammunition."

Mitch's face flushed. "Who cares what your friends think?"

"I do!" Omar shouted. "Some are guys I played football with. And, yes, I played on the high school team. And by the way, I was pretty damned good. Now, those guys are off in college and I'm running errands and doing odd jobs at an anti-terrorist camp."

Mitch nodded. "Your mom kept me up to speed about you and the others. But I've had obligations that kept me away from those kinds of things. Now, my new obligations have given me the chance to be home."

"Like what, Dad? What's so important? What was always more important than your family?"

Mitch didn't flinch. "You're right, son. I do owe you an explanation. And I want to make you an offer." Mitch glanced away. "I guess this is as good a time as any."

Mitch stood and walked over to the wall behind his desk. To Omar, the judges' panels of oak were as solid as stone, but Mitch pressed a release and the wall swung out. Inside was a safe, several rifles and pistols hanging on the wall, and a row of drawers with names on them.

When Mitch motioned Omar over, Omar stood reluctantly, suddenly he seemed more curious than resistant. There were twenty-four drawers labeled with male names and around the same number with female names. Mitch pulled one of the drawers out and passed Omar a Polish passport. Omar examined the passport, especially the photo inside. He looked back up at his dad, waiting for an explanation. What he saw, when he looked up, was the man in the photo in his hands. Mitch had donned a wig of rough-looking, course hair, thick-framed glasses, and a mole on his cheek.

Mitch finally broke the silence. "I do things on behalf of the government. I traveled a lot over the years and have had several identities. That went with the job."

Omar shook his head. "You're CIA?"

Mitch pulled the disguise off and shrugged. "Let's say, I'm affiliated."

Mitch passed Omar another passport—Canadian this time. When Omar opened it, his own face was looking back. But the name was "Oliver McCallan."

Before Omar could ask, Mitch said, "I have these for all of you. In case we have to leave in a hurry."

"What? What do you mean 'leave in a hurry'?"

Mitch shrugged. "Sometimes this job can go sideways. And I will never leave my family in the lurch. I have contingencies in place to take care of us—all of us."

Omar frowned. "Won't the government take care of us?"

"It doesn't work like that. As far as the government is concerned, I don't have any connection to them. They will turn their back on me."

"Then where do these fake passports come from? Didn't the government give them to you?"

Mitch shook his head. "They taught me how to procure them, sure. But I found an expert forger to make these. They have been processed in a way that will make it almost impossible to detect as a fraud. But thanks to 9/11, that kind of document is getting harder to secure."

"Then what do you do for the government? Do you get paid? I don't understand how this works."

Mitch poured a second scotch, smiling ruefully when he realized his son's Canadian pseudonym had originated with the brand. "I do things the government wants done, but can't have a hand in. And I do it without government help."

Omar still seemed puzzled. "So, who gives you orders?"

Mitch chuckled. "Your mom."

"I'm serious."

"I was in the military for a short time. A man came to me and offered me the opportunity to serve my country in a different way. They saw I had potential in other areas." Mitch paused, clearly omitting something. "I did a couple of jobs in South America. Some of those jobs involved smuggling guns to freedom fighters. People who didn't have money to pay for the guns they needed to fight communism."

"You gave them guns?" Omar was beginning to see where the story was going. "Like Iran–Contra?"

"No, son. Like you, your sisters, and your brother, I believe that if you give someone something, it has no value.

You did chores around here when you were younger, and I paid you for that. Now, you do real jobs around this place that help me keep things going. The errands you run and the odd jobs you do have a purpose. The money you earned then, and the money you earn now, was a value for work done, not a gift. Money has a value to you, in sweat and work. You see, I had to buy those guns with my own money, so I had to get something of value in return."

"You mean drugs?"

"Cocaine was all they had to offer. And the value of that payment here in the United States was substantially more than it was worth to anyone in those jungles."

"You were a drug dealer."

"Drug smuggler—there's a difference. I took something our friends needed and then I took the product they gave me in return and brought it back here. In the process, I made my investment back and a whole lot more." Mitch smiled.

"Where did all that cocaine go?"

Mitch shrugged. "Mostly to people I had connections with in Hollywood. I could have smuggled in tons of the stuff, and they would have bought every speck."

"You're smuggling cocaine now? That's what you're doing in here all the time?"

Mitch shook his head. "No, son. I wouldn't bring that business into our house. No, this farm is just for training freedom fighters. No smuggling."

Omar looked like his world had been upended. "You still haven't answered my questions. You're telling me the US government sends you out on these missions? You get some kind of orders to go out and do this stuff?"

Mitch spoke carefully, "Sometimes, I get a clipping from a newspaper in the mail or a link to a story on the internet. I know, based on past experience, that the stories have been sent to me by 'friends' in the government. It's my job to put a plan together, find the right people, and make it happen. And it's up to me to finance the operation. So, I make sure I make a profit."

"And the government protects you?"

Mitch shrugged. "They give a wink and a nod. And if I happen to clash swords with US law enforcement, they run interference." Mitch grunted. "If I get caught outside the US, however, it's every man for themselves."

Omar seemed even more confused. "The government won't send help?"

Mitch laughed harshly. "If it suits their purpose."

Omar's eyes narrowed. "Why are you telling me this now?"

"I have other business interests. That's the process. The government is totally hands off—we do a job they want done, they pay nothing, and I absorb all the risks."

"But why now? Why bring me in on it?"

"I have a project going that you may be able to help with. One of my other interests happens to be on the US-Mexican border. I have businesses that earn our family money, just like the farm. Both are *mostly* legitimate," Mitch said as he looked over the top of the glass of scotch.

"Could I end up in jail over this?"

Mitch shook his head assuredly. "I take lots of precautions. But as I told you, I also have friends in high places. Most of what I do is sanctioned on the highest levels, son."

"Most?" Omar asked.

"To make the kind of money we enjoy, you have to do some things that others might think of as, um . . . questionable. I have bills to pay, like everyone else." Mitch tipped back the scotch and finished it, then took a second glass out and poured two scotches. He handed one to Omar.

"This is eighteen-year-old Macallan Scotch whisky—the good stuff. Let's have one together."

Omar took the offered glass. He took a sip.

Mitch finished his glass off, then said, "I think you are ready to become more than a helper in this business of mine. It's time for you to run an operation. At least a part of it."

"You want me to become some kind of undercover agent? Doing what?" Suddenly, Omar seemed interested.

Mitch laughed. "You won't be going undercover. You'll be using your real name and working out west on a project. But I need to use the talent you have for flying airplanes. I want to ferry radios that we modify to our customers on the border. Technically, those radios and phones can't leave the US. *Technically.*"

Omar seemed disappointed. "I was hoping this was going to be like *Mission Impossible.*"

"The old TV shows?" Mitch asked.

"The movies with Tom Cruise. He's a government agent who works off the books."

Mitch smiled. "I guess if they made a movie of my life, it would be sort of like *Mission Impossible.*" Mitch continued, "I need someone I can trust in Texas, at an office I have in El Paso. It'll just be for a few months. If you pack in the morning, I'll arrange a ride for you."

"A ride? No flight?"

"First trip, I want you to get to know the area. You'll be doing plenty of flying later if our services are as useful as I think they will be. And we can never forget, there are some rough customers on the border. If you drive out, you won't have any issues with you carrying a gun, and I want you to take several sets of our latest secure radios. I'll have them boxed up and loaded for you and Adam to leave early tomorrow."

"That sounds good. Will Adam know what needs to be done?"

Mitch nodded. "He's been my right hand since before I married your mother. He will walk you through everything, just listen to what he says and follow his lead."

Omar was all in. "This sounds like an adventure!"

"It will be, son." Mitch poured a third scotch. Then he passed a heavy package over to Omar.

Omar opened the box to find a Glock 19 in a holster, a DEA badge, and a set of DEA credentials with his photo. "You already had this made up? What am I supposed to do with these?"

Mitch pointed at the box. "Like I said, there are some rough folks on the border. This will help you along if one of our competitors were to give you a problem. And if the local lawmen give you a problem, just use the badge and ID. They won't stand up to the TSA's scrutiny, but they are good enough for some local cop who finds you're carrying."

Omar nodded, examining the false credentials carefully.

"If you need to rent a plane while you're out there, I want you to rent it in the company name using the credit card you have. The card can't be traced back to us. You're still current in the 182, aren't you?"

Omar nodded. "And most other single-engine stuff."

"Good. I may want you to fly back and forth with some radio gear. We have a customer who buys the radios and sells them in Mexico. His requirements are very specific, and he prefers his products to be hand delivered."

Mitch knew Omar hadn't expected this when he ran into the room.

Omar sat the box down. "I'm good with the Glock. Looks like I'm better than you—at least I never shot a desk. But if we're not doing anything illegal, why would I need any of this?"

"We're on the verge of some big money. Shipping goods from Texas to Georgia and back, not just radios and specialty trucks. It could be enough income for all of us to live on for many years." Mitch shook the glass and the ice rattled around. "Just supplying people and vehicles to ship these goods. We never even have to touch the goods. Once the wheels are in motion, all the work is done on the phone or by one of our secure radios."

Despite being excited, Omar still seemed skeptical. "What's the catch, Dad?"

"The people we will be supplying are involved in drug smuggling. We don't do any of the movement of the drugs. We just furnish secure comms and offer them specialty vehicles for whatever use they make of them."

Omar looked intrigued. "You're sure there's *no chance* I could get arrested for what we're doing?"

"These people are smuggling marijuana, which will be legal in this country soon. They grow it cheap in Mexico, but it's still illegal to import into the US. No heavy stuff. No reason for the government to even look at us twice."

"No cocaine involved, then?"

Mitch laughed again and slapped his son on the back as they walked out of the office. "No cocaine. I promise."

Mitch poured his fourth scotch as he watched his son jog up the stairs. He wondered if Omar was as excited as Mitch had been on his first assignment. Mitch decided Omar would be a natural for this next phase of the operation. *No cocaine,* he thought. *Methamphetamine is certainly not cocaine.*

CHAPTER 5
WHAT A METH

WEDNESDAY, NOVEMBER 17, 2004
8:19 A.M.
NORTH OF EL PASO, TEXAS

Montana Worley was a new member of the Texas Highway Patrol and like a child, she was expected to be seen and not heard. She couldn't initiate a call to the big ranger she had talked with—that would be overstepping.

She decided to take a more subtle route. When Montana saw Sergeant Helen Camos pull to the side of the interstate, Montana decided to meet with her. Montanan nosed her black-and-white patrol car behind her supervisor's marked unit. The two women stood under a highway bridge out of the afternoon sun. Even when the temperatures were cool, the sun could burn you.

Montana liked her sergeant and valued her opinion. "Sarge, I noticed you didn't seem to like that ranger. I was kind of wondering if anything came of the investigation of that truck?"

Helen took her hat off and wiped her head. She looked off for a while. "It may have seemed that way. That wasn't my intent."

Montana waited. Sergeant Camos turned back to her.

"Troop, I guess I'm a little touchy about that particular ranger. I was close to his wife. She was a good woman who was taken too soon."

Montana nodded and said, "He told me his wife died. He seems like a good man. I just wondered if there was something else going on."

Helen laughed. "If you mean, do I have my eye on him? The answer is no." She held up her left hand and pointed to her wedding ring. "My husband is a good man, and more patient than I deserve. You'll find out soon enough that working for the Highway Patrol can lead to family problems. Hell, just to make sergeant I've been in three different districts."

Montana pursed her lips. "I've heard that about working in state law enforcement. Is your husband in law enforcement? I've never heard anybody mention him."

"He works for a technology company here in El Paso. He travels so much that the company has let him work in most of the places I have been stationed. Most of the time it has worked."

Montana hung her head. She was uncomfortable asking the next question but really wanted to know the answer. "Do you regret going into this career?"

Helen looked far away again. "Troop, you make sacrifices in life. Working for the State, you make more than most, I think."

Montana noticed that Helen's voice had cracked. Helen pushed her hat back on her head and moved to stand.

Montana was surprised. "Sarge, I'm sorry. Did I say something wrong?"

Helen leaned back against her patrol car. "No, Troop. You didn't. I guess nobody has told you about me?"

"I've only heard good things about you, Sarge." Montana

was honest. She hadn't heard any negative comments about her boss. Helen was recognized within their district as a hard charger.

Helen Camos wouldn't meet Montana's eye. "I heard you got shot back in Georgia."

Montana nodded. "My vest saved my life."

"You're lucky. I got hit twice in the vest. The third bullet went into my abdomen just below the vest. A stupid traffic stop for a burned-out taillight."

"God, I know that sucks. Do you have any health problems now?"

Helen's laugh was bitter. "I had only been pregnant a month. I wasn't even sure I was, at the time. He killed the child and left me unable to have any more."

Montana's heart sank. She thought about reaching out to Helen but knew she wouldn't want her to do that in public.

"That big ranger was a trooper then. He was coming to back me up when the guy shot me. A coyote with a car full of illegals. Clete rolled up and shot the son-of-a-bitch and then loaded me in his patrol car and took me to the hospital. By the time another car got to the scene, the coyote was gone, along with the car he was in."

"Did you find out what happened to him? Did he ever turn up?"

She nodded. "I heard a story. But I don't know for sure."

Montana waited. The Sergeant took her hat off and tossed it in the air. She spun the hat around her left hand as she turned back to face Montana.

"Rumor is that Clete snuck into Mexico and dragged him back to stand trial. All anybody knows for sure is that he ended up dropped off in front of the El Paso county jail in handcuffs. He tried to fight the case, but shooting an officer is a big deal here. The jury took less than an hour to find him guilty, and the judge gave him twenty years for each bullet he fired. A total of sixty years. He's going to be a guest of the State of Texas for a long time."

Montana grabbed Helen's hand and squeezed it. Helen squeezed back.

"Has he called you?" Helen asked.

"No, ma'am. I guess he's busy."

"I'll make sure he calls you tomorrow. You would be good for him."

Montana mumbled, "Thanks."

Helen put her hat back on and climbed into her black-and-white car. As she pulled up beside Montana, she lowered the window. "Don't break his heart. I owe him."

Montana thought about protesting that her interest was professional. Then she realized that her Sergeant would be insulted. She tipped her hat as Helen drove away.

WEDNESDAY, NOVEMBER 17, 2004
10:04 A.M.
CANTON, GEORGIA

The CMANS offices were unusually quiet. Word that Torres had lost a major amount of drug evidence had spread within minutes. Now Wally Demopolis, the Commander of the CMANS, was sitting at his desk listening to Freddie Torres explain the chain of events.

Demopolis, a big man with a clean-shaven head and goatee, was slumped over his desk. "What did the jail say when you checked on the driver of the van?"

Torres shook his head, something he had been doing

for most of the meeting. "It looks like the same guy who told me he was DEA picked the guy up."

"The jail just gave him up?"

Torres nodded his head. "He had a court order to take him into federal custody. But it looks like, on closer inspection, the order is a forgery. I had the jail fax me a copy." He passed the piece of paper to Demopolis who examined it and passed it back.

Demopolis shifted in his seat, swung his legs up onto his desk, crossed his ankles, and stared at the ceiling. Torres recognized this as Demopolis's pondering position. He would be evaluating all the angles and figuring out the best way to deal with the problem.

Without looking down, Demopolis asked, "Do the folks at the jail know the whole story? Do they know we lost the drugs? Do they have any idea that the court order was bogus?"

"I doubt it. No one outside our office knows about the missing drugs. And we didn't have any outside support, so no officers outside of this office know about the original arrests."

Demopolis kept staring at the ceiling. "What about the old woman?"

Torres rubbed his face with both hands. "She was released. We couldn't prove she was involved in selling sex. She said she was there of her own free will, and there wasn't anything we could find in the apartment to link her to it."

Demopolis rocked back farther in the chair, to the point Torres was afraid the chair would tip over.

"I guess at this point, her being out is a good thing. Things could turn into a circus if we had to present what we have in any kind of hearing. Do you know if the sheriff is aware of what's going on?"

Torres laughed. "I hear he hasn't drawn a sober breath since he lost the election. I doubt he gives a shit to be honest."

Demopolis dropped his feet to the floor. He knew what he had to do. "Sit here while I call him. If he has any questions I can't answer, I want you here."

Demopolis dialed the phone number for Sheriff Haggin. Haggin picked up on the fourth ring.

"What?" was the raspy response.

"Sheriff, this is Commander Demopolis at CMANS. I need to brief you on a matter."

Haggin responded immediately. "Call someone who gives a shit." With a *click*, the connection was broken.

Demopolis shrugged. "Well, I checked that block."

Torres was anxious. "What did he say?"

Demopolis thought for a moment. "Did you play sports when you were a kid?"

Torres nodded, confused at the question. "Sure, mostly *futbol*, or soccer as you guys call it."

"Did you line up and shake hands and tell the other team 'Good game'?"

Torres nodded. "Something like that."

Demopolis laughed harshly. "The sheriff was the guy who folded his arms and pouted when he lost."

Torres got the picture. "What now, boss?" he asked.

"Now, I'll make some phone calls to the DEA and see what they can tell me about this mess. Maybe they know about people running around using fake DEA badges, but I certainly haven't heard anything about it."

Torres had been in the drug enforcement game long enough to have doubts. "You really think the DEA will tell you the truth?"

Demopolis shook his head. "They won't tell me the time of day. But once I put this out to them, they'll make some inquiries. I might hear about the real story through a back channel I have."

Torres frowned. "What kind of back channel?"

Demopolis winked as he said, "I wasn't always married."

Torres waited, but Demopolis wouldn't tell him anything else.

WEDNESDAY, NOVEMBER 17, 2004
11:44 A.M.
EL PASO, TEXAS

Texas Ranger Clete Petterson strode into the barbeque restaurant and joined Trooper Montana Worley at a table near the rear. Clete enjoyed the status the job gave him. Texans seemed to hold his organization in reverence, except along the border where the rangers had a reputation for cruelty and intolerance of the people of Mexico. Clete knew his silver star could be as much a target as a symbol of justice. He had worked hard to build his personal reputation, first as a trooper, then as a Texas Ranger in El Paso.

Walking with his back straight, and with purpose, Clete wore a starched white shirt with dark, western-cut pants. He had two belts, both high-quality leather that had been hand-tooled by a state prison inmate. Both belts were fixed with silver buckles bearing the star of the Texas Rangers. He wore his pistol—a Colt .45 semiautomatic with the hammer locked back—in a matching, old-fashioned thumb-break holster.

He took a position at the table that gave him a view of the entire room. He scanned those around him, looking for obvious weapons, and then set his hat on the table. He noticed

Montana's hat on the table sitting on the brim. He took her hat and turned it over to match his.

"Is that the wrong way to lay your hat on a table?" Montana asked, amused.

Clete nodded. "It lets the good luck run out."

She chuckled. "Okay."

"And it gets the brim all catawampus."

"What? I've never heard that word. Is it real?"

Clete looked at her suspiciously. "How long have you been in West Texas? It means to be all out of order, out of alignment."

Montana said, "Duly noted. And I haven't been here that long. It seems like I just got out of the academy in Austin. I still have a lot to learn."

Clete nodded. "Do you speak any Spanish?"

Montana shook her head. "I wish I understood more. We had a crash class in the academy, and some of my classmates were fluent. I can stumble through a traffic stop, but I don't think I would say I spoke the language by any stretch."

Clete pressed his lips together. "One of the things I tell every boot who comes in here is, learn Spanish. Or at least the border version of Spanish. Some folks call it Spanglish, because a lot of English words have been thrown into the mix over the years. It lets the people out here know you want to be a part of the border."

"Do you speak Spanish? No offense, but you look like a big ol' redneck farm boy to me."

He laughed. "Dang, girl! You say what you think."

She just shrugged.

Clete continued to smile. "And you're right. I'm a big ol' country boy who grew up out in the sticks in the piney woods of East Texas. On a farm, no less. When I went to college I took a couple of semesters of Spanish, but really couldn't speak a lick. Then the big hats in Austin decided a big ol' farm boy would fit in just fine in El Paso. This was my first post of duty. Then I got promoted to corporal and moved to Falfurrias. From there, I went to Odessa as a sergeant. I was top of the list for lieutenant when the opening came up in the rangers. I took a rank and pay cut, got sent back here to El Paso, and the rest is history. I've spent all my career dealing with the people out here, and in the process, I became fluent in Spanish."

Montana was impressed. "Good job. I'm not sure taking classes will help me that much. But I plan to try."

Clete leaned near Montana and said, "Okay, it didn't hurt that my wife was Mexican, and she and the kids all speak fluent Spanish."

Montana shook her head. "You won't do."

Clete frowned. "What the dickens does that mean?"

"You're a mess is what it means."

They shifted gears as a server came and took their orders. No business was ever discussed when civilians were nearby.

Once the server went to deliver their food order, Clete said, "It seems that the truck you followed was abandoned near Midland. The emblems and all are still on it, so it was pretty easy to spot. A compartment, big enough to hold two large suitcases, was left open and empty. A radio of some kind had been installed, but it was ripped out and the bracket and the wiring were left behind."

Montana nodded. "You think it was a load of dope? I don't guess there was enough room for illegals to have hidden inside the truck."

Clete shook his head. "Nope. But here is something interesting. I faxed photos to the CSX Railroad Police. The truck is a dead ringer for one of their authentic work trucks, down to the shop numbers on the fender."

Montana frowned. "They had pictures of the real truck then. Someone had to do some research on this side of the border."

Clete nodded. He fell silent as two iced teas were dropped at the table. As soon as the server left, he said, "And Customs says the truck hasn't been in or out of Mexico."

Montana said, "You think it was loaded here, then?"

"Yep. And I think this deal is connected with a crew we have been keeping an eye on here in the city."

Clete lowered his voice. "A group with ties back to Georgia." He watched her face. When she reacted, he said, "I thought that might pique your interest."

"Where in Georgia?"

"Ever heard of Bowens Mill?"

She shook her head. "Nope."

"What about Jasper?" he asked.

"Jasper, I've heard of. It's just north of Canton, where I policed. It's a little mountain town just outside of Metro Atlanta."

"Do you have anybody you trust who could help us out with running down a couple of addresses we have in that area? We want to hand this off to someone who'll cooperate with our case and not try to grandstand. This case will end up being a multinational conspiracy."

Montana pulled out her pad with a list of her important phone numbers. She scanned it, then look up and said, "I know a GBI agent who works up in Jasper. He is as solid as they come. I can reach out to him if you'd like."

Clete looked her in the eye. "I hope this doesn't piss you off, but could I have the number? Some of the things I have told you are very sensitive. It would look better in his report and mine if you aren't mentioned."

Montana wasn't happy, but she understood. She wrote the number on a napkin and handed it to him.

Montana clicked the pen a couple of times and then stared at Clete. After a moment, she said, "You invited me here to get a phone number from Georgia?"

Clete appeared flustered as his face turned red. "No, I was just . . ." he stammered.

"Just what?"

"I wanted to talk to you . . ."

"Spit it out, Ranger. 'Cause if you don't ask me out before we leave here, I will be forced to ask you out."

Clete sat, face red, trying to decide what to say. "Okay, damn it! Let's go out to dinner. I want to get to know you." Clete wiped the sweat from his forehead. "I would be honored to take you to dinner."

Before Montana could respond, two orders of brisket arrived. Clete seemed as if he had never been so happy to see a plate of food.

CHAPTER 6
TEXAS IS THE PLACE
I REALLY WANT TO BE

WEDNESDAY, NOVEMBER 17, 2004
2:51 P.M.
NEAR MOBILE, ALABAMA

Omar Warren had been sitting on the passenger side of the truck for several hours. The man who drove seemed sullen and the man behind him was quiet.

"You know who I am?" the man said, never taking his eyes off the road.

Omar nodded. "You're Captain Benjamin. You've worked for my dad for a long time."

Benjamin nodded. "I've worked for your dad in a lot of capacities." He glanced over at Omar. "And cut the 'captain' shit. I'm Adam. That's all."

He nodded. Omar didn't know what to say other than, "Yes, sir."

The man in the back seat ignored them. He had been sleeping most of the time since they left the farm.

Omar had seen Adam Benjamin around the training center and knew he was one of his dad's most trusted people. He was over sixty, but in shape, Omar had observed.

He dressed in jeans and flannel and always had a cap on his head. His hair was much longer than Mitch Warren usually tolerated, but he had no doubt of his dad's trust in the man.

Adam glanced back at Omar. "You know why your dad picked the name Adam Benjamin for me?"

"He picked your name?"

"My work name," he said. "Adam was the first man. And Benjamin means 'son of the right hand.' That means I'm his right hand. Do you understand?"

Omar shrugged. "You're his go-to guy?"

"I've been with him longer than your mom, that's what it means."

Omar nodded and kept his eyes on the road.

The route they were taking was mostly country roads for the first two hours. Now they had intercepted I-10 and were covering more ground. The pickup they were in was comfortable, but the miles seemed to drone on. When the truck crossed into Alabama, Adam looked at Omar and said, "You got any cash on you?"

Omar nodded. Mitch had given him cash and a credit card to use. He had even thought to give Omar a Canadian passport, which matched the name on the credit card. "A little. Why?"

"Didn't your dad tell you? Rooms and meals are on the company credit card he gave you. We don't want to use any personal cards or identification for any of this travel to prevent a paper trail. We only buy gas with the card I have, which is owned by a holding company from Norway. We use that card till we're in El Paso, then we'll ditch it. I have a second card as backup. When we get settled in, we put our rooms on your company card."

Omar nodded. "That makes sense, I guess."

"So, if he didn't tell you how things go, are you supposed to be running this show?"

Omar cut his eyes over. "I'm supposed to be learning."

"And snitching to your dad?"

Omar shook his head. "I'm not a snitch. Even if I am the boss's son."

Adam cut his eyes over. "We'll see."

Omar saw a sign welcoming him to Mississippi. The land seemed low and wet from the window of the truck.

Adam shot the truck up the second exit inside Mississippi and rolled to a stop at the top. He turned right and followed a paved road taking them away from the interstate. He followed the road for less than a mile and turned onto a tar and gravel road bracketed by tall pines and scrub brush up to the road.

"Where are we headed?" Omar asked.

"I need to pee. I'm just getting off the main drag," Adam replied.

After a quarter mile, Adam pulled off the path and put the truck in park.

The sleeper in the back grumbled as he crawled out of the back seat and stretched. Adam and Omar stood and relieved themselves. The man from the back seat ambled over and did the same.

Adam zipped up, then walked behind the other man. He pulled a small automatic pistol from his waistband and pointed it at the man from the back seat.

The man threw his hands up and said, "Hey!"

Adam shot him once in the head. Adam watched him drop and draw his last breath.

"Help me drag him into the woods," Adam said.

Omar, shocked at the sudden turn of events, helped Adam pull the dead weight of the man into the high grass beside the road. Adam methodically emptied the dead man's pockets.

Omar watched in silence as Adam readied to resume the journey. Adam motioned for Omar to get back in the truck. Omar climbed into the seat, waiting for whatever would come next. Then Adam pulled the pistol a second time and pointed it at Omar. Omar recoiled, but the door was locked and his only retreat was to press against it.

Adam put the gun to Omar's head and then pulled a flask from his hip pocket. "Take a drink."

Omar shook his head. "What is this?"

"Just some whiskey. Not that expensive shit your dad drinks. But it'll do for the road."

Omar opened it and sniffed. Once the top was off, the whiskey smell was strong. He wrinkled his nose but took a sip.

"Take a hard pull," Adam said.

Omar turned the flask up and took a long drink, closing his eyes when the raw-tasting liquid burned his throat.

Adam smiled. When Omar sat the flask down, Adam handed him the pistol. Omar grabbed the gun in his right hand and held it near his leg.

"What do you want me to do?" Omar asked.

"Point the gun at me and make me take a drink."

Adam laughed at the joke. Omar laughed in relief. Then he took another sip from the flask before he handed it back.

Adam finished the flask and tossed it into the back seat. He winked at Omar and pulled the truck back on the road. "That man was forcing one of the female students to have sex with him. He told her she would be sent home if she didn't, and for her, that would mean death."

"So, you killed him? Couldn't you just fire him?" Omar asked. Omar's mouth was dry as dust. He was having trouble getting the words out.

Adam shook his head. "First, *we* killed him. You were a part of this, like it or not."

Omar thought it over. "Did my dad have this done?"

Adam frowned. "We have an operation that depends on people doing as they are told. Your dad asked me to handle a problem, and I recommended that you be a party to it."

"To see what I would do?"

"No," Adam said. "To show you what you're getting into. This life isn't a game."

"And you kill for my dad?" Omar asked.

"I kill so we can continue this life. We do jobs for people of power. In this world, there is no slap on the hand. If you fuck up, you die—that includes you, son."

Omar stared out the window of the truck. "I guess I knew that."

Adam looked over at Omar. "You're about to become a member of the side of our business that can be hard. The jobs your dad wants us to do aren't strictly legal, at least in America."

Omar leaned back and sighed. "So, what are you supposed to do if I say I'm out? That I can't do this job?"

Adam didn't reply.

Omar nodded. "That's what I figured. And it wouldn't matter—I'm in. Just don't ask me to do what you just did."

Adam didn't smile. "I don't know what you're talking about."

WEDNESDAY, NOVEMBER 17, 2004
4:22 P.M.
CANTON, GEORGIA

Wally Demopolis got the call on his personal cell phone while he sat at his desk at the CMANS. He recognized the number and stepped out of his office to answer. "Hey, girl. Are you still the training guru?"

There was a laugh on the other end. The woman's voice was sharp, and gravelly. "Still in Quantico. The place the DEA sends people when they're afraid they are too dysfunctional for DC." She paused, then said, "You still the head semen?"

"It's called CMANS, darling." He imagined her smiling.

"And passing out at our office Christmas party is called a medical condition. But it kept me from getting fired."

"But you're still on the wagon? Right?"

She snorted. "Most of the time. I dinged up my shoulder in the gym and got a little sideways with some pain pills the docs gave me."

"Damn, girl. You're living a hard life."

"Maybe, but a couple of Percocet and a fifth of Crown will make you forget the stupid shit you do to yourself. I had to go on the bench for that one. Thank God the DEA has good benefits. No, I'm back to only abusing alcohol and my body."

It was Demopolis's turn to laugh. "Let's not talk about your body; I'm still married."

"Me, too," she said. "At least on paper."

Demopolis wanted to change the subject. "Did you get my text?"

"Wally, I have gotten texts from you and the whole top brass of the DEA. It seems the bigwigs in DC ran your name through our system when you reported the guy posing as one of our agents. When you popped in the computer as one of my character references, everybody and their brother has been calling or texting. They want to know what kind of guy you are." She paused. "I didn't tell them the truth."

Demopolis laughed. "I bet you didn't."

"The folks in DC are all shook up. They wanted a full-blown investigation to find this joker. Calling in the big guns from around the country. DEA still has a few people who can actually investigate, you know!"

Demopolis wasn't surprised. "I figured they would be coming down on this hard. I was surprised they haven't called on us for help."

She lowered her voice. "Don't hold your breath waiting. It seems that some phone calls were made on secure phone lines, and then the word came from on high to monitor the situation. Don't take any action."

Demopolis frowned. "That's odd. You mean they're sitting on their hands on this?"

"Uh-huh."

Demopolis was shocked. "Why in the hell would the DEA let something like this go? Forget about the dope we lost. What about some guy running around with fake credentials? Damned good copies of DEA credentials, from what I hear."

She was still quiet. When she spoke, it was almost a whisper. "In Mexico, they called it *las tres letras*. You know what that is?"

"Three something?"

"The three letters. It's what the Mexicans called all of us American *federales*. We wear those raid jackets, just like the rest of the law enforcement world in the Western Hemisphere. Ours have three big gold letters on the back."

"Okay, I get the three letters thing. But I'm missing something. You're saying it's one of your own?"

"Nope. We use the expression inside the DEA. But when we use it, it refers to the agencies that don't exist." When Demopolis didn't respond immediately, she said, "CIA, DIA, or NSA. And they are probably listening to me tell you this right now."

Demopolis thought about what she said. Maybe she was just being paranoid. "They can't work in the US. I know enough to know that. The Church Committee put an end to that."

"Right. We're from the government and we're here to help. Your best bet is to let this drop."

Demopolis didn't like that. "What's my next best bet?"

The line went dead.

CHAPTER 7
HAVE I GOT A DEAL FOR YOU

WEDNESDAY, NOVEMBER 18, 2004
9:42 P.M.
WEST OF BEAUMONT, TEXAS

Omar was restless. They had been on the road for just over twelve hours and had just crossed into Texas. Omar was surprised that the murder of his father's employee hadn't really bothered him.

Omar assumed that, once they were in Texas, El Paso would only be a few hours away. The two men had traveled almost exactly seven hundred miles, stopping only for fuel, snacks, and the occasional bathroom break.

When Omar saw the road sign on his right, he was shocked. The sign read "EL PASO: 855."

Omar slumped in the seat. "How much longer are we going before we spend the night?" he asked Adam.

"We'll stop between Houston and San Antonio. The best place will be something right on the interstate, but not in any big city. You check in late and leave the key in the room. It's rare that any of the staff would even pay us any attention."

"Why are we worried about being seen?" Omar asked.

"We aren't—now. But I always try to consider how we

can move around without leaving any signs behind. We call it 'tradecraft.'"

"What does it do for you?"

Adam glanced over at Omar. "It worked a lot better before 9/11. We could get driver's licenses, passports, credit cards, and could get any of those things in just about any name you wanted. Now it's very tricky. Motels want you to provide a valid ID and credit card. The names need to match, and sometimes the card company won't issue you a line of credit on a name they haven't vetted."

"That's why the fallback is cash?" Omar asked.

"Right. But as you have seen, you draw more attention by using cash for things like gas or motels. So, we'll spread the costs out among several cards. The rule when I went through training was 'never tell a lie that can be broken with one phone call.' Now, we just try to keep things where some prosecutor can't get the whole picture on one subpoena."

Omar turned to look at Adam. "My dad says we don't have to worry about going to jail. He said he has friends who will get us out of trouble."

Adam shrugged. "I'll just be honest with you: Your dad can lay it on a little thick. None of that is guaranteed. Your dad and I have been involved in operations the government put into play and then decided they didn't want to go to the trouble of following through. Politics might change or the politicians might change. Sometimes that can happen in the middle of an operation. That's why you want to have an exit plan and then a couple of backups to that. Don't trust the government, particularly when it comes to your life or your freedom."

Omar nodded. "I want to be a sponge. The more I can pick up the better."

Adam found an exit with a large truck stop advertised. "Good, you want to pick up as much as you can? Pick us up another bottle of whiskey and a big bag of pork skins. We'll be driving for a couple of more hours at least."

Omar nodded. "That I can do. Will they have whiskey in the truck stop?"

"Nope, but if I recall correctly, there is a liquor store across the street. Don't get hit crossing the street." Adam looked at his watch. "And don't delay. The liquor stores in this state close in about twenty minutes."

Omar jumped out of the truck as soon as Adam parked at a pump.

THURSDAY, NOVEMBER 18, 2004
3:46 A.M.
CANTON, GEORGIA

Rose Mitchell slipped out of bed and tiptoed into the bathroom. She wanted to clean up and get dressed. Spending the night seemed less attractive once her date passed out beside her.

She spent several minutes in the bathroom, washing herself and redoing her hair. She turned the bathroom lights out, hoping she could dress in the glow of the night light. She got her underwear on and was pulling on her dress when she heard the rustling in the bed.

Daniel Byrd rolled to his right and mumbled, "Die, you son-of-a-bitch."

He shifted again, groaned, and then slumped onto his back.

Rose shook her head. *I can't deal with his shit!* she thought.

She adjusted her dress and was making one last check in the mirror when Byrd called to her.

"Rose, are you leaving?"

She turned, startled that he was awake. She shrugged. "Danny, I don't think this is working out. You scare the hell out of me."

Byrd rolled off the bed and stood beside her. He was unsteady on his feet and grabbed the wall for support. "Rose, I know I'm a mess in a lot of ways, but my therapist says I'm getting better."

Rose shook her head. "She's not sleeping with you, is she?"

Byrd scowled. "She's a professional. And she seems to know more about me than I do."

Rose laughed harshly. "Well, it doesn't take a professional to know that you don't know much about yourself. Hell, I know you better than you do. And I don't have time to be your backup counselor."

Byrd leaned into her. "Rose, don't go. At least stay the night. Maybe we can talk in the morning."

"You mean, when you're sober?"

Byrd hung his head. "Sorry, I guess I got a little carried away last night."

Rose gave him a hug. "You went on about how the bodies are stacking up and you're trying to keep all your cases caught up. You need to take a break. You're working too hard, and you need to slow down. Maybe take a vacation?"

Byrd nodded. "I have been keeping a hard pace, but we're short on agents in the office and we're covered up with work."

Rose was stern. "There will always be cases. People kill each other; it's been going on since Cain killed Abel."

"Rose, would you go off with me for a weekend? Maybe a getaway to the mountains?"

She shook her head. "Danny, I live in the mountains. Besides, I have my kids to deal with."

He nodded. There was nothing else to say.

Rose squeezed his hand. "You know we get together mostly for the sex. No entanglements. You're a good guy and you treat me well, but there is no future in our relationship."

Byrd's laugh was hollow. "I'm your boy toy?"

Rose was blunt. "When you can stay sober. You need to take a look at that. You drink like it's a job. It makes me feel cheap."

"Like being used for sex?"

Rose turned away. "This isn't going anywhere. Go back to bed."

Byrd smiled a crooked smile. "Can we get together again?"

She stood at the door. "I don't think that's a good idea for either of us. I think it's time to move on."

She opened the door and quickly stepped outside, pulling the door shut as quietly as she could.

THURSDAY, NOVEMBER 18, 2004
10:19 A.M.
BOWENS MILL, GEORGIA

General Mitchell Warren had been sitting at his desk for over an hour. He despised waiting on others he saw as his inferiors. And the man he was waiting for was that. Uneducated, violent, rude, and crude. But he was also one of the richest men in Mexico. Maybe *the* richest.

Warren checked the clock on the wall. Warren refused to wear a watch, relying on his ability to know the time of day within a few minutes. An ability that had abandoned him several cases of scotch ago. Warren was tempted to get up and leave the room.

"Drug lord," he said aloud. "Bullshit."

As if on cue, the phone rang. Not the house phone, but the special secure phone.

Warren picked up on the second ring. He waited for the three beeps that told him his caller was on a secure phone also.

"General Warren. Who's calling?" Encrypted calls had no caller ID function.

"General. This is your friend in Mexico." Rojo's voice was distinguishable, even with the buzz the encryption device generated.

Warren tried to sound jovial. "Good to hear from you, my friend. I got the message that you would be calling."

"*Sí, Señor General*. I believe we have business that needs to be resolved."

Warren waited. He didn't plan to rise to the bait.

"I am referring to the trucks. The special trucks you furnish to my people," Rojo said.

"Were the trucks satisfactory?" Warren knew it wasn't.

"Unfortunately, no, they are not. That is why I call you. I have people who are waiting for deliveries. The trucks were to be a major business venture. Now, my customers are without."

"Unfortunate, but was the problem due to one of the trucks?"

"It was. My people in El Paso intercepted the radio talk with the highway patrol. A lady trooper spotted the last truck you provided."

Warren knew the truck had been intercepted, but he didn't know why. He was curious.

"How would a trooper know such things? The last truck was a perfect copy of the real thing."

"The trooper, she is from where you are—Georgia. And my operatives have learned that her papa was a worker on the railroad."

Warren shook his head at the bad luck. "I had no way of predicting that."

"I am sure you have no way to know this. My operatives on the US side are quite efficient." Rojo's voice sounded patronizing.

Warren smiled. "I have connections of my own. I was able to recover some of your product intercepted by the police in Georgia. A place called Canton. Is that of help?"

Rojo was surprised. "Yes, can one of my people collect it?"

Warren said, "Of course. It belongs to you. I only provide a service."

Rojo was suspicious of the man on the phone. "You must have good friends to be able to recover my product. I am most appreciative. But we have other business."

"Then what is our business? If I'm not at fault, which I am not, what do you want me to do."

Rojo's voice was harder. "No matter the fault, I need this product delivered to Atlanta. You are near Atlanta. I would consider it a gesture of mutual respect if you made the delivery on my behalf."

Warren was prepared. "How much?"

"Two or three hundred kilos."

"No, how much for the job?"

"I pay you a quarter million for these trucks that I buy. Now, I cannot be sure they will be effective. And you want more money to make this right?"

Warren waited, as did Rojo.

Rojo blinked first. "I'll pay you twenty-five thousand for a guaranteed delivery in Atlanta."

"By when?"

"The day after tomorrow. No later than four days. This is a difficult timeline to achieve, no doubt, but I am under some pressure to deliver."

Warren smiled. "One hundred thousand, by day after tomorrow. If it's late, or intercepted, you owe me nothing."

"My people have the product in El Paso now. Where can they meet your representative?" Rojo asked.

"My people will use an airplane this time. No highway patrol to worry about," Warren said.

Rojo covered the handset momentarily. "There is a long, straight, paved road north of Fabens. My people will wait for your plane to land about ten miles from I-10. I will have El Gordo call you with the exact location and time."

There was a click as the line disconnected. Warren waited until he heard the three beeps again. The line was disabled.

He had climbed out on a very thin limb, but he was confident that Adam and Omar would pull his fat out of the fire.

CHAPTER 8
THE PAST IS HERE AGAIN

FRIDAY, NOVEMBER 19, 2004
12:12 A.M.
CANTON, GEORGIA

Daniel Byrd was startled by the phone ringing. He had dozed off on the couch after a few drinks.

"Hello?" Byrd said.

"Danny? You okay?"

"Sure. Who's this?"

"Bobby Wilton."

Byrd sat up on the couch. "Sorry, Sheriff. I fell asleep on the couch watching a movie." Byrd shook the cobwebs out. He should have recognized the Pickens County sheriff's voice.

"Did I catch you at a bad time?"

"No, I'm good. What's up?"

"You sure you want to talk right now?"

Byrd cleared his throat. "I'm okay, Sheriff. As long as you don't need me to drive anywhere."

Wilton laughed. "Not this minute. I had something unusual happen today. I wanted to get your thoughts on it."

"Sure. Do I need to pull my pants up for this?"

Wilton laughed again. "Not as long as we aren't on

video." Wilton got serious. "Have you ever heard of a cop named Carl Hollander?"

Byrd sifted through his memory. There was a shadow flitting around in the back but he couldn't put his finger on it. "Bobby, the name rings a bell, but I can't tell you why."

"He was a cop in South Georgia. We used him to do some advanced training up here a couple of times. He did an advanced class on handcuffing techniques and also did a class for our drug guys on hidden compartments in cars. I think he worked for Tifton PD at the time."

Byrd said, "The Tifton PD thing is ringing more bells than the training."

"Right," Wilton said. "He was canned after the police department got complaints of racial profiling. He was a right-wing nut job, and the complaints the department got were the tip of the iceberg."

Byrd felt the pieces click into place. "Right, the GBI investigated him and found out he was taking money from illegal immigrants who were working in the fields down there. He beat the immigrants up and basically robbed them. And he was also taking money from the members of the Black community he stopped. Most of the victims were afraid to complain. The district attorney was stuck because most of the victims wouldn't testify, but at least the bureau got his Peace Officers Certification pulled."

"That's the guy," Wilton confirmed. "He called me today," Wilton said.

"Is he still doing training?"

"I'm not sure," Wilton said. "But that's not why he called. He said he wanted my help in getting the folks at the airport to work with him on something."

"What?"

"He said he wants to bring in some equipment and the

flight might look suspicious. He just wants to be sure he doesn't run into problems with the airport people or my deputies."

"You think he has something up his sleeve?" Byrd asked.

"Something other than his arm. He's up to something. I'm just not sure what."

"You think he'll call back?"

"He coming to my office tomorrow afternoon at three. Said he wants to meet in person. He even told me he was worried about talking on the phone."

"Okay," Byrd said. "I'll be in your office tomorrow morning."

"Okay, Danny. I'll see you then," Wilton said. "And one more thing."

Byrd waited.

"If you need to talk to anybody, let me know. I'm always available."

"You heard about Rose?"

"Courthouse gossip travels faster than the speed of light."

"I'm okay."

"You don't sound okay," Wilton responded.

Byrd was quiet for a moment. At last, he said, "Thanks, Bobby. You're a good friend."

FRIDAY, NOVEMBER 19, 2004
2:54 A.M.
EL PASO, TEXAS

Omar had heard Texas was a big state but now he thought "big" was such an understatement. When Adam Benjamin pulled the truck into the lot of a cheap motel,

Omar was exhausted. Sitting in the truck seat, without doing a whole lot else, had been miserable.

"Wait in the truck," Adam said as he climbed out and walked on stiff legs into the motel lobby.

Omar could see him doing the paperwork associated with renting motel rooms. While Adam was paying with a credit card, Omar saw him pull out the flip phone he seemed to carry everywhere.

He stood by the entrance to the motel and carried on an animated conversation. At times, Omar caught Adam looking at where he sat in the truck. Omar noticed that Adam's head was bobbing up and down, now. Adam closed the phone and put it in his pocket. He walked back to the truck and said, "Son, are you ready for a shower and some sleep? I damned sure am."

Omar stepped down and grabbed his duffle bag. He followed Adam up to the rooms on the fourth floor. Once Adam had passed Omar a room key, he ambled down the hall toward his own room. He pushed the plastic card into the door slot and then turned to Omar. "Rest up. I've got some things to take care of first thing, then I'll meet you at the office your dad has here in town. Your dad has a job for us."

Omar started to ask a question, and Adam said, "Get a cab from here." He tossed Omar a brass key marked Do Not Duplicate. "That'll get you in the front door. Just find a place to settle in and wait on me."

Omar opened his own door. As an afterthought, he asked, "What time do I need to be there?"

Adam looked at his watch and saw that it was four a.m. back in Georgia. "Sleep till noon if you can. Be sure to get something to eat. We could have a long day."

FRIDAY, NOVEMBER 19, 2004
6:58 A.M.
WOODSTOCK, GEORGIA

Anne Kuykendall had agreed to meet Byrd early that morning. She normally didn't see patients before eight a.m., but she had a soft spot for troubled cops.

At seven, she had turned on the lights and ushered Byrd into her private office. Byrd took his usual station on the couch and she took the recliner. "You sounded bad last night. What happened?"

Byrd hung his head and looked at his hands. His voice was soft. "Rose left me yesterday."

"Left you? I thought you two were just bed buddies, that there wasn't a serious relationship between you two."

Byrd rocked back and forth. "That's what I told you. And that's what Rose believed. I guess I had a different opinion. I guess I thought it was more."

Anne pulled her left foot up under her in the chair. "Daniel, you told me this was a casual thing. And from the look of you, I'd say you're drinking more than you told me. What happened to a strict two-drink limit?"

Daniel looked up and grinned like a child caught with his hand in the cookie jar. "I guess I slipped off the wagon."

She shook her head. "It looks to me like you jumped off and then set the wagon on fire."

Daniel hung his head again. "What am I supposed to do? I can't sleep without a few drinks, and if I don't sleep, I'm an even bigger mess."

Anne leaned toward Daniel and said, "The thing you love the most, more than you ever said you loved Rose or any other woman we've talked about, is your work. What are you going to do when the day comes and you can't work, or worse get fired, over this drinking problem of yours?"

He became defensive. "What makes it a problem? I have everything under control. I'm dealing with this."

She was sarcastic. "If you're dealing with things so well, why am I here early? Why do you pay me for my time if everything is roses and unicorns?"

He slumped back on the couch. "Then what should I do? And don't say quit drinking."

"Quit drinking. You can't handle moderation. At least for now, you need to cut out the alcohol."

He closed his eyes and nodded. "I know. I just feel lost right now."

"The circumstances that led to you and Rose being intimate have caused you to have a strong connection with her. Even if she doesn't reciprocate. Now, let's talk about how you two met."

"You know that story," Byrd protested.

"I want to hear it again. I want to hear it while you are feeling this way."

Byrd stretched out on the couch and told the story again.

CHAPTER 9
HAVE I GOT A DEAL FOR YOU II

FRIDAY, NOVEMBER 19, 2004
9:54 A.M.
JASPER, GEORGIA

Daniel Byrd pulled into the parking lot behind the Pickens County Jail. He parked his Crown Victoria and navigated past the locked doors and access control devices. He picked up a cup of hot coffee and sat in Sheriff Bobby Wilton's office.

"Sheriff, how goes it?"

Wilton smiled. "It goes. Election season is over, so now we move into crazy people doing crazy things season. I can't decide if Carl Hollander wants to sell me a vacuum cleaner or offer me a bribe. And the hell of it is, my wife actually needs a new vacuum cleaner."

"Well, I can leave and come back after you guys cut a deal."

"Funny guy. Do you have any thoughts about what he's up to?"

Byrd opened his folder and looked at his notes. "I checked with GBI Intelligence. They actually had a couple of reports on him since he left the police department. He's mostly working for some kind of anti-terrorist academy in Ben Hill County."

Wilton looked puzzled. "Ben Hill County is way south. Who has an anti-terrorist academy in that area? The feds?"

Byrd shook his head. "It's a private operation. Run by a guy who moved in and bought a ton of land several years ago—General Mitchell Warren. He says he was a government operator during the Gulf War. He built this place out in the middle of nowhere. He has a firing range, training rooms, and even a grass landing strip."

"Wow! Is he legit?"

Byrd looked over his notes. "The guy has been arrested once in the US. He was caught smuggling hi-tech radios to a group associated with Pablo Escobar. The intel folks were able to find copies of the stories that were run in national publications, with details about the arrest. They even found a copy of his mug shot from back in the day."

Wilton nodded.

Byrd continued. "Funny thing is, there is no record of his arrest on NCIC. Nothing. And the military denies that he ever served."

Wilton frowned. "You think he was a federal informant."

Byrd shrugged. "Could be. GBI Intel did find out that he calls his operation 'the farm.' Like the CIA training center in Virginia. And he calls his business the Counter Insurgency Academy. Again, the CIA."

"You think he works for the CIA?"

Byrd closed his folder. "If he does, he didn't get the memo about keeping it a secret."

Wilton stood up and Byrd followed him out the door of the office. They stood in the hall where Wilton leaned against the wall. "If this was a couple of months ago, I would have been sure it was a political trap of some kind. Now that the election is over, I don't see what Hollander is up to. I barely know him. He started training for us when I first came into this office. I was broke after running for election for the first time. He was doing me a favor by training my staff, and he did it for a reduced fee. And I let him stay at my house while he was here to save the county money. I never thought he could be a crook. But then, I barely knew him."

Byrd crossed his arms. "Bobby, you couldn't have known he was a dirty cop. And he sure wasn't going to tell you that he was ripping off people in his home area. Let's just wait and see what he has to say."

Wilton was glum. "Are you going to sit in on the meeting?"

Byrd shook his head. "No, he won't open up with me there. I was planning on having you wear a wire."

FRIDAY, NOVEMBER 19, 2004
11:54 A.M.
JASPER, GEORGIA

Bobby Wilton watched Carl Hollander walk into the café across the street from the courthouse. He was wearing black tactical pants, a gray shirt with a logo of some kind on it, and a heavy black military-style jacket. He exuded arrogance, looking the room over as he stood at the door. Bobby Wilton thought the only way he could look more like a prick was if he were wearing a turtleneck.

Hollander spotted the sheriff and pushed his way through the late lunch crowd to join him. Wilton didn't stand up.

"Sheriff, good to see you again."

Wilton nodded. "How have you been?"

Hollander smiled. "Doing great." He pointed at the

logo on his shirt. "I work for the Counter Insurgency Academy down in South Georgia. It's over in Ben Hill County." Hollander said, "You know the area?"

Wilton leaned back in his chair. "I went through a training class with the sheriff from down there. He was a farmer who was going broke and decided to run for sheriff. I guess his situation wasn't unique. People loved him though, and still do. I talk to him occasionally. He's a good man."

Hollander wasn't interested. "Uh-huh."

"How can I help you?" Wilton asked.

"Right to it."

"Yep. We have court going on across the street, and I need to get back to the courthouse."

"I have a coworker who is bringing some expensive equipment in by plane tomorrow or the next day. They're coming into the Pickens County airport. And this equipment is highly sensitive."

Wilton frowned. "It can't be bounced around much."

Hollander looked around the room. "No, I mean the secret kind of sensitive."

"Government kind of sensitive?" Wilton asked.

Hollander nodded. "Top secret. Federal-level secret. As secret as it can get." Hollander reached into his front pocket and pulled out a federal shield. The badge looked to Wilton like a Bureau of Alcohol, Tobacco, and Firearms badge, but he only got a glimpse.

Wilton smiled. "We always like to help the feds."

Hollander said, "This isn't a favor. The company shipping these radios has a lot of money. They are a major government contractor and have authorized me to pay you to cover this shipment."

"Cover?"

"We want to be sure that no one tries to hijack this load.

I want to pay you to be our man on the ground. Our local eyes, so to speak. I want you to be there with me when the plane arrives and make sure nobody tries anything. I figure you know the locals who might try anything."

"I doubt that anybody around here would try anything. The crooks around here are more into meth than high-tech equipment."

Hollander shifted gears easily. "And that's the other service you can offer. You know the locals who hang around that airport, don't you?"

Wilton nodded.

Hollander continued. "If you see somebody who doesn't belong, I'd like to know it."

Wilton sat back in his chair. "What does a job like this pay?"

Hollander smiled.

"Would a thousand dollars make it worth your time?" Hollander pulled an envelope from his hip pocket. He placed it on the middle of the table. "I remember how you were struggling to pay the bills after your first election. I thought cash might help you this time."

Wilton didn't touch the envelope. "All you want from me is to be with you and look for anyone out of place?"

Hollander smiled broadly. "That's it, Sheriff."

Wilton moved the envelope to his side of the table using a single finger. "When do I need to be there?"

"Can I call you tonight? I'll know more by then."

Wilton stood and put the envelope in his hip pocket. "My number is in the phone book."

Hollander stuck out his hand to shake, but Wilton pretended to be waving to a friend at the front of the café.

As Hollander turned and walked out of the restaurant, the surveillance team watched as he got into a small pickup truck and fired it up. Hollander backed out of the spot and pointed the truck toward the motel he was staying in. The team followed behind.

FRIDAY, NOVEMBER 19, 2004
11:59 A.M.
EL PASO, TEXAS

Omar walked into the offices his dad rented in El Paso. The space was in a strip mall on the northwestern edge of the city, upstairs by an insurance agency. The front window looked past the campus of the University of Texas at El Paso, and directly into Mexico.

Omar had used his key, the one Adam gave him at the motel, to get in the front door of the office. Adam had already had someone stack the secure radios in the corner of the front room. And that was all that was in the front room.

Omar had slept later than he thought he would, road weary from the near-eighteen-hundred-mile trip. His legs were wobbly as he got out of the cab and struggled in the high desert sun to find the office Adam had described.

He checked out the other rooms, all of which were empty. Omar had found a chair and plopped into it. He busied himself examining the boxes of radios they were to deliver.

Omar knew the radios were police surplus which his dad's people had converted. There was a black box with cables attached added to each device. Some of the radios were small walkie-talkies and others were designed to be mounted under the dash of a vehicle. He had clicked one of the walkie-talkies on when Adam came rushing through the door.

Out of breath, Adam asked, "Have you talked to your dad?"

Omar shook his head.

"Well, I did. You need to get out to the airport and rent a plane that will carry me and you and about two hundred pounds of luggage and freight. We need to be able to leave this afternoon or tonight."

Omar stood up. "I'll probably have to take a check ride. They won't let me just take off in one of their planes."

"That's already arranged. They'll need a copy of your pilot's license. Use the one your dad gave you. I've arranged payment on a card I have. Just make sure you get us a solid plane and get it loaded with fuel."

"Where is the airport? And how long will we be gone?"

Adam pulled one of the walkie-talkies out of a box. He turned back to Omar. "I have the address on this piece of paper. There is a billboard right up the street for a cab service. You can see the cab service number from the stairs."

Omar nodded.

"Don't worry about packing clothes," Adam continued, "we'll only be gone a couple of days."

Omar stood in the middle of the office, watching Adam as he turned the knobs on the radio. Adam turned back to him. "Get going. We need to get in the air as soon as we can. We have to be in Georgia by this time tomorrow."

Omar remembered the ride out. "How long is the flight?"

Adam thought about it. "We'll want to stay around three thousand feet for the trip. So, about fourteen to sixteen hours by the time we refuel once in Louisiana. Then, adjusting for the time change, means we'll need to be on our game. Are you up for this?"

Omar nodded and headed out the door. He took his new cell phone out and dialed the number he read off the billboard. Then he hustled down the stairs to meet the taxi.

CHAPTER 10
THANKS FOR NOTHING, WRIGHT BROTHERS

FRIDAY, NOVEMBER 19, 2004
12:58 P.M.
EL PASO, TEXAS

Clete Petterson sat in his truck slumped over near the door to minimize his silhouette. He had been sitting here, quietly, since before daybreak. The storage building he watched was quiet, too.

Clete was dressed in jeans and a shirt. No hat and no star on his chest. The DEA agents he was working with had asked him to watch the facility and wait for a truck to show up. He didn't have much confidence in the information. If the lead had been solid, the DEA agents would be sitting here with him.

Petterson's thoughts drifted back to last night's dinner with Trooper Worley. He realized that he still, awkwardly, thought of her as Trooper Worley. He was surprised how comfortable their time together had been. She had been surprised it was his first real date since his wife died. He was surprised, as he mulled over the evening, that his wife's specter didn't hover over the night.

Montana had been warm and funny. He had listened to her talk about her childhood and when she talked, guardedly, about the day she was shot by the fleeing murder suspect and her decision to leave Georgia, to make a clean break. They had laughed easily, as though they had known each other a long time. She had seemed so natural. He felt the most comfortable he had in a long time. Sharing with anyone was tough for him.

When he dropped her off at the little apartment she rented on the north edge of town, she hesitated at the door. He felt awkward and shy and stood stiffly as they said their good-nights. She finally gave up on him, leaned in, and kissed him on the lips.

He was embarrassed that he had stood there, shifting from one foot to the other, while she took the initiative. She had stepped back after the kiss and ordered him to call her. He intended to do that as soon as he was off this surveillance.

He sat through the noon hour and was about ready to call it quits when a van pulled up to the storage building door. Clete sat up in the seat and grabbed his binoculars. The van had pulled up so quickly, he didn't have time to bring the binoculars to his eyes before the two—he thought there were two—men were behind the van and rolling up the door.

He was wondering about getting out of his truck to get a look at the license plate when the two men—he had been right—came out with two large pasteboard boxes. They loaded them in the back of the van and then jumped in. The entire transaction had taken less than five minutes before the van pulled out onto the street.

Clete fired up his truck and fell behind the van in the thick midday traffic. He kept the van in sight as it maneuvered around the downtown streets toward I-10. The van was traveling just below the speed limit on the surface streets, and Petterson was able to pace them without effort as the van turned east on the interstate route and merged with the other cars. Traffic in the center of El Paso was heavy at midday, but the big Texas Ranger was able to negotiate around the big trucks and keep the van in sight. He considered calling one of the DEA agents on the phone but he doubted the men could catch up to him. He assumed the load would continue east, and he could easily have a highway patrol trooper "traffic stop" them along the way.

Petterson was patient as the van rolled farther eastward. The number of cars around them was much less now. He had drifted back several places but could still see the van making its way in the flow. He knew they were nearing Fabens and was surprised when the van signaled for an exit. Petterson had been in the middle lane and had to quickly jump over a lane to hit the exit.

He had one car for cover when the van stopped at the top of the ramp and signaled a left turn. He decided to make a right turn and double back when the van was out of sight. He watched the van in his rearview, and once it was safe, he looped the truck back and looked to the horizon. The van was there, as he thought it would be.

The road was dusty, and the van left a cloud as it worked north. Clete tried to remember where the road intersected with a major highway when he saw the van brake and stop on the side of the road. He quickly backed just out of sight. Looking over his shoulder, he saw a rocky path leading out into the rough ground to his right. He rolled his truck up and parked it in a low spot. Grabbing his field glasses, he jumped out of the truck and jogged toward where the van had stopped.

When he found a vantage point, he looked for cover. Several scrub brushes were nearby, and he chose one that was at the highest point on the sandy ground. He carefully checked the area for rattlesnakes before he laid down and got comfortable.

The West Texas sun was still hot in November, and Clete was without his hat to protect his shaven head so he fashioned a headcover from his bandana.

The big Texan considered making his way back to the truck for water when he heard the airplane coming in low from the west. He rolled onto his back and used one hand to shovel sand onto his body. He heard the plane zoom past his spot, but the pilot was flying so low Clete didn't get a look at it.

Clete looked all around, then he heard the plane, a single-engine high wing, coming back south. It had barely come into view when he saw the landing gear extending, and the plane touched down on the rural road.

The van quickly moved up near the plane and the two men got out. They unloaded the boxes from the storage building. Clete watched as another man got out of the plane as it idled and helped them load the boxes in the back hatch. Clete made a note of the tail number of the plane as the pilot swung it around and departed the same way it had come in.

Clete wrote the number displayed on the rear of the blue and white airplane in the palm of his hand with an ink pen. The numbers ended in 87Y. He lay back down and watched as the van drove away. Soon, the desert was quiet.

FRIDAY, NOVEMBER 19, 2004
2:08 P.M.
JASPER, GEORGIA

Byrd stared at the ceiling of Bobby Wilton's office. He shook his head. "Sheriff, it just has to be dope. You don't fly anything else around like that. Probably marijuana out of Mexico."

Wilton nodded. "That would be my guess. Nobody tracks planes once they're inside the US, do they?"

Byrd sat up. "I was in a class this past summer where they told us about a Federal Aviation Administration program working with Customs and Border Patrol. They track planes that might be smugglers. But the hitch is, you have to know where they originate."

Wilton nodded. "What do we do?"

"I'll contact the GBI Regional Drug Office. We'll get some agents to help us out with surveillance on the airport. And I'll get a couple of them to sit up on Hollander's motel."

"What do you think?"

Byrd shook his head in frustration. "Bobby, I wish I knew. But we just have to play the cards we're dealt."

"I'll pull as many deputies as I can. But that will only be four or five."

Byrd said, "Get with GSP and see if you can get some troopers. They'll be happy to help."

Wilton laughed. "You planning to chase this airplane?"

Byrd shrugged. "I've been accused of stupider things. I'm going to head out. We need to be in place at the airport by six. I'll have to get up around five."

Byrd left Wilton's office, and when Byrd walked into his apartment, he went directly to the cupboard and sat out a cocktail glass. He dropped ice cubes in and looked for his vodka bottle. Then he stopped.

I have to be up early, and I need a clear head. Tonight is as good as any to take a break, Byrd thought.

Byrd dumped the ice in the sink and headed to bed.

FRIDAY, NOVEMBER 19, 2004
2:10 P.M.
NEAR FABENS, TEXAS

Clete Petterson stared at his palm. He held the phone in his right hand and looked where he had written the tail number of the small high-wing plane. "That can't be right. I'm sure I got the number down," Petterson said to the watch officer at the El Paso Intelligence Center.

"Ranger, I have checked and double-checked. That tail number is issued to a Robinson R-44 helicopter."

"Put it on watch, anyway."

The watch officer didn't argue.

Clete Petterson's next call was to the FAA Control Center in Albuquerque. He had attended a conference with an FAA investigator and asked for him by name. The mere fact that he had the confidential phone number got him transferred to a supervisor.

"Center Operations. What can I do for you?" the voice on the other end of the line said. The voice was male, professional, and measured.

"Sir, my name is Clete Petterson. I'm a Texas Ranger in El Paso. Earlier today, I watched a cache of drugs loaded onto a plane north of Fabens, Texas. I wanted to see if any-one there could help me track that plane."

"Ranger, are you asking us to search our recorded ra-dar information from several hours ago?"

"Yes, sir." Clete waited.

"Do you have a time?"

"It was exactly 11:47 a.m. The plane landed at that time. About ten minutes later, it departed."

"From the airport there in Fabens?"

"No, sir. From the highway about ten miles north of Fabens and just a little to the west."

"That makes it easier. We flag flights that go off radar in that area. Let me see if our special services controller was working then. We assign someone to work with Customs on a regular basis." Music came on the line as Clete waited.

Clete was weighing other options when the music stopped.

"Who is this?"

"Texas Ranger Clete Petterson."

"Hey, buddy. I hear you asked for me by name."

Clete laughed. "I still have your business card. I don't meet many investigators for the FAA."

"What do you need?"

Clete explained the request again. The voice on the other end of the line didn't respond right away. He could hear a computer keyboard clacking.

"Here we go. I have a plane leaving a rental facility at Dona Ana County Airport in New Mexico. Tail number given on departure was six-seven-Yankee."

Clete interrupted. "Did you say six-seven?"

"That's affirmative. Departed and skirted north of El Paso and Fort Bliss. We lost radar contact for about ten minutes about twenty-five miles east of El Paso near the

Fabens regional airport. Our Customs guy called the airport and they said no one had landed. By the time he got them on the horn, the plane was back in the air. We put a track on it and passed it off to Fort Worth."

"That's a lot of work."

"The plane is on a DEA watch. Fort Worth may still have it. We were getting a decent track earlier."

Clete called the El Paso Intelligence Center watch desk again, feeling vindicated.

FRIDAY, NOVEMBER 19, 2004
4:52 P.M.
NEAR WAXAHACHIE, TEXAS

Adam was dozing as Omar negotiated the airspace between Dallas and Austin. Omar had taken off his headset and rubbed his ears, something that seemed to help about every hour or so. He was watching fuel consumption closely, worried about the four hundred and forty pounds of meth crammed into the airplane.

Their route had taken them south of the Dallas-Fort Worth metroplex, near Waco, and then they planned to intercept I-20 near Tyler. He had flown between the two terminal control areas and was well on his way to Louisiana. The drone of the airplane engine could become hypnotic, as Adam had discovered, but Omar was scared his heading would drift and he would cross into the flight path of another plane. The Cessna 182 his dad had procured was the retractable-gear version and was solid as a rock.

They had been cruising at about 140 knots at 3,000 feet. Adam had told him they would land outside of Shreveport,

Louisiana, at a small airport for more fuel. The big question was, could they make the last leg on the single fill-up?

About three hours into the flight, Omar insisted on landing and peeing. Adam produced a plastic juice bottle and held the control yoke while Omar relieved himself. Otherwise, the flight had been uneventful.

It was near Longview, Texas, that the trouble started. Omar was comfortable with the controls and noticed almost immediately when the rented plane began to turn ever so slowly north. He first attributed the change to wind currents, and he applied trim to maintain his heading. Realistically, he had abandoned the navigation heading for simply keeping I-20 out his left window.

It wasn't long after that when the rough air started. Omar decided that he should climb a few thousand feet, thinking the air would smooth out. Adam woke up as the plane shuddered through buffeting winds.

"What's going on, kid?" Adam said as he looked around the cockpit and outside for clues.

"Rough air. Nothing to worry about. We've been flying close to the interstate, and sometimes the heat of the asphalt will cause a bumpy ride."

Adam shook his head. "Not this time of year. Hell, the outside air looks to be around forty degrees. Have you checked the weather radio lately?"

Omar felt a cold chill. Everything was clear when they left the airport outside of El Paso. But they were over eight hundred miles from there.

"Shit. I haven't checked in a while."

Adam grunted. "Out here, a storm can blow up from the west in a matter of hours, not days. I'll get the weather service tuned in on the radio. Are we getting anything else? Any wind shears?"

"That's only a problem in a thunderstorm."

Adam frowned. "Clear air-wind shear can hit you up to fifty miles ahead of a fast-moving thunderstorm."

Omar was sweating.

Adam turned in the seat, looking behind them. "Damn it! We have a big thunderstorm bearing down on us. It looks to be about thirty miles behind us. We need to make some time."

Omar pushed the throttle forward. "We may have to land before we hit Louisiana. I've been nursing the fuel, but if I have to gun it, we'll run dry before we get there."

Adam shook his head vigorously. "No can do. We have to go to the airport I told you about. No other options."

Omar went wide-eyed as he felt the plane buck and roll to the right. "Shit, we're not tracking. The plane is trying to turn to the south."

"Hell, yes! Wind shear will do that. It must be coming from the southwest. You'll have to correct." Adam was busy. He had pulled a calculator out of his bag and was figuring how much fuel it would take them to make the country airfield.

Adam almost lost his calculator when the plane ducked right and dropped over a hundred feet in a second. Adam grabbed the yolk and put his feet on the pedals. "I'll hold this thing as steady as I can. You figure out for sure if we have enough fuel. And don't bullshit me with some conservative number. You have to squeeze every inch out of this bitch."

Omar didn't agree. "No, we have to go into an airport soon or we'll be unsafe."

"Unsafe!" Adam spat. He turned to face Omar. "We can't."

"Can't?"

"Those boxes we loaded are filled with two hundred kilos of the purest crystal methamphetamine you will ever see. Enough to put us in federal prison for life."

"Dad did this to us?"

Adam shook his head. "We bought the ticket. Our payday will cover the stress and strain—if we make it. Otherwise, the cost of failure is high."

Omar shook his head. "That son of a bitch. He did this."

"You can deal with your family issues later. Right now, you have to get us to that airport."

Omar shook his head from side to side. "It can't be done."

Adam grabbed Omar's right arm and shook him. "If it was easy, anybody could do it."

Omar glanced over and sat up straighter in the seat. He had run the numbers and thought they might have a couple of gallons to spare if the weather didn't get a lot worse. But this was completely contrary to the safety measures he was trained in. Omar took a deep breath and crossed his fingers. They would need a lot of luck to make it to the backwoods airport.

Then the rain started. Sheets of rain washed over the little plane, and the engine struggled to keep up. The steady, heavy layers of rain were causing the RPMs of the propeller to drop. The controls were getting heavy in Omar's hands as he pulled on them. The sky had gotten progressively darker, and the interstate highway below them was obscured by the rainfall.

The cockpit temperature on the instruments was fifty-seven degrees, but to Omar, it felt tropical. Omar wiped sweat off his forehead and worked the navigation aids and found a navigation beacon near his destination. He determined that he was closer to the correct heading than he thought. "We're in good shape," Omar said. "I've got the

VOR, and we should be able to use the beacon to get us to the airport."

The weather broke for a minute, and Omar made out a water tower to their south with the word "Marshall" in big letters. He reckoned they were less than thirty minutes from the field.

He pointed the plane north of Shreveport and adjusted the navigation receiver. He was crossing into dangerous territory because he was afraid to risk going lower than fifteen hundred feet, but going higher would mean the Shreveport Regional Airport's tower would be painting them on their radar. He was willing to chance it since the Shreveport airport had announced they were on a weather hold.

As he got closer, Adam tuned the aircraft radio to a frequency he had been given by Mitch. Once the numbers were rolled in, he gave Omar the thumbs up. Omar pressed the button on the yolk to activate the aircraft radio. "Cessna 87Yankee to Timber traffic."

"This is Timber fixed-base operations." The voice on the radio sounded to Omar like some crotchety old man. "We have no traffic in the area. You are cleared to land on runway eighteen. We have winds gusting out of the west, and our lights are doing the best they can. Can you see them, Cessna?"

"This is Cessna 87Yankee. Is there another runway, since the wind will be blowing directly on my right side?"

The reply was less than he had hoped. "Nope. We got one runway, north and south. But once you get down under a hundred feet the wind won't bother you as much. The pine trees'll block the wind. Taxi to the open hangar with the lights on. I can refuel you in the dry."

Omar shook his head and wiped the sweat from his

eyes. "That old bastard sounds like getting this plane a hundred feet off the runway will be a piece of cake. This thing is shaking like a dog shitting a peach seed."

Adam grabbed the cowling on the bulkhead and tried to see the runway ahead. "You got this, kid."

Omar thought he didn't sound convincing.

Omar had picked up the glimmer of the runway lights at the private airport laid out for the logging company. He could see, even at a distance, the runway had been intended for temporary use. He hoped the rain hadn't washed the asphalt out anywhere.

Omar pulled power and rolled right to line up with the runway. When he did, the wind pushed the plane off course. Omar tried dropping his right wing, but then he began to drift to the west.

The plane was anything but steady, rocking left and right and suddenly losing altitude. Omar worked the throttle and kept enough power applied that the plane was close to the heading he needed. He checked the gauges when he was ten miles out.

The sound of the rain pounding the plane was louder than the engine. Omar was doing his best to concentrate on the job at hand. He saw that his altitude was higher than he wanted but pulling power would send them off course. He weighed his options, and then he tightened his seat belt and pushed the throttle forward.

"What are you doing, kid?" Adam asked.

"Flying us onto the runway, I hope."

"What happens if that doesn't work?"

"We'll slam into the ground." Omar took deep breaths. The plane was on line, more or less, and the runway was coming up ahead.

"Not funny," Adam mumbled.

Omar's hand hovered over a lever on the dash. "This is where it gets interesting."

Omar pushed the lever, and they heard the landing gear extending. Immediately, the plane slowed and seemed to pitch forward. Omar pulled the yolk toward his chest, working it left and right to keep the plane level. He kept one eye on the airspeed indicator as they dropped steadily out of the air.

The first touchdown was hard, and the plane bounced back in the air. Omar fought the pedals and alerions to keep the plane on the hard-packed runway. He had not used any flaps for fear the plane would drop out from under him.

The plane had touched down at sixty miles an hour faster than it should have. Omar struggled with the controls, trying to stick the plane to the runway. Gravity and drag helped the plane slow, but their speed was not bleeding off as fast as Omar had hoped. Omar pushed the toe breaks with all the force his legs would muster, telling Adam to stand on the toe breaks with him. The uneven brake application caused the little plane to zig and zag along the runway. The men rolled to a halt sixteen inches from the dirt at the end of the asphalt.

Hands shaking, Omar took his headset off and hung it on the neck of the control yoke as he taxied over to the World War II–vintage hangar with the big light hanging in the center. Two hundred feet from the safety of the shed, the airplane engine shuddered and died. The ashen men quickly dropped to the ground and pushed the plane out of the weather.

An old man stood in the shadows until the plane was rolled to a stop by the fuel pump. Then he walked over and used a step ladder to get to the wing tanks. Soon aviation-grade gasoline was pouring into the wing tanks. The old man looked down from his perch as Omar and Adam stretched and turned. "Boys, I been working here nearly fifty years, and I ain't never seen nothing like that landing y'all just did. Which one of you is the stunt pilot?" He laughed at his own joke.

Adam frowned and said, "Just fuel us up. We're on a tight clock."

The old man pointed at the sky. "I reckon you'll need to tell the man upstairs about your clock. There ain't no way you'll be flying out of here before this rain lets up. And the weather service is saying this storm won't pass for a couple of hours."

Omar took the opportunity to use the restroom. Once inside, he sat on the toilet and tried to calm down. His hands shook and he felt like he would vomit. He slumped in the narrow stall and took deep breaths. By the time Omar stood up in the stall, his hands had stopped shaking. He went to the dirty sink and washed his face. Looking in the broken mirror, his face was pale, but it looked better than when he entered the room.

He ambled back out to the airplane and did a visual inspection of the control surfaces. As the old man finished pumping the aviation fuel, Adam motioned for Omar to step away to a corner of the old building. They navigated around the standing water where the rain had blown in.

Adam turned to face him. Omar waited, expecting to be chewed out for his performance so far. Adam narrowed his eyes. "You done good, kid. You didn't panic. I'm glad you didn't try to land this thing at an airport we don't control."

Omar was pleasantly surprised. "Thanks. I did the best I could."

"Your old man would be proud. This is the kind of flying we used to have to pay top dollar for."

Omar smiled. Despite his fear, he was proud of what he had done today. "Adam?"

"Yeah, kid?"

"Were you worried?"

Adam nodded. "I may need to change my drawers before we leave. I think my asshole sucked them up into my body!"

"Adam, I had to read up on this when I was taking my flight lessons. Do you know what the cause of almost all aviation accidents involving private light planes is?" Omar asked then laughed. "Flying too close to the ground."

Adam didn't laugh.

The two men found a couple of worn-out recliners and settled down to wait out the storm. Both men fell into a fitful sleep.

CHAPTER 11
WHAT GOES UP

FRIDAY, NOVEMBER 19, 2004
11:58 P.M.
EL PASO, TEXAS

Clete looked at his watch and decided to dial the phone anyway, even though it was midnight in El Paso. That meant that it would be two a.m. in Georgia.

"Hello?" The voice sounded like he had been asleep.

"Sorry to be calling so late. Is this Agent Kyle Goodwin?"

"Who's this?"

"Clete Petterson. I'm a Texas Ranger."

"No shit?"

"No shit."

"Well, what the hell can I do for a Texas Ranger at," Goodwin paused, "after two in the morning?"

Clete asked, "Are you the agent who listed a plane with the tail number ending in six-seven-Yankee?"

"Why are you asking?" Goodwin was cautious.

"Because I think someone has changed the tail number to eight-seven and is using it to fly a load to Georgia," Clete said.

"What I'm about to tell you is highly classified. It comes from a court-ordered wiretap from an FBI case out of New

Mexico. They are working a national security case on a questionable plane rental company in Santa Teresa."

Goodwin gave Clete the rundown on the airplane rental operation at the Dona Ana Airport. He said it was a fly-by-night—no pun intended—operation run out of a van. The company wasn't officially on the airport, since the airport authority had thought the operation was probably illegal. The plane had been rented by a company from Georgia, with offices in a place called Bowens Mill. Clete knew he couldn't use the information for a search warrant, but he made notes anyway.

"I've been talking to a GBI agent," Goodwin said. "He had inquired about the company renting the plane. The GBI agent had run an inquiry through EPIC on the company in Bowens Mill."

"Can you give me the agent's contact information?"

"Hang on." Clete heard the rustling of papers. Then Goodwin came back on the line. "The GBI Agent is named Daniel Byrd."

Clete flipped back in his notes and found where Montana had given him the name and number for a Danny Byrd. The numbers were the same.

"Small world. He is a friend of a friend."

Goodwin said, "Well, it was worth it to be woken up by a Texas Ranger. That sure is impressive."

Clete said, "Thanks, pardner."

"*Pardner*. I'll be damned."

Clete laughed as the line went dead.

SATURDAY, NOVEMBER 20, 2004
2:27 A.M.
CANTON, GEORGIA

When Daniel Byrd's phone rang, he looked at the clock by his bed and groaned. *At this time of the morning, it has to be a murder,* he thought. And his alarm had been set for four a.m. to be able to get to Jasper early.

"Hello?"

"Sorry to call you at this time of the morning, Agent Byrd, but I'm in the middle of a hunt. I've got an airplane headed to Georgia that I think is loaded with drugs, and I need some help."

Byrd dropped his feet to the floor and turned on a lamp. "Who is this?"

"I'm a friend of a friend. Trooper Montana Worley gave me your name."

"Wow! How's Montana doing?"

"She seems to be doing great. She is going to be a good trooper, for sure."

"You're a trooper, then?" Byrd asked.

"Texas Ranger. My name is Clete Petterson."

Byrd smiled. "Clete is sure enough a Texas name."

Clete laughed. "I get that a lot. And I'm sorry for waking you up, but I need some help out your way."

Byrd pulled his notepad onto his knee and said, "Fire away. What can I do for you?"

"I watched a plane take off today. Well, it was yesterday. It looked like it was taking on a load of dope. It was out in the desert near Fabens. I got a tail number off the plane, and it turns out they had altered the number."

"Georgia is a big state. Not as big as Texas, but the largest east of the Mississippi River. Any idea where it is headed?"

"The plane is connected to a company doing business in Bowens Mill, Georgia."

"Shit!"

"What?" Petterson asked.

"We're setting up surveillance at the Pickens County Airport this morning. That's near Jasper, Georgia. We have a plane coming in just after daybreak."

"Is it connected to Bowens Mill?"

"It is," Byrd said. Then he told the Texas lawman about the meeting with Hollander.

"I think we're onto something. We have an investigation on a business near Bowens Mill, and there are connections to Jasper," Clete offered.

"What kind of connections?"

"Lots of calls to the area, but all the numbers are pay phones. We don't know who they are talking to. Any ideas?"

"Not really. Can you tell me anything else about the plane?" Byrd asked.

"It's a Cessna 182, blue and white. And it's about fifteen miles north of Shreveport, Louisiana, right now."

"Does anyone have eyes on it?" Byrd asked.

"FAA Special Agents are working with us to track it. The plane landed in the middle of a rainstorm. We think it will probably take off once that front moves out."

"Give me a number where I can reach you. I'll keep you posted on my end."

SATURDAY, NOVEMBER 20, 2004
2:58 A.M.
NEAR BENTON, LOUISIANA

The men slept less than they would have liked, but more than they intended. The storm had passed by midnight, but they wanted to give the storm some time to get out of the area.

At three a.m., Omar fired up the plane. Adam finished paying the old man off before climbing into the passenger seat. The plane rolled out of the hangar and Omar checked the gauges, worked the pedals and yoke, and adjusted the propeller for correct function as they rolled down the taxiway.

When Omar felt sure the plane was ready, he looked over at Adam and gave him a thumbs-up. Both men put their headsets on and tightened their safety belts. Adam gave him a nod, and Omar pulled the plane onto the runway. He pressed the button to transmit on the local channel when Adam knocked his hand away. Adam shook his head and said on the intercom, "Radio silence. We'll fly around the Jackson and Birmingham TCA. Stay to the north of both and then we'll hit Atlanta to the north, too. The airport we're headed for is on the north side. I'll vector you in as we get closer."

Omar frowned. "You know how to work the VOR?"

Adam smiled. "Think of this as a test."

Omar's face was red. "You know how to fly?"

Adam shrugged. "I don't have a license, but I've done a good bit of flying in my life."

Omar shook his head and pushed the throttle forward.

The plane began to roll and bounce on the rough asphalt. Omar waited until the airspeed was good and then pulled back on the control yoke. He retracted the landing gear and put the plane in a hard climb.

Adam spoke. "Keep us around three thousand feet. Nobody will pay any attention to us at that altitude. I'm going to switch the transponder off—no need to be more than a blip on the radar in Atlanta Center."

Omar nodded. "That'll burn more fuel. Are we going to gas up again before we get there?"

Adam pulled out a map with their route marked in pencil. "We should be okay. I figure we should hit the Georgia line about daylight. Then we'll know for sure how much range we have."

Omar nodded, leveled the plane off, and set the trim. With an adjustment to the throttle, the plane was cruising at maximum efficiency for the altitude.

SATURDAY, NOVEMBER 20, 2004
4:53 A.M.
JASPER, GEORGIA

Agents and deputies were gathering in the visitation room at the Pickens County jail, the largest room in the building.

As the agents, deputies, and troopers made their way into the room, Daniel Byrd wondered how this would end. He waved at the Region Eight people as they wandered in and spotted Doc Farmer near the back of the room.

Byrd was in front of the room, meeting with the Assistant Special Agent in Charge of the GBI drug office.

Terry Cromwell had been in the same Special Agents class as Byrd, and the two had remained friends. Cromwell had bounced all over the state, working undercover in some of Georgia's worst communities.

"So, Byrd-man, you think this deal is some kind of drug thing? What got you spun up at the last minute."

"I got a call about an hour and a half ago from a Texas Ranger. He says the plane we're looking for loaded up with dope in West Texas."

"You think this is for real?"

Byrd nodded. "Real enough that I sent Jamie Abernathy to Kennesaw to meet a DEA pilot. Apparently, the FAA has been tracking this guy since he left El Paso. He's over Mississippi right now, and they are tracking him on radar. He looks to be headed our way."

Cromwell nodded. "GBI Jamie Abernathy? What are Jamie and the DEA guy going to do?"

"They can make direct contact with the FAA Area Control Center. All the centers are linked with other centers so they can coordinate air traffic nationwide. So far, they have been able to track this flight, even though they aren't using a transponder. They should be over Alabama soon. The DEA pilot plans to intercept the plane and follow it into Jasper."

Cromwell was skeptical. "What if it doesn't come here? They could land in a whole lot of places other than here."

Byrd frowned. "I wish we could be more certain. There is a lot that we don't know, but Hollander being here and the plane being somehow connected to Bowens Mill adds up to something. It's worth setting up on this place."

Cromwell said, "I'll figure out a way to cover all this overtime if things don't pan out. But your name will be featured prominently in the memo!"

"I don't blame you. The way the Bureau is about OT, I'd be looking for a fall guy too."

"Seriously, is there a plan if the plane lands somewhere else? Can the DEA pilot get to them?"

Byrd shrugged. "It will depend on how far away they land. They'll call the cavalry and do the best they can."

Cromwell chuckled. "I guess pulling off miracles is what they pay us for."

Byrd slapped him on the back. "That's the truth. So, let's go tell all these agents, deputies, and troopers what we know and listen to them ask the same questions we'd like answered."

SATURDAY, NOVEMBER 20, 2004
6:12 A.M.
NORTH OF BIRMINGHAM, ALABAMA

Adam had figured out the path through all the controlled airspace with precision. But he hadn't counted on a strong headwind. The plane had begun to surge and fall just north of Birmingham. Omar had let the little plane buck gently for a while, then he tried losing altitude to see if the air was smoother. He knew he could drop to 2,500 feet and still be safe. But nothing was helping. The best course would be to climb to an altitude where the winds were calm, but he didn't have that option.

Adam was watching the fuel gauge and running calculations that gave answers he wasn't happy with. Their fuel consumption rate had been higher than predicted. Adam had run the numbers several times. The result was the same each time: they would have enough fuel to get to the airport, but not enough to waste any time.

"We'll need all the fuel we have, but we should be just under the wire," Adam said.

Omar looked over at Adam. "I was trained to always have plenty in reserve. I don't know how much of this kind of flying I can do. Can't we just land and get fuel on the way?"

"No. We have enough. I just prefer we have extra fuel to loiter in the area for a few minutes and check the airport out. We should have enough fuel to divert to Canton or Ellijay if we have to. Don't get in a sweat, we won't run dry."

Omar checked the gauges and tried to relax and focus on the job ahead.

Adam smiled at his pilot. "Get us back up to three thousand. We're good with fuel. No need to attract attention."

CHAPTER 12
SATURDAY IS A GREAT DAY FOR FLYING

SATURDAY, NOVEMBER 20, 2004
6:19 A.M.
NORTH OF CENTER, ALABAMA

"Atlanta Center, this is Flint 355. I am eighty miles northwest of Atlanta at ten thousand feet. I am squawking the DEA code. Do you have me on radar?"

The response was quick and precise. "Flint, we have you with positive contact. The unknown aircraft you are tracking is about twenty miles due north of you at 2,500 feet. The target appears to be heading for Jasper."

"Center, has the target passed the Rome VOR?"

"Roger, Flint. The target is east of the Rome VOR and climbing. Radar altitude is not precise. The aircraft is not squawking any code, so our altitudes will be approximate."

"Center, would you continue to monitor on this guard channel?"

"Flint 355, I am yours. I am still painting your target on our radar."

"Thanks for the help, Center."

"Here to serve, Flint. Will there be any other Omaha

flights in the area?" The controller was using the code for federal law enforcement flights.

"Negative, Center. I'm the only Omaha unit on this mission. Just little ol' me."

"Understood, Flint. We're standing by on guard."

Arlow Turner was one of a growing number of DEA agents who were full-time pilots. He had been the third member of this elite group and had flown out of Atlanta for most of his time with the DEA.

Arlow brought his airplane around and sat himself above where he thought the Cessna should be. The DEA Aero Commander was faster than the 182, and he estimated he should be able to intercept the flight from Texas in just a few minutes.

GBI Agent Jamie Abernathy was sitting in the right seat, wearing a headset and using a long-range video camera to try to spot the suspects. Jamie wasn't the average GBI agent. She had worked occasionally as a model for women's clothing and accessories. Then she tried her hand at real estate. Her good looks had carried her a long way in those businesses, but she found them boring. After briefly serving as a Dawson County deputy sheriff, she had been hired by the GBI. She had excelled in academics and was the best and most tactically proficient shot in her class.

Arlow pointed out the front of the plane.

"Look at about our two o'clock," he said on the intercom. "If he's flying the VOR, he should be about there."

Jamie swiped her blond hair aside and put the device up to her eyes. After several tense seconds, she said, "You're good, Arlow. I see them."

"Hit the button on the top left. That should give you a range."

Jamie nodded. "Range is indicating sixty-five hundred meters."

Arlow corrected their course slightly. They were now directly behind the 182 and above them. Arlow was comfortable there was no way the occupants of the Cessna could see them.

"Flint 355 to Atlanta Center. We have the target visual. Stay with me if you can."

"Flint, Atlanta Center is standing by," came the terse response.

Arlow adjusted something on the panel of the plane, then said, "Atlas, this is Flint 355."

The response was hollow and staticky. "Flint 355, go."

Arlow looked over at Jaime and said, "This is DEA Flight Operations in El Paso. I'll have them relay to your agents on the ground. What is Byrd's radio number?"

Jamie took her eyes away from the viewer and blinked. "Danny is GBI eighty-nine."

"Atlas, contact Georgia Bureau of Investigation radio and have them relay to GBI eighty-nine that we have visual on the target aircraft and expect them to be in sight over the airport in about twenty minutes." He paused. "And tell your boss that we need radios in our aircraft that'll talk to the locals."

The response was quick. "I'll be sure to make a note of that. And I'll ask for raises for everyone while I'm at it."

Jamie laughed at the exchange. "Everybody has a wish list."

She returned to the viewer. "He's crossing I-75 on a track for Fairmount. Sure looks like he's headed to Jasper."

Arlow nodded and started to descend. "We should probably get a little closer," he said to himself.

SATURDAY, NOVEMBER 20, 2004
7:37 A.M.
JASPER, GEORGIA

Omar pulled the throttle back on the 182. He could see the Jasper airport off his nose, but knew he was too high to enter the pattern. He reached for the gear lever when Adam grabbed his hand.

"Let's look things over first. We have enough fuel left. Fly an orbit at three thousand feet and let me take a look around." Adam leaned over and scanned the area around the airport.

Omar was skeptical. "We're on fumes now." Omar leaned over and tried to look, too. "I thought we had a guy grease the skids for us."

He said, "We did, but you can't be too careful."

Omar rolled the plane into a gentle turn. "What am I looking for?"

Adam kept his eyes on the ground. "Police cars. Or unmarked cop cars. Or for that matter, too many cars in the parking lot. I've flown in here a few times, and there aren't normally a lot of cars in the parking lot."

Omar tilted the plane and drifted toward the middle of the airport. Adam spoke into the intercom. "Careful of the approaches. We don't want to get hit."

Omar nodded. The airport seemed quiet, and Omar had monitored the Unicom frequency since they came into Georgia. He hadn't heard anyone taking off or landing from Jasper.

SATURDAY, NOVEMBER 20, 2004
7:39 A.M.
JASPER, GEORGIA

Byrd was holding the radio microphone in his lap.

"Nine hundred to eighty-nine. DEA advised the plane is circling the airport. The DEA airplane is on their tail."

Byrd responded, "Clear, nine hundred."

He switched the radio over to the Pickens sheriff's channel. "GBI eighty-nine to all units. Don't move until the plane is on the ground."

SATURDAY, NOVEMBER 20, 2004
7:40 A.M.
JASPER, GEORGIA

Arlow took the DEA airplane north and lined up with the south-facing runway. He planned to land the twin-engine plane behind the Cessna 182. He saw the smaller plane drifting over the airport and rolled around to the left to compensate for the delay.

Jamie came on the intercom. "I've lost them."

Arlow struggled to pull the plane around in a full circle. He looked around at the mountains to his east and decided his best bet was to climb. As Arlow applied power to the engines, he said, "Sorry, Jamie. He's checking things out, so I ended up a little too close. We're going to climb a little bit and then line back up with the airport."

SATURDAY, NOVEMBER 20, 2004
7:42 A.M.
JASPER, GEORGIA

After the second slow loop, Adam said, "Call us out on the Unicom. Let the area traffic know we intend to land."

"Pickens County traffic, this is eight-seven-Yankee, landing on runway one-six. Preparing to turn downwind."

Adam was looking all around.

Omar started looking, too. "What's wrong?" Omar asked.

Adam shook his head. "I thought I saw an airplane. It was back to the north. Now it's gone."

Omar shook his head. "I can't see anything. Was it higher or lower?"

"Higher. It looked like it might be headed into Pickens County."

SATURDAY, NOVEMBER 20, 2004
7:42 A.M.
JASPER, GEORGIA

Jamie Abernathy was feeling the tension in the cockpit. Arlow worked the controls, trying to keep the faster DEA plane behind the 182. Jamie watched as the DEA pilot switched between radios.

"Flint 355 to Atlas. Our target is on final to Pickens County."

"Atlas to 355. Clear, the target is on final. GBI eighty-nine is aware."

SATURDAY, NOVEMBER 20, 2004
7:43 A.M.
JASPER, GEORGIA

"Pickens County traffic, eight-seven-Yankee is on final for runway one-six." Omar was focused on putting the plane down. He checked and rechecked the instruments.

Without turning, he asked Adam, "Any sign of that plane you saw?"

Adam was watching the parking area off to their right. The plane was fifty feet above the ground, passing the north end of the runway when Adam noticed several cars in the airport parking lot were moving. That set off alarms for Adam. He focused on the cars, barely conscious of the bark as the plane touched the tarmac.

Adam counted at least four cars in the parking lot moving toward the airport ramp, normally reserved for airplanes.

Adam shouted to Omar, "Abort! Abort! Abort!"

Omar was stunned. He had feathered the propeller and was slowing the plane down. Adam pushed the throttle forward and readjusted the propeller pitch.

Omar rallied and raised the flaps. Omar said, "We may not have enough runway!"

"You've got to use what you've got, kid."

Omar pushed the throttle to the firewall. He shouted a steady stream of expletives.

Adam was watching the cars as they came toward them. He wondered if they would be able to intercept them. When Adam saw the blue and gray GSP unit come out of the wood line headed for the end of the runway, his heart sank.

Omar saw it at the same time. The marked GSP car with blue lights flashing was headed for the end of the runway, right in front of them. Omar shook his head, verified that the throttle was wide open, and then gripped the yolk.

"Adam, when I tell you to, I want you to pull up the gear."

Adam was impressed. "You got it, kid!"

Adam watched the airspeed indicator as their speed climbed slowly. Adam was focused on the end of the runway as Omar shouted, "Gear up."

Adam pulled the lever up, and for a moment the airplane sank. Then, ever so slowly, the airspeed crept up. Adam was tempted to close his eyes as the GSP unit parked right in front of them.

They both felt the buffet as they passed over the GSP unit with inches to spare. Omar struggled to gain altitude as the plane swept over the end of the tarmac. The plane shuddered and then seemed to gain strength. Omar noted they were five hundred feet above ground level as the engine screamed with the strain.

SATURDAY, NOVEMBER 20, 2004
7:43 A.M.
JASPER, GEORGIA

Arlow lowered the landing gear and reached for the switch to lower his flaps. He was still watching the smaller plane when he saw something unusual. The other plane had slowed on contact with the runway, but now it was picking up speed.

"Shit!" Arlow said without the intercom.

"What!" Jamie said as she looked at the pilot.

"They're going to run. They saw something!" Arlow said as he raised his landing gear and prepared the Aero Commander for a chase.

"Flint 355 to Atlanta Center!"

"Center, go!"

"Our target is on the run. Do you have radar contact?"

"Roger, Flint. He is directly south of Pickens County Airport. He is climbing at this time."

"Stay with him."

SATURDAY, NOVEMBER 20, 2004
7:44 A.M.
JASPER, GEORGIA

Byrd was storming along the driveway to the airport when he got on the radio. "GBI eighty-nine to surveillance. I'm going to circle around and try to find them in the woods at the end of the runway."

Cromwell came on the radio. "Danny, they just cleared a trooper car and are climbing out."

"Aw, fuck! I'm headed to the Cherokee County Airport. It's due south of here." Byrd activated the lights and siren on the Crown Victoria. He heard the engine roar as he pushed the accelerator pedal to the floor.

Cromwell took charge. "All units, head to the Cherokee County Airport."

Byrd pushed the car as much as he could, the speedometer hovering around 125. In his rearview mirror, he could see more blue lights trailing behind him.

SATURDAY, NOVEMBER 20, 2004
7:44 A.M.
JASPER, GEORGIA

Omar let out the breath he realized he'd been holding since they had throttled up. "Shit, that was close."

Adam looked over his shoulder. "It isn't over, kid. We got a plane on our tail, and we've got no fuel to speak of."

Omar slapped the cowling. "Damn. What do we do?"

"We have to put this bitch down somewhere we can run. This guy on our tail has to be a cop."

Omar shook his head. "What about the load?"

Adam grunted. "Can you run with a hundred-pound box to lug around? I can't."

Omar understood. "You're right. We've got fuel for, maybe, five minutes."

Adam looked at the air chart he had used to map the flight. "Cherokee County Airport is off our nose. Try to get us away from the buildings and we'll run for the woods."

Omar nodded. As the plane climbed, he could see the next airport just ahead. Omar was in the process of pulling the power when the engine stopped.

"Fuck!" Omar shouted.

Adam kept calm. "We're okay, kid. Just keep us on track with that runway. Try to squeeze as much glide time as you can from her."

SATURDAY, NOVEMBER 20, 2004
7:46 A.M.
JASPER, GEORGIA

Jamie was looking through the viewer once more. "I think his propeller quit turning. I'm not sure, but it looks like it's stopped."

Arlow scanned the horizon. "They've been in the air for a while. That last takeoff must have sucked their tanks dry. He'll have to ditch at Cherokee County. It's the only airport in sight."

Jamie nodded. She pulled her M4 rifle out of the floor and put the sling over her shoulder. "Can we follow it in?"

Arlow glanced over. "We're going to give it a shot. Pull those straps tight, and plan on a bumpy ride." Jamie flinched and Arlow shrugged. "I've crashed before. I've always walked away."

Jamie shook her head. "That's not what I wanted to hear."

"Flint 355 to Center, our target is going into Cherokee County Airport. We will be following. Can you contact local authorities?"

"Doing it now, Flint."

SATURDAY, NOVEMBER 20, 2004
7:46 A.M.
CANTON, GEORGIA

Omar was sweating as the plane sank. He sawed the control yoke back and forth to get the plane lined up with the runway. Without power, it was hard to fight the drift the plane was experiencing. But the plane was sinking faster than either of the men anticipated. Omar shook his head. "The wind is pushing us out of line with the runway. If I try to correct, it may increase our sink rate."

Adam gripped the cowling. "Just keep us out of the woods."

Omar nodded. "Just as soon as we clear the trees, give me full flaps. And I'm going in with the gear up. I'm afraid the gear will snag on something before we get to the runway."

Adam looked at Omar. "You're the boss."

Omar felt a surge of pride. He focused on the runway, which was farther away than he would like. The plane skimmed a couple of trees at the extreme end of the airport. *We'll never make the runway*, Omar thought.

"Hit the flaps."

He could hear the motor that extended the flaps grinding and feel the plane balloon up, but it wasn't enough. The plane dropped to the ground and started skidding to the left. Omar felt the edge of the pavement slide under the plane as it lost momentum.

Omar fought the controls but realized nothing he did had any effect. The plane made a grinding sound as it leaned to the right and came to a stop.

SATURDAY, NOVEMBER 20, 2004
7:48 A.M.
CANTON, GEORGIA

"Flint 355 to Center. The target aircraft is down short of the north end of the Cherokee County Airport. The aircraft is down. Send emergency services."

"Flint, I have Cherokee 911 on the phone. What are your intentions?"

"Standby, Center. I'll advise."

Arlow rolled the Aero Commander into a sharp turn, using his momentum to carry the plane toward the south end of the airport. With the runway blocked, Arlow aimed his plane at the taxiway.

Then he applied the left rudder and right aileron to slip the twin onto the tarmac in a maneuver reserved for crop-dust pilots. The plane dropped like a rock, then at the last moment, Arlow leveled the controls and bounced onto the south end of the taxiway. He pulled power but didn't brake until they were nearing the crashed 182, which was scattered over the pavement.

Before he could get the plane stopped, Jamie grabbed her rifle and was climbing out the door. She sprinted across to the crumpled aircraft.

"Police! Show me your hands!"

Her knees flexed as she sidestepped toward the downed plane. As she got closer, she could tell the occupants were gone. She dropped the barrel of her rifle and shook her head in frustration. Her blond hair swirled around her head as she jogged back and climbed in the door.

Arlow waited for her to get strapped in. He spun the plane around onto the taxiway.

"They're in the wind," Jamie said. "Fuck!"

Arlow pressed the radio button. "This is Flint 355 to Cherokee County traffic. Flint will be departing the taxiway."

"Flint, this is Cherokee County ground. You will be leaving the taxiway?"

"Negative. I will be departing from the taxiway."

"Flint, I can't let you do that."

Arlow smiled. "Then close your eyes."

The Aero Commander lunged into the air and Arlow rolled to the right as soon as he cleared the hangars. The plane rocketed up and he swung in a tight curve to get a look at the woods near the crash site.

"Center to Flint 355, are you departing Cherokee?"

"Center, we are going to be doing a ground search. Please help us with local traffic."

"I have Cherokee Airport on the line. Did you take off from the taxiway?"

Arlow glanced over at Jamie and smiled, then responded to the Atlanta Center. "Center, that would be me."

It took a moment for Center to respond. "I'm impressed."

CHAPTER 13
ALL'S WELL THAT ENDS—WELL

SATURDAY, NOVEMBER 20, 2004
8:01 A.M.
CANTON, GEORGIA

Byrd slowed to take the ramp off the interstate to Airport Road. He slipped the car off the ramp and onto the street. When he did, he saw flashing red lights ahead of him. By the time he rolled into the airport, the gates were swinging open for the fire trucks. Byrd followed them onto the tarmac, and when the fire trucks hesitated, he shot past them. He could see the crumpled airframe near the north end of the runway.

The fire trucks followed him, and they pulled up together. Byrd ran to the downed plane and looked for survivors. He was surprised to see the plane was empty. As he looked around the cockpit, more officers arrived. The firefighters had run a line out, but there was no fire.

Just then, Doc Farmer waved from the wood line at the edge of the airport. "I've got a blood trail here. It's going into the woods."

Byrd looked over his shoulder. He gave Doc a thumbs-up as other agents responded to help. Byrd figured the best idea was to wait for a tracking dog. He turned back to the boxes in the back of the crashed plane. He ripped the lid off one and saw plastic airtight containers. They were pale blue with dark blue lids. He had seen the same packages before. Each contained a kilo of crystal methamphetamine.

Byrd stood up with his hands on his hips and turned to see Terry Cromwell. Cromwell looked into the plane.

He turned to Byrd. "Is that what I think it is?"

Byrd nodded. "If you think it's pounds of crystal meth, you would be right."

Cromwell stood back. "I've never seen that much crystal. We usually get the homemade powder. How much do you suppose this is worth?

Byrd shook his head. "I don't know, but I'd have to guess about ten million."

SATURDAY, NOVEMBER 20, 2004
8:04 A.M.
CANTON, GEORGIA

Omar watched from the wood line as the cops circled the crippled airplane. Blood was dripping from a cut on Omar's forehead. Adam Benjamin was bleeding from his right hand, the one he used to force the airplane door open. Both men had smaller scrapes and scratches from scaling the security fence around the runway.

Adam pulled a clotting agent from a small pack he had pulled from the plane. He applied it to Omar's head and his own arm. Then he took a cotton bandage roll and wrapped his arm. Adam looked at Omar's head. "That stuff will stop the bleeding, but there's not much in this kit to cover your cut up."

Omar gingerly touched the gash. "I'll make it till we get back to the farm. What is that stuff?"

Adam held up the kit. "When you're in the thick of things, the only rescuer you have is yourself. I keep a couple of tourniquets and this clot powder with me all the time. I'll fix one up for you when we get home."

Adam grabbed Omar's arm and the two men started working their way through the rough mountain terrain away from the airport. The trek would be difficult, but Adam had escaped pursuit over rougher terrain in South America. He motioned for Omar to stay close behind and they started working their way north. Adam planned to work their way back toward the interstate. He remembered a gas station where they could get food and arrange a ride.

They had escaped by pure luck, and he didn't like to depend on luck. When he was sure the airport was far enough behind them to take a break, they sat near a creek and rested.

"Kid," Adam said, "you did some real pilot shit today."

Omar stared straight ahead. "But we didn't accomplish the mission. We failed."

Adam laughed. "We survived. We didn't go to jail. That's success."

Omar slammed his fist into the muddy ground. "Next time, I'll be ready."

Adam smiled to himself. *Knowing your dad,* he thought, *there'll be a next time.*

SATURDAY, NOVEMBER 20, 2004
10:01 A.M.
CANTON, GEORGIA

The GSP helicopter was circling again. It was flying low and slow, and the sound of the blades was deafening. Daniel Byrd was propped against his government ride, frustrated that the pilot and passenger had gotten away. His car was idling near the crashed plane.

He watched as Doc Farmer and the Cherokee sheriff dog handlers came out of the woods. The men were covered in dirt and sweat, and the dog handlers wanted to rest their animals. The men sat on the back of one of the firetrucks still on the scene and gulped down water.

Byrd was confident the suspects had simply made it into the woods and gone to ground. He figured they would wait until dark and get a ride.

He shook his head and wondered if there was anything else they could do. The DEA pilot had flown for almost an hour, circling the airport in wide circles. In spite of everyone's efforts, the manhunt was winding down.

Doc Farmer came over and stood beside Byrd. "Those boys are out there somewhere. But I'll be damned if we can find them."

Byrd nodded. "They're probably watching us right now. But I don't know what else to do." Byrd shook his head. "The GSP pilot says their forward-looking infrared is worthless because the ground is fairly warm. They could probably find them in December."

Doc laughed. "Teddy, none of us wants to wait that long."

Byrd had to agree. "Were the Pickens folks able to arrest Hollander?"

Doc nodded. "They caught him trying to leave the airport. He's at the Pickens County Jail."

Byrd watched sullenly as a local wrecker came onto the airport grounds to move the wreckage off the only runway. The airport manager had been out to talk to Byrd several times, angry because the airport had been closed for so long.

As the rollback wrecker pulled the remains of the little airplane on the tilted bed, Byrd dropped into his car and pulled into gear.

Now, he thought, *I guess we have to do some of that detective stuff.*

SATURDAY, NOVEMBER 20, 2004
10:15 A.M.
EL PASO, TEXAS

Petterson had dozed off at his desk. He was snoring when the phone rang.

"Ranger Petterson." He sounded groggy.

"This is Dan Byrd."

"Yes, sir. Any news?"

"Your boys are in the wind. They crashed the plane after a short chase by a DEA plane. We've been searching for several hours, now, with no luck."

Clete rubbed his face. "Damn! Was there any dope in it?"

"Looks like about two hundred pounds," Byrd said.

"Weed?"

"Nope. Crystal meth. The most I've ever seen."

Clete sighed. "We're getting word the Mexican mafia is making it and shipping it into the US. And they're selling it dirt cheap."

Byrd moaned. "It'll sell like wildfire then. Hell, if it's cheap enough, it'll put our meth labs out of business."

Petterson thought back to the people on the plane. "Any leads you get, give me a call. I can run down anything out this way."

"I'll do it. And tell Montana I said hey. I'm glad she's fitting in out there."

"You need to come to El Paso sometime. I'd like to meet you. Come on out and we'll get you a hat and some cowboy boots," Petterson said.

Byrd laughed. "I always wanted to meet a Texas Ranger. Maybe I will come out sometime."

CHAPTER 14
AFTER THE FACT

SATURDAY, JANUARY 1, 2005
10:25 A.M.
CANTON, GEORGIA

The Cherokee County sheriff's office was a beehive of activity. Daniel Byrd dodged around people moving furniture and running around the area. At the front door, he had been met by a deputy who was scraping the previous sheriff's name off the door. As Byrd made his way back toward the inner office of the sheriff, inmates in work clothes, guided by deputies, moved couches and desks between offices. In the short walk, Byrd met several deputies who rushed past him and headed toward the parking lot.

Byrd walked into the sheriff's suite and saw Willie Nelson, the newly elected sheriff of Cherokee County, on his knees by a pile of keys. Willie looked up as he walked in and broke into a grin. "Hey, buddy. Welcome to the chaos."

Byrd watched, puzzled, as Nelson dug through the keys on the floor. "What happened, did a cabinet get dumped?" Byrd asked.

Willie shook his head. Before he could answer, a deputy came rushing in and pulled a couple of silver keys from behind the sheriff.

"My predecessor's last official act was to dump every key in the building into a pile on the floor. I got here at midnight, and we couldn't get inmates out of their cells. We didn't have the key to the first patrol car. I actually had to kick in my office door to get in here." Nelson still seemed in good spirits.

"Patrol cars, too?" Byrd repeated.

Nelson nodded. "He called in all the deputies who were working last night. Fired them and took their keys away. He took the labels off and tossed them in a pile. When I came in this morning, most of the deputies had stayed. I swore them in and then we started getting back to work. Since midnight, we've gotten all but a couple of patrol cars back on the road."

Byrd shook his head. "What a dick."

Nelson laughed. "Well, that's what got him the boot."

Byrd laughed, too. "You reap what you sow." Byrd changed the subject. "Congratulations, Sheriff! You're going to do a great job."

"Thanks. It's still hard to believe all that hard work paid off."

Nelson got awkwardly to his feet. "Hey, there is someone I want you to talk to. Our drug Task Force Commander is down the hall. He told me a story last night, and I want to get your opinion on it."

Byrd followed Nelson as he led him through a light green-painted hallway. "A couple of months ago," Nelson said, "our guys made a big drug bust in the city. They got a bunch of crystal meth." Nelson stopped and turned to Byrd. "Have you heard of any crystal around this area?"

Byrd nodded. "I don't know how much you heard about it, but the airplane we chased from Jasper to the Cherokee County Airport was loaded with crystal. About two hundred pounds."

Nelson's eyebrows shot up. "My god. I thought the old-school crank was bad enough. Now we're getting the crystal that's coming out of Mexico in our area?"

Byrd nodded. "How much did your drug folks get?"

Nelson frowned. "I'll let Wally Demopolis explain that to you. He's the drug commander here. He's a good man."

They turned a corner and Byrd saw a sign on the wall that said "CMANS."

Byrd followed Willis Nelson past the sign and into a suite of offices. He looked back at Byrd. "I'll be getting them out of this building as quick as I can. It's crazy to have undercover officers coming in and out of the jail like this."

From behind a desk, a big man stood and stuck his hand out to the sheriff. "How's it going, sir?"

Nelson shook his hand and said, "The first day has to be the worst."

The big man nodded. He had a genuine smile as he motioned the visitors to a seat. Nelson was quick to say, "I've got to get back to sorting keys. I wanted you to meet Daniel Byrd, he's the GBI agent for this area."

Sticking his hand out to Byrd now, he said, "Wally Demopolis. Good to meet you."

Nelson stood at the door and said, "Tell Danny about the deal where the DEA stole drugs from you."

Demopolis rolled his eyes and sat back in his swivel chair. "Sure, Sheriff."

Byrd sat across from Demopolis. "DEA coming in and taking a case after you do the work isn't a new thing. Did they screw you over some other way?" Byrd asked.

Demopolis blushed. "They screwed us, but we're not one hundred percent sure who 'they' are."

Byrd leaned back. "This must be good."

Demopolis drummed the end of a pencil on his desk. "It was more like an unarmed robbery."

Byrd waited.

Demopolis hit a button on his phone and shouted into the receiver. "Torres, can you come up to my desk?"

He hung up the phone. "I'll let you hear it from the horse's mouth. Although, honestly, I think he feels like he was the other end of the horse after he gave our evidence away."

Another man worked his way around to Demopolis's desk, and he was introduced to Byrd as Freddie Torres. Once the niceties were attended to, Freddie told the story from memory while Byrd listened without commenting. When Torres had laid out the circumstances, he waited for Byrd.

"Damn, the guy had legit-looking DEA creds?" Byrd asked.

Demopolis and Torres both nodded.

Byrd made notes as he looked up and asked Torres, "The people y'all arrested, where were they from?"

Torres dug out his notes. After a couple of seconds, he found what he was looking for. "The guy who ran the house was from Doraville, and his mattress cleaner was, too. The old woman was from Forest Park. The one they got out of jail was from someplace called Bowens Mill. I think it's down in South Georgia."

Byrd nodded. "Can I get a copy of the Bowens Mill guy's mugshot and book-in information?"

Both CMANS agents nodded.

"Whatever you need," Demopolis said. "Have you ever heard of anything like this?"

Byrd thought about his response. "Not *just* like this. But we did chase an airplane into the Cherokee County airport recently. In that case, we had a guy with BATF credentials and a badge."

SATURDAY, JANUARY 1, 2005
11:15 A.M.
CANTON, GEORGIA

When Byrd got back to his apartment, he dug a phone number out of the little book he kept in his car. He dialed the home number of DEA Agent Walt Stone. Walt had been assigned to the GBI Drug Unit Byrd had worked on in 2001.

Stone was a six-foot-six former high school teacher. With a voice that seemed to swell up from his barrel chest, and jet-black hair, he had worked undercover assignments around the world. He looked nothing like a kid who came out of a mill village in Rome, Georgia.

"Hello?" The voice was deep and guarded.

"Did I interrupt your New Year's Eve cookout?"

"Is this one of those GBI birds? The kind that flocks around on a working man's holiday?"

"You got me. Sorry to bother you on a holiday," Byrd said.

"And yet you did," Stone said.

"Yep. And I really do apologize, but I needed to run something by you."

"So run it. I'm just sitting here watching football, and Dallas isn't doing well," Stone said.

"About a month and a half ago, one of the local task forces up my way got about twenty pounds of crystal meth on a human-trafficking investigation," Byrd said.

"Wow, crystal in the suburbs. We've been seeing it in Atlanta, but this is the first I've heard of it outside I-285."

"Apparently, the dope was taken by someone with DEA credentials and a badge. The name on the creds was David Clemente but the agent who took the dope, and the suspect out of jail, was an imposter," Byrd said.

The line was quiet for a moment. "I remember hearing about that. There was talk around the office. You don't want to know what the talk was."

Byrd took the bait. "What did you hear?"

Stone had lowered his voice. "The cousins."

"What?" Byrd asked.

"When we work outside the US, we have our federal law enforcement brothers who have offices in the US Embassy. The 'feebs' are the FBI, because the FBI is always special. Then we have the brothers—that's Customs, IRS, and a couple of other agencies depending on the country. Then we have the cousins."

"Let me guess," Byrd said. "Would another name be *las tres letras*?"

"You win the prize," Stone said.

"Can you check with them and see if they have some kind of operation involving a guy named Warren?" Byrd asked.

"You don't want to do that," Stone said.

Byrd frowned. "Why not? Or is it that they won't tell you?"

"They won't tell us," Stone said. "And anything they tell us will be a lie. And if he is one of their assets, they'll tip him off."

"You just ruined my day," Byrd said.

"Seems fair," Stone said. "You just ruined mine. Take a day off, Danny."

PART 2
TRADE SCHOOL

CHAPTER 15
SUCKING AND BLOWING

THURSDAY, JANUARY 20, 2005
3:15 P.M.
BOWENS MILL, GEORGIA

Omar Warren crawled from the rear of the airplane his father had bought. The interior of the plane was strewn over the floor of the hangar, and Omar had to dodge around the various pieces to get to his coffee. He took a long drink then sat on a stool. He was tired but satisfied.

The surplus O-2 Skymaster had been easier to procure than Omar or his dad thought possible. The Skymaster's chief distinction was one engine mounted on the nose of the aircraft, and the other was mounted in the rear in a push/pull configuration. Servicemembers referred to it affectionally as the 'suck and blow.'

The plane they had found was in poor condition, having served honorably in Vietnam. This particular Skymaster was one of twenty rebuilt after the war and flown by the California Department of Forestry and Fire Protection. Omar had trucked it to Bowens Mill on the back of a borrowed flatbed truck and unloaded it in the hangar the week after Christmas.

Omar had worked for hours on end, repairing some

parts and replacing others. Thankfully, the plane was rugged enough that the airframe was still in serviceable condition. Omar had worked alone to reattach the factory auxiliary tanks, which increased the fuel capacity by a third. A week had been burned getting the two engines to start and run efficiently.

Omar had gone to a store in Valdosta to buy an eighty-gallon waterbed. It would soon reside in the rear of the passenger compartment and would almost double the range of the warbird.

As Omar finished his coffee, he saw his father and Adam coming toward the hangar to get a look at his work.

Mitch looked things over and then stepped back. "This thing reminds me of the ship on *Star Trek*." Mitch continued to examine the cockpit. "What are those hoses in the back for?"

Omar wiped his hands. "Adam, what was one of our biggest problems in getting from El Paso to Georgia?"

Adam frowned. "The police?"

Omar groaned. "Other than that."

Adam guessed again, "Fuel management. We basically ran out twice."

Omar nodded. "Right. We couldn't hold enough fuel to make the flight in one hop."

Adam climbed into the open hatch and looked the inside of the airplane over. "So, what's your answer?"

Omar pointed to the box under the tail of the airplane. "Waterbed," Omar said.

Adam looked at the box, then back at Omar. "Where do you plan to put that thing? It'll need to go near the center of the airplane, won't it?"

"In the back of the cockpit, where the payload goes," Omar said with a proud grin.

Adam shook his head. "You plan to put fuel inside the airplane?"

Omar nodded then pointed at the hoses he had added. "The fuel will run into the wing tanks, so I'm not making any significant changes to the fuel-supply system."

"You plan on using an electric pump to get the fuel up top? Won't that cause a fire risk?"

Omar shook his head. "No electric pump. I thought it would be too dangerous. Fuel vapors would most likely escape near the fittings, and catching fire in the air would be a disaster."

Adam frowned. "Then what good is all this work?"

Omar smiled again. "I'm using gravity."

Adam examined the hoses again. "Are you planning to fly upside down to get the fuel into the wings?"

Omar pointed to the floor of the plane. "Nope. We put the waterbed in the back with the hoses connected to the fuel tanks and put the drugs on top of the waterbed. The weight forces the fuel up into the wing tanks, and we double our range."

Adam turned back to Omar. After several seconds, his face split into a grin. "Damn, son, that is ingenious. Have you figured out the weight and balance issues?"

Omar slapped the wing and said, "These things were built for six passengers and extra avionics. The extra fuel shouldn't be a problem. The balance should be okay since I'm putting the waterbed directly underneath the wings. There's enough room behind the two front seats to attach it with straps. We'll fuel up at a friendly airport to get all that fuel on board. Then we can ditch the waterbed if we need to. I added a panel in the ceiling that will hide the extra hoses. If someone were to check us out at any point, they won't see anything unusual."

Mitch nodded his head up and down. He looked at Adam and said, "The boy seems to have thought of everything."

Mitch looked the airplane over again and then stopped to examine the tail numbers. "Who is the plane registered to?"

Omar smiled again. "I found one of these for sale in Ocala, Florida."

Mitch asked, "You plan to buy another one?"

"Nope, I plan to use the tail number of that airplane down in Florida on our plane." He slapped the fuselage. "If the cops check us out, they'll find a perfectly legitimate ownership."

Mitch stood back. "How soon can you have this thing operational?"

Omar thought it over. "I can have it up and running by the end of February, but I'll need a couple of weeks to make sure there aren't any problems that I missed. I think it would be safe to commit to a run by the second week in March."

Mitch nodded, deep in thought. "That will probably work. I'll let the Mexicans know." He turned toward the house.

Adam slapped Omar on the back. "Good job, kid. You're going to fit in here just fine."

MONDAY, JANUARY 31, 2005
11:13 P.M.
CANTON, GEORGIA

Byrd climbed the stairs to his apartment like he was going up the steps of a gallows. Each step seemed to be harder to climb. He turned the key and let himself into the dark apartment, kicking the door shut behind him.

As soon as he was in the door, he saw the light on his answering machine flashing. With a deep sigh, he pushed the button and waited to hear the only message.

"Danny, this is Bobby Wilton. Call me when you get in. You'll want to hear this sooner than later." The recording was rough, probably from Bobby Wilton's new cell phone.

Byrd turned on a light and sat on his couch. He dialed the Pickens County jail and waited for the night operator to answer. "Pickens County sheriff's office. How can I help you?"

"This is Daniel Byrd with the GBI. Is the sheriff in?"

"Yes, sir. Hang on."

The line clicked and buzzed and then he heard the connection made. "Hey, Danny. Were you out on the town tonight?"

"If you call looking for a missing college student out on the town, then I was."

Wilton sounded concerned. "Are you doing okay?"

Byrd closed his eyes. "Yeah. We found this kid tonight. Her car had gone down an embankment. She died when the car hit a tree. She was probably twenty years old."

Wilton sighed, too. "It takes the starch out of you to see things like that."

Byrd leaned back. "You didn't call for a therapy session, so what's going on?"

"A name from your past. Carl Hollander."

"Yeah, he tried to bribe you and then he was there when the plane loaded with crystal meth tried to land."

"Right," Wilton said. "I told you the DA wouldn't go for charging him when the people in the plane didn't turn up."

"You're calling to tell me Jerry Mason is cutting Hollander loose?" Byrd asked.

"Sort of. Mason plans to go before one of the judges on Monday and have him released. They think they don't have enough to charge him."

Byrd slapped the couch. "I should have expected this."

Wilton continued. "I didn't call you on a Monday night to give you bad news."

"What then?" Byrd asked.

"Hollander wants to talk to you. He asked me today if I could get in touch with you. He's pissed that his buddies are letting him rot in jail."

Byrd frowned. "Does he know the charges are about to be dropped?"

Wilton laughed. "Not as far as I know. He says he can give you the names and places of the players in this operation."

Byrd sat up. "Wow!"

"I told him I would reach out to you, and you'd see him tomorrow."

Byrd stripped his jacket and tie off as he talked. "I'll be there bright and early in the morning."

"I figured," Wilton said. "See you in the morning."

Byrd hung up the phone and finished taking his clothes off. He walked into the bathroom and took a cold shower. Looking in the mirror afterward, he had considered a drink to help him sleep—he couldn't get the young girl in the Mustang out of his mind.

Byrd was limiting his alcohol intake. He had found a judo academy, a sport he had practiced in college, and resumed training. He was feeling better than he had a few months ago.

After he brushed his teeth, Byrd climbed into bed where he tossed and turned for a while before finally drifting off to sleep around midnight.

CHAPTER 16
NEVER GIVE A SUCKER AN EVEN BREAK

TUESDAY, FEBRUARY 1, 2005
8:22 A.M.
JASPER, GEORGIA

The deputy brought Hollander into the visitation room at the Pickens County jail. He was handcuffed in front and dressed in an orange jumpsuit. He looked miserable.

"You can take his cuffs off," Byrd said to the deputy when he sat Hollander in front of Daniel Byrd.

Once the cuffs were off, Hollander rubbed his wrists. "Thanks," he said.

Byrd leaned back in the chair he had positioned across the little table from Hollander. "Do I need to advise you before we talk?"

Hollander shook his head. "I know my rights. I've read them to other folks enough to know them by heart."

Byrd waited.

Hollander leaned forward and began rocking. "I've got to get out of here."

Byrd shook his head. "I'm not buying a pig in a poke. You'll have to tell me what you know, at least enough for me to evaluate, then I'll decide if it's worth my time to go to the DA."

Hollander continued to rock. "I can tell you about the general and his place in South Georgia."

"What else?" Byrd asked.

"I can tell you about his contacts in Mexico and what I think he's up to. I can tell you who was probably on that airplane back in November. And I can tell you how he keeps getting away with it."

"*Probably on the airplane?* You don't know who you were meeting?" Byrd asked.

"Not for sure. We didn't have secure comms, so I never talked to anybody on the airplane. But I'm pretty sure who the general sent. There ain't but a couple of people at the farm who can fly an airplane."

Byrd leaned forward. "Okay, let's start with that. Who do you think was on the airplane?"

Hollander sat up and leaned forward. "All I know him by is his work name, but the one I figure was in charge was Adam Benjamin. He's the general's most-trusted operative."

Byrd pursed his lips. "The name you know him by is not his real name?"

Hollander lowered his voice. "Everybody there, except a couple of folks like me who are ex-law enforcement, are government operatives. They have all kinds of false names and passports and everything else."

"Where do they get those things?" Byrd asked.

Hollander shook his head. "I don't know for sure, but I know they can get just about anything they need. You know that BATF badge and credentials y'all took off me when I was arrested?"

"Yes," Byrd said.

"I got them from the farm. The general gave them to me

so I could carry a gun wherever I needed to. Anytime I went on a mission for the general or Benjamin, they gave me the creds."

Byrd sat back. "Where did they get them? Do they make them?"

"I don't know for sure. All I know is all of the people that go on missions with the general have some kind of government ID to allow them to carry a gun when they want to."

"Who sends them on these missions?" Byrd asked.

Hollander wiped his mouth. "I know what they tell me."

"What's that?" Byrd asked.

"The government sends 'em. They go on these missions, and they get all their supplies and different identities from the CIA."

Byrd snorted. "The real CIA or that bullshit company that Mitch Warren had?"

Hollander waved his hands. "The company is his cover. He really does work for the CIA. That's where all the students come from—they are funneled in by the CIA."

"Can you prove that?" Byrd asked.

Hollander shook his head. "But, if you'd seen what I've seen, you'd know I'm not lying. He has people who show up at that training camp who are connected all the way to Washington. I've seen them."

"Can you go with me and show me around the place? Maybe act like I'm a prospective instructor. An ex-cop you met in jail?" Byrd asked.

Hollander seemed to think it over. "Can you get me out of jail?"

Byrd nodded. "I'll meet with the district attorney in the morning, and I should be able to have you out by tomorrow night."

"You get me out of here and I'll do whatever you need," Hollander said.

Byrd stood up and motioned for the deputy to take Hollander back. "We'll talk more tomorrow, after I see if the DA will go along," Byrd said.

TUESDAY, FEBRUARY 1, 2005
10:22 A.M.
LAS CRUCES INTERNATIONAL AIRPORT, LAS CRUCES, NEW MEXICO

Omar taxied the Skymaster to the end of the longest runway at Las Cruces International Airport. He rolled to a stop at the end of the runway and ran his preflight checks. His stomach was in knots, and the tension was building as he revved both engines and waited for clearance. *Today should be a piece of cake*, he thought.

Just over a week ago, Omar had flown this route without a hitch. The fuel bladder had performed flawlessly, and the trip had been quick and without event. All the work he had done was paying off. If today went well, he could be running a regular route in no time.

This morning, a discreet fuel truck had met him on the airport ramp and filled the Skymaster to the top, including the extra capacity. The man running the fuel truck had noted the amount of gasoline needed to fill the tanks but made no comment.

Now, Omar had asked for runway three-zero.

The tower's response was concise. "Skymaster Twenty-two-November, maintain runway heading and contact Las Cruces Departure Control on one-one-niner point one-five when airborne. Cleared for runway three-zero."

Omar rushed through the checklist, excited about the adventure to come. "Las Cruces tower, this is Skymaster Twenty-two-November, ready to depart runway three-zero." The roar of the two engines made headsets a necessity, not a luxury.

The tower responded in clipped, brisk terms. "Skymaster Twenty-two-November, roger, cleared for takeoff. Maintain runway heading and contact departure control on one-one-niner point one-five."

"Skymaster Twenty-two-November, copy one-one-niner point one-five?"

"Affirmative, Twenty-two-November," the tower operator said.

Omar double-clicked the microphone button and taxied onto the end of the runway. He took a deep breath and started to roll.

The airplane was definitely heavier with a full load of fuel, and Omar had anticipated he would need extra runway, but he wouldn't worry for a few hundred more feet.

As soon as the wheels were no longer touching the tarmac, he flipped up the gear and gently eased the plane upward. He switched to the departure control frequency and gave them a call. He could tell the air traffic controllers were busy, something he had counted on.

Omar talked into the boom microphone on his headset. "Las Cruces Departure Control? Skymaster Twenty-two-November checking in VFR and climbing to 1,500 with a request."

"Skymaster Twenty-two-November, El Paso Center. Go ahead with your request."

Omar pressed the button on the control yoke. "Center, Skymaster Twenty-two-November is requesting VFR Flight Following to Horizon Airport-T27."

"Skymaster Twenty-two-November, squawk 3225 and ident."

Omar adjusted the aircraft transponder and pressed the ident button.

"Skymaster Twenty-two-November, radar contact, five nautical miles NW of Las Cruces International. Turn right and proceed on course to T27. Altimeter two nine point nine eight."

Once he was east of the Fort Bliss military reservations and east of El Paso, he canceled VFR flight following with El Paso Center, switched the transponder to squawk 1200, and descended as low as he thought he could handle. The plane, heavy with fuel, shot across the barren landscape at a hundred feet above ground level. The radar altimeter would help him avoid terrain.

He switched his transponder to "Standby Mode" when he was near Horizon Airport. On the FAA's radar, it would look like he had landed at Horizon.

He dropped even lower as he crossed the border into Mexico. The plane was barely skimming the desert sand as he turned to follow the Rio Grande River until he could see his real destination.

At the low altitude, the runway came up suddenly, but he had anticipated it and was able to pull power and drift down without incident. He was relieved the airstrip was extra long. He got the plane stopped farther along the runway than he had hoped, but taxied back up near a hangar and met the pickup truck waiting on him.

Omar idled and feathered both engines then climbed into the back of the plane. The men in the truck lifted a box with much effort and passed it to Omar. Omar dragged the box into the Skymaster and placed it on top of the waterbed mattress. He was shifting the box into the best position when the men brought a second box. Omar was concerned at the weight, but he dragged the second box into place. He was comfortable that the plane could handle the fuel load and the 440-pound payload with ease.

Using nylon straps, Omar fixed the boxes in place, carefully tightening them and checking his work. He was preparing to climb into the front when the men brought a third box.

Omar waved them away. "I can't carry this much. You'll have to take that back."

The leader of the two shook his head. "Rojo says you must take it all. The General agreed to this."

Omar shook his head, but he let them slide the box into the plane. He took his last strap and tied the box down as best he could. "My fucking father," he mumbled as he slid into the cockpit and buckled into the seat.

As he taxied the Skymaster, the tires felt mushy from the extra weight. He pulled the plane to the very end of the runway and revved the engines until the needles on the gauges were almost in the red. Then he crossed himself and said a prayer before shoving both throttles to the max and releasing the brakes.

The heavy airplane bounced and shook as it slowly gained speed. Omar was beginning to wonder if he could manage to get out of the cockpit if the plane crashed. He considered releasing the seat belt, but the airplane took off at the last moment and sluggishly crawled into the sky. Once he was about thirty feet in the air, the plane was more responsive to the controls. He waited to retract the landing gear until the Skymaster was moving easily through the air, as he knew the gear doors would dramatically increase the drag during their cycle. When the airspeed indicated over eighty knots, he retracted the gear.

He rolled the airplane to the north and kept the plane as close to the ground as he could, crossing the Rio Grande for the second time. Once he was back in the USA, he nosed the Skymaster upward and let out his breath.

After passing Horizon City Airport on the east side, Omar started heading east and called El Paso Center.

"El Paso Center, Skymaster Twenty-two-November with you five miles east of Horizon City. VFR climbing to twenty-five hundred feet—looking for flight following to Dallas."

The reply was immediate. "Skymaster Twenty-two-November, El Paso Center—squawk 3150 and ident."

Omar adjusted the transponder settings and pressed the ident button as he continued to climb.

"Skymaster Twenty-two-November, radar contact, six miles east of T27. Altimeter two-nine point nine-eight. Proceed on course to Dallas."

Omar double-clicked the microphone and worked his way up to three thousand feet. After reaching cruising altitude, Omar disabled the transponder. He would take the same route he had used for the ill-fated flight in November. This time, he hoped he had better luck.

He planned to cruise at around 150 mph and expected the flight to take nine or ten hours. Checking his three thermoses of coffee and the bag with two sandwiches, Omar settled into his seat and prepared for a long ride.

TUESDAY, FEBRUARY 1, 2005
11:16 A.M.
EAST OF FABENS, TEXAS, ON I-10

Bundled up in a thick jacket and with the heat off—it made getting out for traffic stops less painful, she had found—Trooper Montana Worley cruised in her black-and-white Crown Victoria, heading to a gas station in Sierra Blanca for lunch. She had discovered the place served fried chicken that tasted like it could have been from Georgia. She was traveling at fifty miles an hour, which gave her a chance to observe the traffic around her.

Montana, at last, was feeling comfortable in West Texas. The terrain no longer felt foreign to her, and the border lifestyle was comfortable. She had been happy to discover that tequila was one of the healthiest liquors made, and it was served in abundance in every watering hole in the high desert that was now her home.

The night before, she had gone to dinner with Clete Petterson at Rosa's Cantina, made famous by Marty Robbins's ballad about El Paso. The food was authentic Mexican and served in abundance. After, they had gone back to Clete's house, up on a hill overlooking the city. When they got home, Clete paid his babysitter and ushered Montana inside. Clete's children were in bed, so they sat in the living room and got comfortable. She joined him on the couch and leaned against his chest as he used a remote to turn on classical music on the radio.

"No country music?" she asked.

He laughed. "I usually listen to *narcocorridos* this time of night."

She frowned and asked, "What is that?"

Clete put his head on her shoulder. He said, "They are literally drug ballads, usually about a specific trafficker, that tell a romanticized version of their lives. The music is popular on both sides of the border, despite it glorifying murder, rape, and kidnapping."

"You're a smooth talker, Clete. A girl wants to enjoy a quiet evening with a guy talking about ballads glorifying rape."

He looked over with raised eyebrows. "Murder, too."

She shook her head. "No more shop talk. We can do that when we're at work."

He pulled her close and kissed her on the mouth. When they broke, she smiled. "That's better."

He kissed her again, this time with more feeling. He put his right hand behind her head and ran his fingers into her hair. They kissed longer this time, Montana wrapping her arms around Clete and pulling him close.

He pulled his head back and looked her in the eye. "Are we getting serious here?"

"I'm feeling pretty serious. We've been dating for a few months now, and your kids didn't run away screaming when I spent the night a couple of times."

Clete looked away for a moment. "Montana, I have strong feelings for you. I've dated some, since my wife died, but I haven't felt this way about anyone else. And I'm not sure what to make of it."

She sat up and held his hand. "Honestly, I haven't felt serious about a man since my divorce. I understand what you're going through. Maybe we should go slow."

Clete kissed her again. Then he held her face with both hands and looked deep into her eyes. "I don't say this lightly, but I think I'm in love."

Montana started to cry.

Clete was confused. "Did I do something wrong?"

"No, you big lunkhead. But you don't tell a girl you love her and then expect her to sit and act like nothing happened."

Clete wiped the tears with a finger.

"I guess I should go ahead and tell you this," she said. "I love you too. I didn't think I could love another man after the asshole I was married to, but I do love you."

Clete kissed her face where her tears had left moisture.

They moved to the bedroom and lay together in bed, holding each other until they fell asleep.

Montana was suddenly snatched from her reverie when a red-and-white airplane shot in front of her car. She slid her car to a stop and tried to get her binoculars into play fast enough to read the tail numbers as the plane banked and climbed. Getting out of the car, she stepped onto the shoulder of the road and focused on the rear of the airplane. The numbers were small and difficult to read. What she did notice was the odd configuration of the airplane. It looked like a standard high-wing airplane but it had two big tail rudders.

She jumped back in the car and hopped into the interstate traffic. She needed to find a pay phone and let Clete know what she had just seen.

TUESDAY, FEBRUARY 1, 2005
6:15 P.M.
NORTHWEST OF BIRMINGHAM, ALABAMA

Aviation fuel has a distinctive smell and for a good reason. The scent was added to the combustible liquid so that it was easy to detect a leak inside the airplane. Omar knew it was not unusual to get a whiff of that aroma simply from walking in and around airplanes. Fuel would get on shoes or on baggage placed near a plane on the tarmac.

But Omar was surprised to smell fuel over the strong chemical smell of his cargo—the final step of manufacturing crystal meth involved soaking the ingredients in paint thinner. The acetone smell had been strong inside the cockpit when the boxes were loaded. Now, Omar thought the fuel smell was too strong to be casual transfer. The aroma had gotten more pungent in the last hour.

The air outside the airplane was clear and turbulence free. Omar checked the area around him for other air traffic and didn't see any other flyers in the area. When there seemed to be no alternative, he set the autopilot and climbed into the back of the plane. He saw immediately that the waterbed was leaking. The boxes were tied down, but the vibration of the engines had rubbed part of the mattress thin. The rubber material had held as long as it could before a pinhole leak had developed. Fortunately for Omar, the fuel in the mattress was almost gone.

He reached into his emergency kit and pulled a roll of duct tape out. He pulled off a foot-long strip of the silver tape and tried to cover the leak. But the liquid on the bladder kept the adhesive from sticking.

Damn it! he thought. *I should have planned for a leak.*

He pulled out the aviation map and looked at his alternatives. His offload crew would be meeting him at the Dalton, Georgia, airport at about nine p.m. There was no friendly place to get the leak fixed before he got there, and the leak was small. Omar decided to soldier on toward the landing. He shut off the overhead fuel valve, isolating the built-in tanks. Once the bladder was no longer feeding the wing tanks, he folded the leaking area over onto itself and taped the mattress together. That would keep the smell down and slow the leak.

He had chosen nine p.m. as the landing time to give him a view of the parking area from the air. If police cars were about to come for him, he would see the brake lights and the headlights clearly from the air.

Starting to feel nauseous from the aviation fuel smell, Omar popped open the air vent near his head and felt immediate relief from the rush of cold air. He also felt the temperature drop inside the cockpit.

TUESDAY, FEBRUARY 1, 2005
9:09 P.M.
DALTON MUNICIPAL AIRPORT, DALTON, GEORGIA

Omar was tired, his hands were stiff from the cold, and his eyes were burning from the fuel vapor still trapped in the cockpit. He could see the stream of headlights and taillights cutting a swath across the horizon and knew it was I-75. He could make out the lights of Chattanooga to the north, and the city of Dalton was off the nose of the twin-engine airplane. He rechecked his navigational aids and confirmed he was on a direct course to the local airport.

Omar took a deep breath. It was showtime. "Dalton Unicom, this is Twenty-two-November approaching from the north for full stop on runway one-four."

He waited for an answer. When none came, he started to pull power and begin a gentle descent into the local runway. "Dalton Unicom, Skymaster Twenty-two-November will be making a straight-in approach to runway one-four."

The radio remained quiet. Omar pulled the throttles back, dropped his landing gear, and angled the plane into a path for the runway. He dropped flaps and began to scan the area adjacent to the runway. He couldn't even see a car or truck in the parking area. But he wouldn't relax until he was on the ground and in the clear.

Omar's head swiveled left and right as he brought the airplane into line with the lighted runway. He pulled all the power from the front engine and used the rear engine to guide the plane the last mile. He heard the satisfying bark of the tires on the runway and gradually brought the Skymaster to a halt. He kept the engine RPMs up, just in case a police car came into sight, but continued to taxi until he was in the shadow of the southern hangar by the parking pad. When he came to a full halt, he pointed his flashlight at the minivan parked on the apron. He could see the two men inside, and the men started moving toward the stopped aircraft.

Omar unstrapped and scrambled into the back, having the boxes unstrapped before the men could get the access hatch open. He noted that the men were different this trip, but the van was the same. He pushed as they pulled each box out and shuttled it to the van. The men were dressed in dark clothes and Omar didn't get a good look at them, but their accent made him think they were Mexican.

When the process was finished, he turned the plane around and pushed the power back up. He taxied near a dumpster at the rear of the quiet airport. He then dragged the waterbed out of the cargo area and onto the ground. Then he wrestled the makeshift fuel bladder into the green dumpster. He was able to find a garden hose that was connected to water and washed the leaked fuel out of the inside of the Skymaster.

In a couple of minutes, he climbed in and shut the door, then guided the airplane back out to the asphalt. He ran through his checklist at the end of the runway and then pointed the Cessna toward the centerline. Soon, he was thundering along the runway, the airplane now lighter and more quickly knifing into the air.

Checking his watch, Omar estimated he could be back in Bowens Mill around midnight.

CHAPTER 17
UNDER THE COVERS
IS WHERE I BELONG

WEDNESDAY, FEBRUARY 2, 2005
8:22 A.M.
TEXAS RANGERS OFFICE, EL PASO, TEXAS

Texas Ranger Clete Petterson had been in his office since seven a.m. He could look out his window and see the sluggish traffic on I-10 he had gotten to the office early to avoid. Rather than spend the morning waiting in traffic, he opted to spend it waiting on the phone. He had been on the phone for almost an hour, but he felt like he was finally getting somewhere.

He had called the FAA Office of Investigations and got through to an agent after being passed around for about ten minutes. Once he got someone from investigations on the phone, he explained about the airplane Montana had seen.

The investigator worked away at his computer for a few minutes as Clete tried to wait patiently. He could hear the clicking sound of keys.

"You know, I think this sighting might be related to another notice we got from over in New Mexico. The tower controller sent this in as a suspicious flight, and we had done a little research on it already."

Clete tightened the phone to his ear. "What was suspicious?"

"The pilot requested the longest runway in the airport. They do that sometimes if the plane has been recently repaired and they want to check it out, or if they are carrying several passengers and want the safety margin the longer runway gives them."

"This pilot wasn't any of those, I'm guessing."

"No, he was alone. And he had an off-airport fuel company fuel his airplane. It got our tower guy curious, so he reported it in our system and one of the special agents ran the tail number down."

"Who did it come back to?" Clete asked.

"A man in Ocala, Florida."

"Anything come up when you ran his name?"

"Just that he's a licensed pilot and has been for several years. He is type rated in twin-engine airplanes, which he would need for the airplane with that tail number," the FAA agent said.

"The trooper didn't mention that airplane was a twin engine. We may be talking about another airplane."

The FAA man continued. "The plane the number comes back to is a Cessna Super Skymaster. To the average person, if you see it in the air, it looks like a normal single-engine airplane. There is an engine in the nose, and then one in the back. They were used in Vietnam as forward observation planes."

"Well," Clete said. "I guess I can start running information down on the owner. That's a place to start."

"You can. But we did some checking on our own. The airplane in question was out of commission in Florida.

One of the agents here called the tower at Ocala—he was going to put a watch on the plane—but the controller in the tower happened to know the owner and the airplane. He verified that the plane was torn down for an engine repair and had been in the hangar in that condition for over a week."

Clete nodded. "You think it was a false tail number?"

The FAA man said, "It had to be. No other explanation."

Clete rubbed his chin. "Any idea where the plane went?"

"It took off from Las Cruces International and the pilot said he was headed for Horizon Airport. Do you know where that is?" The FAA man asked.

"Sure, it's just north of where our trooper saw the plane crossing over."

"Okay, that makes sense. He probably dropped off radar and crossed over. We do know he crossed into Fort Worth Center's airspace. He kept moving to other centers' airspace until we lost him north of Birmingham. The airspace up there gets really busy, even on a Sunday night."

Clete grunted. "That gets me a lot further than I would have thought." The ranger changed gears. "What type of plane did you say it was?"

"We were able to confirm it was a Cessna Skymaster. The people on the ground said it looked like an old military model that had been repainted," the FAA agent said.

"Are there a lot of those around?" Clete asked.

Clete heard the clicking again. The FAA man said, "Probably less than two hundred were ever converted to civilian use. I would imagine, just because of their age, less than a hundred are flying. If that."

Clete thought it over. "Can you send me a dump of the current ownership records? I'll get one of the DEA intelligence analysts to run information on the list of current owners."

"Sure. Give me your email, and I'll get it over to you. It should be current."

Clete gave him his department email address. Before he hung up, he saw the information in his inbox. Confirming the email, Clete hung up the phone and pulled up the spreadsheet. He saved a copy on his desktop and then began to sort the information it contained. He ran a version sorted by names, and then he scanned it to see if a name popped out. Then he ran a version sorted by address. He rolled down the list and was about to run another version when he stopped. He scrolled back toward the top and looked for a name that had caught his attention.

He found the entry and read it with interest. The owner of the airplane he was looking at was a business in Bowens Mill, Georgia. The plane's ownership had been transferred on January 10, 2005.

Clete leaned back in his office chair, mulling over his options. Then he sat forward and started looking for a phone number.

WEDNESDAY, FEBRUARY 2, 2005
11:11 A.M.
GBI REGION 8 OFFICE, GAINESVILLE, GEORGIA

Daniel Byrd sat in front of Tina Blackwell's desk. His Special Agent in Charge was reviewing the draft copy of Hollander's statement.

"He knows the DA isn't going to file charges?" Blackwell asked.

Byrd nodded. "I plan to come clean with him this afternoon. That's assuming the DA hasn't changed his mind.

Sheriff Wilton is working with Jerry Mason this morning to get the charges officially dropped."

Blackwell leaned back in her chair. "Let me guess why you're here instead of there. You want to go undercover with this guy to Bowens Mill?"

Byrd smiled. "I'm the best candidate. He is comfortable with me and I can pose as a recently fired deputy."

Blackwell was skeptical. "How are you going to make that story fly? These folks can run an internet search on you in ten minutes. They'll know you're a fraud."

Byrd took a deep breath. "I have a plan. Bobby Wilton fired a deputy a couple of weeks ago. I'll use his name. If anyone searches the name, they'll see the newspaper article about the firing. If anyone were to call the sheriff's office and ask questions, Bobby can cover that, too."

Blackwell laughed. "You've got it all figured out."

Byrd shrugged. "I think it will work. And I don't plan to do any kind of deal with the folks there. I just want to get a look around and then get out of Dodge."

Blackwell nodded. "I'll call the Inspector. If he's okay with it, I'll let you know. In the meantime, go round up Jamie Abernathy and get her up to speed on this. I want her to go with you and act as cover."

Byrd protested. "This isn't a high-risk operation. I hate to tie up another agent. I'll be fine on my own."

Blackwell looked over the top of her glasses. "Do you want to go?"

Byrd sighed. "Yes, ma'am."

She picked up her office phone. "Then we'll do it my way. Now, close that door on your way out."

Byrd stepped out and closed the door. He had taken two steps toward his desk when he heard Machelle Stevens call his name.

"Yes, ma'am," Byrd said.

"There's somebody on the phone asking for you," she said. "He says he's a Texas Ranger. I thought that was a cowboy thing. Do they still exist?"

"Yep. What line is he on?"

"Hmm, are you sure that's a real thing? I thought that Chuck Norris show was made up."

"What line, Machelle?"

"Line two," she said. Byrd saw her turn to her computer, searching the internet to confirm that the Texas Rangers were real.

"Byrd," he said into the phone.

"Danny, this is Clete Petterson. How are you doing?"

"I'm good. What gets you on the phone to Georgia this early in the morning?"

"We've had another plane spotted here that looks like it's tied to that place in South Georgia."

"Bowens Mill?" Byrd asked.

"Yep," was the reply.

Clete spent the next ten minutes detailing the story as Byrd took notes.

WEDNESDAY, FEBRUARY 2, 2005
12:01 P.M.
BOWENS MILL, GEORGIA

Omar Warren woke up in his own bed, happy to be back in South Georgia. He threw the covers back and got on his feet. The floor was cold, but not as cold as the airplane had been last night. He pulled on a pair of sweats and a T-shirt and headed for the stairs. He didn't realize how stiff he was until he started moving.

Sitting in an airplane loaded with drugs for almost twelve hours sure takes it out of you, he thought.

When Omar was on the main floor, he searched for his dad. He checked his office in the house, without any luck. He pulled on a pair of shoes and headed for the training center.

He met his dad leaving the training building. "Welcome home, son!" Mitchell Warren exclaimed.

"Have you spoken with Big Red? Is he pleased?" Omar asked.

Mitch was all smiles. "I haven't spoken to him directly, but I guarantee you he'll be happy. The trips you made were the fastest, most trouble-free shipments he has ever gotten."

Omar beamed. "I found a couple of issues that I need to fix on this last trip. I had a small fuel leak from the bladder, but I didn't have any major problems. That old airplane is solid as a rock."

Mitch slapped Omar on the back. "Come on, son. Let's go to my office and fix a drink to celebrate."

Omar glanced at his watch, and then shrugged. This was a day of celebration after all.

They walked together back to Mitch's office in the house. Once inside, he closed the door and opened the secret cabinet. Mitch looked at Omar. "I think I'll check in with Red and see if he is pleased. Stay quiet, but I want you to listen in."

Omar sat in one of the plush chairs across from his dad's desk. He hung his left leg over the arm and let it dangle. "Sure, I'll keep quiet."

Mitch made the connection on the secure phone. El Gordo answered after the second ring. "El Gordo. Is this Señor General?"

"It is. Is Señor Rojo available?"

"No, señor. He is at a meeting with a customer. But he did ask me to tell you something if you called."

Mitch was wary of the mercurial drug runner. "What would that be?"

El Gordo said, "He was very happy with the shipments you have handled so far. He says we can do much business together. He will be calling with arrangements to have you paid for your work. He also wants to know how soon you can take another shipment for him."

"That will depend on how much he's paying for these shipments. Did he tell you that?" Mitch had a figure in mind.

"Rojo says he will pay you one hundred thousand US dollars for each hundred kilos you deliver across the country. Is that satisfactory?"

El Gordo had more power than Warren had thought if he could negotiate prices.

Mitch smiled and winked at Omar. He said into the phone, "Tell him I will confer with my pilot and get back to him. The pilot is very skilled, and his skills come with a cost."

El Gordo didn't push. "We will wait for your counter offering."

Warren hesitated. "We have many expenses on this end, but we think we can meet that goal of a couple of hundred kilos every other week, maybe more."

El Gordo was pleased. "If you can deliver one hundred kilos every other week to our people in Atlanta, we will be willing to sweeten the offer. We need very much to get our product to this place as quickly as we can."

Warren was satisfied with the negotiations. "Good," he said. "I will call back in twenty-four hours. May I speak to Rojo then?"

The man said, "Sí," then the phone went dead.

Warren was all smiles. "Five hundred thousand dollars for the two trips."

Omar was up, pacing the floor. "My God. I could have loaded more product on the plane, I was just being ultra-cautious. Hell, I might be able to get four hundred keys a trip if I can work out the bugs in the fuel delivery system."

Mitch nodded. "You think you can make a trip every three or four days?"

Omar laughed. "Nothing to it if I can get the fuel issue squared away."

Mitch stood. "What would it take?"

Omar thought out loud. "A fixed tank or maybe a couple of tanks that could be mounted where they wouldn't affect the weight and balance. They would need to be plumbed in a way to make them feed the wing tanks direct."

Mitch poured two scotches. "Let me make a call to the broker who sold us that Skymaster to begin with. He may know a way to do it."

Mitch passed Omar one of the glasses. Omar held his high. "To future endeavors," Omar said.

Mitch laughed and clinked the glasses together. "Omar, you need to get dressed and start looking at what we can do to that airplane. We're about to be sitting pretty."

Omar sipped the scotch. "There's something I want you to ask Rojo."

Mitch waited.

"We need to control the offload site. They had me land at an airport I knew very little about. We should be able to find a place near Atlanta that we can control. If we had a runway up there, it would make the entire operation safer."

Mitch thought it over. "Okay, I think that's sound logic. And I think we can work it so Rojo foots that bill."

They clinked glasses again.

WEDNESDAY, FEBRUARY 2, 2005
2:21 P.M.
GBI REGION 8 OFFICE, GAINESVILLE, GEORGIA

Byrd sat in Tina's office again, this time giving her a rundown on the call with Ranger Petterson. She took notes as he talked, occasionally asking for clarification.

"This should be enough to tip the scales," she said. "The Inspector is going to meet with Director Hicks this afternoon. I'll email him this update. He was hesitant at first. Then he remembered the drug office for the area near Bowens Mill is knee-deep in a wiretap investigation. They're not going to be able to help for the next month or more."

Byrd sat up. "Will our office need to send a cover team, then?" Byrd was aware that Tina Blackwell had worked in a drug office twice on her path up the leadership ladder in the GBI, so she understood the dynamics of a successful undercover operation.

"Do you think you can get what you need in a couple of days?" she asked.

Byrd nodded. "I doubt we could sustain the operation any longer than that. I figure I'll be lucky to get on the property. I'll be damn lucky to look around. And I'll be shocked if I get more than that."

Blackwell nodded. "I think you're right. If I send a couple of agents with you for cover, can you wrap it up and be back by Friday?"

Byrd stood up. "I don't see why not. Who can I take?"

Blackwell sat back in her chair. "Who do you want?"

Byrd didn't hesitate. "You mentioned Jamie earlier. How about I take Doc and Jamie."

Tina nodded. "And why Doc?"

"When he was a Revenue Agent, he worked all over the state, just like I have. He won't be off his game down south."

She turned in her chair and started typing the email to Inspector Will Carver. "Okay, talk to both of them and make sure they can be out of town till the end of the week."

"Yes, ma'am," Byrd said as he left the office. He found his desk and logged into his computer. He had talked to Jamie and Doc when he came in, so he didn't need to chase them down. Now he just had to wait on a call from Atlanta.

He was reviewing case reports when Tina came into his office. "You better get moving," Tina said. "They gave you till Friday."

Byrd closed his work and stood up. "Thanks, Tina. I know you went to bat for me."

"Just don't screw this up," she said as she turned to leave.

CHAPTER 18
MOODY BLUES

Wanting to get an early start, Byrd pulled up to the Jasper Elite Motel, known as the "e-light" by locals and was everything you could ask for in a rundown motel. Byrd had arranged for Carl Hollander to spend the last few nights there.

Byrd went to the door of the room and banged. He was surprised when Hollander opened it, dressed and ready to go. Hollander was wearing green fatigue pants and a sweatshirt and pulled on a military-style field jacket as he grabbed his bag and closed the door behind him.

Byrd laughed. Byrd was dressed in black fatigue pants, a black sweatshirt with the logo of the Georgia Public Safety Training Center silk-screened on the front, and a green military pilot's jacket.

"You ready to go?" Byrd asked.

"I sure am," Hollander replied. "I took a shower for about an hour after I got in this room. I slept the best I have in months. But a couple of nights on my own here was enough."

"Jail ain't for sissies," Byrd said. "We're going to ride down in your truck. Is that okay?"

Hollander nodded. "Sure. It'll give me somebody to talk to. It's about a four-hour drive."

"Okay," Byrd said. "Our cover team is meeting us at the jail. I'll leave my car there."

Hollander crawled into the worn-out Chevy truck Byrd had helped him get out of impound last night. Hollander followed Byrd around the back way to the Pickens County Jail. Byrd parked his Crown Victoria in the front lot and waved to Jamie Abernathy and Doc Farmer. They had their clothes for the week loaded in Doc's Crown Vic.

Hollander seemed concerned when he saw Doc's car. "Are they going to follow us in that car?"

Byrd shook his head. "We're not the FBI. We're going by GBI Headquarters to get an undercover car. They have one waiting."

Hollander seemed to relax. He followed Doc out onto the parkway for the trip to Atlanta. Once they swapped into a seized Ford pickup truck, the pair of trucks pushed south. Over two hours later, the scenery had turned to farmland and forest, flat and low with swampy areas here and there along the road.

In one of the trucks, Jamie looked at the area as the sun was coming up to their left. "This looks like Florida, without the pretty beaches."

Doc nodded. "Compared to where we work, it might as well be North Florida. It's got all the creatures and none of the amusement parks and sandy beaches."

Jamie didn't seem pleased. "How far do you think we'll have to walk in the woods to cover him?"

Doc shook his head. "We won't be able to get close enough through the woods to do any good. I checked the topographic map for the area where the Warren guy has this training center. He put his place right in the middle of a couple of hundred acres. A body bug won't do us any good either. We're here mostly to make Tina feel better."

Jamie was confused. "Where will we wait, then?"

Doc shook out a cigarette. He rolled the truck window down, and in seconds the inside of the truck was frigid. "The property is bracketed with cemeteries, one on each side. We'll pull around to the back of one of them. If somebody shows up, or there is a funeral at one, we'll just move to the other one."

Jamie laughed. "Two cemeteries out in the country like this?"

Doc nodded. "Both have the same name on the map. They must belong to the church that's on the west side of the property."

"How far are we out from the farm?" Jamie asked.

Doc shrugged. "About thirty minutes, I'd guess. We'll turn onto a state route and follow it about five miles to the entrance to the compound."

The two fell silent.

In the other truck, Hollander made the turn onto River Road. He slowed on the tar and gravel surface and pointed the truck southeast. Hollander was nervous about what he was about to do. In the mountains of North Georgia, the idea of bringing an undercover agent onto the property seemed like a good idea. Now, he was beginning to have second thoughts.

Byrd must have sensed the fear welling up in Hollander because he asked, "Do you remember our cover story?"

Hollander nodded, his expression glum in the morning light.

"Tell me the cover, then," Byrd ordered.

Hollander glanced over at Byrd. "I met you at the jail. You were a deputy at Pickens County where you worked in the jail. You smuggled me extra food and weed from time to time. Then, last week, you got caught having sex with a female who was in jail on drug charges. The sheriff didn't want to prosecute you, for fear it would make him look bad, but they fired you. Is that about it?"

Byrd gave him a thumbs-up. "Keep it simple. You don't know me well, just know that I'm a bent cop. If they want to know about my background, you let me do the talking."

Hollander was grim. "These aren't people who should be trifled with. They are connected to some big folks. I don't want to end up in the pond out back."

Byrd raised his eyebrows. "He has a gator pond, I guess?"

Hollander nodded. "I've seen the beasts. They are huge. I want nothing to do with that."

"I read that gators, even big ones, rarely attack humans," Byrd said, obviously trying to reassure Hollander.

Hollander grunted. "I hope the gators read the same article."

Hollander slowed the truck and turned off the highway. He drove down a path leading to a farm gate. The red-painted gate was locked and had a wooden bird's nest on the fence near it. Hollander took a proximity card from his wallet and waved it near the wooden box. The gate clicked loudly and moved out of their way. Hollander pulled the truck forward and waited for the gate to close.

"What are you waiting for?" Byrd asked.

Hollander glanced over. "Policy. You always wait on the gate to close back and latch. That way no interlopers can get on the property."

Hollander rolled the truck forward along the roadway. It was dirt and grass but was surprisingly smooth. Hollander let the truck idle along as they came into a pasture. The area was long and about the width of a football field. Byrd saw an aluminum building ahead that he assumed was a barn.

Hollander elbowed Byrd as they neared the building. "We're on the runway now, and this building is their hangar." There was a large door, big enough he realized for an airplane, open a few feet. As they rolled along the pathway, a man ran toward the truck, coming from the hangar.

Hollander said, "This is Omar. He's Mitch's oldest son."

Byrd asked, "You call him Mitch?"

"Hell no! I call him General Warren."

The young man ran up to the truck window, leaning in as Hollander rolled down the window.

"Hey, Carl. Glad to see you!"

Hollander shrugged. "Glad to be here. You act like you knew I was coming."

Omar nodded. "Your lawyer called my dad last night. He said the charges against you were being dropped. Dad is worried you might have talked. I told him I didn't think you were a snitch."

Hollander coughed. Byrd leaned toward the window and stuck out his hand. "Hey, I'm Herman Moody. I rode down with Carl to get away from that place up there."

Omar shook his hand. "How did you guys meet?"

Byrd looked embarrassed. "I was a jailer at Pickens County. I had a little misunderstanding with the sheriff, and he fired me."

Hollander smirked. "He misunderstood that he couldn't get a blow job from an inmate. She ratted him out to her lawyer."

Byrd hung his head. "She was a tweaker, but she looked pretty good, I'll have to say."

Omar laughed. "Are you looking for work?"

Byrd nodded. "I need something to make a dollar or two."

Omar looked him over. "You know anything about flying?"

Byrd shook his head. "Not much. I was in a small plane a time or two, but I can't drive one of the things."

Omar slapped the door and stood back. "Well, I'm sure Dad would like to see you. Nice to meet you, Mr. Moody."

Byrd leaned over again. "What are you working on?"

Omar's face lit up. "Have you ever heard of a plane called a 'suck and blow'?"

Byrd laughed. "That's what got me fired."

Omar's face reddened. "Sorry."

Byrd shook his head. "No worries. So, what is it?"

Omar pointed. "A twin-engine airplane."

Byrd stepped down from the truck. "Can I take a look?"

Omar shrugged. "Sure."

As Hollander stayed in the truck, Byrd walked over to the hangar door and peeked inside. The hangar was dark, but he could see a red-and-white airplane with twin tails. "Wow, it looks in good shape."

Omar was enthusiastic. "It is. Everything on it works like it's supposed to. These things are tough as nails."

When Byrd tried to get closer, Omar stepped in his way. "You guys probably shouldn't keep Dad waiting. He saw your truck come through the gate."

Byrd reluctantly climbed back into the pickup. "Well, thanks for letting me check it out."

As they drove away, Byrd wondered how Omar, way out here in this hangar, knew what his dad was doing in the main house. Byrd didn't have a good feeling about things.

The old truck pulled up in front of a house, which sat

farthest away from the highway of all the buildings. The house was big and white and seemed to suit the property. Byrd knew, from looking at maps, that the house had a view of the Ocmulgee River, only fifty yards behind the structure.

Before the men could get out, they saw a slim, fit man with salt-and-pepper hair coming down the front steps toward them. Hollander leaned over to Byrd and said, "That's Adam Benjamin. The general's right-hand man."

Byrd sat still. He said, "Two first names?"

Hollander shrugged. "Neither one is real."

Benjamin came to the driver's door and opened it for Hollander. "Welcome back, Carl. Glad to see you were able to get out."

Hollander didn't offer to shake with Benjamin. The two men stood uneasily for a moment. Then Hollander said, "Is all my stuff still here?"

Benjamin nodded. "Sure. We didn't move anything. It's all just where it was."

"Thanks. I appreciate that."

Benjamin looked at Byrd, who was still sitting in the truck. "Who's your friend?"

Byrd answered, "Herman Moody. I met Carl while he was in jail."

Benjamin looked Byrd over. "What were you in for?"

Byrd laughed. "Being too stupid to get another job. I worked as a jailer."

Benjamin's eyes narrowed. "Why'd you leave?"

"I had a difference of opinion with the sheriff."

Hollander interrupted. "He got caught getting a blow job from a woman who was in on drug charges."

Byrd shrugged. "When they hired me, they said the job had benefits. I just thought that was one of them."

Benjamin grunted. "Omar said you were a deputy in Pickens County. I guess you're looking for work.?"

Byrd shook his head. "Not so much. I'm just going to kick around till I go back north. I need time away for things to cool down."

Benjamin seemed relieved. "Is Carl going to put you up?"

Byrd shook his head. "No, he's taking me to my cousin's house in Douglas. He was just so proud of working at this place, he offered to show me around. If y'all don't mind, that is."

Benjamin looked over at Hollander. He seemed to be thinking things over. "Sure, show him around, and then come back to the main house. The general may want to meet him."

CHAPTER 19
HANDS ACROSS THE BORDER

THURSDAY, FEBRUARY 3, 2005
11:02 A.M.
BOWENS MILL, GEORGIA

Mitch Warren dialed the secure phone, waiting for the three beeps, and then for the connection to be made.

The man on the other end answered with a grunt and then said, "*Momento.*"

Rojo came on the line. "My friend, it is good to talk with you. I am very pleased with your recent work."

Warren chuckled. "That is the work of my son. He did a great job. I am very proud."

Rojo's tone softened. "My son is my pride and joy. He was not raised like me—I was raised in poverty with no education. My son has always known wealth and is college educated. But he has opened my eyes to the business that we do. He has made ways for our profits to increase. They are our future."

Warren smiled. "Yes, they are. And in that regard, my son has recommended some ways that our operation can be improved. I wanted you to consider these recommendations. We will need some additional funding."

Warren could sense the caution in his voice when Rojo asked, "For what, may I ask?"

"My son believes we should have an airstrip close to Atlanta which we control. In that way, the loads can come at times we decide upon. No more landings late at night or at locations where unforeseen problems may crop up."

Rojo asked a muffled question to someone else, likely from placing his hand over the phone. Warren waited while the discussion went back and forth. Then Rojo said, "I understand your concern. We agree that a private location would be better. Was the arrangement in Mexico satisfactory?"

Warren was relieved. "Mexico was most satisfactory. But law enforcement in the United States can be treacherous. We can have more influence if we choose the location."

"How soon can this be accomplished?" Rojo asked.

Warren gave that some thought. "I'll get back with an answer in a week, if not sooner."

"Good. We have more product ready to go. We are making plans to get as much as we can across the border. That will make the pickup easier. Your son should be able to run a regular route if he wants. There is much money to be made."

"I look forward to that," Warren said.

THURSDAY, FEBRUARY 3, 2005
12:20 P.M.
BOWENS MILL, GEORGIA

Hollander had walked Byrd through the training building first. The men stood in the back and watched as students were lectured on the latest techniques for camouflage. Byrd nudged Hollander and they went back outside.

A gentle rain started to fall, so Byrd pointed to the

hangar. When they shuffled into the hangar for cover from the cool droplets, they were both wet.

Omar was crawling from the inside of the airplane. "Raining, I see."

Byrd shook his jacket off. "Yep. Mr. Benjamin suggested that Carl show me around. We were leaving the training center when it started. We just came in here to get in the dry."

Omar walked over and looked out the door. "This time of year, it may pass over in a couple of minutes, or set in for a couple of hours."

Byrd and Hollander stood near the hangar door. Byrd didn't want to seem too eager to get a look at the red-and-white airplane. He took a moment to memorize the tail number on the airplane in the shadows.

Omar waved for them and Byrd walked up to the plane. "Problems?" Byrd asked. "Or are you making improvements?"

Omar grabbed a flashlight from the toolbox. "I guess you could say both. I want to extend her range, but I don't want to mess up the balance of the airplane."

"How much fuel are you planning to add?" Byrd asked.

"About five hundred pounds, roughly eighty gallons." Omar shone the light around the cockpit.

Byrd stood behind him and looked over his shoulder. "I guess you'll need room for a payload, too."

Omar looked back at him. "Yeah. I need to be able to carry about four or five hundred pounds."

Byrd raised his eyebrows. "Will this bird carry that much weight? I would think that would be a heavy load for her."

Omar smiled. "This thing is stouter than you'd think. It may max her out, but she can do it. She's as solid as a rock."

Byrd nodded. "All these old military planes are like that. I worked as a fuel jockey at an airport when I was a kid. I saw some that flew in World War II that could still be around today. They made them solid."

Omar slapped the wing spar and smiled. "Yep!"

The rain was letting up, and Byrd didn't want to push his luck. He looked everything over once more and then said, "Carl, we need to let this man get back to work."

Hollander nodded, and then they jogged back out toward the house.

THURSDAY, FEBRUARY 3, 2005
12:44 P.M.
BOWENS MILL, GEORGIA

After going deep into the cemetery to relieve herself, Jamie walked back to the truck and climbed into the passenger seat, shaking the rain out of her long blond hair. "I hadn't planned on getting wet."

Doc chuckled. "It may be the most action we see today."

Jamie nodded. "They don't mention all this waiting in Special Agents School."

Jamie grew concerned. They hadn't heard anything since Byrd and Hollander turned into the compound. Jamie looked over at Doc. "What do you think?"

Doc pursed his lips. "Danny is okay. He can talk his way out of anything he might run into in there."

Jamie wasn't satisfied. "He can be reckless. I know you've seen that."

Doc nodded. "He can be . . ." Doc thought about the right word. "He can be impetuous."

Jamie mulled that over. "Impetuous would be a polite way of saying reckless."

"And I'm nothing if not polite."

Doc was, in fact, worried that Byrd had been out of contact so long, but he wasn't going to alarm Jamie. He turned and looked in the direction of the big house. Doc stepped out in the light rain, cupped the end of a cigarette in his right hand, and lit it. "I know you haven't worked with Danny as much as I have. He can be a loose cannon at times. But you'd have to admit, no matter what, he's a cannon all the time."

Jamie leaned her head back and closed her eyes. "I would certainly pick him to be beside me if I had to kick in a door, that's for sure. But, Doc, we kick doors less than I thought. It seems like we spend most of our time on a computer."

Doc took a deep puff on the cigarette. "We've become slaves to our computers. But you can't ever forget, a law enforcement agency needs people who can kick doors. Someone will always have to do that."

Jamie opened her eyes to look at Doc. "I guess I missed the best time to be an agent. Seems like the cowboy days are over."

Doc finished the cigarette and crushed the butt with his foot. "The days aren't changing. It's the cowboys who are changing." He climbed into the truck and looked at his watch. "Danny's still a cowboy."

"He never wears boots," Jamie observed.

"A pair of boots and a hat don't make a cowboy."

THURSDAY, FEBRUARY 3, 2005
1:02 P.M.
BOWENS MILL, GEORGIA

The General looked Byrd over. "What was your name again?" he asked.

"Herman Moody, sir." Byrd stood near the door of Mitch's office, examining a couple of the plaques displayed on the wall, but they were mostly in foreign languages.

"Mr. Moody, please have a seat." The general motioned to the chairs across from his desk.

Byrd sat down. "Thanks."

"I understand from my people that you are recently unemployed." It was a statement, not a question.

Byrd nodded but kept quiet.

"Would you be interested in a small job that might help you until you get back on your feet?" The General watched Byrd closely.

"Not down here. I have family down this way, but I don't want to live down here again. I hate the heat and the snakes."

Mitch pursed his lips. "And if the job was near Atlanta?"

Byrd wasn't prepared for this. "It would have to be something legal. I want to stay clean. This has been the most embarrassing thing ever for my family."

Mitch turned in his chair and pulled a bottle of scotch from the twin bookcases behind him. Byrd watched as he poured a large drink. He spotted an arc of worn carpet under the bookcase and realized the bookcase must swing out.

With his back still turned, Mitch asked, "May I offer you a drink?"

Byrd waived his hands. "No, thanks. Since I got arrested, I've been trying to quit."

Mitch took a sip. "I'm not a quitter."

Byrd laughed. "Good for you. I'm sure you've earned that right."

"I'm looking to rent some land near Atlanta. I'm looking for a scout."

It was possible the offer was some kind of setup but Byrd didn't want to let this opportunity pass. He nodded but didn't leap at the bait.

"I'm not a realtor, but I could do some looking around for you. You want to rent something for a couple of months, or longer?" Byrd tried to sound disinterested. "I'm sure there are lots of places around if you're willing to pay the price."

Mitch leaned back. "My needs are pretty specific. I want a horse farm, with at least a couple of hundred acres. I plan to move several show horses onto the land. It needs to be secluded, but close to a major highway. I can pay you well if you locate a place for me."

"I don't mean to look a gift horse in the mouth, but why not just call one of the big real estate agencies?"

"I want someone who is looking out for me. Not looking for a commission. I can pay you a good price for going to a realtor and looking at land on my behalf. I have a couple of other wants, but we could get into those if you find any prospects."

Byrd leaned in and met Mitch's gaze. "Why should you trust me? You barely know me."

Mitch laughed. "I don't trust you. At best, you're a bent law officer. At worst, you're a crook and a conman. I have several irons in the fire, and I need someone in Atlanta."

Byrd shrugged. "Herman Moody isn't a crook. He's a guy who likes blow jobs."

"Sounds like just a guy to me," Mitch said. "Let's do business." Mitch stood and walked around the desk. "There's just one last thing. Would you mind emptying your pockets?"

THURSDAY, FEBRUARY 3, 2005
2:13 P.M.
BOWENS MILL, GEORGIA

Doc was lighting another cigarette when Carl Hollander's truck went by the cemetery. Doc jumped back into the seat, fired the truck up, and set off on Hollander's heels. He pushed the undercover truck hard, and soon they were overtaking Hollander's truck. They could see two heads in the truck.

Doc glanced over at Jamie. "I think that's Danny's noggin on the passenger side."

Jamie nodded. "I think you're right. I wish we could talk to him about how things went."

Doc grunted. "I can see his head moving, so at least he's still alive."

Doc dutifully followed Hollander at the same pace. Doc carefully checked his rearview mirror and hadn't seen a car behind them since they left the cemetery.

THURSDAY, FEBRUARY 3, 2005
2:38 P.M.
BOWENS MILL, GEORGIA

Hollander stepped on the brake pedal. "They missed us. They must not have seen me turn in."

"Relax," Byrd said. "They're just checking our tail. Pull as far from the road as you can and find a place to stop."

The truck bounced as they drove to the back of the cemetery. They passed weathered marble spires marking the last resting place of someone important in their time and Byrd motioned for Hollander to stop and wait. He turned in the truck seat and got the best view he could of the area. They only waited a couple of minutes when the undercover truck came back into view.

Byrd waited for the GBI vehicle to pull in behind them, then he hopped out of Hollander's truck. As soon as Doc got out, Byrd said, "Come shake hands like you haven't seen me in a couple of years, Doc. Jamie, come out here and give me a hug. I don't think anybody followed us, but it won't hurt to be safe."

Doc shook his hand vigorously. They smiled at each other like long-lost relatives do. Jamie came behind Doc and threw her arms around Byrd. She was smiling from ear to ear. Byrd leaned in and whispered, "We could be kissing cousins, don't you think?"

Without breaking her smile, Jamie said, "Don't be a dick. If you want to kiss someone, you should have kissed Doc."

Byrd laughed.

Byrd pulled his overnight bag from the back of the

truck and transferred it to the undercover vehicle. Byrd waved Hollander over by the GBI vehicle.

"Carl, what are your plans from here?" Byrd asked.

Hollander was glum. "I guess I'll go start looking for work. I don't suppose the GBI would vouch for me if I tried to get back in law enforcement, would you?"

Byrd shook his head. "We can't do that, Carl."

Hollander grinned. "It was worth a try."

Byrd nodded. "You need to stay as far away from the farm as you can. These boys strike me as people who don't play. Call my office when you get settled, and make sure we know where you're living."

Hollander nodded and lumbered back to the truck. He drove out of the lot and Byrd watched him turn south on the highway.

Doc watched, too. As soon as Hollander's truck was out of sight, he asked, "What happened?"

Byrd headed for the rear door of the truck. "Let's talk as we drive."

"Should we head back to Jasper? It's not very late." Doc asked.

Byrd thought about it. "There's nothing here to see. They're looking for a place to bring a plane in, but they want something closer to Atlanta."

"Are they looking for another airport to land at?" Jamie asked.

Byrd slumped in the back seat. "They want me to find some land they can rent. I actually sat down with Mitchell Warren himself. He didn't say he was looking for a runway, he made it sound like he was looking for a horse farm."

Doc glanced back. "Do you think all that was on the level?"

Byrd shook his head. "I'll be damned if I know. But he

gave me a cell phone to contact him on. It's a bag phone with some kind of box attached to it that makes the calls secure."

Doc whistled. "That says something."

Byrd continued. "I'm glad I didn't take a bug or recorder though. He made me empty my pockets."

Doc looked back, startled. He ran the truck onto the shoulder of the road. "He didn't find anything, did he?"

Byrd sighed. "I took precautions. I locked my gun and badge in the trunk of my car. I made sure to leave my driver's license and any credit cards with my name on them back there, too."

Jamie turned to him. "He looked through your wallet?"

Byrd nodded. "Yep. I missed the handcuff key on my key chain, but I told him I kept it when I got fired. He was curious why I didn't have anything with my name on it in my wallet. I just told him the sheriff took all my stuff when they booked me in and didn't give it back just to piss me off. He seemed to buy that."

"Wow," Jamie exclaimed. "That's crazy."

Byrd looked at her. "No, the crazy part is that he took down my name and date of birth."

Doc looked into the rearview mirror and met Byrd's eyes. "I hope you mean that he took your undercover name."

Byrd nodded. "I memorized Moody's full name and DOB. I didn't think to memorize his Social Security number. When he asked for that, I told him I didn't plan to report any income from him. He laughed and said he could find out what he needed from my other information."

Doc nodded. "He's got a cop on the hook. He must have someone who can run names through the computer system."

Byrd nodded. "That's my guess."

"What can we do about it?" Jamie asked.

Byrd closed his eyes again. "It's too late to change anything in the real Moody's driver's license or criminal history. But we can tell if someone makes an inquiry. That'll tell us something."

Doc looked at Jamie. "We'll be going by the entrance to the farm. Grab your camera and take as many pictures as you can."

She nodded as she dug into her bag. She had brought a camera with a powerful zoom. "And we should probably stop by the GBI office in Perry and get a call in to the Crime Information Center. We can get them to set up a flag if any of Danny's information is run through the system."

Byrd nodded, without opening his eyes. "Yep, and I need to make a phone call."

Jamie laughed. "Got a date tonight?"

Byrd shook his head. "Nope. But I know something that is going to make a Texas Trooper and a Texas Ranger very happy."

Byrd slumped over on his bag and tried to nap.

CHAPTER 20
I LOVE IT WHEN A PLAN COLLAPSES INTO PLACE

THURSDAY, FEBRUARY 3, 2005
4:58 P.M.
PERRY, GEORGIA

The GBI Office in Perry, Georgia, is located immediately adjacent to I-75, right on the way home. Doc parked the truck out front of the one-story brick building and the group hustled to the front door. The office investigative assistant was in the process of locking the office when they got there. Doc displayed his credentials, and she ushered them in, using her access code to get them into the main part of the office.

"Sorry to disrupt your evening. I know you're getting ready to go home, but we need to use one of your phones," Doc said.

She was not bothered. "Come on in. One of the agents is still here, so I'll leave you with her. Phones are on all the desks, and the restrooms are in the main hall."

The IA shouted down the hall. "Janet, we have some visitors here to use the phone! They're from Region Eight!" She turned back to Doc. "We don't have an intercom."

Jamie perked up. "Is that Janet Oliver? We were in Agents' School together."

The IA pointed down the hallway. "That's her, second door on the left."

"How did you know we were from Region Eight?" Byrd asked.

"I heard our SAC talking to Inspector Carver. Bowens Mill is on the edge of our territory," she said as she headed out the back door.

Byrd found a phone on a desk in a dark office. He pulled the agent's chair around and propped his feet on the desk as he dialed.

"DEA Atlanta Field Division. How may I route your call?" said the voice on the phone.

"Walt Stone, please," Byrd said.

"Hold, please."

In seconds, Stone picked up the phone. "Agent Stone."

"Walt. This is Danny Byrd."

"Hey, man," Stone said. "I'm getting ready to do a dope deal with some of your GBI narcs and a couple of folks from Atlanta PD. What are you up to?"

"I need your help," Byrd said.

"Do you need Arlow to fly for you again?" Stone asked.

"No," Byrd said. "This is more a radio technology question. A guy I was undercover with today gave me a bag phone he said was some kind of super-secret spy phone. I was wondering if you could take a look at it?"

"Sure. Call my cell phone when you get into Atlanta. Are you coming from Canton?"

"No, I'm in Perry. Give me an hour and a half."

"See you soon," Stone said.

Byrd sat up and dialed a second number from memory. Clete Petterson answered on the third ring. "Petterson."

"How are things in Texas?"

"When I went out for lunch it was eighty degrees. By the time I leave, the prediction is for it to be twenty-eight degrees. Got to love the high desert," Clete said.

"Well," Byrd said. "I'm about to tell you something that will warm you up. You and Montana both."

"What have you got?"

"I found a red-and-white Cessna with twin tails. And I was able to get the real tail number."

"Hot damn!" Clete said. "Lay the numbers on me."

Byrd recited the tail numbers from memory. He heard Clete typing on his computer. "Are you able to run tail numbers directly on your computer?" Byrd asked.

"No, but I've called FAA investigations so many times, they have given me an email address for their inquiries desk. They respond pretty quickly," Clete said. "Was the airplane up in Jasper?" Clete asked.

"No," Byrd responded. "I saw it in a hangar in Bowens Mill. On a property belonging to a guy who says he's a spook. He runs a mercenary training center down here in South Georgia."

"Do you think we should put a lookout on the airplane?" Clete asked.

Byrd thought it over. "No, I think we should put it on the EPIC watchlist."

The watchlist from the El Paso Intelligence Center was available to drug cops worldwide who needed to track an airplane or a boat. Byrd had used the list once to keep tabs on a private jet he suspected of being involved in trafficking young girls from Thailand. The FAA centers around the US had access as well.

Clete agreed. "I'll call over there and get that done. I'll make sure they notify both of us."

"Great," Byrd said, leaning forward to drop the phone into the cradle.

"One more thing," Clete said.

Byrd stopped. "Sure."

"I just wanted to tell you something," Clete said.

Byrd waited. Curious.

"Montana and I are getting married."

"To each other?" Byrd asked. The line went quiet. "I'm kidding," Byrd said. "Buddy, that's great! I wish you the best."

Clete sounded awkward. "I know you guys had dated."

Byrd became uncomfortable. "We were never involved. We just went out a couple of times."

Clete stammered. "It's okay. She said you guys never slept together, but that you got really close after the shooting. She thinks the world of you."

"I really care for her, too. She's special. Don't screw her over," Byrd said.

Clete paused. "I wouldn't—"

Byrd cut him off. "She needs a good man. You sound like you are one."

"Thanks," Clete mumbled as he hung up the phone.

THURSDAY, FEBRUARY 3, 2005
8:01 P.M.
ATLANTA, GEORGIA

Byrd used a phone at GBI Headquarters to set up a meeting with Walt Stone while Doc and Jamie dropped off the undercover truck and loaded their gear in Doc's car.

He bounced down the concrete steps in front of the GBI

building and climbed into Doc's car. "We have a meeting in twenty minutes on the south side of the CNN Center."

Doc groaned. "Us old folks need to get home."

Jamie cut her eyes over. "Okay, this old man needs to get home. I need my beauty sleep."

Byrd tried to sound upbeat. "I'll be quick."

"Right," Doc said. He didn't sound convinced.

The law officers worked their way through downtown Atlanta, dodging evening traffic as best they could.

Doc looked back at Byrd. "Where are you taking us?"

Byrd was looking out the window for his friend. "Pull up behind this Atlanta PD car. The Zone Five Precinct is in the CNN Center. Walt is here somewhere."

As they pulled to the curb, Byrd saw Walt Stone coming out of the building. Standing six feet, six inches tall, he was hard to miss. Byrd waved and Stone rushed over to them.

"Three GBI agents in one place! Must be planning a raid," Stone said.

"Any DEA agent sober this time of day is equally shocking." Byrd turned to Jamie. "Do you know what DEA stands for?" Before Jamie could respond, Byrd said, "Drunk Every Afternoon."

Stone smirked. "That wasn't funny ten years ago. It might have been true, but it wasn't funny."

"So what brings you out to this part of our capital city?" Byrd changed the subject.

Stone pointed to the west. "Ever heard of the Bluff?"

Byrd shook his head. "No. Is it a place or a club?"

Stone waved at the area in front of them. "It's the area just past the Dome, and it's where someone goes to procure heroin in this fair city."

"In sight of the federal building?" Doc asked.

Stone nodded. "We have been threatening to shoot video of a buy from the windows in the US Attorney's office. The resolution wouldn't be great, but it could be done."

Byrd was shaking his head as he reached into the truck and pulled out a small nylon bag.

"What do you have there?" Stone asked.

Byrd handed the bag over. "The man said it was a secure cell phone. Said we could talk freely on it. But it's a prototype and may be finicky."

Stone held the phone in his hand. "Mind if I open it up?"

Byrd said, "Be my guest."

Stone opened the case and sat the phone and its parts on the trunk of the Atlanta PD car. He pulled a small screwdriver Byrd had seen him use on everything from guns to meth labs. He used the blade to push some of the parts around. "Okay, let me give you a quick class on encryption. Ready?"

Byrd nodded. "I have some fundamental understanding but go ahead."

Stone pointed at two boxes attached to the phone that seemed out of place. "To transmit effective encrypted communications, the signal needs to be digital. An analog signal is too easily scrambled up and significantly reduces the range of a device."

Byrd nodded, as Jamie stood beside him, listening intently. "I understand so far," Byrd said. "The year before the Olympics, the GBI switched to digital radios. We work all our channels encrypted."

"Good. In order to secure a cell phone, you'd have to generate a signal that would trick the system into thinking it is analog. I'm guessing here, but I think this small box the antenna is hooked to does that."

Byrd looked at the box. "That makes sense. But the cell towers in Atlanta went digital prior to the Olympics in '96."

Stone nodded and pointed to the second box. "Right. And in the metro area, the first box is just for looks. It will still work in the suburbs, but not so much in downtown."

"A call on this phone could be intercepted with the right scanner now that digital is becoming more common."

Stone pointed to the second box. "In the federal government, we call this an STU device—stands for Secure Telephone Unit. They can make calls. But when you call another STU phone, you ask whoever is on the other end to initiate a secure transmission. They press a button on both phones and after a fifteen-second delay, their call is encrypted."

"I've heard of those phones. But I thought the government regulates them. How does some toy soldier in South Georgia get his hands on them?" Byrd asked.

Jamie looked at the phone as Stone examined it and asked, "How do you know about this stuff?"

Stone lowered his voice. "I was assigned to the El Paso Intelligence Center for a few years as their tech person. I assigned the STU phone sets at EPIC. I've actually seen one of these."

Byrd looked stunned. "Really? Who makes them?"

"A guy named Warren. The US buys them for use in countries that have limited infrastructure." Stone continued to examine the device.

Byrd was staring into space. *Was this even possible?* he asked himself.

"Who gave you this?" Stone asked.

"The main target of our case. A guy named Mitch Warren."

Stone stared. "Old guy who has scotch for breakfast?"

Byrd nodded.

"Is this connected to the case you called me about on New Year's Day?"

Byrd nodded.

"He's a cousin," Stone said.

Jamie looked confused. "He's your cousin?"

Stone shook his head. "A federal cousin. From the agencies that don't exist. He has connections with CIA and NSA, I think."

"Is there any way to be sure?"

Stone said, "Hold on." He turned the bigger box over and examined it. Like most electronics, it had a thin metal label. This one read "DIGITAL SUBSCRIBER VOICE TERMINAL; TSEC/KY-77 CELLULAR; SERIAL ASN-B1-27; MEETS ISO/IEC 18033-3 STANDARD."

Pointing at the label, Stone said, "These guys, the ones like Mitch, hate to be in the shadows. Notice that the thing is labeled *ASN*. That's NSA backward. It's beta version one, item twenty-seven. This is a VINSON-level encryption device. We think the cousins provide them to drug-trafficking organizations they work with."

Byrd was incredulous. "They work with? You mean the US government is working with the same DTOs we try to bring to justice?"

Stone nodded, frowning as he said, "They do. CIA agents have impaired DEA investigations for years. They tip the groups we are working on, then they tell us that the groups are onto us. They play both sides against the middle. And I'm pretty sure Warren is one of their contract employees."

Byrd stared at the box for a minute, then he shrugged. "That doesn't make him exempt from the law."

Stone handed Byrd the box back. "He may think that it does. You be careful!"

CHAPTER 21
WORKING TOGETHER TO GET IT DONE

FRIDAY, FEBRUARY 4, 2005
2:58 P.M.
DECATUR, GEORGIA

The Director's conference room was just barely large enough for the assembled mass of investigators. There were GBI agents from Region Eight, Region Thirteen where the farm was located, and the Major Violators Squad of the GBI Drug Enforcement Section. The agents were spread around the big conference table, talking about old relationships and current cases when GBI Director Buster Hicks walked into the room.

Everyone quieted as he circled to the head of the table and took a seat. Several people mumbled, "Director," as Hicks sat up and waited. SAC Tina Blackwell took the lead.

"Director," Tina Blackwell started, "I asked for this meeting to bring everyone who has an interest in this investigation to the same table."

Hicks nodded. "Can someone bring all of us up to speed on how this case was started and what the latest developments are?"

Blackwell pointed at Daniel Byrd. "Agent Byrd knows

the most about the investigation, and he did the undercover operation. I'll let him explain what has happened
thus far, and then let everyone know the concerns we have
going forward."

Hicks acknowledged Byrd. "Danny, you have the floor."

Byrd stood and cleared his throat. "Thanks, Director."

Byrd outlined the case of the airplane from Texas and
the investigation by the Texas Rangers. Then he brought
everyone up to date on the details of his undercover meeting in Bowens Mill.

Garry Rothchild, the SAC from the Perry Office, asked
the first question. "Why are we working this case?
Wouldn't the DEA be in a better position to do what needs
to be done?"

Byrd started. "I have reached out to DEA. They are
willing to support our investigation—"

Will Carver interrupted, "And they'll be happy to take
credit for the investigation!"

Byrd nodded. "That, too. The DEA says their bosses
don't see this as a priority."

"Tell them why we think it is a priority for Georgia,"
Tina Blackwell said.

Byrd pointed out the window. "Every ounce of crystal
meth coming to Atlanta—and right now we are talking
about a few hundred pounds—is being brokered by a man
we know only as 'Rojo.' That's 'red' in Spanish. We have
intelligence that links our friends in Bowens Mill to Rojo."

"Can you give us an idea how that link was made?"
Director Hicks asked.

"Sure," Byrd said. "We managed to get phone tolls for
Rojo that were subpoenaed by the Texas Rangers. There
are numerous calls between a number linked to the compound in Bowens Mill and Rojo's place in Juarez. The

rangers tried to go up on a wiretap of Rojo's phone, but they discovered the phone calls were encrypted. Probably by a phone like the one Warren gave me."

SAC Rothchild nodded. "Well, I can tell you that we've never had a single bit of information on that place. As far as we have been able to tell, no problems have ever come out of the training center he operates."

"Is he connected with the sheriff in the county?" Byrd asked.

Rothchild shrugged. "He's a big landowner, so I'm sure he has some connections in the courthouse. I've never heard any talk about him being a big contributor to any campaigns."

"Is the sheriff on the up-and-up?" Byrd asked.

Rothchild nodded. "As far as I know. We have a good working relationship with him."

"Not all sheriffs are bent, Danny," Director Hicks said.

Byrd nodded. "I know a sheriff I trust who vouches for him. But it never hurts to ask."

"Where do we go from here?" Terry Cromwell asked. Terry was representing the GBI Drug Enforcement Section in the meeting. "I know from the plane we caught in Cherokee County that these people are legit. This probably should be a drug investigation, but Danny is up to his neck in it." ASAC Cromwell turned to Inspector Will Carver.

Carver glanced at the Director, then he pointed at Byrd. "I think you've hit the nail on the head. Danny is onto them with his undercover approach, and there is no reason to rock that boat. Danny knows all the players, not just the crooks but the cops in Texas as well. My thought would be to detach him to Terry's unit for thirty days or so. What do you think, Terry?"

Cromwell nodded. "That would work." He turned to Byrd. "What would you need?"

Byrd leaned forward. "An undercover vehicle for starters. But there is one more thing I'd like to ask for: Could I get Agent Abernathy detached, too?"

Tina Blackwell coughed. "Are you planning on asking for any more of my people?"

Byrd smiled. "I know this could make our office very shorthanded, but Jamie used to be a licensed realtor. She knows the lingo and the inner workings. If we try to approach Warren with a piece of property, we need to have someone undercover who can talk the talk."

Hicks looked to Blackwell. "Can we make that work, Tina?"

Blackwell nodded. "What he's proposing makes sense. It's the only way to go forward. I just want to wrap this up as quickly as possible."

Hicks turned to Carver. "Make it happen, Will. And keep me up to speed."

The meeting broke up and the agents filed out of the room. Director Hicks motioned for Daniel Byrd to stay behind.

Once the room had cleared, Hicks asked Byrd, "You know I worked for the FBI?"

"Of course, Director," Byrd said.

"Then you have some idea that I've had some history with the intelligence community?"

"The cousins?" Byrd asked.

Hicks nodded. He pulled a business card from his wallet. It only had a name and a phone number imprinted. "I reserve this for high-ranking law enforcement executives and the staff in the governor's office. It's my private cell phone number. Call it if something goes wrong. I'll help any way I can."

Byrd took the card. "I hope I don't have to call, but I appreciate the support."

Hicks clasped his hand. Byrd shook back. Then Hicks said, "The cousins are like teenagers working in the drive-thru, if you don't check what you get in the bag, you're liable to get screwed."

Byrd chuckled. "I've heard that from a lot of people."

FRIDAY, FEBRUARY 4, 2005
8:19 P.M.
BOWENS MILL, GEORGIA

Omar was inside the cockpit of the Cessna Skymaster. He had spent the afternoon updating the navigation gear in the rugged red-and-white twin-engine plane. The only hurdle left was to extend the fuel range to be able to fly from El Paso to Georgia in a single hop.

Omar wasn't happy with the options he had identified. There was a small void around the tail, but the fuel capacity it offered would make the airplane tail heavy. The other option, more aerodynamically attractive, required an aluminum tank to be installed on the floor behind the seats. The tank would feed to wing tanks but would require several connections inside the cockpit. After his last experience, the thought of potential fuel leaks filled Omar with dread.

Mitch Warren wandered into the hangar and walked to the side door of the airplane. "How's it going?"

Omar sat up and shrugged. "I guess it's going as well as can be expected. I've upgraded the navigation system. Take a look at this." Omar pointed to a box integrated into the instruments.

Warren craned to get a look. "What is it?"

Omar chuckled. "Essentially a fuzz buster. It will detect radar from any government chase planes."

Warren frowned. "Won't the ground radars have it alarming all the time?"

Omar nodded. "I modified the unit. The band the feds use is military. And I turned the sensitivity down so low that it should only pick up signals generated a couple of miles from me."

Warren smiled. "Good thinking, son. You've got a knack for this kind of work."

Omar smiled back. He was enjoying his father's praise. "Thanks."

"What about the fuel range issue? Where does that stand?" Warren asked.

Omar hung his head. "I have a couple of options, but I'm not crazy about either one. I'm just not an expert at fuel systems. I wish I knew more about them."

Warren mulled that over. "I know a guy from the Air Force. His specialty was plumbing extra tanks, but he was working in much larger aircraft. Maybe I could give him a call."

Omar nodded. "That would be a big help."

Warren slapped his son on the back. "This is good work, son."

"Thanks, Dad."

"If we can work out the fuel problem, are you ready to make another run?" Warren asked.

Omar nodded. "Yeah. I'd like to see how everything works."

Warren wondered aloud, "What airport could we use, do you think?"

"You don't think Moody can come up with a landing strip?" Omar asked.

"I'm still looking into his background. We need to be sure he can be trusted," Warren said. "In the interim, we need to make a few dollars."

Omar shrugged. "What about Cartersville? Didn't the CIA once run air ops out of that airport?"

Warren nodded. "Yes, they did. That could be a good choice. I'll make some phone calls."

"Plumber first," Omar said to Warren's back.

MONDAY, FEBRUARY 7, 2005
10:19 A.M.
CEDARTOWN, GEORGIA

Byrd sat at the desk of Sheriff Jim Garrison of Polk County. Garrison had been sheriff of the growing county for over a dozen years. He was recently reelected and was comfortable in the job.

Byrd made his pitch. "Sheriff, we're looking for a piece of land with an airstrip on it, or one where an airstrip could be built. The targets want the land to be close to Metro Atlanta, and they're against using any public airports. We were hoping you might be able to help us out."

Sheriff Garrison looked at Byrd over his reading glasses. "I'm always willing to help the GBI any way I can. Would the people want to use the place for anything other than landing airplanes?"

Byrd shook his head. "I doubt it. They are smuggling crystal meth from the border to here in Georgia."

"Damn! If I had the money, I'd buy a place for you to use. Meth has ruined a lot of lives in my county. Give me a day or two to look around. I think I might be able to find you a place that fits the bill. How soon do you need something?"

"Yesterday," Byrd said.

Garrison smiled wanly. "I'm coming down with a cold, but I'll get my major to look into it for you."

"Who's the major?" Byrd asked.

"Robert Davids. Do you know him?"

Byrd smiled. "I sure do."

Byrd shook hands with the sheriff and went into the hallway. He saw the name of his old friend on one of the doors. Robert Davids had been a drug agent for Polk County for a number of years before he returned to lead criminal investigations for the sheriff's office.

He stuck his head in the door. "Robert, glad to see you're still working."

Davids stood up and greeted Byrd with an outstretched hand. "Danny Byrd. I'm surprised to see you're still alive!"

They shook each other's hands and laughed. Byrd pointed to the nameplate on Davids's desk. "Major?"

Davids was embarrassed. "They had to give me a title. I was more interested in the pay that went with this job. Titles are for books."

Byrd nodded. "Well, I hear you're doing a good job over here."

Davids raised an eyebrow. "So, what brings you here? I thought you had transferred to Gainesville. This is a little outside your stomping grounds, isn't it?"

Byrd told him what he was working on and that the sheriff thought he might help find land. Davids looked pensive.

Davids said, "I may know a place." He looked at Byrd. "How much runway will they need?"

Byrd shrugged. "With a good approach, they could do with less than three thousand feet, I guess."

Davids walked over to the county map on his wall and gave it a look. He seemed to be trying to remember something.

"When I was a kid here, there was an old dirt runway out in the west side of the county. Marijuana smugglers used it back in the day. As far as I know, it's still out there on some private land."

"Is it still in the hands of the smugglers?" Byrd asked.

Davids laughed. "No, I wouldn't do that to you. It belongs to a man who managed country singers for a while. He made a lot of money and bought the land to build a ranch. His wife died young and he abandoned the idea. Last I heard, the property was just sitting there. They still call it the Thomas place."

Byrd was intrigued. "Do you know how to get in touch with the owner?"

Davids nodded. "Yeah. He works for us."

Byrd raised an eyebrow. "He works for the sheriff's office?"

Davids nodded. "He got out of the music business. He had made plenty of money, and he wanted to give back to his community. He went to work for the sheriff as a bailiff in the courthouse. He's still there."

Byrd motioned for Davids to lead the way. "Let's go talk to him."

Davids grabbed his hat and led the way.

MONDAY, FEBRUARY 7, 2005
11:44 A.M.
I-10, EAST OF SIERRA BLANCA, TEXAS

Trooper Montana Worley pulled the black-and-white Crown Victoria off the pavement and waited for the traffic backed up behind her to pass. She had gotten used to the phenomenon. Like the pace car at a race, people refused to pass the marked highway patrol car.

She waited patiently, then pulled the car back onto the roadway. She used the time she wasn't focusing on driving to admire the high desert view. On both sides of the interstate, she could see mountain peaks in the distance. With no hundred-foot-tall pine trees to block the view, as she remembered Georgia, the landscape was spectacular.

Soon she was back up to her favorite patrol speed: fifty miles an hour. She was watching her mirror when the rough-looking truck took to the fast lane and began to creep up on her. The Nissan truck was dull from being in the sun and looked like it hadn't been washed since the day it was sold as new.

As the truck got closer, she recognized the front license plate bore the pattern of a Mexican tag. It looked like one issued in the Mexican State of Guerrero. Fleetingly, she wondered what a truck from deep central Mexico was doing on this side of the border.

The truck was occupied times two, in police speak, as it slowly drew alongside the state police car. The driver was laser-focused on the task of driving the truck. Montana saw that both hands were locked on the steering wheel, and the man was looking straight ahead. He wore a baseball cap and sunglasses.

The passenger had on a similar ball cap, this time one from the Atlanta Braves. She recognized the logo on the front as the truck got closer.

Montana decided to take her foot off the gas and let the truck pass. As she did, she saw the AK-47 pointed out of the window.

Immediately, she jabbed the brake pedal and felt the deceleration. The truck shot past her, and the passenger withdrew the rifle.

She flipped the switch for her lights and siren and

gripped the radio microphone. She said, "Forty-four twenty-nine to El Paso."

The radio operator responded immediately, "Go forty-four twenty-nine."

Montana pushed the gas pedal down as she spoke. "El Paso, I am in pursuit of a Nissan truck, occupied twice. The passenger just pointed an AK-47 at me as they passed. I am westbound I-10 passing mile marker one-fourteen."

"El Paso to One-oh-four. Are you clear on the pursuit?" The dispatcher said, as she alerted the air unit.

The sound of the helicopter blades beating the air was clear as the pilot responded. "One-oh-four is responding."

More troopers alerted the radio dispatcher that they were headed toward Montana. "El Paso, Forty-four twenty-nine, say your location."

Montana drove with her left hand as she talked into the microphone. "We are passing mile marker one-sixteen. Traffic is light. Suspect vehicle speed is in excess of one hundred. No shots have been fired."

Just then, Sergeant Camos called on the police radio. "Forty-two-oh-three to Forty-two twenty-nine, I am in front of you, coming from the direction of Van Horn."

Suddenly, the truck driver slammed on the brakes. The tires smoked as the truck skidded and was surrounded by a cloud of burned rubber.

Montana used the anti-lock brakes to drive around the stopped truck as she tried to get her car stopped. Montana was able to thread the needle, shooting between the truck and the cable barrier in the center of the highway. She swung the steering wheel hard to the right as she slid to a halt, putting her patrol car between her and the men in the truck.

Montana rolled out of the driver's seat and pulled her

patrol rifle, a Bushmaster M4, out with her. She took a position behind the engine block and pointed the gun over the hood. She saw the men crouching next to the door of the truck. The first shot from the AK-47 was louder than she had anticipated, and she saw the flame come from the barrel.

Without thinking, acting on long hours of training, she fired two shots from her patrol rifle. The rifle bullets penetrated the truck door and struck the shooter, but the frangible rounds didn't kill him. He fell over backward, AK-47 still clutched in his hands, and rolled to get back on his feet.

Once the man was in the clear, Montana fired two more shots. This time the man went down. She thought she saw blood after the second shot but couldn't be sure. She kept one eye on the downed man as she looked for the driver.

She heard a patrol car stop behind her. She glanced over her shoulder to see a trooper jumping the cable center divider and running toward her. She recognized the voice of Sergeant Helen Camos as she shouted, "You okay, Troop?"

Montana nodded. "I'm good. I've got one suspect down. He's the shooter."

Sergeant Camos took a position near the car door. They could hear the DPS helicopter coming from the west. Helen spoke into the microphone for her portable radio. "Forty-two-oh-three to One-oh-four, we have one suspect not accounted for. We think he is hiding behind the truck. Can you give us a hand?"

The pilot tilted the nose of the helicopter up to bleed off speed. The noise and down draft from the spinning blades drowned out the sound of the radio for a moment. Then they heard the pilot say, "Your other occupant is spread eagle on the pavement behind the truck. I think he wants to surrender."

Montana advanced on the truck and worked her way around to the driver as he lay on the concrete roadway. She had to divide her attention between looking for the suspect and dodging impatient drivers using the shoulder of the road to pass. She slung her patrol rifle on her back and handcuffed the man as he lay perfectly still.

She dragged him to his feet and shoved him toward her patrol car as more troopers arrived on the scene. As she did, she noted her hands weren't shaking and her breathing was steady.

MONDAY, FEBRUARY 7, 2005
12:34 P.M.
CEDARTOWN, GEORGIA

Byrd and Major Davids were in Byrd's Crown Vic. Following Davids's directions, they had found the property with the old runway. Byrd drove the Crown Vic along a dirt path that led to a pole barn.

Davids pointed out the front windshield. "The area right in front of us is where the runway was laid out. You can see, when we get out of the car, how the ground lays."

Byrd followed along as Davids walked through knee-high grass and uneven ground toward the middle of the field. Once they got near the center, Byrd noticed that the ground beneath their feet was hard-packed.

"I can feel it," Byrd said.

Davids nodded. "I was just a kid when all that happened with the Pot Plane. That's what everybody called it."

"Have you been here before?" Byrd asked.

"Nope, but there were pictures of the plane on the

ground from every direction. They were posted all over the sheriff's offices. Everybody had one on their wall."

Byrd looked all around. "One way in and one way out."

Davids nodded. "Unless you're on foot."

Byrd stood and took the area in. "Do you suppose we could get a crew out here to cut this grass?"

Davids smiled. "For you? Of course."

CHAPTER 22
PLUMBERS DON'T JUST WORK FOR NIXON

MONDAY, FEBRUARY 7, 2005
2:01 P.M.
BOWENS MILL, GEORGIA

The pickup truck pulled up to the hangar in a cloud of dust. The man who stepped out was barely more than five feet, seven inches tall, and was round as a beach ball. He wore faded jeans and a work shirt, covered by a heavy canvas jacket. He walked up to the hangar and stood for a moment to let his eyes adjust.

Omar stared at the man and waited for him to say something.

The round man said, "I understand you need a plumber."

Omar nodded. "I sure do. Are you the man my dad called?"

The man ignored the question. He strode over to the airplane. He pulled a powerful flashlight from his pocket and pointed it inside the cockpit. "I hear your last system was leaky."

Omar craned his head to see where the man was looking. "Yeah," Omar said. "I still have lines running to the wing tanks, but the waterbed I used wasn't tough enough."

The man raised an eyebrow. "That sounds like some rag-tag shit right there."

Omar shrugged. "It worked."

"It leaked!"

The man ran a tape measure along the floor of the cockpit. He was muttering to himself as he glanced around the space. "How much room will you need for cargo? Can I use the space behind the seats?"

Omar nodded. "That's where the waterbed sat. How far back would you need to go?"

"About thirty inches should do it. And about a foot tall. Will that leave you enough room?" The man didn't stop examining the inside of the airplane, even to talk.

"Can I put anything on top of it?" Omar asked.

The man nodded his head. "Sure. I'll mount a sheet of aluminum flashing over the tank. You should be good to put a couple of hundred pounds on it, just be mindful of the fuel lines. We'll use an internal pump that should keep the system sealed, so we shouldn't have any leaks."

"That damned waterbed sure did," Omar said.

The man glanced over his shoulder. "I bet it did!"

"Do you have the tank?" Omar asked.

The man shook his head. "No, but I can have it in twenty-four hours. It's a fuel cell for stock car racing."

Omar nodded. "That sounds good to me."

The man walked back to his truck. "I'll see you about this time tomorrow."

MONDAY, FEBRUARY 7, 2005
10:30 P.M.
CIUDAD JUÁREZ, CHIHUAHUA, MEXICO

Little Red—"Pequeño Rojo" as he was known to his friends—was a "narco junior." That is, the adult-child of a major drug dealer. He had been raised in privilege and was feared by the people who knew and partied with him.

Pequeño Rojo was barely twenty years old and dressed in designer clothes from head to toe. He stood several inches taller than his father and spent long hours in a full-featured gym in the house his father owned near the center of the city. His dark hair was styled, and he got regular moisturizing treatments to blunt the parchment skin others endured from so much time in the sun.

He wanted to run his father's business and felt like he would be able to do the kinds of things his father was afraid to do. One of those things was to take the war onto the American side. But his attempt hadn't gone well.

His father, Rojo, was pacing the office he kept in their palatial residence on a mountaintop in Juárez. "You should not have done this without talking to me. This act could escalate our problems on the other side."

Pequeño Rojo was young and brash. He tried to show patience with his father's outdated ideas, but he was sure his own ways were the best. "Father, I have done nothing more than pick at a scab. That policewoman is nothing to us, but it sends a message to those who would try to damage our business."

"But she is something to the police in Texas. They will think this is a declaration of war. We keep them pacified on their side of the river and they don't come for us on this side. That is the way it has worked for many years!"

Pequeño Rojo stood up. "The old ways aren't always the best. It is time we stopped kissing the asses of the Americans. We have money and power. We have the drugs the Americans love and will pay much money for. And when the Americans give up their war on drugs, we will have the women and children to smuggle. The American appetite for things their government prohibits is voracious. We must push the police to give us room to grow."

Rojo shook his head. "The governor of Texas is a madman. Much is being said about the border troubles, and any escalation on our part will make his rhetoric more empowered."

Pequeño Rojo grimaced. "He is a big, stupid gringo. We can have our way on the border if only we push the gringos. They are weak and have little appetite for a shooting war. Just like their war on terror, they will eventually lose interest and give up the cause."

Rojo walked up to his son and put a finger on his chest. "If you continue down this path, I put you on notice that your methods will not work. You cannot push the American police like we do in this country. Even with the help of their intelligence community, we cannot fight an open war on the American side. We must continue to infiltrate our people, to work in the jobs the gringos find too unpleasant. Our workers on the American side are many, and the American police are few and hamstrung by their own rules."

Rojo continued, "We are richer than anyone in our family has ever dreamed of being. I will not lose all that I have earned. You must stop this thing."

Pequeño Rojo stomped to the door. "You will see that

your ways are finished. There will be narcocorridoes written about me, very soon."

As he pushed the door open to leave, the young man thought it might be time for his street name to change to just Rojo. Maybe his father had outlived his usefulness. Pequeño Rojo saw the prize in reach as he left his father standing alone.

Alone, Rojo shook his head. He waved his son away and sat at his desk. He laid his head on the massive oaken desk he had skilled craftsmen build for his office. It was identical to the desk used by US presidents. He stretched his arms out, pleading with God to give him guidance. Then he sighed heavily, pushed himself up, and looked at his hands. There was much blood there, but he didn't think he could bear his son's blood on them.

Rojo felt a wave of sadness as he contemplated killing his own son. But the life of a privileged child was not worth the empire he had built with those same hands.

TUESDAY, FEBRUARY 8, 2005
3:35 P.M.
BOWENS MILL, GEORGIA

The installation of the fuel cell had gone quickly. The plumber rolled in just after daybreak and set to work. Omar watched, occasionally asking questions, as the fuel cell was bolted into place and the connections were made to the fuel system. Then, the man carefully connected the internal fuel pump to the electrical system. He spent the next hour adding a circuit breaker and a gauge on the panel near the pilot's left knee. Then he finished with a switch on the console.

When he stood up, the plumber pointed to the switch and the breaker. "These are for the fuel pump. Once you run this tank dry, cut the pump or it will eventually seize up. The gauge will give you an idea of the percentage of fuel in the tank, but it's not designed for use in an airplane. You'll need to estimate your usable range and base everything on that. If the breaker trips in flight, you'll have to leave it until the system can be inspected." The man shrugged then continued, "That's never happened to anyone I know of, but you can't be too safe with fuel and electricity."

Omar climbed into the cockpit and touched the switch. "The location feels good."

The man cleaned his tools and put them back in their spot in his toolbox. "Fuel up the cell—gravity should take care of that—and see how you think it's feeding. I'd run her on the ground for a while and use various power settings. Otherwise, call me if you need anything else."

"What is the total capacity with the new tank?"

"Forty-two gallons. Not as much as the waterbed, but every ounce should be usable. That should put you at a range between sixteen and seventeen hundred miles on a fill-up. Does that do it for you?"

Omar nodded, looking over his shoulder. "That should do it."

The plumber loaded his tools into his truck and left without another word.

Omar examined the cockpit, touching each one of the new controls. After several seconds, he seemed satisfied that the refinements were exactly as he needed them. He could fly to El Paso in a day, get some rest, and make the trip back early next week. In fact, he thought he could make the trip once a week if need be.

Omar climbed down and admired the plane. There was

nothing unusual about the outside of the airplane and nothing to draw the attention of any cops who might come around. A detailed inspection by an aircraft mechanic might catch the illegal fuel cell, but he didn't plan on that happening.

TUESDAY, FEBRUARY 8, 2005
5:15 P.M.
EL PASO, TEXAS

Clete Petterson stopped by the ranger office to check his mail. He had waited to do so until he figured the office would be empty.

When he saw the bulky package with the return label from the FAA Data Center in Washington, he excitedly ripped the package open. He found two CDs and several aviation charts with information written on them. Then he found a letter from the specialist who had recovered the information.

The CDs were downloads of the raw data from the FAA radar for the flight path of the Skymaster Montana had seen. There were audio recordings of the pilot obtaining clearances along the way. The most interesting part, according to the letter, was the fact that close examination of the radar returns indicated the flight had entered Mexican airspace and landed at an airport with a runway parallel to the border.

Clete loaded the first CD into his desktop computer and began to scan the information. He took the time to look at each file and listen to the audio. The voice of the pilot was hard to make out, but Clete thought he sounded young.

Clete made careful notes of the path the airplane had flown. He wasn't a pilot, but he had flown with Department of Public Safety pilots on several occasions. He understood the significance of the navigational beacons pilots used.

He took a large aviation chart he had purchased just for this purpose and taped it to his office wall. He started in New Mexico and drew a line from point to point as the airplane crossed half of the United States loaded with high-powered stimulants.

Once he got to Georgia, he followed the trail to a place called Dalton. He hadn't heard of the city, but he could see on the map that it was situated north of Atlanta. Clete was just finishing the chart when he heard someone come into the office.

Clete looked out to see Major Stetson Crosby come in the door. The big ranger was dressed in jeans and a patterned shirt. Standing at six feet, seven inches tall, he looked every bit the part of a ranger. His jeans were pressed and his work boots had a highly polished sheen.

Crosby looked at Clete. "What are you doing working so late?"

"I needed to get out of the house. How about you?" Clete asked.

"Why?" Then Crosby caught himself. "Oh, I guess it's difficult to be in the same house with Montana and not spend all your time talking about the shooting." Crosby headed for his office. "I was taking a leave day until I got a call from the Director's office. I ran by to answer an email."

Clete followed Crosby into the Major's office, where Crosby motioned for him to have a seat. "Thanks," Clete said.

Crosby sat in his big chair and turned to face his computer. He spent several seconds logging into the DPS network.

While he waited, Clete saw an intelligence report on the middle of Crosby's desk titled "Trooper M. Worley, Assassination Attempt." Clete's chest pounded. He was not aware that Montana had been targeted. He leaned forward and read the report upside down. Apparently, there was information that the two men who had tried to shoot Montana were associated with Rojo's organization.

He was going over some of the details when Crosby spoke, without turning around. "It's an important skill for an investigator to be able to read documents when they're reversed."

Clete's face flushed.

"I know you well enough to know you wouldn't come into my office uninvited. I also know you've been kept out of the investigation of Trooper Worley's attack. Since you have been insulated, you couldn't possibly tell her anything our intelligence folks have learned." Crosby turned back around. "But you might just recommend that she be extra cautions for a little while."

"Should we ask for troopers to sit on the house?" Clete asked.

Crosby pursed his lips. "We would be asking already if we thought they'd try again." He flipped the report over and exposed a second sheet.

Clete leaned forward and read the second report. A confidential source had told a member of the Narcotics Service that Rojo's son contracted the attack on Trooper Worley. The source alleged that Rojo put a stop to any more violence on the American side of the Rio Grande. Rojo had gone so far as to ask the source, whom he believed to be an informer, to pass the word to the "*Tejanos diablos.*"

Clete muttered, "The devils from Texas."

Crosby nodded. "They still refer to the rangers that way."

Clete stood up. "Thanks, Major."

Crosby looked innocent. "For what?" He turned back to the computer.

CHAPTER 23
SIGNING ON THE FAKE DOTTED LINE

WEDNESDAY, FEBRUARY 9, 2005
11:15 A.M.
DECATUR, GEORGIA

Daniel Byrd sat in a small room—actually, more of a closet—in the Technical Investigations office in GBI Headquarters. He had the secure phone Mitchell Warren had given him, and the techs had attached a recording device. Byrd mulled over his approach to Warren, trying to decide how aggressive he needed to be.

After much thought, he pressed the record button on the machine and turned to the controls for the phone. He had a cheat sheet provided by Warren, but the operation seemed to be pretty straightforward.

Byrd turned the Function Select switch to OP position. He removed the handset and listened for a dial tone. After he dialed the number Warren had provided, Byrd listened for the beeps and then waited for someone to answer.

"Yes," the voice on the line said. The voice was digitized, and Byrd didn't recognize who answered.

"General Warren?" Byrd asked.

"Who's this?" came the response.

"Herman Moody, from Pickens County," Byrd replied.

"Herman, this is Omar. Dad is down the hall. Can you hold on?" Even when he identified himself, Omar's voice was difficult to identify.

"Sure, I'll wait."

Byrd heard a loud noise as the phone was laid on something.

Mitchell Warren came on the line several minutes later. "Mr. Moody," Warren said. "Have you had any success finding an appropriate location?"

Byrd made sure to sound upbeat when he answered, "I have. I found a farm in Cedartown, Georgia. That's less than forty miles northwest of Atlanta. It's the Thomas place. And—you're going to love this—it was used for smuggling marijuana back in the eighties."

Warren laughed, at least Byrd thought it was a laugh. With the garbled sounds, Warren could have been strangling. Warren said, "I sense a bit of symmetry here. I am not a drug smuggler, but I will be using the runway for clandestine purposes."

Byrd slapped himself on the head. *What was I thinking?*

"The owner is in a nursing home, and he is willing to do a really cheap deal as long as you don't make any changes to the property," Byrd said.

"What is he asking for the use of the land?" Warren asked.

"Two thousand dollars a month," Byrd replied.

"How soon can you bring a contract?" Warren asked.

"I have a realtor who can do all the contract work," Byrd replied.

"How soon?" Warren was on the hook.

"What's in this for me?" Byrd asked.

Warren went silent for a moment. "I'll pay you a thousand-dollar fee. For that amount, you will bring all the necessary paperwork to me here at the farm. I'll pay three thousand for two months. But I'll pay that to the realtor, and they can pass the money on to the owner as they see fit."

Byrd intentionally hesitated. After a couple of beats, he said, "That sounds fair. I'll call you within the next hour and set a time we can bring the paperwork to you."

He walked out of the room and looked at Jamie Abernathy. "Are you ready to go to South Georgia?"

Jamie was dressed in a business suit, her long blonde hair pulled back. She gave Byrd her best smile. "Ready when you are."

After grabbing lunch with Jamie to delay the call, Byrd sat in the closet again.

He dialed the number, heard the beeps, and waited for the ring. This time Warren picked up on the first ring. "Yes?"

"General? We'll be there in four hours. I'm bringing the realtor, so if there is anything you don't want her to see, tell me now. I can arrange to meet somewhere tomorrow."

Warren sounded pleased, if Byrd could make anything out over the secure phone. "It will be fine to bring the realtor to my office at the farm. Give me a time I should expect you."

Byrd looked at his watch and did some quick math. It would be a three-hour drive at best, and he wanted a little time to look things over. "Let's shoot for five this afternoon. We'll have to get out of Cedartown and negotiate Atlanta traffic."

"Great," Warren said. Then the connection was broken.

WEDNESDAY, FEBRUARY 9, 2005
1:03 P.M.
EL PASO, TEXAS

Montana was curled up on the couch with Clete. It felt odd to her for them to be home together midday in the middle of the week. She was on the verge of dozing off when Clete jerked. She snuggled closer and said, "I think you fell asleep."

Clete hugged her in response. "I need to call Danny Byrd tonight. I did some charting on the track of that airplane you saw. It ended up in a place called Dalton."

Montana turned to look at him. "That's a place north of Atlanta. It's the carpet capitol of America."

Clete smiled. "You think he's smuggling carpet from Mexico?"

She slapped at his chest good-naturedly. "Kiss my ass!"

Clete ignored the attack. "I'd love to, but I need to call Danny."

"You're a laugh a minute. You should do standup."

Clete took a deep breath. "There is something we need to talk about."

Montana sat up. "This sounds serious. Am I in trouble?"

Clete looked into her eyes. "You can't tell anyone you know this, but it looks like Rojo's son is the one who set you up to be shot."

Her mouth hung open. "How do you know?"

He shook his head. "I can't tell you that. I also know that his dad is mad about it. We've known for years the mafia doesn't want to bring the fight into the US. It will cause them more trouble than it's worth."

"Should I be worried?" Montana asked.

He scowled. "You live with a Texas Ranger. What else do you need?"

Montana's left eyebrow shot up. "What more indeed."

Clete grabbed the phone on the end table. "Listen in while I call Danny. You might hear some things I'm not supposed to tell you about."

Clete called the GBI Headquarters phone number and was surprised to learn Byrd was in the building. The call was routed to a desk Byrd had commandeered.

When Clete heard Byrd answer, he said, "Wait till you hear this."

WEDNESDAY, FEBRUARY 9, 2005
5:25 P.M.
BOWENS MILL, GEORGIA

Daniel Byrd checked the recorder in Jamie Abernathy's purse one last time. He planned to have her turn it on as they walked from the car to the house. Once they felt like everything was ready, Byrd turned the car onto the paved road and made the short drive to the entrance to the farm.

They bounced over the rutted entrance lane and came to the box at the gate. But before he could alert the house, he heard the mechanism click and the gate began to move out of the way.

Byrd glanced at Jamie, shrugged, and said, "I guess we're expected."

Byrd could tell Jamie was nervous. She had been an agent for several years but was considered a poor choice for an undercover assignment. Her good looks—a benefit in some ways—were a problem for an agent working undercover. Agents wanted to be nondescript and forgettable to blend in with the environment.

As they went past the hangar, Byrd tried to see if the Skymaster was inside. He couldn't make anything out as they slowly advanced on the manor house. Byrd pulled the undercover car up in front on the gravel drive and put it in park.

As Jamie activated the recorder, Byrd recognized Adam Benjamin coming down the steps to greet them. He extended his hand to Byrd, and Byrd shook. Then Byrd pointed to Jamie. "This is my realtor, Jamie Benson."

Jamie came around the car to where the two men stood. She put on her winningest smile. "Hi, I'm Jamie. It's a pleasure to meet you. Are you the one who'll be signing the lease?"

Adam shook his head. "I wish. I'm just hired help around here. The boss is inside."

Byrd touched Jamie on the elbow. "Right this way. The General will be the one signing the paperwork."

Adam watched with his hands on his hips as the pair climbed the steps to the veranda and walked to the front door. Byrd glanced back and caught Adam examining his license plate.

By the time they reached the door, Mitchell Warren was waiting to greet them.

"Come in please," Warren said.

Jamie extended a hand. "I'm Jamie."

Mitchell Warren shook her hand and held on. "It is a pleasure to meet you, Jamie."

Warren barely acknowledged Byrd as he escorted Jamie to his office. They took seats around a conference table and Jamie pulled the legal documents from her purse. She was careful not to snag the audio recorder.

"I am Mitchell Warren, late of the United States Army," Warren said.

Jamie turned the smile on again. "My daddy was in the army. I wasn't born then, but I've seen pictures."

Byrd said, "This fellow was a General in the army. He's leasing the Thomas place."

Jamie laid the paperwork on the table. "This won't take long. I understand you want to pay in cash?"

Warren smiled. "I hope that's not a problem."

Jamie turned on the smile again. "It most certainly isn't. What Uncle Sam doesn't know won't hurt us."

"My thoughts exactly," Warren said.

Warren glanced at the documents and then, quickly signed at the points Jamie had highlighted. He seemed thoroughly disinterested in the contract.

"Do you plan to make any changes to the property?" Jamie asked. When Warren glanced at her, she continued, "If you are, I'll have to get approval from the owner."

Warren shook his head. "No changes." Warren pulled a bottle of scotch and three glasses from a drawer. "May I offer a congratulatory drink?" Warren asked.

Jamie stuck out a hand and waved the glass away. "I can't. We have a long ride back, and I need to get this paperwork filed as soon as I'm back home."

Byrd looked at the offered glass for a moment. He looked back at Warren. "I'm driving," Byrd said. Byrd heard the regret in his own voice.

"What brought this property to your attention?" Warren asked Byrd. "You were able to find it pretty quickly." Warren watched him over the top of the glass.

Byrd laughed. "Jamie having the contract for the place helped. I called her and asked if she could think of a place that would fit the bill. When she mentioned the Thomas place, I had to agree it was what you were looking for."

"How so?" Warren asked.

"I'd heard of this place when I was a kid. It was in all the newspapers back then. In the eighties, some drug runners cut a runway on the property. They used it for years, until they got caught. After Jamie mentioned the place, I remembered the history. They were like pirate stories to a kid living out in the country. Those stories about drug running in Georgia got me interested in law enforcement."

Warren chuckled. "The tales of our youth."

Byrd nodded. "I went out to the Thomas place—that's what it's called by the way."

"Yes, you mentioned the Thomas place." Warren seemed in a hurry.

"Right. Well, I looked it over and I think it's perfect," Byrd said.

Warren took two envelopes out of his top drawer of the desk he had gotten the scotch from. He handed one to Jamie and the other to Byrd. Neither checked the contents.

"Would you care for some food after your journey? I'm sure my wife can rustle something up," Warren said.

Byrd and Jamie said in unison, "No, thanks." Then they looked at each other and laughed.

Byrd said, "I think we've been in the car too long. Thanks, General, but we'll take a rain check. Maybe next time we come to visit, we can do that."

Warren nodded. "You look anxious to get back on the road."

Jamie nodded. "My husband expects me back tonight. It's a long drive, so we need to get going." The two GBI agents had worked out the cover story on the way down. They wanted to spend as little time as possible in the house.

Warren, ever the southern gentleman, ushered Jamie

out into the hallway. "Jamie, will you excuse Mr. Moody and I for just a moment? I promise you, I'll be quick."

"Of course, Mr. Warren," she said.

Mitch returned to his office and stepped close to Byrd. "Is the runway you mentioned usable?"

Byrd smiled slyly. "I figured that might be what you were interested in. Yes, it needs to be mowed, but the runway is hard-packed Georgia clay. It might as well be paved."

Warren nodded. "I have some tasks you should be able to help with."

Byrd shrugged and waited.

"I want someone to mow the landing strip on the property. And Adam will be coming up soon to check it out. Can you have the cutting done in the next two days?" Warren watched Byrd closely.

Byrd thought it over. "I don't see why not."

Warren smiled. "Good. I added a bonus to your package that should cover any costs and your additional time."

Byrd shook Warren's hand again. "That's great. I'll see to it that this land is just what you want."

Warren walked out with him to join Jamie. As Byrd and Jamie headed for the door, Adam came into the house. He held the door for them as they passed.

Jamie turned to Adam and said, "It was a pleasure to meet you."

Adam smiled. "The pleasure was all mine."

Adam was openly admiring Jamie as the agents left the house and went down the steps.

"What do you think he was up to? Or is he not allowed in the house?" Jamie asked under her breath.

Byrd kept walking. "He was checking out our tag. We need to check with the Headquarters Communications Center to see if someone did an inquiry."

Jamie scowled. "How could he run our tag? He'd have to have access to NCIC. The FBI has so many restrictions on access to that system, there's no way he could do that."

"We'll see," Byrd said. He fired up the undercover car and started back down the driveway. "If he can't, then I spent an hour for nothing. I had the registration on this car changed to 'Herman Moody.'"

WEDNESDAY, FEBRUARY 9, 2005
6:22 P.M.
BOWENS MILL, GEORGIA

Adam sat down in the chair he assumed Jamie occupied. He hadn't sought out her chair, but he appreciated the lingering scent of her perfume.

Warren waited. "What were you able to find out?"

Adam shrugged. "The car is registered to a Herman Moody with a Jasper address."

Warren nodded. "But you're not satisfied?"

Adam shrugged again. "I can't find any reference to Moody in any of the federal data bases. He's not acting as an informant for the FBI or the DEA. But I still get a bad feeling when I'm around him."

Warren poured a scotch. "You're seeing things when nothing is there. He is what he seems: a useful grunt. Nothing more."

Adam stood. "Well, he sure does know how to pick a realtor."

Mitchell Warren laughed. "That he does."

Adam changed the subject. "Will this property be something we'll hold onto?"

Warren sipped the liquor. "Probably not. Omar is concerned about letting Rojo's men do the offloading. But in the end, I think we should do our business in public. These boxes Rojo sends aren't big, are they?"

Adam shook his head. "No."

Warren continued. "Omar will just need a little more convincing. We can always use our people for the airport meet and do the exchange with Rojo's people somewhere else." Then Warren changed the subject. "How do you think Omar is doing?"

"He's doing well. He's a good pilot, like the ones we've flown with in some of the worst parts of the world."

Warren seemed pleased. "Yes, he has the right spirit for our work. In another age, he would have been a pirate. Mr. Moody mentioned pirate tales when we spoke."

"We might all have been," Adam said.

Warren laughed. Adam realized that laughing was something he hadn't seen Mitch do in a while.

"What do we hear out of Mexico?" Adam asked.

"That's why I asked you to come down," Warren said as the smile faded.

Adam knew something was up. "I saw Omar busy with the airplane this morning. Is he headed back to El Paso?" Adam was relaxed and confident in Omar's flying skills. The long-range weather report seemed in their favor, too.

Warren nodded. "He plans to fly out and then do the return day after tomorrow. I just signed a contract for the temporary use of some land near Cedartown, Georgia. Do you know the area?"

Adam shrugged. "Generally. I used to have family in Cartersville."

Warren sat forward at his desk. "We had looked at Cartersville as a landing site. But the land deal went through faster than I expected. We will have a private runway for use outside of Cedartown."

Adam still had doubts. "Do you trust this guy Moody? He found the place awfully fast from my view. Is the airstrip on his family's land?"

Warren chuckled. "He knew about it from his childhood. It was used by drug smugglers back in the eighties. He read the story when he was a kid and wanted to get into law enforcement because of it. Ironic, wouldn't you say?"

Adam wasn't convinced. "He lied to his boss and did something against the rules. How can I trust a guy like that?"

Warren gave Adam a look. "Do you realize how hypocritical that comment makes you sound? That is our lives, is it not?"

Adam had to admit those characteristics had made up his adult life. "Okay. What do I need to do to help?"

"I want you to handle the offloading of the airplane in Cedartown. Find a location to pass the shipment off to Rojo's people in Atlanta. I'd go with a big parking lot, or something of that nature." Warren seemed more involved in the details than usual.

"I can do that," Adam said. "If Omar flies overnight like the first time we can have him cleaned out and deliver the product by lunchtime. He plans to be back in Georgia by Monday morning?"

"That'd be the plan," Warren said.

"Have Omar touch base with me before he leaves, and we'll set everything up."

Warren looked at his watch. "He's out at the hangar now. Run out there and work things out. Set up a comms plan and all the little things you know need doing that Omar might not think of. He's leaving in the morning."

Adam stood up. "I'm on it."

WEDNESDAY, FEBRUARY 9, 2005
9:15 P.M.
CIUDAD JUÁREZ, CHIHUAHUA, MEXICO

Pequeño Rojo sat in front of his father's desk. He focused on his new cellular phone, ignoring what Rojo was telling him. Rojo thought his son was more focused on his hair, his clothes, and the expensive alcohol he consumed in large quantities than he was their business.

"My son, you must listen to what I am telling you. You will one day lead this business, and then the lessons you have learned will keep you out of prison." Rojo slammed his open palm on his desk for emphasis.

Pequeño Rojo looked up with a sneer. "Your *money* will keep you out of prison, not tales of past successes. Times are changing, Father, and you are not the future. You are the past."

Rojo stepped around his desk and stood in front of his son.

"You don't scare me," the young man said.

Rojo slapped his son with an open hand. Pequeño Rojo's chair tipped over and he fell to the floor. His face was red and he had inadvertently thrown his phone across the room. He picked himself up and did his best to stand tall in front of his father. "When I resort to violence, I am wrong. When you resort to violence, it is from anger. You are the old angry past, my father. I am the future, where problems are met with violence because that is the most effective way. One day, you will learn to listen to those smarter than you."

Rojo flicked out the knife faster than his son could

imagine. Rojo held Pequeño Rojo by the collar and brought the tip of the knife to his throat. He growled, "You will not take any more action on the US side. Is that clear?"

The younger man's eyes were wide with fear.

"You are my son. If not, I would be preparing to replace this carpet since it would be covered in your blood. I cannot make you honor me or respect me, but I can make you fear me."

Pequeño Rojo responded weakly, "You wouldn't kill me."

Rojo released his grip. "You are right."

Pequeño Rojo relaxed.

"It would give me pleasure to kill you right now," Rojo continued. "But your mother would never forgive me."

Pequeño Rojo straightened his clothes.

Rojo returned to his seat. He leaned back in his chair and locked eyes with his oldest child. "You should not assume that simply because I won't kill you, I might not hire someone to kill you."

Rojo watched with contempt as his son stormed out of the room. Rojo shook his head, then held his head in his hands. *What have I done?* he thought. *This can't go on. He will destroy us all.*

Rojo stood and looked out the window of his estate. He controlled the police, the judges, the politicians, and every powerful person within his community. And yet he couldn't control his own son.

THURSDAY, FEBRUARY 10, 2005
10:32 A.M.
BOWENS MILL, GEORGIA

Omar felt a flutter in his stomach. Now he knew it wasn't fear; it was excitement. He looked forward to the challenge, he realized. The adventure of the game.

He and Adam had gone over the plans in detail. Adam had suggested they pick an airport in the area he could divert to if there was a problem in Cedartown. They had worked out a communications plan, the frequencies they would use, and code words, just in case.

Omar was impressed with Adam's planning skills. He even felt more comfortable knowing Adam would meet him when he got back to Georgia.

He fired up the old warbird and rolled onto the runway. He had enough fuel to make Texas, and then he'd stop, top the tanks off, and recheck the weather forecast. It would be better, he reasoned, to spend as little time in the El Paso area as possible. One small mistake could draw the police to him, and that could spell disaster.

As the Skymaster bounced over uneven ground to the grass runway, Omar checked and rechecked each gauge. Everything looked good, and the engines were both running as smooth as silk. He took a sip from his travel mug, steered the plane around to line up with the runway, and did one more engine performance check.

Omar took a last look toward the hangar, gave a salute to whatever angels might be looking out for him the next couple of days, and applied power to the propellers.

The aircraft picked up speed, and with a bounce, the

rugged plane was defying the laws of gravity. Omar smiled at the thought of the other laws he was breaking at the same time.

As he climbed into the South Georgia sky, he looked out the window and enjoyed the view. He took in the trees, the Altamaha River, and the swamp lands as he slowly pointed the airplane west. He knew from experience, he would be looking at a lot of sand very soon.

THURSDAY, FEBRUARY 10, 2005
11:23 A.M.
GAINESVILLE, GEORGIA

Daniel Byrd read the email again. It didn't make sense. The undercover license plate on the car he and Jamie took to Bowens Mill had been queried on the National Crime Information Center computer system. The NCIC is the national hub, but each state manages their own data. Byrd knew anyone looking into the undercover car would leave a trail through the GCIC system managed by the GBI.

Byrd had emailed the GCIC investigative desk and requested the contact information of anyone who might have tried to check out the license plate in the last couple of days.

The teletype read "INQUIRY ON UC PLATE; DATE 02/09/2005 AT 18:18:34. TERMINAL PHYSICAL LOCATION: DOJ WASHINGTON, DC; OPERATOR J. GORE."

Byrd didn't like the sound of that.

THURSDAY, FEBRUARY 10, 2005
12:13 P.M.
BOWENS MILL, GEORGIA

Adam wasn't happy with this operation the General was running and decided to voice his concerns before he left for North Georgia. He caught the General in his office in the big house.

"Mitch, we need to talk," Adam said.

Warren extended a hand. "Come in and have a seat."

Adam remained standing. "Why are you letting Omar get so deep in this operation? He's a kid. A talented pilot, but a kid."

"My son is perfectly capable of running his side of the operation. You were his age when you got into this game. Why don't you have faith in Omar?" Warren blustered.

Adam stood in front of the General's desk. "I was recruited into the US Army, not this bullshit we're in now. And when I was first recruited, I was in the game for the action. I had no family to speak of; my mother died young, and my father was distant at best." He paused to look into Warren's eyes as he spoke.

"The only bright spot in the last year had been the opportunity to coach Omar. I know that Omar is the child I never had, and to a certain extent, Omar was looking for a father figure in his life."

Warren stood up. "Don't you think I know that? Do you think I'm oblivious to what this life has done to my family?"

Adam stood his ground. "I'm never sure what you know, Mitch."

Warren poured a scotch for himself. "Omar turned out good in spite of me."

Adam stepped closer to Warren. "You want me to take a trip and maybe it will mend my soul? What makes you think I have a soul left? All the jobs we've done. All the people who've died at my hands." Adam watched Warren's hand shake as he took a sip of scotch. "And your hands, too, Mitch."

Warren didn't look up. "I know that. I know the things we've done."

Adam turned to leave. Before he closed the office door, he turned back to Warren. "Then let's not ruin his life. Let's get him out of this before it's too late."

CHAPTER 24
WELL, WHAT A SURPRISE TO SEE YOU HERE

MONDAY, FEBRUARY 14, 2005
5:15 A.M.
CEDARTOWN, GEORGIA

Adam Benjamin walked the edge of the pasture that would, at least for today, resume its role as a runway. The moon was full and high, and it lit the runway.

He and one of the men he had brought from the farm were ramming tent pegs into aluminum pie plates. Then, about every ten to fifteen yards, they jammed the pegs into the ground, creating a reflective border on the side of the runway.

Moody had been true to his word when he told the General the runway would be mowed and prepped. The once-tall grass and weeds had been trimmed to within an inch of the red Georgia clay. As they forced the tent pegs into the ground, Adam noted that the ground was well packed. Some places had been too hard to get a peg into, but the placement didn't need to be precise. This wasn't going to be a night landing.

As he walked, Adam sniffed the air. And every few

yards or so he would stand perfectly still and listen. He had learned from experiences in dangerous parts of the world to use his senses to warn him of trouble. The new mown grass smell was strong, and the sounds of the forest seemed normal. He could hear a bullfrog croaking from the pond near the front of the property.

Adam came to the fence at the west end of the property. He looked back at the pie plates and figured they would do the trick. He ambled toward where their vehicles were parked and wondered if it was time for him to get out, to find a place to live his last days in peace.

The radio in his hip pocket chirped. He looked at the display and saw that it was Omar.

"Where are you, kid?" Adam said.

"I figure I'm still about on pace to get to you by around nine." The signal was thready and garbled.

"How are you able to reach me?" Adam asked.

"I'm at fifteen thousand feet. I've got to get back down right away, but I thought we might be able to talk from here."

"Get your ass back to three thousand feet. The oxygen at that altitude won't last long. Call when you get closer to the Alabama-Georgia line."

"Will do," Omar said.

Adam stuck the radio back in his hip pocket. He looked around the farm, enjoying the last hours of the dying night. Then he knew it was time to get the men organized.

5:25 A.M.

The briefing room was full of law enforcement officers. Byrd knew most of the participants, and when he heard someone call his name, he turned to see Jim Reaves, an agent with the US Customs Service. Reaves and Byrd had worked a case undercover on the Georgia coast in 1998.

Reaves was tall, lean, and muscular. His head was clean-shaven, but he sported a goatee. He would brag that you couldn't see a single gray hair on his head. "Danny, how are you?"

Byrd stuck out his hand. "Great, thanks for coming."

"My SAC was intrigued by the information you've developed. We don't usually use our inspection authority over here on the East Coast for people and things coming out of Mexico. There are too many stops in between. But this sounds like it fits the bill," Reaves said.

Byrd nudged Reaves. "You'll be able to take this to the US Attorney and be a superstar. Drug ring, Mexican connections, airplanes, the whole shooting match."

Reaves smiled. "You are welcome to help my career any time you'd like."

Byrd shrugged. "You Feds are all alike. Let the State and locals do the work, and then you take the glory."

"If you knew the hell I just caught from my wife for being here on Valentine's Day." Reaves shook his head. "And anyway, I thought you said I was walking in with you to this secret runway?" Reeves asked.

"Oh, yeah," Byrd said. "I guess you are going to have to work today."

5:55 A.M.

Byrd led the team through the woods along the route he had scouted. Jim Reaves was right behind him, and Jamie Abernathy brought up the rear.

When he had surveyed the location to see if it would fit the bill, he found an old roadbed that ended up parallel to the airstrip. It would help the agents get close surreptitiously and keep them from accidentally wandering in circles in the woods.

The team did everything they could to move silently through the early morning stillness. Each was armed with a long gun, their service weapon, and a radio to communicate with the other teams in cars. The GSP helicopter was at the Cedartown airport, and the pilots told Byrd they could be over the runway in under five minutes.

Byrd hefted his M4 rifle as they crossed the remains of a fallen pine tree. He estimated they would be at their observation post in about fifteen more minutes.

6:05 A.M.

Sheriff Jim Garrison rolled out of his bed and worked his shoulder joints. He had been in the bed for two whole days, and though he didn't feel well, he felt well enough to get out and move around. He sat on the bed and dragged his pants on with considerable effort. He pulled a sweatshirt on and slipped on his favorite boots.

He walked to his garage and started to climb into his county patrol car. Then, after consideration, he decided he was technically still on sick leave. He went back into the kitchen and got the keys to his old pickup truck. He stopped to cough, then went on to the reliable Chevy he drove when he wanted to get away from it all.

He decided to head down to Cedartown and talk to his personal pharmacist. Bob had given him sound advice in the past, recommending over-the-counter medications to help shake a stubborn cold or sinus infection.

The sun would be up in less than an hour, peaking over the eastern horizon. As a young deputy, and then later as the high sheriff, he loved driving around this time of day. People were out headed to work, school buses were picking up children, and the day was a blank sheet of paper.

He was passing the Thomas place when he thought he saw headlights on the property. He slowed and pulled into the driveway of the old farm and tried to see what was going on. He pulled out the "seeing glasses" he kept in the glove box. He refused to wear the glasses in public but kept them for night driving or when rain made it difficult for him to see well. He pushed the glasses into place and focused on the headlights, trying to make out what was happening.

He decided to roll the truck down nearer the activity, then scrambled in the console for his spare badge, wishing he had put on his gun, but he didn't expect any real problems.

7:01 A.M.

Major Robert Davids dialed the sheriff's cell number. He was surprised when he didn't get an answer. The sheriff had been out of work with what he said was a bad cold or the flu. Davids decided to call his house number, worried he would wake the sheriff's wife but not willing to face his wrath if he was unaware of the drug bust about to go down in his county.

The sheriff's wife answered on the second ring.

"Sorry to wake you up, but is the sheriff available?" Davids asked.

After a couple of seconds, she said, "No, he must have

felt better this morning. He's not here and his pants and boots are gone. I guess he's been sitting at home too long."

Davids hung up and thought his options over. He decided to have the radio operator send him an email. As soon as the sheriff checked in on his phone, he would get word about the operation.

7:10 A.M.

Byrd noted that his exhaled breath made a misty cloud around his face. The sliver of light coming over the horizon was giving them enough illumination to navigate the piney forest. But he was too focused on the job at hand to enjoy the golden halo the hardwood trees gave the trail he was following. Byrd thought he could make out the runway from where they were.

He had a powerful set of binoculars stuffed in his backpack and had a spot picked out that would give them a good view of the activity on the runway. Byrd used hand signals as they got near the pasture with the improvised airport.

When he found the high spot, he dropped his pack and retrieved the field glasses, laying down in the damp grass and leaves that bordered the field. Abernathy and Reaves joined him. Once he was prone at the edge of the woods, he was able to get a clear view of the men at the pole barn near the edge of the landing strip. Two were stocky, dressed in rough clothes, and had long guns slung across their backs. He recognized Adam Benjamin propped against a new model pickup truck. He could see a pistol in a holster on Adam's waist.

Then he saw a set of headlights coming from the road to the runway.

7:15 A.M.

Adam Benjamin watched the headlights advance slowly down the driveway leading into the pasture. This wasn't good. The truck was probably too old to be the police, but there was no way to be sure.

Adam motioned to the other men to get inside the vehicles and stay out of sight. He ambled in the direction of the truck as it slowly continued toward him. In a moment he was bathed in the front headlights. He would have to make a decision soon.

He made sure his pistol was accessible and walked toward the approaching truck.

7:15 A.M.

Sheriff Jim Garrison knew he had stepped in it. He had thought the lights out at the old farm were vandals. It was as he was driving down the rutted road to the field that he remembered the GBI was going to use this property for a sting.

Garrison had no doubt that the man in his headlights was not a GBI agent. He looked like he had a military background, but something looked sinister about the man walking toward his door. He had made a point to look at the mug shots of every felon arrest in Polk County, so this man didn't ring any bells.

Garrison dropped his badge behind the truck seat and rolled his window down.

"Hey," Garrison said preemptively. "You the new owner of this farm?"

The man was bland. "Just getting started on some improvements. Why do you ask?"

"I live right down the road. I knew the last owner, and I guess I'm just being nosy," Garrison said with a laugh.

Before Garrison could react, Adam stuck a small Glock 9mm in his face. "Curiosity killed the cat, my friend."

Garrison's mind raced. There was no way he could take the gun away from the man. He looked like he was a fighter. The sheriff decided the best bet was to be a good witness.

Garrison started making mental notes of the dress and appearance of the men he could see. A couple of men got out of a truck and came to support the military man.

Garrison was pulled from his own truck and handcuffed. The man with the Glock gave the inside of the truck a cursory look, made an attempt at patting Garrison down for weapons, then shoved the sheriff toward the pole barn standing near where they were parked.

The sheriff was pushed along until they came to several bales of hay. The man kicked two bales together and pushed Garrison back, where he sat down hard on the hay.

"Friend, if you keep quiet and don't give us any problems, you'll live to stick your nose into someone else's business."

Garrison cocked his head to one side. "Mister, have you ever seen an old movie called *No Time for Sergeants*?"

The man nodded. "A little before my time, but I love those old classics. Andy Griffith, before he was the sheriff of Mayberry, right?"

Garrison smiled. "That's it. Do you remember when the sergeant talked to Andy about not making waves? He said if you make waves, you rock the boats."

The man nodded again.

Garrison hung his head, and said, "Right now, I know I've got the smallest boat on the lake. Even a little wave would do me in. You don't have to worry about me making any waves. I just want to be able to paddle my little boat for a while longer."

The man then patted the sheriff on the shoulder. "Keep that thought in mind, old timer. We'll be gone soon. And you'll have a story to tell your neighbors."

Garrison smiled. "You won't have any problems from me."

7:17 A.M.

Davids and a small team of GBI agents were hidden behind a church just up the street from the Thomas place. He, like everyone else on his team, was anxious for the operation to get underway. When the response to the tag request came over the GBI radio, he was only half listening.

"The current owner is James Tilman Garrison, of a Cedartown address," the dispatcher said, responding to someone's question regarding the pickup.

Davids stared at the radio microphone, mouth open, expecting the radio operator to correct herself. Seconds ticked by until he grabbed the radio mic and spoke into it. "This is Major Davids with Polk County. That truck belongs to our sheriff. Can anybody see the driver?"

Davids recognized Daniel Byrd's voice when he spoke. "GBI Eighty-nine to all units. The driver of the truck looks like it is the sheriff. One of the off-load crew just pointed a gun in his face. They are taking the sheriff out of his truck and searching him."

Davids swore. "Fuck! What can we do?"

"We have to let this play out, unless they make a move to hurt the sheriff," Byrd said.

Davids wasn't happy. "He's been out sick, so I don't know what his condition is. How well can you see him?"

Byrd sympathized. "I'll move as close as I can. He looks okay, just pissed off. He and the guy who looks to be in charge are having a talk."

Davids slumped in his seat. The sheriff wasn't just his boss, he was a friend, and he wondered how he would hold up under the strain.

9:45 A.M.

Omar had been sitting in the same position for over eight hours. The flight had been smooth, but he had learned a few things.

The radar detector was worthless. There were far too many military bases between West Texas and Georgia for the receiver to do any good, he guessed. It had alarmed nonstop from the time he took off until he switched it off near Fort Worth.

He was still tense, but he couldn't wait to get out of the airplane and stretch his legs. He checked and rechecked the gauges, then started looking toward the rising sun, trying to will his eyes to find the runway waiting for him.

The airplane had performed better than he hoped. The fuel system worked flawlessly, and the airplane had been as comfortable as a living room while he crossed four states to get to Georgia.

He took a sip of the little bit of coffee left in the thermos. It was cold, but it was wet. Omar had eaten his last sandwich three hours before, and he felt his stomach growling.

He checked his watch and decided to give Adam a try. He estimated he was less than thirty miles from the grass runway.

Omar pressed the transmit button and waited for an answer.

"Go ahead, kid."

"I'm less than thirty out, Adam. Is everything cool?"

Adam sounded irritated. "A busybody old man showed up and we had to put him on ice for a little while. We'll have to find another place to bring you in next time, but that's no big deal."

"You didn't do anything permanent, did you?" Omar asked.

"I'm not that guy," Adam responded.

Omar was relieved. "Good, I'll see you soon. Everything has been as smooth as glass."

CHAPTER 25
HIGH-FLYING FUN

MONDAY, FEBRUARY 14, 2005
9:48 A.M.
CEDARTOWN, GEORGIA

"Flint 355 to Atlanta Center," Arlow called on the UHF military radio in his DEA Aero Commander.

"Atlanta Center to Flint 355. Please squawk the law enforcement ident code," came the reply.

Arlow leaned down and rolled in the numbers for a law enforcement aircraft on a priority mission. The number changed every few days for security purposes, and Arlow had his fingers crossed that the number he keyed in was up to date. He pressed the ident button.

"Flint 355, radar contact, 8 nm SW of the Rome VOR. Current altimeter twenty-nine point fifty-five. What help do you need, sir?"

"Flint 355 request flight following for safety only. Flint is shadowing another aircraft and will be involved in enforcement activities."

"Roger, Flint. Any idea what area? We can vector flights if necessary."

Arlow was reluctant to give specifics, even on a private military channel. Scanners could intercept the conversation, and this smuggling group was capable of doing just that. "Flint 355 will be in the area."

"Affirmative, Flint 355. We do have a few targets painted on radar in your area."

Arlow craned his neck around. He could see his target about two miles out, but it never hurt to verify. "Center, do you paint a target about two nautical miles off my nose?"

"Affirmative. The target is not squawking, but radar indicates an altitude of thirty-five hundred feet."

Arlow adjusted the pitch of the propellers and let the Aero Commander slow slightly. "Thanks, Center. If you'd be kind enough to lock on that target for me, Flint 355 will be standing by."

Arlow heard the *click-click* as the channel went quiet. He tightened his seat belt and took a couple of deep breaths. A DEA plane from Dallas Air Support had picked up the Skymaster just after it left Mexico. Using the fighter-plane radar system the DEA had procured, the pilot had followed the target to near Meridian, Mississippi. Arlow had been waiting at the Naval Air Station and, once alerted, had taken the handoff near the Alabama state line.

Flying alone, there had been some challenges staying behind the in-line twin-engine airplane. The new radar was a big help, but the Aero Commander cruised at a higher speed than the former military plane. Arlow had twisted and turned to slow his own progress, and twice the radar lock had been lost as he jinked around. But the target plane had maintained the same heading after crossing north of Birmingham, and Arlow had been able to reestablish contact each time.

Arlow double-checked every resource on the government airplane as he anticipated the action to come.

Arlow used his police radio to call the GSP pilots in Cedartown. "Flint 355 to GSP Aviation."

"GSP 715 to Flint 355, go ahead."

"GSP, you can start moving this way. Our target is less than five minutes out."

Arlow recognized the whine of the turbine start in the background as the GSP pilot responded, "We're on the way!"

"Arlow?"

The pilot recognized Daniel Byrd's voice. "Yes, sir."

Byrd's voice was soft. Arlow assumed he was in an observation post on the runway. "FYI, our targets have taken the local sheriff hostage."

Arlow took another deep breath. "Copy."

10:01 A.M.

Omar didn't bother to circle the airport; he knew Adam would be on the lookout for any problems. He set the Skymaster on the runway as if he had practiced it a hundred times. The warplane coasted up to the trucks parked by the pole barn.

Adam motioned for the ground crew to pull the boxes out of the back of the airplane as Omar stepped down to stretch his legs. The engines idled noisily as Omar leaned on the door frame and arched his back.

Adam walked over to join Omar when Omar saw the alarm in Adam's eyes. "What's wrong?" Omar asked.

Adam turned his head all around as the two men he'd brought were busy loading the boxes of meth into the back of Adam's truck, working as quickly as possible.

Then Adam pointed his nose like a birddog. "Shit," he said.

"What?" Omar asked.

"Helicopter," Adam said as he looked around.

Adam pointed to one of the men. "Take these boxes and find a place to go to ground. I'm flying back with the kid." The men stared at Adam. "Right now! Go!"

The two men turned, closed the camper top, and got in Adam's truck. Adam found his backpack on the ground.

Omar could see the helicopter now. "Could it be a corporate chopper, or maybe the National Guard?"

Adam shook his head. He watched the men fire up his truck. "They're flying too low. Cops! Got to be. Let's go!"

Omar throttled up the airplane. His hands began to shake. Adam climbed into the back, pulling a MAC-10 machine pistol from his backpack.

The fun and games were over. Omar took a deep breath and focused on his job.

10:03 A.M.

Arlow slowed the Aero Commander as much as he could as he tried to keep it in the air. He planned to block in the Skymaster on the runway. But he didn't want to alert them to his presence too early.

Arlow could see the GSP helicopter flying at treetop level, the red light on the belly of the repurposed Huey flashing, as he lowered flaps and gear and felt the airplane slow and balloon up. After the initial rise, the airplane settled into a glide slope that would put Arlow near the end of the runway.

He could see the men at the other end of the runway and strained to see what was going on.

10:04 A.M.

Byrd ran while staying in a crouch. "Hit it, hit it, hit it!" he shouted into the radio on his vest. He was surprised how slick the ground still was from the morning dew. He brought his rifle up to this chest and looked over the sights as he advanced.

Byrd instinctively ran to the left, with Jim Reaves and Jamie Abernathy fanning out to his right. Byrd ran to the shed where Sheriff Garrison sat, feeling the prop wash from the Skymaster as he ran behind it.

10:04 A.M.

Omar didn't bother to check the gauges on the plane. He raced the engine and used the pusher prop to taxi out on the runway. He guessed he had a minute before the helicopter would try to hover overhead, preventing a takeoff.

He saw two men and a woman with long guns running around near his airplane as he bounced along to the packed runway. He could see cars with blue lights flashing on the single road to the property when he looked over his shoulder.

10:04 A.M.

Arlow dropped the high-wing plane onto the rough runway, pleasantly surprised how hard the ground was. He could see the Skymaster sitting facing away from him at the other end of the runway.

In front of him, he could see police vehicles, marked and unmarked, surrounding two trucks. In one truck, the occupants were out at gunpoint; in the other, the driver was slumped against the door while deputies helped him.

Then the Skymaster turned onto the runway, facing the DEA plane.

10:05 A.M.

Byrd ran to where Sheriff Garrison sat in the pole barn. "Sheriff, do you have the keys for your truck?"

Garrison nodded as he watched Byrd unlock the handcuffs. Byrd continued, "Get in it and when you see a chance, get the hell out of here."

Byrd turned back to the airplane as he heard the engines roar and the plane started to move. Byrd ran toward the airplane, hoping to get in a position to block their path. Byrd saw that Jamie and Reaves were trying to make a similar maneuver, but they were too far away.

Jim Reaves and Jamie Abernathy ran past the pole barn, motioning the police cars streaming into the property to block the runway.

Byrd was thirty feet from the Skymaster when the window behind the pilot popped open. He recognized Adam Benjamin crouching behind Omar. In slow motion, he saw Adam stick the barrel of a submachine gun out the window. Then he heard the bee-buzzing sound of a bullet passing over his head. Byrd was so surprised at the turn of events, he didn't react immediately.

When the second bee-buzz passed his left ear, Byrd swung the M4 rifle around and brought it to bear. The next bee-buzz seemed closer.

Byrd used the iron sights to line up the gun at where Adam was crouching. He pulled the trigger and heard the zing of the recoil spring—*pull, pull, pull,* and only the sound of the spring zinging next to his right ear.

Byrd saw Adam fall backward. He heard someone shouting in the radio, "Shots fired! Shots fired."

Byrd drew a bead on the plane again and pulled the trigger once more.

10:07 A.M.

Omar gunned the engine and applied full power before they were even on the airstrip. The higher grass and rougher ground caused the warplane to bounce around as Adam tried to find a stable position in the rear. Omar glanced back and saw Adam folding out the machine pistol and forcing a magazine into the bottom.

Omar turned onto the hard ground and manicured grass just as he saw the Aero Commander sinking onto the landing strip from the other end. The DEA airplane was down quickly, stirring up considerable dust with the turboprop engines.

Omar looked over his shoulder once more. Adam had kneeled beside the auxiliary fuel tank for stability. Adam looked at Omar, winked, and gave a thumbs-up. "Let's do it, kid! You've got to get us out of here!" Adam shouted above the roar of the engines.

Omar took a deep breath and started the takeoff roll. The airplane was sluggish at first, slow to pick up speed. Omar applied every bit of power available, using every trick he'd heard of to get the plane in the air. As they gained momentum, Omar said to himself, "Come on! You can do this!"

Omar heard the loud banging as Adam fired at the police running like ants on the ground. *Bam-bam-bam*, came the report. Then he heard the sound of something banging into the airplane, and a sound that reminded him of a steak being slapped onto a kitchen counter. He heard a grunt but couldn't look away from the runway. Two more times, something slammed into the airplane and on the second one he felt a piece of hot metal or plastic burn his neck.

Suddenly, the plexiglass window beside his left ear shattered and a chunk of the window flew through the air.

10:07 A.M.

Arlow's eyes widened as the Skymaster got closer. The two planes were less than five hundred feet apart. There was no room on the makeshift runway to get off the hard clay for fear of damaging the Aero Commander.

Arlow heard the *pop-pop-pop* of gunfire and decided his only course of action was to play out the game of chicken.

Less than two hundred feet away, the Skymaster jumped into the air and Arlow saw the landing gear retracting. Then the belly of the airplane flashed over his head as he stood on his toes to bring the DEA plane to a halt.

Arlow looked for a suitable place to turn the plane around. He saw a wider segment of the hard clay runway and began the process of making a U-turn. As he did, he saw Daniel Byrd running toward him.

Byrd grabbed the door handle and launched himself inside. "Do you have room for one more?" Byrd asked.

Arlow spoke through gritted teeth. "Close that door. We're in pursuit!"

Byrd muttered, "Smokey and the Bandit."

Arlow got the Aero Commander lined up and applied power. It was a powerful craft, but they were midway on the runway. The big twin-engine bird was gaining speed, but the available airstrip was running out.

Arlow focused on the instruments. "When I give the word, raise the gear," he said as he pointed at a lever.

Byrd nodded. "Are we going to make it?" Byrd asked.

Arlow glanced over. "It'll be close."

The plane bounced up and Arlow held the nose down to gain speed. "Gear up."

Byrd threw the lever up, then tightened his seat belt. He watched with concern as the trees ahead got closer and closer.

"Arlow?" Byrd said.

Arlow grimaced as he held the control yoke and kept the airplane in the air. "It's going to be close."

Slowly, the Aero Commander forced itself into the air. Arlow let out a long breath. Byrd did, too.

Arlow activated the mic on his headset as Byrd reached around and put another one on. "Flint 355 to Atlanta Center. Flint request immediate support."

The calm voice of the man sitting in Hampton, Georgia, came right back. "Atlanta Center to Flint 355. State your situation and your request."

"Were you able to paint the aircraft departing just in front of me?"

"Standby, Flint. I'll run back the tape." There was a pause from the controller. "I have your bogie, Flint. What can I do?" the controller came back.

"Keep me vectored to it, please," Arlow said into the mic.

Byrd then used the microphone on his walkie-talkie to let the ground team know what was going on. "GBI Eighty-nine is in the air with DEA. Our target appears to be headed south. Jamie, can you alert Region Thirteen to have agents headed to meet us at the farm? Tell them we have exigent circumstances and we're in hot pursuit."

"I'm clear. Keep us advised," Jamie replied.

Arlow looked to Byrd. Over the intercom, Arlow said, "Sounds like you know where he's headed."

Byrd nodded. "I've got a pretty good idea. A place in Bowens Mill."

Arlow shook his head. "Never heard of it."

"It's about two hundred and fifty miles from here, just northwest of the Okefenokee Swamp."

Then Arlow clicked over to a second radio. "Atlas, this is Flint 355."

The voice that responded was hollow and slightly garbled. "355?"

"Atlas, can you please alert Customs Air Support in Jacksonville? I am in pursuit of a bogie headed in their direction. Our ETA is less than two hours."

The voice on the end of the secure communications network asked, "Do you have a location?"

"Affirmative. The target is headed for Bowens Mill inside Georgia. Have Customs call me on the UHF guard channel when they get fifty miles out."

10:10 A.M.
SOUTH OF CEDARTOWN, GEORGIA

Omar was shaking. Adam had struggled into the front seat and was holding his abdomen, where blood flowed at an alarming rate. Adam scrambled around, trying to reach his backpack. "I need to get something on this wound or I'll bleed to death."

"Tell me what to do," Omar said, feeling terrified.

Adam spoke through gritted teeth, but the wind rushing in the window made it hard to understand him.

"What?" Omar asked.

Adam motioned with great effort at the backpack on the floor. Omar released his seat belt and stretched out to grab the pack from behind his seat. "I've got it," Omar said.

Adam was pale and sweating profusely. "Find the green pack with the red cross on it."

Omar set the autopilot for straight and level and focused on the task at hand. He found the green pack and unzipped it, finding the contents so tightly packed they spilled out in his lap. He immediately saw the green pack—coagulant powder—and opened the package with his teeth. Pulling up Adam's blood-soaked shirt, Omar shook the contents of the package out onto the wound.

"What do I do next?" Omar asked.

On the verge of unconsciousness, Adam's head rested against the seat, his eyes squeezed tight. "See if I have any more holes in me. We need to stop as much bleeding as possible."

Omar ripped the shirt up but couldn't see any more bullet wounds. "I don't see anything," Omar said.

Adam groaned. "Check my back. Don't worry if I pass out, it has to be done."

Omar leaned Adam forward. As soon as he did, Adam's eyes rolled back and he passed out. Omar gripped Adam's shirt and felt for dampness. Looking his hand over, Omar didn't see any more blood. He then manhandled Adam back into the seat and strapped him in.

Omar refocused on the task at hand, getting them to safety. He looked out of the cockpit and saw they were passing over I-20. He looked left and right, hoping to see a water tank with a city name on it. Then, there it was: "VILLA RICA" painted on a white tower to his right.

He grabbed a bloody chart from the floor, doing his best to wipe Adam's blood from it, then started figuring the heading he would need to get back to Bowens Mill.

12:02 P.M.
BOWENS MILL, GEORGIA

Omar flew the Skymaster straight onto the runway at the farm. He could see the sheriff department's cars and unmarked police cars near the hangar and in front of his father's house, but he had no other option—his fuel was almost exhausted and Adam hadn't moved in the last hour. Omar was sure he had stopped breathing.

As he let the airplane sink down, he saw a Blackhawk helicopter headed straight for him. The Blackhawk turned and came to a hover over the other end of the runway where Omar would end up. The dark green helicopter bore a gold band along the side reading "US CUSTOMS." Omar knew it didn't matter at this point.

Omar taxied up to the hangar. As he did, he saw the DEA Aero Commander taxi up behind him. Omar switched the airplane off and sat in his seat. He didn't know what else to do.

He heard the door of the Skymaster being ripped open and looked around to see a familiar face pointing a rifle at him. Omar stared at the man in surprise.

"You're Moody?" Omar asked.

"My therapist say's it's just how I express my anxiety," the man with the rifle replied. He could tell Omar didn't get the quip. "My real name is Byrd. I'm with the GBI."

12:10 P.M.
BOWENS MILL, GEORGIA

The farm looked like a three-ring circus. GBI agents crawled over the house, sheriff's deputies secured the airplane while stringing yellow tape around the area, and a med-evac helicopter had come to transport Adam Benjamin to a trauma center in Savannah. Omar had been placed into the back seat of a deputy's car and watched the proceedings sullenly.

SAC Gary Rothchild directed his agents as they searched for anyone who might have been in the house, the training center, or any of the other houses on the property.

Byrd was glum as he waited with Arlow to see if anyone was found. They sat on the front veranda as deputies and agents passed back and forth. An agent stopped by Byrd and said, "There's nothing much in the house. Just personal stuff."

Byrd look up. "What about his office?"

The agent shook his head. "Clean."

Byrd stood and walked inside as the agent and Arlow followed. Byrd headed directly to the bookcase and started pulling on books. After a couple of tries, he found the book that was attached. When he pulled on the copy of *The New Centurions*, the bookcase slid open. Byrd stepped in and saw secure phones, a safe, several rifles and pistols hanging on the wall, and a row of drawers with names on them.

Byrd counted twenty-four drawers labeled with male names, and around the same number with female names. Byrd pulled one out and passed Arlow a Canadian passport. Arlow examined the passport then passed it back to Byrd.

"Who is that? I've never heard of Miles Groulx," Arlow remarked.

"Me neither," said Byrd. "But the picture is Mitch Warren."

Byrd and Arlow left the agent to conduct a complete search of the hidden room. They walked back to the veranda to wait.

Arlow nudged Byrd. "What did they get in Cedartown?"

Byrd looked up. "Jamie called on the radio. They got about three hundred kilos of crystal meth. The guys in custody aren't talking, but they're going to be housed in the common jail of Polk County for quite a while. They've been charged with kidnapping the sheriff and trafficking meth. That should hold them for a while."

Arlow nodded. "What about the spook who lives in this house? Warren?"

"One of the agents inside told me it looks like he and the family dropped everything and hauled ass. He said there were half-full coffee cups on the table and the refrigerator door was standing open." Byrd dropped his head again.

Arlow tried to be upbeat. "We'll catch him, soon enough."

Byrd smiled. "That's not why I'm down."

"What is it then?"

Byrd stood and stretched. "I won't be working cases for a while. I'm the one who shot Adam Benjamin."

3:22 P.M.
FITZGERALD, GEORGIA

Daniel Byrd looked around the room he sat in. It was painted an ugly green that was not found in nature. In some places, it seemed the paint had been applied with a trowel. The cinder-block walls were bland and without accents or decorations. In other words, the Ben Hill County Jail was the same as most others.

Byrd laid his Miranda waiver form and his ID data form at his left and placed his pocket recorder front and center. He had everything the way he wanted when Omar was brought into the room.

Omar looked like a scared child when the deputy sat him in the chair across from Byrd. Byrd looked him over; the orange jumpsuit and the handcuffs made Omar look more vulnerable. But Omar was neither sullen nor defensive. He sat in the chair, looking scared, and listened to what Byrd had to say.

Byrd began by getting Omar's full name, date of birth, and home address. Omar seemed happy to talk. When Byrd read the Miranda form, Omar signed it without hesitation.

"You know that you're under arrest?" Byrd asked.

Omar nodded. "How is Adam?"

Byrd watched for a reaction. "He's going to make it. He was hurt pretty bad, but you did a good job keeping him alive till you got back to Bowens Mill, kid."

Omar shuffled around in the chair. "He's tough. I bet he'll be fine. Do you know how long I'll be in here?"

Byrd shrugged. "For a while. Your current charges are trafficking methamphetamine. The weight of the meth we got in the truck will put you on the top tier of charges. There won't be any bond, and you may be facing federal charges to boot."

Omar nodded again. "I should be getting out soon. My dad will be able to fix this."

Byrd laughed. "Your dad will be working miracles if he can fix this. Your buddy Adam tried to kill an agent."

Omar nodded. "Yeah. We were just trying to get away. Adam said it's easier if we get away on our own."

Byrd scowled. "I'm the agent Mr. Benjamin tried to kill."

Omar looked sincere. "I sure do hate that. Adam was just doing what he had to do. Nothing personal. He's a good man, just trying to do a job that has to be done."

Byrd raised his voice. "You think the fact they claim they are working for the government excuses the things that were done? You think your dad is a patriot?"

Omar met Byrd's stare. "My dad is a businessman. He sees me as an asset. That's all."

"Is that how he sees Adam? Just an asset?"

Omar squinted at Byrd.

Byrd leaned forward. "Son, your daddy is not getting you out of this mess. You're looking at spending the rest of your natural life in prison."

Omar shrugged, trying to look surer of himself than what he must have felt. Byrd could tell it was taking every bit of his resolve to hold it together. "We'll see."

Byrd leaned back in his chair. "Kid, the best thing you can do is tell me everything you did. Maybe I can get the district attorney to go lighter on you. Otherwise, you're fucked."

Omar rocked back and forth in the chair. "I can't give my family and friends up. I can't."

Byrd slammed his folder shut. "Okay, I guess there isn't anything more to talk about, kid."

Omar smiled. "Adam calls me kid."

CHAPTER 26
YOU AGAIN?

WEDNESDAY, FEBRUARY 16, 2005
9:05 A.M.
DECATUR, GEORGIA

Daniel Byrd sat slumped in the interview room chair. He felt good physically but was nervous about the interview coming up.

The routine for a GBI agent–involved shooting is that an office the agent is not associated with conducts a thorough investigation of any use of force. The case is then evaluated by the office supervisors and forwarded to the appropriate district attorney for review.

Since Byrd was involved in a shooting in Region 1, the Calhoun office's territory—Byrd was assigned to the Region 8 office in Gainesville, and he was detached to the Drug Enforcement Office—Director Hicks had assigned Inspector Robert Sullivan to investigate the shooting.

This development had Byrd worried. Even though Adam Benjamin had survived, Sullivan had a reputation as a shrewd investigator, deft at confrontational interviews, who marched to the letter of the GBI Policy and Directives Manual. A former Marine, Sullivan was tall, with tousled blond hair, a broad smile and a thick accent that was a holdover from his formative years in Boston.

"Agent Byrd, may I remind you of the GBI Use of Force Policy?" Sullivan asked.

Byrd sat up in the chair. "I think I have a pretty good idea what it says. Is there something specific?"

Sullivan leaned into Byrd's personal space. "How many shootings have you been involved in?"

Byrd leaned back again. "I've only been investigated for having shot one other person. That was ruled a good shoot."

Sullivan frowned and said, "You make it sound like there were other shootings that weren't investigated."

Byrd was defensive. "I've been shot at, but I've only returned fire twice in my life. This time and the last time, in Canton."

Sullivan stood and leaned against the wall of the small room. "But you understand my concern. Most agents in the GBI never pull their weapon. It's rare for an agent to use their weapon at all. Even more rare for it to happen more than once."

Byrd shook his head. "I did what was necessary under the circumstances. I won't back down when I'm being shot at."

Sullivan's face showed no emotion. He sat back down with his knee touching Byrd's. "And the GBI Policy? You know it's a violation of Policy to fire at a moving vehicle? Isn't that exactly what you did?"

Byrd shook his head. "No, sir. It is not!"

Sullivan examined the report in front of him. "I am reading the report the agents at the scene wrote and your investigative summary. What I see says you fired at a moving airplane."

Byrd dug his heals in. "That's not what it says. That's your interpretation."

"How could I interpret it any other way?"

Byrd placed both hands on the table and said, "It says

that I shot the man who was shooting at me. He happened to be in a moving vehicle. I didn't put him in there, but he ended up there. I only shot at the individual who was threatening the life of all the agents on that runway."

Sullivan raised his voice. "How do you justify shooting all those rounds? He was hit with the first couple of shots, wasn't he?"

"Damned if I know. All I know is, he was still a threat in my view until I knew for sure he was down." Byrd's voice was raised now.

Abruptly, Sullivan stood and walked out of the room.

Suddenly, Director Hicks walked into the room, and Byrd stood up.

"How's it going, Danny?"

Byrd smiled warily. "Good . . . I think."

Hicks smiled, too. "I know the investigation still has a couple of pieces left to be filled in before it is officially finished, according to Inspector Sullivan."

Byrd nodded.

"I just wanted to tell you, unofficially, you did a good job out there. Go home and get some rest."

Byrd laughed, a relieved laugh this time. "I sure could use a day or two. Thanks for the encouragement; it never hurts."

Hicks shook his hand. "The Inspector will be back in here in just a minute to give you the official word, but I wanted to speak to you before you got out of the building. Now I'm off to do one of those political jobs I hate to do. This one is especially loathsome."

"I'm sorry you have to do the baby-kissing and back-slapping part of the job. I'm sure it's no fun." Byrd tried to sound sympathetic.

Hicks nodded. "This one is worse than usual."

Byrd gave him a quizzical look.

"I'm headed over to see Linda Pelfrey sworn in as a judge of the Court of Appeals."

Byrd sat back down.

Hicks opened the door of the claustrophobic room. "You're welcome to join me," he said over his shoulder.

"Thanks, but I'm late for a colonoscopy," Byrd said.

Hicks laughed. "Assholes involved, either way," the Director said as he let the door close behind him.

MONDAY, FEBRUARY 20, 2005
9:25 A.M.
CANTON, GEORGIA

Daniel Byrd had been cleared to go back to work over a week ago. He was in his office in Canton when the phone on his desk rang.

"GBI, Agent Byrd."

"Danny, this is Jerry Mason. What are you doing this fine morning?"

"Paperwork. And not in nearly as good a mood as you. What gives?"

"Your friend, the new Judge on the Court of Appeals, is already paying dividends."

Byrd sat up at his desk. "What has she done now?"

Mason chuckled. "It's more what she didn't do. You remember our friend Brandon Fisher?"

"Yeah," Byrd grunted. "Her meth hookup."

"Allegedly," Mason said, enjoying himself. "Anyway, with her now on the bench in Atlanta, he got sentenced for all the crap we've thrown at him the last few years. Our new judge dropped the hammer on him."

"Wow! What did he get?" Byrd wondered.

"Twenty, do ten." Mason said—the shorthand for a twenty-year sentence, of which ten is to be served in prison. The remainder would be spent on probation.

Byrd groaned. "He'll be out in five."

Mason laughed. "More likely, he'll be out in three. But that's more than we've been able to get him in the past, Teddy."

"Doc must have told you about his nickname for me?" Byrd mumbled.

"Everybody in the northern third of the State knows your nickname! It could be worse."

"Yeah. Thanks, and thanks for the information."

"Anytime," Mason said as he broke the connection.

PART 3
ALL OVER BUT THE CRYING

CHAPTER 27
EVERYBODY HANGS OUT HERE

TUESDAY, MAY 3, 2005
3:17 P.M.
DAWSONVILLE, GEORGIA

Daniel Byrd stood looking at the remains of Otis Clifton.
The clearing in the trail where the body was found was
far enough away from the highway for the birds to be sing-
ing in the trees. Byrd had seen deer tracks as he had
walked in, led by Sheriff Chester Reagan. The trail led
from behind Otis's house out into the area known as
Dawson Forest, a 10,130-acre public-use forest southwest
of Dawsonville. Doc Farmer was the agent who usually
covered Dawson County but he was in the middle of a
murder trial in Union County.

The clearing was a fifteen-foot circle of worn ground.
Byrd saw signs that several beer cans had been discarded
nearby. Otis was found by his father, a stooped eighty-
three-year-old man who had worked as a laborer all his
life. The old man sat quietly, rocking back and forth on a
fallen tree. His face was the picture of sorrow.

The old man looked up at Byrd. "He didn't come get
me for my doctor's appointment. I came to check on him,
but he wasn't in the house. I decided to look down here

and found him like this. Someone has done killed him, for sure."

Byrd pulled his issued camera from its black bag. He began taking photographs of the scene and the surrounding area. Once he had taken photos from the trail he had followed in, Byrd made his way through the woods, always looking for disturbed leaves, until he was on the opposite side of the body.

Without concern for the sheriff, coroner, and two deputies who stood around the senior Clifton, Byrd photographed the scene from every angle he could conceive. Their presence at the crime scene would be forever recorded in the photo log of the criminal investigative file.

With a deep sigh, Byrd moved up to the body. Otis Clifton was hanging from a tree limb by a common fiber rope that had been weathered for some time. He was nude and the body was not yet cold or stiff. Byrd photographed the knot around Otis's neck. He photographed the tree limb above the body, over which the rope had been thrown. The limb had been worn over time, with bark twisted off and hanging loose.

Byrd began documenting the body as it hung in the clearing in the forest. Otis's hands hung straight down by his body, and his feet touched the ground. Byrd observed the elongation of the neck, common with death by hanging. Otis's face, hands, feet, and legs were a slight blue color. His eyes bulged from his face—Byrd was tall enough to see the petechial hemorrhaging—and his tongue protruded.

The most unusual observation was the object, which appeared to be a wooden leg from a small table, that protruded from Otis's rectum. The end of the wooden peg had long construction nails sticking out, bent at an angle so that they pierced Otis's buttock.

Next, Byrd took pictures of the ground beneath the body. He sighed again as he noted the worn area where Otis's feet had fluttered back and forth, trying to gain purchase and relieve the pressure the rope must have exerted on his throat. The feet, which now touched the ground as Otis's body settled, had worked hard trying to get relief before the oxygen deprivation had ended Otis's life.

Byrd then examined the wooden box near the feet. The box was less than a foot long on each side. He saw signs of wear on the top of the box and found disturbed ground where the box tilted and moved from under Otis's feet. There were signs that the box had tipped over, since it was now several inches away from the victim's feet.

Once Byrd felt he could move closer to the body, he examined the hands. There were remains of body lotion on the right hand. And he saw a bottle of lotion near the upended box.

Byrd finished his assessment of the scene, then motioned to the coroner. "You can cut him down now. But be sure not to cut through any of the knots," Byrd said.

Byrd walked over to Clifton Sr. "Sir, if you would like to, you can go back to the house and wait. There's no reason for you to stay here."

The old man looked up at Byrd through watery eyes. "My wife's been dead for twelve years. My son was my caregiver. Now, I got no one."

Byrd nodded. "I'm very sorry for your loss. We'll give your son dignity, as much as we can, while we determine what happened here."

As the old man tried to stand up from the log, he tipped backward. Byrd extended a hand and helped the old man to his feet. "Be careful on this trail, don't get hurt."

The man looked at Byrd, tears finally rolling down his

face. "I've walked these hills for most of my eighty-three years, son. I've seen good times and bad. I've lived through a lot, but for the life of me I can't fathom why someone would kill my boy like this."

Byrd patted Clifton's back as he began the trek to his son's home. "We'll figure this out."

Sheriff Reagan watched the man retreat. When he was sure it was safe to talk, he asked Byrd, "What do you make of all this? Who would murder a man like this?"

Byrd shook his head. "This is probably not a murder."

The sheriff looked doubtful. "We had figured someone did this to get him to tell where he has his money hid. Talk in the community was that he kept cash hidden in his house."

Byrd shrugged. "I won't know for sure till the pathologist finishes his job, but I'd be willing to bet this was an accident."

The sheriff's eyebrows shot up. "Accident?"

Byrd nodded. "Based on what I see here, Otis came out here pretty often. He could walk out here naked since there are no neighbors in sight. There aren't any clothes piled up out here."

Reagan looked around as Byrd pointed at the rope in the tree. "The rope up there has been here a while, and the tree limb has been worn down over time as the rope hung with weight on it. There are scabs and scars on his butt cheeks that tell me this is not the first time that thing with the nails has been in his ass. The lotion on his right hand is the last piece of the puzzle."

The sheriff stood looking at the body with new eyes. "You're saying he was out here masturbating?"

Byrd nodded. "He probably stood on that box and masturbated while he flexed his knees. The rope would tighten enough to get him where he wanted to be." Byrd pointed to the box and the ground around it. "When things got good for him, he probably was moving around and the box tipped over."

"Damn," the sheriff said.

Byrd pointed to the wear on the limb. "And like I said, this wasn't his first time."

"Double damn," the sheriff said.

Byrd sighed again. "He struggled for a little while. He could stand on his toes long enough to try to get the box back under him. But in the end, the oxygen flow gradually decreased, and he dropped. When his weight pulled the rope tight, it was all over."

The sheriff stood by Byrd, looking things over. Then he turned and asked, "Any chance you would go tell the family what you think?"

Byrd smiled. "Not a chance in hell."

The sheriff nodded and struck his jaw out. "I guess this part falls to me?"

Byrd nodded. "I work my side of the street; you work yours." Byrd looked the sheriff in the eye. "If it makes you feel any better, the old man knows."

"What?" the sheriff asked as he pushed his brown hat back on his head.

Byrd shrugged. "No way he would have looked this far in the woods unless he knew. Or at least suspected."

The sheriff was the one who sighed deeply. "I'll get his preacher out here to help me. He works in town at the service station. I don't want to do this alone."

Byrd squatted by Otis's feet to take closeup photos of the furrows the man's feet had worn. The sheriff turned and started back up the trail, the two deputies trailing behind him.

Byrd looked around the woods and suddenly felt very

tired. He looked at the coroner, a local funeral director who had been elected last year. "Is this job everything you hoped it would be?"

The other man shrugged and waited for Byrd to finish with the body.

WEDNESDAY, MAY 4, 2005
1:22 A.M.
DAWSONVILLE, GEORGIA

Daniel Byrd pulled his GBI car into a spot in the front of a twenty-four-hour country store near the square in Dawsonville. He switched the car off and took a deep breath. He needed more coffee for the rest of the drive home. Stepping out of the car, he took a moment to examine the inside of the brightly lit business.

Byrd saw the cashier behind the register looking relaxed and bored. Byrd noted a single customer standing near a coffee pot. Everything looked in order. Byrd's legs seemed heavy and stiff as he stepped up on the curb and pulled the glass door open. He checked each aisle as he angled toward the waiting coffee, relaxing as he noted the walkways were empty.

The lone customer looked up as Byrd walked toward him. For the first time, Byrd registered how big the man was. While he looked to be in his late seventies, the man was as big as a house. He stood at least six feet, six inches tall, and his shoulders were almost as wide as a door frame. He was dressed in wool slacks, a dress shirt, and a dark gray fedora.

Byrd made eye contact and nodded. He was suddenly uneasy as he approached the coffee pot.

"Are you Byrd?" The voice cracked like a whip.

Byrd froze, his right hand involuntarily sliding toward his handgun.

The man towered over Byrd. "Well, is that who you are?"

Byrd moved his feet apart. He tried to act casual as he glanced up at the man's face. "You have me at a disadvantage, sir."

The man stuck out his right hand. "The name is Chuck Page. I retired as a Squad Commander with the GBI."

Byrd immediately recognized the name. He grabbed Page's extended hand. Suddenly, Byrd's hand was crushed as the bigger man applied bone-breaking pressure.

Byrd worked his hand away and flexed his fingers. "Yes, sir. I've heard about you. They even warned me about shaking hands with you, but it slipped my mind. You headed the Smuggling Squad for the GBI back in the seventies and eighties, right?"

The big man nodded. He pointed toward a small table with chairs near the door. "Grab a cup of coffee and join me."

Byrd noted Page favored his right leg as he strode toward the chair with the best view of the front door. Byrd poured the dark coffee for himself and joined the bigger man.

Byrd sat uncomfortably and tried to angle his chair to get a clear view of the door for himself. Page smiled. "Don't worry, I've got your back."

Byrd didn't relax. "How do you know me?"

Page locked eyes with Byrd. "I'm a trained investigator, son."

Byrd nodded uncomfortably. He sipped his coffee as he watched the older man over the rim of the cup.

Page leaned back and smiled. "I'm just screwing with you. I spoke to our sheriff earlier and he said you were in town working a death. When I saw you pull up out front, I guessed who you were."

Byrd brushed his hair back from his forehead and said, "And here I thought I was a real hotshot."

Page laughed. "Hell, in some ways you are. I heard you're the first agent to catch a smuggling plane since I had to retire in ninety-four."

Byrd relaxed a little. "I got lucky."

Page leaned in. "All agents get lucky, son. But you have to *make* your luck. Hard work gets you lucky." Then Page frowned. "So, what have you heard about me?"

Byrd thought about it. "You were a hard charger during your days with the Bureau. Hired as an undercover agent the same year as Phil Peters."

Page sat up straighter. "Phil Peters was the best Director the Bureau ever had in my opinion."

"Your team worked all over the southeast. Your squad tailed a crew of smugglers from Miami to Chicago on one case," Byrd continued. "And that was when nobody had cell phones. You had to do everything either by radio or pay phone."

Page nodded but kept quiet.

Byrd resumed. "In 1988, you led a team in taking down a plane loaded to the gills with cocaine. The copilot didn't want to go to jail, so he turned a machine gun on your guys. One agent almost died. You took a round to the leg that almost took out your knee. After several surgeries, you took a medical retirement."

Page smiled broadly. "I zigged when I should have zagged. We got the load that night though. And killed the bastard who shot us up."

Byrd raised an eyebrow. "That was the last dope plane the GBI caught."

Page took a long sip of coffee. "Right—until your deal."

"Were you waiting on me?" Byrd asked.

Page shook his head. "No, I just have trouble sleeping some nights. This leg will throb and I toss and turn. I end up getting out of the house and coming down here. The only place in the county open twenty-four hours."

Byrd sat back. "Any advice for a young agent from a veteran?"

Page pushed his hat back. "You've proven you have the instincts. Listen to your gut, it seldom steers you wrong." The older man looked around the room despite being able to see that no one else had entered the store. "I heard a rumor that one of the three-letter agencies was up to their eyeballs in your case," Page said, almost whispering.

Byrd wiped both hands over his face. After taking a deep breath, Byrd leaned in and said, "You heard right. Did you hear which one?"

Page glanced around again. "The letters I heard started with a *CI* and ended with an *A*."

Byrd chuckled. "Did you ever run into them in one of your smuggling cases?"

Page nodded and pursed his lips. "Had a guy who was a legitimate machine-gun manufacturer. He smuggled guns south and brought dope north. We arrested him with a truckload of machine guns and the Alcohol, Tobacco, and Firearms guys took the case. We were told later that a US Attorney came down and ordered the guy released. He was never charged with the guns or the drugs we got."

Byrd's eyebrows shot up. "That sounds familiar. Were you able to ever get anything on him?"

Page squinted at Byrd. "He disappeared." Page looked around the room again. "But I did get the satisfaction of shooting his brother. He was the one in the plane who shot me."

Byrd laughed and shook his coffee cup. "Is there any chance you'd be willing to tell me the rest of the story?"

Page stretched his legs out, grunting as he got the pressure off his right knee, and got comfortable. Byrd didn't get home for another two hours.

WEDNESDAY, MAY 4, 2005
3:25 P.M.
CIUDAD JUÁREZ, CHIHUAHUA, MEXICO

Rojo smiled to himself as the special phone rang. He picked up the receiver for the device and listened as El Gordo watched.

"Señor Rojo, please?"

"I wondered if you would call," Rojo said.

Warren sounded chipper. "I have been rearranging my business assets. As you know, some of my most trusted people have been detained by our friends in law enforcement."

"And you lost a shipment of mine," Rojo reminded.

"Yes, we lost a shipment. We had a Judas in our midst. That will be addressed."

"And my shipment?" Rojo asked. "Will you be addressing that matter?"

Warren didn't miss a beat. "I am in negotiations to get your product back to your people in Atlanta. I may not be able to do it the way I did last time, which is not a concern of yours, but I may be able to get the drugs back."

"And your son? Can you get him released?"

"Also, in the works. I have made certain calls and expect to be able to work that out very soon." Warren continued into his sales pitch. "And in the process, we have learned many lessons. I plan to correct our mistakes and begin to deliver product for you on a larger scale very soon."

Rojo gave El Gordo a puzzled look. El Gordo, hearing both sides of the conversation, shrugged in response.

"I still need that service," Rojo replied. "Do you think you can deliver this time? You seem to be jinxed."

Warren chuckled. "Growing pains, we call them. I have a much larger airplane that can haul larger single loads. I will be working out the details in the next few weeks, but I plan to become your delivery service of choice."

"I admire your tenacity. I will wait to hear what the arrangements are."

"The final arrangements will require a few people I have in mind to coordinate on the El Paso end. Then I have people lined up in Atlanta to make the final delivery to you."

Rojo was intrigued. "Might I ask the capacity of the aircraft?"

"I'm not sure how much load the plane can hold, but I'm sure I can ship up to a ton of product in very short order."

Rojo was doubtful. "Will the police not take interest in such an airplane?"

Warren was curt. "That's one of the things I've figured out. I don't own the plane. It will be provided by a sub-contractor of sorts."

"Do you trust this contractor?" Rojo asked.

"They won't know what is in the shipment. They have so many packages being shipped, they'll barely note ours. I'm working with the US Postal Service."

WEDNESDAY, MAY 4, 2005
4:15 P.M.
EL PASO, TEXAS

Adeline Riley and Raelynn Michaels sat in the mini-van parked on the quiet city street. The car was turned off, and the inside was hot in the afternoon sun. In this corner of El Paso, in the shadow of the campus of the University of Texas, the two women in the van wouldn't warrant a second look. At least, that was their hope.

Adeline—"Addy" to her friends—was the senior investigator of the Texas DPS Narcotics Service. She had been assigned to the Narcotics Service after four years working the road as a trooper. She had been a narc for the last ten years but was new to the El Paso area. She sat slumped in the passenger seat of the van.

Raelynn Michaels, known as "Rae," was an El Paso County deputy and had worked in the narcotics unit for less than a year.

The two women had been watching the storage facility for several months, varying their schedules, hoping to catch someone accessing locker 33A. They were tenacious, because they had the word of Texas Ranger Clete Petterson that drugs had been stored in the locker.

Today, they had been watching for almost three hours.

Rae squirmed in the driver's seat. "We might as well pack it in. We lose air support in about twenty minutes."

Addy nodded. "I sure was hoping today would be the day."

Rae slammed her hands on the steering wheel. "I'm beginning to wonder if the bad guys have moved on us. We haven't seen anybody come or go in all the time we've watched."

Addy looked the street over. She was trying to decide if there was a vantage point to hang a camera when a truck with a camper shell pulled into the lot and parked in front of locker 33A.

"Son of a bitch!" Rae exclaimed. "Our patience has paid off."

Without saying a word, Addy stepped out onto the street. With the long limbs of a gymnast, she bounced as she walked down the street. Dressed in jeans and a sweat-shirt, with her long hair tucked into a ball cap, she planned to stride past the storage building, trying her best to get a look at what the truck was up to.

Rae, who was the stronger of the two and preferred CrossFit to ballet, had long curly blond hair and a dark sense of humor. She was content to be the team driver. She started the van and slumped lower in the seat as she called the DPS pilot waiting at the heliport on her phone.

"Eighty-one forty-nine to One-oh-four. We have action. How fast can you get in the air?"

"I'll be with you in less than five," came the crisp answer.

Rae held up her right hand with all five fingers waving when Addy glanced her way. Addy nodded and then stood by the fence, stretching and twisting.

Suddenly, Addy turned and jogged back toward the van. Rae pulled the van into drive and rolled toward her partner. The truck was coming out of the driveway as Addy dropped into the passenger seat.

Rae kept her eyes locked on the moving truck as she accelerated the undercover car. "Could you tell what they were up to?" she asked.

Addy shrugged. "They took a couple of big pieces of luggage out of the locker. I couldn't tell much about them, but both of the bags looked heavy."

Rae nodded, making a traffic light just in time to keep sight of the truck. "If they head to the border, it has to be money. Any other direction, then your guess is as good as mine."

"This close to the border, I'd go with money house," Addy said grimly.

Rae cut off a city bus as she tried to get closer to the truck, closing the gap. "Did you get a look at the license plate?" Rae asked.

Addy said, "Yep, 'State of Chihuahua.'"

Rae glanced over for the first time. "You think it's Rojo?"

Addy didn't answer.

Rae pressed the radio mic. "Eighty-one forty-nine to One-oh-four, we are turning onto North Mesa Street from Shadow Mountain."

"One-oh-four, I'm less than a minute out. Can you get me situated?"

Rae slumped lower as she talked. "We are in a white minivan traveling eastbound. The target is a red pickup with a camper. They are two cars in front of us. We're approaching a red ball at Festival."

"One-oh-four to Eighty-one forty-nine, I have you in sight. What's the plan?"

"If they go anywhere other than the border, we hang with them. If they go for the border, well, that will bring on more talk." Rae leaned into the console as the truck got a green light. "One-oh-four, we have a green ball. He is continuing southeast," Rae said.

Addy frowned at the phone. "I can't get Clete, so we'll just have to do the best we can," Addy said.

"One-oh-four has the eyeball," the pilot proclaimed.

Rae relaxed as the helicopter took the responsibility for following the car. "My money is on the Puente Libre," Rae used the common name for the Bridge of the Americas. The Bridge of the Americas includes two four-lane bridges for passenger vehicles, with two sidewalks for pedestrians. The bridge is one of four international points of entry connecting Ciudad Juárez and El Paso, and is the busiest port of entry in Texas.

Addy frowned. "We're too far away to be sure."

Rae glanced over. "We should call ahead to Customs and get a dog ready to run around that truck," she said.

Addy stared out the front windshield. "We'll see," Addy muttered.

The truck meandered through city streets, continuing southeast. Rae would keep the minivan parallel to the travel route, relying on the helicopter to keep the pickup in sight.

"He's turning east on I-110," the pilot called out.

Rae smiled. "Told you."

Addy made a decision. "Get ahead of him. We'll get to the Port of Entry and let Customs know what's coming their way."

"You got it!" Rae said as she pressed the accelerator. The minivan leaped forward, and Rae swerved left and right around slower cars.

"Do you have lights and siren in this thing?" Addy asked.

Rae shook her head. "The sheriff doesn't want us running around town in undercover cars with lights and siren."

Addy considered having the DPS helicopter pick her up but thought it would be too dramatic. It would be better if the truck appeared to be randomly diverted to secondary inspection.

Rae cut across two lanes of traffic to exit onto I-110, the move met with a chorus of honking horns. As soon as they made the turn onto I-110 leading into the Port, Addy knew they were in trouble.

The line of cars and trucks on the private side of the Port stretched back almost a mile. While the line of cars was daunting, Addy made the decision she was fit enough to jog to the Customs offices at the port. This effort would give them precious time to work out with the federal authorities how to handle the approaching truck.

Addy made sure her identification was tucked in her hip pocket and jumped out. As she slammed the door, she leaned in the window and said, "When the truck shows up, bumper lock it all the way to the border."

Rae gave her a thumbs-up.

WEDNESDAY, MAY 4, 2005
4:25 P.M.
CIUDAD JUÁREZ, CHIHUAHUA, MEXICO

Rojo paced the floor. He didn't know if he was more angry or concerned. The trouble with his oldest son had been brewing for months. Now, it seemed his son had decided to impress, or maybe just embarrass, his father.

He shouted at El Gordo. "Where is my son? I have told him, more than once, that money movements must be carefully planned."

El Gordo wrung his hands. "He did not tell me of his plan. I heard from one of the men who guard the house. He was bragging about making you look foolish for going to so much effort to move cash, when the border is so easy to cross coming back into Mexico."

"Did this man get an idea what the plan was?" Rojo asked.

El Gordo shook his head. "Only that it was a simple plan. I do know he enlisted the help of a man who repairs appliances in the Los Lagos neighborhood."

Rojo shook his head. "My son is a fool! Call his cell phone and tell him he must get back here right away."

El Gordo dialed the number by heart. He waited as the phone rang again and again. No answer.

WEDNESDAY, MAY 4, 2005
6:05 P.M.
BRIDGE OF THE AMERICAS PORT OF ENTRY, EL PASO, TEXAS

Pequeño Rojo was jubilant. He and the peasant were about to bring two million US dollars across the border without a hitch. He slumped in the passenger seat of the old truck and waited as the driver pulled into the long line of vehicles waiting to cross. They had chosen the port because it is the busiest in Texas.

The old man driving seemed unaware of the importance of the mission. Pequeño Rojo had told him the suitcases contained clothes his family could have for simply helping Pequeño Rojo clean out the place he had rented. The old man wasn't nervous, the one tell-tale sign border police look for. All the two men in the truck had to do was wait out the traffic.

Pequeño Rojo wished he had his cell phone on him, but he knew the police on the US side could track phones somehow. He wasn't going to mess this up. But it would sure be nice to call his father and brag of his success.

Addy Riley was struggling more than she had anticipated. The altitude made for thin air, but she jogged most
every day at the university track. It was the noxious fumes
from the mile of cars and trucks that made the trip difficult.

She ran through an underpass and saw the porticos
used to inspect cars and trucks headed into Mexico. To her
right she could see the line of big trucks waiting to be
cleared to exit the country. *Funny,* she thought, *I've been
around El Paso for a few years and never paid any attention to
the area around the bridge.*

She was sweating and coughing when she got to the
pedestrian entry into Mexico. She had guessed she could
get the attention of one of the blue-uniformed Customs
and Border Protection offices there. The Port of Entry was
a beehive of activity. CBP agents walked among the cars
waiting to leave the US, taking time to peer into each one.
Others were walking dogs beside the lanes of traffic, while
others were checking the identification of each person.

She put both hands on her knees to catch her breath before she approached one of the CBP agents checking IDs.
She held out her credentials with the silver circular badge
bearing the outline of Texas.

The CBP agent extended her hand in front of a family
waiting to walk into Mexico. She addressed Addy. "What's
the problem?"

"I'm with the Regional Narcotics Task Force. My partner and I are following a truck we think is about to bring

a couple of suitcases of cash across here. We need your help."

The CBP agent relayed the information to her supervisor and seconds later Addy saw several CBP agents carrying slung machine guns headed her way.

The CBP agent she had approached pointed. "That's our response team. They'll be able to help you."

Addy said, "Thanks," then turned to meet the blue-uniformed contingent.

A compact Hispanic man whose name tag read "SAENZ" extended his hand. "May I see your identification?"

Addy passed her ID to the man, who examined it carefully and handed it back. "Do you have a description or any other information on this truck you are looking for?"

Addy smiled. "We're not looking for it. My partner is behind the truck, and we have a DPS helicopter riding herd. We watched them make a pickup on the US side."

Saenz frowned. "Why do you think this truck is up to no good?"

Addy threw her trump card. "We have connected the location they were seen at with Rojo."

Saenz's eyebrows shot up. "Rojo! You have my interest."

"We watched them load two large suitcases into the back of the truck. I figure it's either dope or money," Addy said. "And nobody smuggles dope back into Mexico."

Saenz nodded. "You've got me there. Can you communicate with your partner?"

Addy nodded. "I'll call her right now." She opened her flip phone and dialed the number.

WEDNESDAY, MAY 4, 2005
6:15 P.M.
BRIDGE OF THE AMERICAS PORT OF ENTRY, EL PASO, TEXAS

El Paso County drug investigator Rae Michaels was breathing as hard as her partner. She had been nervous about missing the truck, but the air unit put her right in behind it. Now she pulled as close to the rear of the truck as she could get. She had no intentions of some hothead cutting in front of her to get closer to the head of the line.

She could see the driver in his left-side mirror, and he looked cool as a cucumber. The passenger was slumped against the door.

Rae was biting her lip when her cell phone rang.

"Yo," Rae said.

She heard Addy on the line. "Rae, when you get to the first inspection station, hit your four-way flashers and honk your horn like a crazy lady."

"Can do," Rae responded. "We've still got a few minutes to go."

"Okay," Addy replied. "When the inspector stops the truck, pull right up to his back bumper, then get out and meet me over by the offices. The CBP will motion them into secondary, but they aren't taking any chances. Their Response Team will be close by and if anything goes wrong, they plan to do a full felony takedown."

Rae's pulse raced and her breathing became more ragged. "I love this stuff," Rae said aloud as she crept closer to the Port of Entry.

CHAPTER 28
CROSSING OVER

WEDNESDAY, MAY 4, 2005
6:17 P.M.
BRIDGE OF THE AMERICAS PORT OF ENTRY, EL PASO, TEXAS

Supervisory CBP Officer Raul Saenz had no intentions of sending one of his men up to the door of the truck. He was going to lead from the front. Just a couple of minutes ago, the DPS drug investigator had pointed out the target truck.

Saenz waited with his arms crossed over his chest, partly to conceal his rapid shallow breathing. As the truck pulled up to the inspection station, he heard the horn of the minivan and saw the lights flashing. *Showtime*, Saenz thought.

He stepped to the window and leaned down. What he saw was not what he expected. The driver was an old man, who seemed calm as the federal official leaned into his window. "May I see your identification please?"

The driver had his Mexican passport in his hand. Saenz looked to the passenger, who was feigning sleep. Saenz took the offered passport from the driver and then said, "I need the information from your passenger also."

Without waking his companion, the old man pulled another Mexican passport from the seat and handed it across.

Saenz looked at both passports and the names meant nothing to him. But when he examined the passenger's paperwork, he recognized the face from a briefing he had attended only a month ago.

He casually walked away from the truck, leaving another officer to stand guard. He motioned to the Response Team members. "The man on the passenger side is Pequeño Rojo, the top man's oldest son. We need to be careful with this one."

The men wore grim faces as they fanned out around the truck.

WEDNESDAY, MAY 4, 2005
6:18 P.M.
BRIDGE OF THE AMERICAS PORT OF ENTRY, EL PASO, TEXAS

Pequeño Rojo watched the mirror as he tried his best to look asleep. When they had stopped for the obligatory inspection, he remained still. He had watched with disdain as the curly-haired American woman started flashing her lights and honking her horn. Then she jumped from her van and ran into the federal office. Some Yankee who couldn't control her bladder.

When the man in the blue uniform asked for their identification, he had kept quiet. But when the man in uniform walked away from the window, Pequeño Rojo went on alert. He couldn't put his finger on it, but something was going on.

He wrapped his fingers around the butt of the Colt automatic he had stashed under the seat. When the uniformed American asked them to step out of the truck, Pequeño Rojo knew things were crashing around him. He flung the door open and looked for a route to the pedestrian bridge. He held the pistol low as he crouched by the truck.

"Gun!" one of the Response Team members shouted.

Several members of the Response Team shouted, "¡Policía! ¡Suelta la pistola!"

Pequeño Rojo turned to the shouts of the Response Team members and as he did, the gun swung around with him. The CBP officer standing behind the door fired three shots from his .45 caliber pistol, each striking the young man in the center of his chest.

Pequeño Rojo fell to the pavement, barely aware of the activity around him.

WEDNESDAY, MAY 4, 2005
6:19 P.M.
BRIDGE OF THE AMERICAS PORT OF ENTRY, EL PASO, TEXAS

Addy was on the phone with the county 911 center before Pequeño Rojo had stopped rolling on the ground. She gave the operator the particulars and asked for an ambulance.

Then she dialed Clete Petterson's desk. This time he answered the phone.

"Ranger Petterson."

"This is Addy Riley. You need to get down to the Bridge of the Americas. We just followed Pequeño Rojo from that storage building you put us on to."

Clete leaned back in his chair. "Did CBP get anything?"

Addy tried to sound calm. "They just killed him. He pulled a gun on one of the CPB guys and they shot him on the bridge."

"On my way," Clete said as he hung up the phone.

WEDNESDAY, MAY 4, 2005
7:33 P.M.
BRIDGE OF THE AMERICAS PORT OF ENTRY, EL PASO, TEXAS

Clete Petterson strode toward the taped-off crime scene. The Customs agents were clumped together in groups, awaiting the arrival of the FBI. Cars and trucks headed into Mexico were being diverted around the body under the white sheet with blood around it.

Addy Riley and Rae Michaels were in the shade near the office doors of the Port of Entry. Each was holding a heavy piece of luggage. They looked like they were running away from home.

Clete joined the narcs. "Ladies, can you fill me in?"

Addy nodded. "Sure, Ranger."

"Call me Clete."

"Sure, we'll lay everything out for you. First, can we get these bags inside and open them up? CBP has turned them over to us without opening them up."

Clete was surprised. "They aren't interested in the contents?"

Addy shook her head. "It's our case, so they gave everything to us. And they are expecting us to charge the driver, too."

"Driver?" Clete asked.

Rae interjected, "Some poor schmuck who does appliance repairs at a big box store on the Mex side. The kid told him the bags were full of clothes that Little Red needed to get rid of. The old man didn't have a clue what he was doing."

Clete pointed to the bags. "Has anyone opened these?"

Both drug investigators shook their head. Clete pointed to the offices. "Let's see if we can get a room with a camera. We'll make sure every step is recorded. I know everything outside here is recorded."

"Good idea," Addy said.

Clete nodded. "Major Crosby is on the way here. He's over this region for the rangers."

"The more eyes the better," Addy said.

Clete went into the offices and a CBP agent helped him locate an interview room they could use to inventory the money and interview the driver. By the time he had completed arranging for a place to work, Major Stetson Crosby was standing with the two drug investigators.

The Texas Ranger Major's slacks and shirt were pressed with razor-edge creases. His white hat was shaped to suit his long face and sat on steel gray hair. His piercing blue eyes took in everything at once. Even other rangers thought of him as the embodiment of the Texas Rangers.

When Crosby saw Clete coming out of the CBP offices, he broke into a broad grin. "Sounds like we might have made a good hit on our old friend Red."

Clete pointed to the drug investigators. "These young drug investigators are the ones who did the work, I just put them on a lead. Have y'all met?" Clete introduced Addy and Rae to the highest-ranking ranger west of Austin.

"Major, thanks for coming out," Addy said. "It never hurts to have someone with rank on the scene. By the time we pass things up our food chain, it can get all jumbled up."

Stetson laughed as he pushed his cowboy hat back. "Well, at least I'll do something for the good of the order today."

Clete pointed to the door. "Let's get these bags, and ourselves, inside."

The group moved into the room Clete had arranged, the drug investigators muscling the bags onto the interview table.

Major Crosby took the lead. "Clete, let's open one bag at a time and deal with the contents."

Clete stepped up to the table and turned a sky-blue suitcase around so the latch faced him. He clicked the latches and opened the case. He was shocked to see brand new women's lingerie crammed in the bag.

Clete looked around the room. Major Crosby looked disappointed, but the two drug investigators were crushed. Clete dug into the mass of thongs, lacy bras and bustiers. He held a handful up for the others to see.

Once he got below the top layer, he found what he was looking for. The next layer was made up of stacks of US twenties and hundreds. The cash filled the suitcase. Clete pulled up a stack of hundred-dollar bills and tossed it to Addy.

"This might fit you," Clete said. Addy blushed then looked at the bundle she had caught.

Her face lit up. "Wow. I thought that kid had died for some trashy lingerie."

Major Crosby blushed, too. "Ranger, I'm going to pretend you didn't do what you just did. And I apologize to you ladies."

Rae spoke up. "We quit being ladies when we became narcs. Ladies don't fish drugs out of a woman's 'prison wallet.'" Crosby blushed again at the reference to hiding drugs in a vagina.

"I see your point," Crosby said, chuckling reluctantly.

When the other suitcase was opened, they found the same contents. Using the CBP's money counter—the same type banks utilized—the final count was $2,566,220.

The law officers completed their paperwork as quickly as possible before taking the cash to the evidence locker in the ranger's offices.

As the officers left the building, exhausted from the long day, Addy looked toward Clete and said, "Interested in a celebratory drink with us, Ranger?"

Clete stopped walking. "Thanks, but I don't think that's a good idea."

Rae spoke up. "Are you worried about being out on the town with two wild women? It could be fun."

Clete shook his head. "Ladies, I'm honored that you would invite me, but there's a trooper waiting at my house who will be miffed if I come home any later than I already will be."

"Trooper?" Addy asked.

Clete nodded. "I'm engaged to Montana Worley, a trooper here in El Paso."

Addy pursed her lips. "Of course, I know her. I guess she's off the road now, after the shootout?"

Clete smiled and said, "She can't wait to get back on the road. She's tough."

The narcs walked back to their minivan. As she hit the unlock button, Rae said, "Well, when I got up this morning, I didn't expect our day to go this way."

WEDNESDAY, MAY 4, 2005
8:10 P.M.
BRIDGE OF THE AMERICAS PORT OF ENTRY, EL PASO, TEXAS

The young girl was dressed modestly. She was barely sixteen and looked it. Her appearance was neat but conservative and she kept her eyes down as the blue-uniformed men of the border checked her identity card perfunctorily and waved her on.

The agents of the CBP knew her well. She, like over two thousand Mexican citizens her age, crossed the border to attend high school. Then she worked at a café until it was time to walk back home. Each school day was the same for her: the long walk across the border and then to the school, hours of studies, then to the café for an afternoon of cleaning tables and washing dishes, and finally, the walk back home.

Each day she met the little man on the way from home to the bridge. He would load the bag that hung from her hips with half a kilo of meth, never touching her or looking in any inappropriate way. And each day before she left the café, another man of equal courtesy would load American cash into her bag. Her education, something her family could never afford, was paid for by Rojo. And he also paid for information.

She was anxious to get over the bridge to give the man she would meet the news of Pequeño Rojo's death. There would be a cash bonus for this. And her description of the big Texas Ranger would be worth even more.

WEDNESDAY, MAY 4, 2005
11:59 P.M.
CANTON, GEORGIA

Byrd sat up in bed abruptly. The phone ringing always did that to him. He fumbled in the dark and grabbed the receiver.

"Byrd."

"Daniel, this is Clete Peterson. How are you doing?"

Byrd glanced at the clock by the bed. "I was asleep. What time is it in Texas?"

"Sorry. It's almost ten here. I forgot the time difference."

Byrd clicked on a light and found his notepad. "It's okay," Byrd said. "I had to get up to answer the phone."

Clete chuckled. "Next time I see you, I'll buy you dinner."

Byrd wasn't amused. "We've never met. I think we'll have to get you and Montana subpoenaed out here to ever meet you."

Clete said, "Have you gotten a commitment from your federal prosecutor to go after everything at once?"

Byrd sighed. "We have an Assistant US Attorney here in Gainesville. I gave him a brief of the investigation over the phone and then I delivered a copy of the file to their office. They are trying to decide if there is a nexus to the border. That's their new way of avoiding drug charges."

"Why would they want to avoid drug charges? That's all the US Attorney's office in El Paso does. That and immigration cases."

Byrd sounded tired. "I may get a chance to meet you anyway. If they do decide to prosecute, they want someone to verify the route that Omar flew from Mexico to Georgia."

"The FAA tracks aren't good enough?"

"They insist, if we go to trial, they'll need someone to be able to testify to the area, the airports and their proximity, and the airport that exists in Mexico."

Clete grunted. "They've never heard of Google Earth?"

Byrd wiped his face. "What's that?"

"CNN used it to follow the invasion of Iraq. It's like a giant photographic map you can move around on. You can also zoom in on terrain and urban areas. It's not real-time, but it shows every structure and mountain the satellite picture can see."

"Wow. I wonder if our office computer can get that. I think it would be pretty easy to find the airport in Mexico. The way it was described, it must be right across the border," Byrd said.

"Good idea. I'll take a look tomorrow. We have the program on one of our office desktops. I can print the pictures out and fax them to you. But that's not why I called you," Clete said, sounding somber.

"What's up?"

"Rojo is a guy in Mexico. We think he ran those loads. His real name is Vincente Acosta-Hernandez."

Byrd was making notes. "Sure, you mentioned him to me earlier. We compared some of his phone tolls to the ones from Warren's farm. I'd like to bring him into federal court on this case." A federal prosecution would wrap all the players into one trial, regardless of state and national boundaries.

"We had a major event tonight. I'm not sure if it helps or hurts our case, but there will be ripples on both sides of the border. I know that for a fact," Clete said with emphasis.

"Does it have to do with the attempt on Montana?" Byrd asked.

Clete sighed. "I hadn't thought about that." Clete paused. Then he said, "Did I tell you our Intelligence Service got word that Rojo's son put out a hit on Montana?"

"You hinted that it went back to Rojo's group, I remember that," Byrd said.

"Well, today I had a couple of drug investigators do surveillance on the storage facility that I saw the load originate from when Montana saw the airplane cross the border. I just wanted to see if we could identify anybody coming and going."

"Good idea. Did they see anything?"

Clete said, "Yep. A couple of guys showed up in a van with a Mexican license plate. A young guy went into the storage building and came out with two suitcases. Big suitcases."

"Meth?" Byrd asked.

"At the time, we didn't know. The investigators got on their tail and followed them to the busiest port of entry in Texas. They figured it sounded like money instead of drugs."

"Makes sense," Byrd said.

"So, the investigators alerted CBP. The long and short of it is that Rojo's son, Pequeño Rojo, was in the van. When CBP directed them to secondary, Pequeño Rojo came out with a gun. A CBP tactical team put him down," Clete said.

"Is he still alive?" Byrd asked.

"He took it hard. He didn't live to get off the bridge," Clete said. "The bags had two million in US dollars in them."

"Holy smokes. Between the money and the son, I guess Mr. Rojo is riled up," Byrd commented.

"Montana is on edge anyway but you're right, this could cause them to make another attempt on her."

"That'd be a big jump, wouldn't it? I thought the dad was more careful of stirring things up on the US side," Byrd said.

Clete paused. "I guess we'll have to ramp up security here at the house for a while."

Byrd understood. "We'll help any way we can. And if she wants to come back to Georgia to visit family, I'll make sure she gets a detail to cover her."

Clete muttered, "You know her. She won't turn tail, even to see family."

Byrd said, "Let me know what I can do on this end."

"Will do. And let me know what your US Attorney says," Clete said before he hung up.

Byrd crawled out of bed and finished making notes on the conversation. Then he took a shot glass and filled it with vodka.

CHAPTER 29
THE WHEELS OF JUSTICE GRIND

Daniel Byrd hung up the phone, wanting to slam it into the cradle until both were smashed into an unrecognizable heap.

He stomped into SAC Tina Blackwell's office. She looked up, surprised at the look on Byrd's face.

"You are not going to believe this shit!" Byrd said.

Tina sat back and waited.

"The Feds never cease to amaze me! The United States Attorney for the Northern District of Georgia has declined to prosecute Warren and company. He says that the Department of Justice lawyers in DC think we can't prove the drugs came from Mexico, so there is no need for the federal government to prosecute the case."

Tina tried to be the voice of reason. "Can we do it in Superior Court here in Georgia? Would Cherokee County or Polk County take the case?"

Byrd nodded. "Paulding would be all over the kidnapping of the sheriff, and Cherokee would take the drug case, but neither one could scoop up everyone involved."

"What about RICO?" Tina asked. The Racketeer Influenced and Corrupt Organizations law had been enacted in Georgia in the 1970s to fight criminal organizations.

Byrd shook his head. "There's no way any of the prosecutors would go after the organizations in Texas or Mexico."

"Let me put in a call to the Director. He might be able to apply some pressure," Tina offered. "In the meantime, why don't you see if the folks in Texas can try the US Attorney over there?"

Byrd nodded. "Maybe that will work. It's worth a phone call."

FRIDAY, MAY 6, 2005
2:17 P.M.
EL PASO, TEXAS

The United States District Court for the Western District of Texas is headquartered in San Antonio, with divisions in Austin, Del Rio, El Paso, Midland, Pecos, and Waco. This district covers over ninety-two thousand square miles and seven divisions, and serves to provide justice for violations of federal law in the broad area.

The federal district courthouse in El Paso is downtown, surrounded by the El Paso County courthouse, other county and city buildings, and the Immaculate Conception Church. The outside of the five-story building is limestone separated by windows with the solid look and ornate features expected in a building where justice is dispensed. The exception was the south lobby, where Clete Petterson and Stetson Crosby stood, waiting to be passed through by US marshals.

When they got to the magnetometers, manned by the "blue coats" — the name given to contract guards who provide security in federal courthouses. The name came from the cheap blue sports coats they wore over cheaper gray slacks—from the US marshal's office, they secured their weapons in lockers. They were directed to the courtroom where the Chief Assistant US Attorney was trying a case. He had asked them to meet him there.

When the two rangers, hats in hand, quietly eased into the courtroom, even the judge stared. They found a bench in the back and took a seat. They settled back and waited for a break in the trial.

They watched with interest as a banty rooster of a man argued a point of law with the judge. He was dressed in a suit that was probably bought in a secondhand store based on the fit. Clete guessed he was barely five-six in height, and was thin as a fence post. But his voice was as loud as a foghorn as he explained the case law he said was the foundation of his argument. Once the government attorney finished his argument, the judge called a recess. He told the defense attorney to come back this afternoon with his interpretation of the law, saying he planned to rule once he had heard from both sides.

In the corner of the courtroom, a US marshal blue coat called for everyone to stand as the judge left the bench.

The banty rooster saw the rangers, gathered his binder of notes and copies of court decisions, and made his way to the back bench. "Gentleman, I'm Douglas Hogan, Chief AUSA for this Division." The men shook hands. Hogan looked at the gold star on Crosby's chest. "Texas Rangers, and a major, no less. How can I help you?"

"We have a joint investigation we have been working," Clete began.

Hogan interrupted, "Are you working with DEA or FBI?"

"GBI," Clete said.

"What is that?" Hogan asked.

Clete grinned sheepishly. "The Georgia Bureau of Investigation."

Hogan smiled. "That will satisfy the need for some interstate aspect to the case. Is it drugs or people?"

Major Crosby spoke up. "Mostly drugs. We stumbled onto a group flying drugs from here to the Atlanta area."

"Is this the case Addy Riley is involved in?" Hogan asked.

Clete couldn't hide his surprise. "You know her?"

Hogan nodded. "We have a case she'll be presenting to a grand jury next month. I called her early this morning to ask a couple of questions and she gave me a thumbnail of what went down at the Port of Entry. I'll be more than happy to grab hold of a case involving the infamous Rojo. He's been a thorn in our sides for as long as I've worked here."

Clete let out a sigh of relief. "That's great news. We appreciate you working with us."

Hogan frowned. "Is there something I'm missing in all this?"

Clete wondered if this question would come up. "The GBI presented the case to the US Attorney's Office in Atlanta but they said the case was too weak because the government couldn't prove the drugs came from Mexico, even though the GBI folks have copies of an FAA radar track that takes the airplane from a runway in Mexico to Georgia."

Hogan shrugged. "Atlanta has a reputation of cherry-picking cases. Is there anything else?"

Clete looked around before he answered the question. He almost whispered when he said, "The group has ties to the CIA and the NSA."

Hogan laughed. "That's not a problem for me. When I was in the Army, I was assigned to the Defense Intelligence Agency. The only people who've lied to me more than the FBI is the CIA."

Stetson Crosby laughed. "You tell it like you see it. I'm glad to hear that there are folks in places of influence who see the FBI for what they are." Crosby paused, and then added, "I helped work the crime scene after the fire in Waco."

Hogan squinted. "Sorry. I can only imagine how hard that was."

Crosby just nodded and looked away.

Clete broke the awkward silence. "I take it the involvement of the US Intelligence Community is not an impediment for you?"

It was Hogan's turn to look around the room. "I met Addy a few years ago when I was still assigned to San Antonio. She was working as a narc assigned to Eagle Pass."

"I knew she had been a narc for a few years," Clete said.

Hogan nodded. "A good one, too. And I guess you know what BORTAC is?"

Clete nodded. "Sure, the Border Patrol Tactical Teams."

Hogan nodded. "The team for that sector was doing a training day at a farm on the border. The landowner was fed up with illegals coming across at night and stomping all over his crops, so the Border Patrol figured they could appease him by running training on his land."

Clete and Stetson nodded. They understood as well as anyone the politics and practicalities of the border.

"Addy and a couple of other narcs were recruited to be the bad guys for the exercise. It was a 'no live weapons' exercise. Everyone on the scene was toting empty weapons."

Clete didn't like where the story was headed.

Hogan continued. "Addy stumbled onto an actual group of people getting ready to run some guns into Mexico. She knew it wasn't part of the training scenario so she drew down on them. Held the whole crew at gunpoint until BORTAC realized what was happening and ran to back her up."

Hogan gathered up his materials. "None of the good guys had a single bullet between them. That woman held four armed men, alone, until the team got there. That's some western stuff, right there."

Crosby spoke up. "She sounds like ranger material."

"I met her when we prosecuted the men. They were all associated with the CIA. We convicted them, but the Department of Justice got them released on a writ. In the interest of 'national security.' All I can say is I did my part."

Crosby said, "That's all we ask."

Hogan started to step away, and then turned back. "Addy was a real hard nose on that case. She made it easier for me to push for a conviction, even though I guessed all along that Washington would intercede."

Clete smiled. "Sounds like Investigator Riley is quite a cop."

FRIDAY, MAY 6, 2005
10:02 P.M.
CIUDAD JUÁREZ, CHIHUAHUA, MEXICO

The old man hung from a rafter in the five-car garage. One of Pequeño Rojo's cars had been backed out to make some room.

The five ugly men had come to his appliance repair

shop with rifles slung on their shoulders. They had come in with such a sense of entitlement and power that the old man had been frozen in place. He barely reacted when the men pointed the rifles at him and told him he must come with them. He stood very still, his mouth hung open.

The leader, who looked to be barely out of his teens, brought his gun barrel close to the old man's face and thrust it almost into his mouth. The man-child threatened to rape the old man's wife and any daughters he might have. Had the young thugs done their homework, they would have easily found that he was a childless widower.

After another nudge with the rifle barrel, he walked toward the door of his shop, stopping absentmindedly to lock it before the men shoved him into the street.

They forced him into the back seat of a dusty SUV and drove him to the home of Rojo. Recognizing the big house, he knew his own death was near. He met the idea with resignation and maybe a little relief.

He hung by his arms, tied and pulled up almost to the ceiling on a pully, his toes just barely touching the floor. He had lost all feeling in his hands and arms some time ago. Now, he simply hung his head and waited for the end.

When he heard footsteps, he wasn't sure where they came from. Out of the corner of his eye he saw someone he knew, beyond doubt, was Rojo. The formidable man walked in front of the old man and looked him over.

Rojo was followed closely by the group of young thugs who had stolen him from his business. They formed an arc in front of the suspended man.

Rojo stepped close. "Do you know who I am?"

The old man nodded.

"And do you know why you are here?"

To this question, the old man shook his head.

Rojo pulled an aluminum baseball bat from behind his back and hit the old man sharply in the abdomen, breaking ribs in the process. The old man winced and cried out. "You drove my son to his death. Do you know that?"

"I did what he asked me. Nothing more." The old man's mouth was dry, the words a croak.

The bat swung again. This time, the blow landed on the old man's right shoulder, narrowly missing his head. "You did what he asked?" Rojo shouted. "That is your excuse?"

"No excuse, patron. No excuse."

The bat swung yet again. This time, the barrel of aluminum came up from the floor and slammed into the old man's crotch. The man cried out in pain, then hung quietly.

Rojo's face was red with rage. "Do you have anything to say to me? Can you say anything that will make up for the loss of my son?"

The old man started to mumble words. Rojo leaned in to try and decipher the declaration. At first, the sound was a jumble of guttural noises. Then he made out what the old man was saying. *"Perdóna nuestras ofensas como nosotros perdonamos a los que nos ofenden."*

Recognizing the Lord's Prayer, Rojo flew into a rage. He swung the bat again and again. The man continued to mumble as his blood formed a pool at his feet.

After a dozen swings, Rojo finally stopped and inhaled deeply as he stood in the old man's blood. Rojo put both hands on his knees, breathing hard, and the old man took his last breath.

SATURDAY, MAY 7, 2005
11:15 A.M.
CEDARTOWN, GEORGIA

The Polk County Jail opened for inmate visitation promptly at eleven a.m., and the line of mothers with children, girlfriends, and friends extended into the parking lot. Saturdays were also the day to put money on the inmates' books, which allowed the incarcerated to purchase snacks and other "premium" items. The line moved quickly, as the deputies knew most of the visitors and most of the people in line knew the protocols for visitors.

The stranger in the line was better dressed than most. He wore khaki pants and a golf shirt and had a vague military bearing. The man waited patiently for his turn, then asked to visit with Omar Warren.

The deputy who signed him into the jail would be hard-pressed to describe the man later, as he was later asked to do. He would only recall the man as "average."

The man was escorted to the wall of booths with thick glass and a telephone receiver. When Omar was taken to the seat opposite the man, Omar looked confused.

The man pointed to the receiver and motioned for Omar to pick it up. Once the connection was made, the man said, "All these calls are recorded. Do you understand that?"

Omar nodded. "Sure. But I don't know you. Are you here for my lawyer?'

The man shook his head. He talked as he unfolded a neatly typed message. "I'm here for your dad. He is working to get you released. He thinks he will know something in the next month. He wants to know if you need anything."

As he watched Omar, the man held up the typed message. Omar read the words.

> *You will be transferred to Federal Custody. Do not worry. Speak to no one about your case or what is happening. Your charges will go away within one month. Don't lose hope. Your mom and I love you.*

Omar almost cried when he read the message. The man looked away for a moment, until Omar was back in control of his emotions.

"Thanks," Omar said into the intercom. "The money that's been showing up on my books has been a big help."

The man nodded as he balled up the paper and tucked it into his pocket. "In our business, people sometimes end up in jail. You're lucky to be in an American jail. I spent a couple of years locked up in Venezuela."

Omar's eyes grew wide. "I guess I am lucky. Tell my dad thanks for me."

The man nodded. "The worst is over. Tight lips and head up. Understand?"

Omar looked determined. "Got it!"

The man stood to leave. Omar wasn't sure what to do, so he touched the glass with his index finger. The man touched the other side with an open palm, then made his way back to his rental car.

CHAPTER 30
SUMMER VACATION PLAN?

MONDAY, MAY 23, 2005
9:07 A.M.
ATLANTA, GEORGIA

Daniel Byrd and Jamie Abernathy arrived at Hartsfield-Jackson Airport with a little time to spare. Doc Farmer had been their driver to save the GBI a parking fee.

Doc pulled to the Departure curb and put the car in park. He stepped out and tried to help Jamie with her bag.

"I've got it, Doc," Jamie said.

"Sorry, I'm old school. I didn't mean any insult," Doc said.

Jamie laughed. "No offense taken; I just like to carry my own bag."

"Well, you two look like you're running away together," Doc said.

Jamie looked at Byrd. "Okay, I do take offense to that."

Doc turned to get in his car. "You two be careful. El Paso sounds like a wild place to me."

"What do you know about El Paso?" Byrd asked.

"I saw a western with Audie Murphy in it. It sounded like a bad place," Doc said as he dropped into his car. He pulled into the flow of traffic and was gone.

Byrd and Abernathy headed for the ticket counter, got their paperwork to travel armed, and headed for security. They showed their GBI credentials and were soon standing at the gate.

"Do you think we'll have any time to look around the city?" Jamie asked. "I've never been to El Paso."

Byrd shrugged. "I came through once on a road trip with a friend from college. I can't remember much, except that it got hot as hell after we got out of Fort Worth. I remember it was hot all the way to San Diego."

Jamie nodded. "I guess 'hot' will be the word of the day. Weather *and* food, I imagine."

Byrd found a couple of seats where he could watch the people at the gate. He knew he was being hyper-vigilant. His counselor, Anne Kuykendall, said it was typical of people who had been in life-or-death situations. No matter where he was, movement attracted his eye. When the movement was a person, his eyes went to their waist, then the area around the arm pits, then to the eyes. He checked for bulges that could hide a gun, then watched to see where the person's eyes were looking. Byrd's eyes seemed, even to him, to be in constant motion.

Jamie sat beside him and put her bag on the floor. "How long do you think we'll be out here?"

"Clete says the US Attorney wants to meet us and go over some gaps he thinks there are in the investigation. Things he may want us to go back and photograph, interviews that might tie up loose ends, that kind of thing."

"Do we have reservations to come back?" Jamie wondered.

Byrd shook his head. "No, but push-come-to-shove we can fly back with Arlow Turner."

"My buddy from DEA?"

Byrd nodded. "He's bringing his plane out here. He'll be at the meeting tomorrow. They want him to help take some pictures from the air of all the locations involved. He offered to video what the flight would look like." Byrd leaned back, trying to unwind. "It'll be good to see Montana again, and to finally meet Clete. But my guess is that by Friday we'll be on a plane back."

"She's the one who worked for Canton PD?" Jamie asked.

Byrd nodded.

"Word is you had a thing with her." Jamie waited for a response.

Byrd was irritated. "The word is rarely right. We went out once and then we spent some time together when I was on the skids from my first shooting."

Jamie poked him. "The gunfighter has to count his shootings now?"

"You know what Wyatt Earp liked?" Byrd asked.

"Women who left him alone?" Jamie asked.

"Ice cream," Byrd said. "When he quit drinking, he had a passion for ice cream."

"Really?"

"I don't know if there was a cause and effect, but he quit drinking early in his career," Byrd said.

"Demons?" Jamie asked.

"Are you asking about him or me?"

Dressed in jeans and a polo shirt, Montana Worley met Byrd and Abernathy at the baggage claim carrousel. She ran up to Byrd and threw her arms around him. "Welcome to paradise, Danny!"

Byrd returned the hug. "You look great. West Texas agrees with you."

Byrd saw a man wearing a white western hat approach. Byrd's eyes locked on him for a second, then he did the customary scan for weapons. He noted the bulge underneath the western cut sports jacket before stopping on the silver star peeking out of his lapel.

Byrd stuck his hand out. "As a trained investigator, I'm going to guess you're Clete Petterson."

Clete broke into a smile. "Don't know the face but I'd know that voice anywhere. We've sure talked on the phone enough."

Byrd turned to Jamie. "Jamie Abernathy, GBI agent extraordinaire, meet Clete Petterson and Montana Worley, a ranger and a trooper of the great State of Texas."

Jamie shook hands with the Texas law officers, then moved toward the exit. When the automatic door opened, the Georgians were stunned by the blast of air. "Damn," Byrd said.

Clete laughed. "Yeah, it's still cool for May. But it's a dry heat."

Byrd was skeptical. "My oven is a dry heat but I don't hang out there."

The Franklin Mountains to the west looked spectacular as they walked away from the stuffy airport building.

Montana grabbed his elbow. "Did you guys eat on the airplane?"

Byrd frowned. "Peanuts and a bit of Coke. And not enough Coke to put the peanuts into."

Clete looked puzzled. Montana said, "It's a Georgia thing. Peanuts in your Coke. But you really need the Coke in a bottle for it to be good."

Byrd turned to Jamie and asked, "Are you hungry?"

"I'm starved."

Clete led the way to his department truck. "I have just the place in mind. We'll get some good Texas barbeque. Give me just a minute to move some things around."

With Montana's help, Clete moved a couple of rifles, a shotgun, an extra pistol, and several cases of ammunition to the rear of the truck. He put each item in carefully, then locked everything inside the covered bed.

Byrd watched the process. "You carry a lot of firepower around with you."

Clete nodded. "West Texas can be a dangerous place."

"That's what we heard when we were leaving Atlanta," Jamie said.

MONDAY, MAY 23, 2005
7:22 P.M.
EL PASO, TEXAS

The food was awesome and plentiful. The eatery sat squarely on the Texas-New Mexico border. The owner of the restaurant recognized Clete and Montana and took special care of them. The owner had commented that he felt safer with the two law officers in his place. Clete reminded him they only had jurisdiction in the half of the dining room that was in Texas.

When they finished eating, Clete led the way back to his truck. "Do you have reservations anywhere?" Clete asked.

"That would be too organized for us." Jamie laughed.

"I'll take you to a motel that's in a good area. You'll have a great view of the border," Clete said as he pulled from the lot.

The hotel looked new, and the front desk was efficient. The GBI agents produced the necessary paperwork to secure a government discount for the rooms, then Byrd and Jamie walked to their respective rooms.

Byrd went inside his accommodations and threw his bag on one of the beds. He took his suit off, hung it in a closet, and jumped in the shower. Soon he was on the bed, wide awake as he remembered the determined look on Adam Benjamin's face as he fired the MAC-10 machine pistol at him. He wondered if Benjamin knew who shot him, or if everything had been a blur. Byrd rolled onto his left side and pulled the covers up tight.

Byrd fell into a fitful sleep an hour later.

TUESDAY, MAY 24, 2005
9:05 A.M.
EL PASO, TEXAS

Jameson Douglas Dagget was a long-time employee of the US Justice Department. He stepped from the American

Airlines flight and weaved his way to the baggage claim area. His suitcase was labeled "PRIORITY," and it was waiting for him as he walked up. He pulled his bag to the curb and hailed a taxi. The driver made no comment when the man directed him, in an officious tone, to the US District Courthouse.

Dagget was a special counsel assigned for many years to the Office of Intelligence Policy and Review. He was cleared to know the most secret of secrets. He had advised presidents, heads of state, and other world leaders of industry, education, and finance.

Today, he was on a clandestine mission. He saw the task as simple but delicate.

He brushed a piece of lint from his suit, a custom-made model from Savile Row, and pondered the best course of action. He didn't want to pull rank—one of these cowboys out here in the middle of nowhere might leak any sabotage of the criminal case to the media. Best to simply poke holes in the investigation, kill the case from within.

Dagget fanned his face. "My good man, can you please turn up the air conditioning?"

The taxi driver, a weathered veteran of life on the border, ignored the request.

The ride was short to the boxy building that houses the US District Courts. Dagget dragged his suitcase into the lobby and was immediately stopped by a blue-coated deputy US marshal.

"Sir, what is the purpose of bringing this luggage into the courthouse?" the deputy marshal asked.

Dagget bristled. "I am a high-ranking member of the Justice Department. I expect a little more courtesy." Dagget dug his official credentials from deep within the pocket of his suit. When he displayed the identification, he started to walk around the magnetometers. The marshal stopped him again. "All bags go through the security equipment, sir."

Dagget ignored the marshal and pulled out a cell phone. He dialed a number and waited. When the party answered, Dagget spoke quietly and firmly. Then he flipped the phone shut and waited.

Five minutes later, the chief deputy US marshal came out into the lobby, Dagget assumed the demeanor of an entitled government functionary, which he was. The Chief motioned for Dagget to walk around the security systems and pointed him to the elevator for the US attorneys' offices.

Dagget sniffed as he got on the elevator. Something in this desert air was making his nose stop up. *God, I hope this trip is short*, he thought as he rode the elevator up.

At the front desk, thanks to a call from the chief deputy marshal, Dagget was escorted to the conference room in the center of the facility. When he entered without knocking, he saw eight people around the table. All of them were staring at him. No one spoke. A man and two women sat on one side, while what appeared to be a Texas Ranger was on the other with a man in a suit and two other women. A final man rounded out the group, sitting at the end of the table.

The suite gentleman broke the silence. "We're in a meeting. Can someone help you?"

Dagget sniffed again. "I'm here for the meeting. My name is Jameson Douglas Dagget, special counsel for the Department of Justice. I have been tasked with making sure this prosecution is done properly and doesn't get involved in matters that may impact the national security of our country."

The gentleman stood up and shook hands with Dagget.

"I'm AUSA Douglas Hogan. I guess we'll need to get you a pass for this floor then, if you'll be working here."

As soon as they left the room, like elementary school kids, the people at the table started whispering to each other. Daniel Byrd leaned over to Jamie Abernathy and whispered, "I don't trust people with three names."

She scowled. "Like who?"

"Lee Harvey Oswald. Or James Earl Ray," Byrd submitted.

"What about James Earl Jones or Dick Van Dyke?" Jamie retorted.

Byrd frowned. "I think Van Dyke counts as one name."

"Jamie Lee Curtis," Jamie hissed.

Arlow Turner, at the end of the table, propped his elbows on it. "The DOJ man's job is to try to sink this case."

Clete looked doubtful. "Hogan seems to have this thing sewed up. I doubt there is much this man can do."

Arlow looked the room over. "I've seen it done. He'll come in here and try to find ways to pick the case apart. If that doesn't work, he'll send you out to get evidence you can't possibly locate. Or it will be too dangerous to get what they want. If any of the cops can't get what he wants, he'll shoot the case down and head back to DC."

Clete had tried more than one case in the federal system and was convinced Arlow was overstating the case. "Let's just wait and see. Maybe this guy is better than sliced bread."

Arlow hung his head.

CHAPTER 31
REVENGE, SWEET REVENGE

TUESDAY, MAY 24, 2005
11:22 A.M.
CIUDAD JUÁREZ, CHIHUAHUA, MEXICO

Rojo listened intently as the informer made her report. The girl had provided detailed information in the past, which had turned out to be true. Why she had not told the information to him sooner, he did not know.

"I saw the big ranger standing over Pequeño Rojo. The big man had shot him many times and left him to die. I witnessed as much."

Rojo's eyes teared up, but the anger was stronger than the grief. "You saw this with your own eyes?"

She nodded meekly. "I did, sir."

"Were there others there as well?" Rojo asked.

He pulled a file folder from his desk and passed it to the girl. She examined the photos stuffed inside, most taken at some distance. She pointed to a photo of Clete taken in the middle of El Paso as he got in his truck. "This is the *Diablo de Texas*," she said, using the old name for the Texas Rangers.

She sorted through the other photos. She found one of two women. "The lady with the dark hair was on the bridge. I did not know she was the police. I am sorry I didn't mention her."

Rojo shook his head. "They are secret police, you could not know this."

She bowed her head. "Thank you, patron."

Rojo opened his desk drawer and pulled out a wad of pesos. He passed the bills to the girl. "Here is twenty thousand pesos. I can give you a thousand American dollars if you would prefer."

The girl snatched the pesos from the desk. "Thank you, patron."

He dismissed her with a wave. Once she was out the door, he turned to the special phone. He had gotten El Gordo to show him how to make the calls. He pushed the buttons and waited for the beeps.

"My friend. It is good to hear from you." Mitchell Warren sounded as if nothing had happened.

"General, I am sorry to hear your son is in custody. And I understand you are in hiding as well," Rojo said.

"Thank you, yes. And my condolences on the death of your son. No man wants to bury his child," Warren said.

Rojo was surprised the American was so well informed. "Thank you. That is the reason for my call. I need your help."

"I will help any way I can," Warren replied.

Rojo had no illusions about who he was dealing with. "I will pay you handsomely for your help."

"What is it you need?" Warren asked.

"You have friends in the US Justice Department, do you not?" Rojo was fishing.

"Some."

"Do you know this man Dagget, who has come to El Paso to oversee the investigation of our mutual business?" Rojo asked.

"I do," Warren responded.

"I am told that the people responsible for the death of my son are a Texas Ranger named Petterson and a narcotics investigator named Adeline Riley. I want to lure them into Mexico. I cannot afford to take action against them on your side of the border, but what happens in Mexico is different."

"Dagget is in El Paso now, as you said. He is a business associate. He might be able to engineer getting these people into Mexico, but it will come at a cost. He will fear being exposed if the plan goes awry."

"I will pay a large sum for his service. It is a matter of honor. What number will this man ask for?" Rojo asked.

Warren did some quick calculations in his head. "For the life of an American police officer, he'll ask a large number. And he may have to go underground if the trail leads back to him. I would estimate one million dollars would buy what you want."

"That is a large sum."

Warren responded, "I have done some looking into Petterson. He's a large man, worthy of a large sum. But if he were to die, the case against my son would be crippled. I would be willing to pay half the cost of Dagget myself."

"That is most kind of you. I will pay you half a million in the usual manner. The funds will be available tonight. Is that sufficient?"

Warren knew he must act quickly. "I'll set the wheels in motion now. I assume you will need time to arrange things on your side of the river?"

"I can be ready by this time tomorrow," Rojo said.

"I'll know by then if Dagget is willing," Warren said as he disconnected the call.

Rojo hung up the phone and looked out the window of his office. He decided he would ask El Gordo the name of a *bruja* to put a hex on the man Warren.

WEDNESDAY, MAY 25, 2005
10:05 A.M.
EL PASO, TEXAS

Byrd and Jamie Abernathy got to the courthouse by taxi and climbed the stairs to the US Attorney's Office. Byrd figured they would be early but was surprised to see Clete and Montana already in the big conference room off the lobby. The officers located a coffee pot and started sorting through the folders of evidence that needed to be organized for prosecution of the criminal case.

The four officers were placing the items in some semblance of order when Addy Riley and Rae Crosby came into the office. Before the new arrivals could find a seat, Arlow Turner pushed his way through the big wooden door.

The team had been working for almost two hours when AUSA Hogan came by the conference room to tell them he and Dagget would be meeting for a while. He recommended the cops grab some lunch and come back around two p.m. Clete suggested they adjourn to Rosa's Cantina, an authentic Mexican restaurant on the west side of town.

Byrd rode in the back of Clete's big truck as they went down streets so dusty, they might have been unpaved. The old rock building was low and looked like it had been on the spot over a hundred years, with a laundromat on one side and a garage on the other.

As they pulled into the gravel parking lot, he could see the border across the railroad tracks. Byrd stepped down from the truck and followed the crowd into the dark café. Clete looked at Byrd's shoes as they went through the door.

"What is that on your feet?" Clete asked.

Byrd frowned. "I brought dress shoes and deck shoes. These are for informal."

Clete shook his head. "We need to get you some boots."

Once his eyes adjusted, Byrd saw the tables were covered with red-and-white checked tablecloths, with white Christmas lights strung from the ceiling and a horseshoe-shaped bar dominating the rear. The server took them to a long table and Byrd worked his way around so he was facing the door. Clete did the same.

Byrd leaned over to Clete. "Is it a law in this state that you have to have something shaped like Texas on display in every building?"

Clete laughed good-naturedly. "I know people who have pools in their backyard shaped like Texas."

Byrd had to admit the people he had met so far were proud of their home state. Even if they weren't from there.

When the food came, it was hearty and flavorful, and not too spicey. The crew of officers had just begun to enjoy it when Clete's phone rang. He fished the flip phone from his pocket, stood to walk outside, and answered the phone.

When the Texan came back, he seemed rushed. "That was Douglas Hogan. This guy from Washington has some kind of special request for photos that need to be done right away. He wants me to come back to his office and make arrangements to get them done."

Byrd had stood up. "What kind of arrangement would need to be made to take some pictures?"

Clete threw cash on the table. "He wants them taken inside of Mexico."

Byrd threw cash on the table, too. "I'm coming with you."

Clete leaned down and told Montana she was in charge

of their guests, then the pair went back out into the sun for the short drive downtown.

WEDNESDAY, MAY 25, 2005
1:15 P.M.
EL PASO, TEXAS

Douglas Hogan looked angry when Byrd and Clete walked in. He sat on the opposite end of the large conference table from Dagget, who had a laptop computer set up in front of him and was working on something.

Clete laid his hat on the table, crown down, and took a seat. "What do you need?"

Dagget didn't look up. "You and one of the narcotics investigators," Dagget said.

Clete glanced at Hogan, who shrugged. "To do what, exactly?"

Dagget pursed his lips. "I have information from a source in Mexico indicating that the airport from which the loads of drugs originated, if your investigation is accurate, has security video. My source says that there may be footage of the suspect airplane."

Byrd was skeptical. "Those video tapes are usually reused. They rarely have more than a couple of months' worth of images."

Dagget looked up. "This particular unit has a solid-state hard drive. I am told reliably that it records for 120 days. There may well be images of prior visits by the suspect's plane as well."

"Can't DEA send someone from one of the consulates to take pictures?" Clete asked.

"I believe that it would be better to have one of our star witnesses perform the task. More direct evidence."

Clete shook his head. "There are a lot of hoops to jump through for a ranger, or any DPS employee, to be able to go into Mexico. And isn't it some kind of violation of the Neutrality Act?"

"I am working as we speak to get approval from the State Department. And the Department has contacted the Chief of the Texas Rangers to get authorization for your visit." It seemed Dagget didn't take no for an answer.

Clete wasn't convinced. "We'll just waltz into Juárez and go out to this airport?"

"I've spoken with the Governor's office for the State of Chihuahua. They will be providing a police escort. I would like to get this done in the next twenty-four hours."

Byrd interjected, "Can I come along? I've seen the airplane and the pilot several times. I could identify it if there are pictures."

Dagget shook his head. "I'm sorry, but this isn't a field trip. I want the two people who have done the most here in Texas to recover the evidence."

Clete frowned. "You think this is worth the effort? It sounds like a long shot to me."

Dagget was dismissive. "It will seal the deal as far as the connections to Mexico go."

Clete came to a decision. "Okay, Addy Riley and I will go. If you can arrange all this. I still think getting all the permissions will be an enormous task."

Dagget looked up from his computer and smiled. "That's what I do, gentlemen."

WEDNESDAY, MAY 25, 2005
6:05 P.M.
EL PASO, TEXAS

"Who do you think Dagget got this hot tip from?" Clete asked the group.

"The cousins," Byrd stated flatly.

"That'd be my guess," Arlow chimed in.

"Who are the cousins?" Addy asked.

"The CIA," Byrd offered.

"You're kidding," Addy asked.

The group had gathered at Clete's house on the outskirts of El Paso. Around beers and nuts, the group of officers tried to figure out what Dagget was up to. The consensus was that this was some sort of trap, but the ball was rolling downhill, and Clete and Addy would have to do their best to outrun it.

Clete looked at Addy. "You don't have to go."

She rolled her eyes. "No way I'm passing on this invitation."

Montana leaned forward. "Why can't I go?"

Clete shook his head. "First, Dagget was very specific about who was to go."

"And second?" Montana asked.

"I didn't have a second reason, but I was hoping you wouldn't catch that," Clete said.

The knock at the door startled everyone. Clete took out his pistol and walked to the front of the house. Everyone listened and waited. When Clete came back, he was trailed by Major Stetson Crosby. The six-foot-seven ranger ducked as he came through the doorway.

"Look who I found in the driveway," Clete said. After introductions, Clete asked, "Major, do you know about this plan for Investigator Riley and I to go to Mexico?" Clete asked.

Crosby frowned. "I hope it's not a fool's errand."

Byrd spoke up, "Or a trap."

Clete shook his head. "Nobody on the Mexican side wants to turn this into a war. They all remember what happened when a cartel kidnapped that intelligence officer, Kiki Camarena. DEA went to war."

"We turned Mexico inside out," Arlow said.

Byrd shook his head. "We're sending two people requested by that three-named pencil pusher from the DOJ—two people who were on the scene when Rojo's son was killed."

Addy said, "But the shooters were with CBP."

Clete nodded. "We know that, but Rojo may not."

Rae stood and stretched. "I can't believe all the technicalities will get worked out. It'll take months to get the Mexican government to agree to you guys coming into the country."

Stetson Crosby shrugged. "Everything has been agreed to. We got word from the governor's staff, and we are waiting on diplomatic passports from Washington. I was told they'll be coming in first thing tomorrow by courier."

"This smells of the cousins," Arlow said. "DOJ wouldn't be able to get passports this fast. This is coming from Langley."

Crosby squinted. "Why would the CIA be helping out?"

Arlow frowned. "There have always been rumors that the cousins were involved in Kiki's kidnapping."

Suddenly, the room went quiet.

Byrd and Petterson laid out the snippets of information

that seemed to point to shadow government involvement. When they finished, Crosby closed his eyes and rolled his head around. Then he looked at Clete. "We need to make sure you two are covered in Mexico. Let me know what you need, and I'll do my best to make it happen. But you know the government—whether in Austin or DC—will not let us mount a rescue effort."

"What do you think we should do, Major?" Clete asked.

"Plan. Make sure the plan is quick and doesn't require government sanctions," Crosby said.

"The biggest hurdle would be getting back across the border if this is a trap," Addy said as she stretched.

Crosby looked over the room. "I can't give you permission to do anything. But I'll fight like the devil if anything goes wrong."

Clete walked him to the door. "Thanks, Major."

"Watch your back." Then Crosby left.

Clete pulled out a legal pad and began putting together a plan. They knew they would be most vulnerable near the border checkpoint, and Clete wanted to have Montana, Rae, and Jamie undercover near the bridge. They planned to rush the bridge decked out in tactical gear, identifying themselves as law enforcement officers, and cover Clete and Addy as they fought their way back to the US side. Clete was confident the Customs officers on the bridge wouldn't interfere.

Byrd agreed to coordinate the efforts from the air in the DEA airplane.

When the planning session began to break up, Addy offered to drop Byrd and Jamie at their motel. The pair climbed into the undercover Jeep and enjoyed the sunset as Addy raced back into the west side of town.

Addy pulled the midnight blue Jeep into the portico and Jamie climbed out. Byrd worked his way out of the back seat and then leaned in. "Can I interest you in coming in and having a drink with us?"

Addy smiled. "Not with the day I have ahead of me. Besides, my husband claims he can barely remember what I look like."

Byrd patted the top of the Jeep and stood back. "Drive safe!" he said as she sped away.

Jamie led the way to the hotel lobby and Byrd followed. "Jamie, could I interest you in a drink?"

Jamie shook her head. "Let's go to my room."

Byrd was surprised. "You don't plan to take advantage of me, do you?"

She punched his arm. Both Agents knew that interoffice romances were a disaster for a career. Byrd rubbed his shoulder as Jamie changed the subject. "Hey," she asked. "Is it true you're banging a married assistant district attorney?

"*Banging*? Do I ask who you're banging?" Byrd said.

"It just seems weird that you only date people who work in a district attorney's office," Jamie said.

"I think I'll drink alone," Byrd said as they stood by the elevator.

Jamie shook her head. "Doc made me promise to keep an eye on you."

Byrd flushed. "Sorry. I forgot I need a keeper."

Jamie winked. "You need more than that. Let's watch some basic cable and talk about your disaster of a love life."

Byrd groaned.

THURSDAY, MAY 26, 2005
10:12 A.M.
EL PASO, TEXAS

The GBI, DEA, and Texas officers were gathered around the conference table in the US Attorney's Office. Jameson Dagget sat near the head of the table, with a manila envelope in his hands. He fished something out of the envelope and handed it to Clete Petterson. Petterson and Addy Riley were dressed in suits; the rest of the group wore casual clothes.

Clete looked at the maroon diplomatic passport he was handed. The photo inside was from the internet, posted on the DPS official webpage. He was wearing his western hat and seated at an angle. He knew enough to know that wasn't permitted in passport photos. He checked the one issued for Addy Riley. Her photo had been an official DPS photo showing her in a trooper uniform.

Dagget pointed at the passports. "As diplomats, you can't be searched. If you choose to be armed, that is your prerogative."

Clete nodded at Addy. "We'll be armed. Will we be escorted?"

Dagget nodded. "The Federal Police will escort you to the location and back. They will wait outside while you examine the evidence and recover it. Please take photos of the recorder in place."

Clete felt resolute. "Addy and I will walk across the Bridge of the Americas. Have the police meet us in two hours. Is that enough time?"

Dagget consulted his Rolex. "I think we can make that work."

Dagget opened his laptop and typed out a quick email. In less than a minute, the computer dinged. Dagget read the response and looked up. "Two hours from now is fine with the Federal Police."

Douglas Hogan watched the proceedings. When Clete prepared to leave, Hogan stood up. "Mr. Dagget, I've arranged for you to fly the route our smuggler used and get an idea how the scheme worked."

Dagget was taken by surprise. "I may need to be near a phone once Mr. Petterson and Ms. Riley are in Mexico."

Arlow spoke up. "I'm taking Agent Byrd anyway. We'll take about an hour. I can have you back by the time they cross the bridge. It'll give you a better picture of the dynamics."

Dagget stood and pulled on his suit coat. "No incursions into Mexico, I assume?"

Arlow laughed. "Even if you gave me a direct order, I wouldn't cross into Mexico. I want to keep my job."

Dagget smiled. "I was joking. I'm well aware of the Department of Justice's prohibitions on travel outside the US."

Clete tossed Byrd the keys to his truck. "I cleared it with the Major for you to take my truck to the airport. You and Arlow can use it."

Hogan spoke up. "Mr. Dagget, I wanted to get you a photo ID from the marshals. It'll only take a minute and then I'll drop you at the airport."

"My regular identification isn't enough?" Dagget asked.

"The marshals have access cards that will make it easier for you to get around in the building when we get ready to prosecute the case," Hogan said.

Dagget shrugged. He couldn't tell Hogan he planned to never come back to this end of the world. He closed his laptop and followed Hogan into the hall.

Clete looked around the room. "Any questions?"

Rae looked around. "Just for the record, if this all goes wrong, I plan to testify. I'm too pretty to go to prison."

Byrd stood and started for the door. "My thoughts exactly," Byrd said.

CHAPTER 32
I SAW THIS COMING

Arlow had based his airplane out of Biggs Field, the enormous runway that was part of Fort Bliss, a military reservation that covers 1,700 square miles to the northwest of El Paso, reaching into New Mexico. Arlow had felt like a BB on a bowling alley when he landed the DEA airplane on a runway that had hosted NASA Space Shuttle transports.

When Hogan dropped Dagget at the airfield on Fort Bliss, Arlow had completed his preflight check of the Aero Commander. Byrd stood near the side door and pointed to the right front seat.

"Mr. Dagget," Byrd said. "You can sit up front. I'll ride in the back. And you might want to shed that jacket. This thing isn't air conditioned."

Two military police officers watched from a marked Humvee. They were a study in disinterest as the three men boarded the airplane.

Dagget took off the suit jacket and carefully folded it. Then he placed it on top a black bag laying in the rear of the passenger compartment. Dagget worked his way into the seat with some difficulty.

When Arlow finished checking the plane over, he crawled into the pilot's seat and handed Dagget a headset while setting the audio channels. Then Byrd buckled himself in, plugged in his headset, and examined the panel used to control the audio only he could hear.

Arlow looked back questioningly, and Byrd gave him a thumbs-up.

THURSDAY, MAY 26, 2005
12:05 P.M.
CIUDAD JUÁREZ, CHIHUAHUA, MEXICO

As Clete and Addy strode across the Bridge of the Americas, Clete turned on the transmitter hidden in his slacks. He looked back at the US side and saw Rae Michaels flash the lights in her minivan.

Clete looked at Addy. "You can turn back now."

Addy didn't slow. "Keep walking, Ranger."

The pair kept a steady pace as they walked the concrete path, crossing under the big green sign with "MEXICO" in white letters. Clete glanced over at Addy, whose jaw tightened.

They approached the green building with porticos over the traffic lanes. Clete noted the facility on the Mexican side was similar to the American border checkpoint, but smaller. When they reached the Mexican border guard, he took one glance at the diplomatic passports and waved them on.

Clete saw the Federal Policemen standing near a white passenger van. The star on the door was faded, as was the paint. The sun was destructive on both sides of the border, Clete noted.

Clete helped Addy into the back seat, then climbed in and pulled the sliding door closed. The two Federal Policemen didn't say a word. They unslung the worn-looking MP-5 machine guns and climbed into the front of the van.

It took two tries to get the engine running. The foursome headed east out of the heart of Ciudad Juárez.

Clete and Addy each noted the streets they traveled, concerned they might have to fight their way out of Mexico. Clete noted the van was headed southeast, parallel to the Rio.

THURSDAY, MAY 26, 2005
12:06 P.M.
EL PASO, TEXAS

The DEA airplane had been in the air for over an hour. Byrd noted Dagget seemed to be enjoying the ride. Arlow had been cleared to fly low over the Rio Grande River, and the Aero Commander headed east out of the city. The view was spectacular, but Byrd and Arlow didn't notice.

Byrd could hear the body transmitter Clete wore in his left ear over his headset, but neither Arlow nor Dagget could.

Byrd was concerned he couldn't hear anyone talking, but he could hear highway noises. The signal was strong as the airplane roared over the river valley. Byrd tapped Arlow on the shoulder and gave him a thumbs-up as Dagget enjoyed the scenery.

THURSDAY, MAY 26, 2005
12:45 P.M.
EL PORVENIR, CHIHUAHUA, MEXICO

The building looked almost new as the van pulled up alongside the large hangar. Modern metal buildings weren't uncommon in the area, and this one didn't look remarkable from the roadway. Once the van stopped, Clete could see the hangar door and the tarmac runway. He was surprised that, from the road, the airstrip was invisible.

The uniformed police officer in the passenger seat pointed to the door cut in the metal building beside the hangar door.

Before he got out of the van, Clete inspected the outside of the building. He saw high-quality video cameras on the corners, over the entry doors, and pointing toward the airstrip.

Clete looked over at Addy. "Well, there are certainly cameras here."

Addy leaned forward in the bench seat, looking for herself. "Yep," she said.

The Federal Policeman on the passenger side got out and opened the sliding door. Clete stepped out and gave Addy a hand. As they stood outside, Clete pushed his hat tightly on his head and looked around. There were piles of building materials discarded on the east side of the hangar and a drainage ditch running along the runway from the taxiway.

Clete took a deep breath and led the way to the door, Addy on his heels. As they walked away, the driver motioned at the van and said, *"Esperaremos aquí."*

Clete nodded and turned to the door, putting his hand on his pistol as he pushed through the door. The hangar was dark inside, with long pillars of light shining from where the hangar door didn't seal.

Addy pressed her back to the wall and waited for her eyes to adjust. The hangar was strewn with wooden crates and pasteboard boxes which threw even deeper shadows in the cavernous building.

Clete moved around the wall toward the west side of the space, with Addy close behind. Clete searched for some clue where to find the recorder for the cameras.

"I hope this transmitter is getting out of this building," Addy said.

Clete looked back. "Me, too."

Clete looked up as Addy saw the first movement. She shoved Clete as a machine gun ripped the quiet. Clete dived behind the nearest crate as Addy fired her Sig Sauer pistol.

"I thought they'd try to kidnap us!" Addy shouted.

"I guess Rojo will be satisfied just to kill us," Clete observed.

One of the gunmen shouted as he fired again. "¡Mataste al Pequeño Rojo, ahora pagarás el precio!"

Clete looked at Addy questioning. Addy grimaced. "My Spanish is rusty, but I think he's blaming us for killing Little Red."

The wooden crate they were hiding behind was thirty feet from the door, which was the only exit they could see. Clete motioned toward the door. He waited to see if the Federal Police officers would come to their rescue. His answer was the sound of the van accelerating away.

THURSDAY, MAY 26, 2005
12:51 P.M.
EL PASO, TEXAS

Byrd prodded Arlow. "Shots fired," Byrd said over the intercom.

"What?" Dagget asked.

Arlow looked over his shoulder. "Where are they?" he asked.

Byrd pointed toward the river. "Sounds like they're in the hangar. Can you swing around? Maybe the *federales* are coming to their rescue."

Arlow banked the airplane and looked for the airport on the Mexican side of the river. The Aero Commander responded like a race car as they rolled south and dived toward the border.

Within seconds they could see the white van racing out of the area.

Byrd shook his head. "Fuck!"

Arlow rolled a knob on one of the radios he monitored. He concentrated for a few seconds. Arlow looked back at Byrd. "If my Spanish is any good, those guys in the van just alerted their pals that the Americanos are fighting back."

Byrd pointed at the airstrip. "Can you put me out down there?"

"If I put you on the runway, do you think you can get to them?" Arlow asked while concentrating on guiding the twin-engine plane along the fastest path to the airport.

"What's going on?" Dagget asked.

Byrd and Arlow ignored the question.

Byrd had the black bag open as the DEA airplane picked up speed. He pulled Clete's issued M4 rifle and laid it at his feet. He pulled a second bag brimming with loaded magazines and slung it over his shoulder.

"What are you doing?" Dagget asked.

Arlow ignored the question. "Can you tell what's going on?"

Byrd shouted back. "Sounds like they're pinned down inside the building. Can you put us at the extreme east end of the runway?"

Arlow nodded. "The runway is almost a mile long, and wide enough for a jumbo jet. I'll land using as little runway as I can, then taxi back to the east end."

"You don't want to just come in by the hangar?" Byrd asked with a smile.

"Not if I plan to fly you back out of here." Arlow turned his focus to flying the airplane.

"Is there a gun in there I can use?" Arlow asked.

Byrd shook his head. "I need you ready to get us out of here. If something were to happen to you, we'd all be screwed."

Arlow started to protest when Dagget turned to face Byrd. "What the hell do you think you're doing?" Dagget shouted.

"Doing what's right," Byrd said. "We're not leaving them to be killed."

"What you want to do is illegal. I'll see both of you in prison." Dagget's face went red with anger and Byrd knew he meant what he said.

Jamie, Rae, and Montana sat in Rae's van, listening to the body transmitter when they heard the first shots. Montana hit the dash with her fist. "Bastard!" she shouted.

Jamie talked into the walkie-talkie Arlow had loaned her. "Danny, are you clear that shots have been fired?"

Jamie got a "two-click" acknowledgment.

Rae remained calm and dialed her flip phone. "Major Crosby, it was a setup!"

"Damn," he said, not a man who cursed often. "We have strict orders not to cross but I'm not going to leave them hanging out to dry."

Rae frowned. "Major, I think it's better I go ahead and tell you something."

"What?" Crosby barked.

"We have a rescue mission underway."

"I can't protect Montana if she goes into Mexico. I hope she knows that." Crosby was controlled.

"She's with me," Rae said.

"Who's doing a rescue?"

"Nobody from Texas, if that makes you feel any better!" She flipped the phone shut. Rae looked at Montana. "I just hung up on Clete's major."

Jamie shook her head. "I wish we could do more."

Rae gunned the minivan and screeched out of the parking lot.

Montana tightened her seat belt. "Give me that phone, Rae. I think we need to get some help out here. Head east on I-10!"

THURSDAY, MAY 26, 2005
12:54 P.M.
EL PORVENIR, CHIHUAHUA, MEXICO

Clete looked at the door. "We've got to get out of here. We need to get to the ditch or that pile of metal."

Addy nodded. "I'm right behind you."

Clete broke into a run, Addy his shadow, as they covered the distance to the door. The pounding of their boots was overshadowed by the roar of machine guns. Clete swung the door open and they ran out of the hangar.

The pile of abandoned materials was closest, and Clete's boots pounded the cement to the discarded steel beams. He plunged down behind a large red girder.

Addy was able to find cover just as the machine guns started up again. Addy fired two more rounds at the advancing assassins, then ducked behind cover.

She looked over and saw that Clete's face was pale. Then she saw the blood running down his arm. "Shit," she said. "You're hit."

"Yep," Clete said, nodding.

Addy reached for her boot. "I'm going to put a tourniquet on you."

Clete watched as she pulled a tactical medical kit from her boot. She took the Israeli tourniquet and applied it to his right arm, then twisted the handle as hard as she could.

Clete groaned. "I need one of those."

She stuffed the kit back into her boot. "You never know when it can come in handy."

THURSDAY, MAY 26, 2005
12:55 P.M.
EL PASO, TEXAS

Montana was doing her best to destroy the dash of Rae's minivan. Both officers had heard that Clete was hit.

Rae drove the van as fast as she could. The traffic was light and she was dividing her attention between the sky and the road. Jamie caught sight of the Aero Commander low in the sky.

"Rae, you watch the road. I've got the airplane in sight," Jamie said.

"I need to do something," Montana said in frustration.

Jamie pointed out the window. "Say a prayer for the folks in that airplane."

THURSDAY, MAY 26, 2005
1:05 P.M.
EL PORVENIR, CHIHUAHUA, MEXICO

The tires barked as Arlow put the airplane on the runway. When he brought the plane to a halt, Byrd pushed out the back door and ran toward the sound of the gunfire, the rifle and extra ammo making the journey more difficult.

Dagget looked over at Arlow as he turned the plane around and rolled back to the east end of the tarmac. "What do you think you're doing? This is an illegal violation of a sovereign country! We have no right to be here! Get me out of here this minute!"

Arlow grimaced. "If we leave here, it'll be with those Texas officers."

Dagget was indignant. "I'll see to it that you are prosecuted for this."

Arlow shrugged. "This was your trip. And I think there are a whole lot of Texas and Georgia officers who will testify for me and against you."

Dagget pulled out a cell phone but Arlow forcefully took it. He tossed the phone onto the runway as he taxied to the end of the pavement.

THURSDAY, MAY 26, 2005
1:05 P.M.
EL PORVENIR, CHIHUAHUA, MEXICO

Byrd felt the effects of the heat and the altitude. His leg muscles burned and he still had a football field to go. Sweat poured off his face, beginning to burn his right eye. His breathing was ragged, but he heard the sporadic gunfire and the adrenaline helped him keep on.

His deck shoes were sorely inadequate for the run he had ahead of him. He pulled the M4 from his back and started to jog again.

He heard the loud report of a machine gun and could see the corner of the hangar as he got closer. The machine gun fire was followed by shots Byrd knew were from a pistol.

THURSDAY, MAY 26, 2005
1:06 P.M.
EL PORVENIR, CHIHUAHUA, MEXICO

Clete knew the bullet hadn't hit a bone, but the muscles in his right arm were filling with his own blood and beginning to contract. Although the tourniquet had quelled the bleeding, he knew it wouldn't stop the swelling.

"I think I heard an airplane," Addy said. "I hope it's ours."

A bullet zinged off the girder in front of them. It was only a matter of time until the gunmen figured out a way to get the advantage. Addy rolled over and fired two quick shots, then retreated behind the steel barrier.

Clete rolled and pointed his pistol in the direction the shots were coming from. When the machine guns fired again, he fired several shots back. His injured arm throbbed with each pull of the trigger.

Addy dropped the magazine from her pistol. "I'm down to six rounds," she said.

Clete handed her his extra magazine. "You've got a better chance of hitting something than I do."

Addy nodded and tried to see over the debris.

When neither of them heard movements or shots for a few seconds, Addy risked another peek.

THURSDAY, MAY 26, 2005
1:07 P.M.
EL PORVENIR, CHIHUAHUA, MEXICO

Arlow powered the twin-engine airplane into a tight climbing spiral. He wanted to stay close to the action but needed altitude to provide overwatch. He had just passed two thousand feet when he saw the line of police cars coming toward the hangar.

"Danny, do you copy?" Arlow shouted into the radio.

THURSDAY, MAY 26, 2005
1:08 P.M.
EL PORVENIR, CHIHUAHUA, MEXICO

Daniel Byrd tried to slow his breathing as he got within sight of the metal hangar. He had no idea where Clete and Addy were and feared he might run up on the shooters.

He heard the radio chirp and pulled it to his ear. "Go ahead, Arlow."

Byrd could hear the anxiety in the pilot's voice. "Bad news. It looks like the shooters are getting backup."

Byrd kept pushing toward the hangar. The news caused him to jog faster. "Any chance they're coming to help us?" Byrd feared he knew the answer.

"I figure it's less than fifty-fifty," came the reply. "I heard the word "*Mátalos*" over the Mexican Police radio. I'm pretty sure that means 'kill them.'"

Byrd concentrated on getting to the Texans.

Then he saw the ditch. He could use it to give him cover

until he was close to the hangar. He jumped into the ditch and crouched as he moved farther west, bringing the M4 rifle up in front of his face.

The rattling sound made his heart stop. He looked down to see the brown rattlesnake coiled near his foot. He used the rifle barrel to scoop the snake up and throw it into the brush.

"Fuck!" Byrd said, then took a deep breath and pushed on.

He neared the end of the ditch where the taxiway connected to the runway, hunkering down and listening. The rattle he heard this time was a machine gun. Byrd took a moment to examine the ground for more snakes before he lay down and sighted the rifle.

The two assassins were hiding around the corner of the hangar, discussing the situation it seemed.

It was then Byrd heard the sirens in the distance. This time the sound wasn't the cavalry coming to rescue him. He pressed the button on the portable radio. "Arlow, how far out are the cops?"

The response was clipped. "I give you less than five minutes."

One of the gunmen looked around the corner of the hangar and fired off a volley. Byrd took the opportunity to shoot the man. He felt the recoil of the rifle and watched the man drop. The second man seemed stunned. He dragged his friend behind cover.

Byrd waited. He felt no immediate remorse for killing the gunman. He was focused on the corner where the other man hid.

He recognized the pistol shots coming from behind a pile of construction material to his left. When the pistol fired again, he anticipated the gunman's return fire.

The second gunman peeked around the corner. "Come on. Step out," Byrd muttered.

The second man was being cautious. Byrd had to be patient.

Byrd saw Addy expose her head and aim the pistol at the corner of the hangar, then fire two shots.

When the second gunman looked around the corner, Byrd shot him in the head. The man went down and lay still.

The sound of the sirens was too close for comfort.

THURSDAY, MAY 26, 2005
1:11 P.M.
EAST OF EL PASO, TEXAS

Rae pulled the van to the side of the highway. Rae, Jamie, and Montana were surprised they could see the Aero Commander sitting on the runway just across the river.

Montana spoke into the police radio. "Sergeant, we need to block the interstate now. Do you have an ETA on the ambulance?"

Helen Camos responded immediately. "I'm ready to shut down the eastbound lane. I have an air unit on the way to transport."

THURSDAY, MAY 26, 2005
1:12 P.M.
EL PORVENIR, CHIHUAHUA, MEXICO

Byrd ran to where Clete lay. Addy was crouched beside him, counting the number of rounds left in her magazine.

She turned and pointed her Sig Sauer at Byrd as he ran up to join them.

"Shit," Addy exclaimed. "Give a girl some notice."

Byrd was out of breath. Then he saw the blood soaking Clete's shirt. "How bad is he hit? Can he run?"

Clete motioned with his left hand. "You two lead the way. I'll be right behind you."

Byrd pointed the M4 toward the hangar and led Clete and Addy toward the runway.

"Arlow?" Byrd called into the radio.

"Go ahead."

"Get down here as quick as you can. Clete is hurt. The two gunmen are down, but I can hear their backup getting close."

Byrd saw the sleek plane bank and almost slam into the tarmac. The DEA airplane taxied up and turned onto the ramp. Addy and Clete ran toward the rear of the twin-engine Commander and began piling inside while Byrd loaded the hardware into the airplane.

Addy looked at Byrd. "Glad to see you, but I wish you had been a little faster!"

Byrd pointed at the men laying by the side of the hangar. "Should we check on them?"

Clete turned and said, "We can take a look at them from the air," through clenched teeth.

Clete squeezed into the seat Byrd had occupied earlier. Addy and Byrd shared the remaining seat. Addy looked suddenly worried. "What happens if we can't get this thing in the air?"

Arlow shrugged. "Every crash I've had, I've walked away from."

"How many is that?"

"Six," Arlow said, then added quickly, "But only two were my fault."

Byrd saw the first police car turn into the airport driveway as he secured the hatch. "We've got to get out of here!" Byrd shouted at Arlow.

Arlow applied power to the engines and the plane picked up speed. Arlow powered the airplane around the ramp and onto the runway.

Byrd involuntarily hunched over when he heard the first bullet slam into the airplane. Another round thudded into the tail of the plane as they became airborne.

Byrd looked over his shoulder as they roared over the metal hangar and turned north. Neither of the gunmen were moving.

"How quickly can we get Clete to a hospital? Can we get an ambulance to the airport?" Addy asked.

Arlow glanced back at her. "We have a Highway Patrol helicopter meeting us on the highway."

Addy craned to get a look. "Who worked that out?"

"Montana has been on the phone calling in favors." Arlow pointed out the window at the black-and-white car blocking the interstate. "The landing should be as interesting as that takeoff was."

THURSDAY, MAY 26, 2005
1:14 P.M.
EL PASO, TEXAS

"Forty-two-oh-three to One-oh-four, do you have an ETA?" Helen Camos called on the DPS radio system.

Deke Waldrip was flying a Eurocopter EC-145 helicopter as fast and low as he could since he had gotten the call from Trooper Worley ten minutes ago. He glanced at his instruments to make sure the helicopter was operating at maximum speed.

"One-oh-four to Forty-two-oh-three, we are less than three minutes from I-10. What am I looking for?" Waldrip scanned the horizon as he talked.

"One-oh-four, I'm blocking traffic at milepost eighty-eight. Be aware that a DEA airplane will be landing on the interstate."

Waldrip triggered the transmitter without thinking. "What the hell?"

THURSDAY, MAY 26, 2005
1:19 P.M.
EAST OF EL PASO, TEXAS

Motorists stood outside their cars on the interstate as the Aero Commander taxied up to the highway patrol car and the DPS helicopter sitting in the eastbound lane of I-10. Montana helped Clete into the back of the helicopter, before climbing in beside him. The helicopter blades whirled faster, dust swirled, and the DPS bird was in the air headed to University Medical Center. Addy and Jamie helped Byrd load Clete's borrowed guns and ammunition into Rae's minivan.

"Good job, GBI man," Addy said. Byrd shrugged.

Addy climbed into the van and Rae accelerated away. Byrd watched the van fishtail as they went. He smiled for the first time, happy to be back in the USA. He nodded his head toward the van and told Helen Camos, "She drives like me."

The Texas Highway Patrol Sergeant smiled back. "She drives like a trooper. I need to recruit her."

Byrd ran back to the Aero Commander and belted himself into the seat, gave Arlow a thumbs-up, and sat back as they raced along the highway and shot into the air.

Dagget sat quietly in the front passenger seat. Byrd looked one more time in the direction of the hangar in Mexico. He couldn't make out anything as the DEA plane rolled to the left and climbed.

THURSDAY, MAY 26, 2005
6:55 P.M.
EL PASO, TEXAS

The ramp at Fort Bliss was blazing hot as the Aero Commander taxied up and Arlow at last shut the engines down. Dagget had been silent for the entire ride back while Byrd had spent the time worried about his future and his career.

Byrd watched a Humvee marked Military Police pull up beside the DEA airplane and saw the passenger's eyebrows shoot up when he saw the bullet holes in the tail of the airplane.

Dagget turned to Arlow. "Well, you're done now!"

Arlow shrugged. "They came because I wanted them here. They will be willing to testify that the three of us left together for an official flight on your behalf. We came back a couple of hours later. Just the three of us."

Dagget was shrewd, but he wasn't stupid. He glared at Arlow for a moment, then unbuckled his seat belt and climbed over toward the rear of the airplane. As he worked his way to the door, he looked for his suit jacket.

Byrd caught his eye. "I think it's back on that runway

in Mexico," Byrd said, "with your DOJ credentials in the pocket."

Arlow met Dagget's gaze. "If it were up to me, I'd have left you with your jacket," Arlow said.

Dagget gave Byrd a dirty look before climbing onto the tarmac, then he waited for Byrd to unlock Clete's truck and get the air-conditioning running. He glanced back at the seat in the back of the DEA airplane, covered with blood, then walked to the truck. Dagget knew when it was time to fold.

CHAPTER 33
TIED UP BY LOOSE ENDS

THURSDAY, MAY 26, 2005
8:05 P.M.
EL PASO, TEXAS

The meeting had been hastily called that night. Major Crosby leaned against a wall, looking at the assemblage.

Douglas Hogan started them off. "Dagget is on the way to the airport. He just called my office and left a message."

Byrd spoke up. "What did he say?"

"He told me he was never here," Hogan said, smiling.

Byrd nodded. "I never saw him."

Hogan turned to Byrd. "What was my part in all this?"

Byrd watched Crosby for a reaction. "You kept Dagget occupied while we loaded Clete's equipment into the DEA airplane. Thanks, by the way." Byrd waited for Hogan to put the pieces of the puzzle together. "We didn't want Dagget to know I was listening in on Clete and Addy's progress. I had to get Clete's bag hustled into the airplane before you dropped him at the airport. I had wanted access to his DPS radio to listen to the transmitter he was wearing. It was good luck that his radio gear was in the same bag as his rifle."

Hogan was excited to have supported the rescue operation. "Well, I spoke to my boss a little while ago. He says we will be prosecuting this case to the fullest. Omar Warren and Adam Benjamin have been transferred to federal custody."

Everyone turned to Crosby as his cell phone rang. He flipped it open and said, "Crosby."

Crosby waited and then said, "Governor, can you and the chief hear me?"

There was a muted response, and then Crosby said, "Ranger Petterson and Investigator Riley were rescued and are back in Texas. Ranger Petterson was wounded, but his injuries aren't life threatening."

Stetson Crosby listened to the voice on the other end. He said, "Chief, I can guarantee you that no Texas officers crossed into Mexico. It was the DEA and the GBI."

Crosby listened and then said, "Yes, Chief. That would be the *Georgia* BI."

The people in the room heard more muttered conversation, and then Crosby stepped back. He was still on a call as he said, "Governor, Clete is at the hospital, but he should be released anytime. No one else was injured. I'll make sure you get a full report."

Crosby folded the phone, then looked at Byrd. "Now, Agent Byrd, you and I need to figure out what that report will say."

Byrd sighed and stood up. He walked over to Crosby and said, "Can I use your phone for a minute? I have to call someone in Georgia."

Crosby handed it to him and waited. Byrd pulled the worn business card from his wallet. The phone rang three times before a voice mumbled, "Hello?"

Byrd turned and made eye contact with Jamie Abernathy. He winced as he said, "Director Hicks?"

"Danny Byrd? Is that you?"

"Yes, sir. I need to bring you up to speed on something," Byrd said.

The silence on the other end of the phone was deafening.

Montana and Clete came in the door as Byrd finished explaining things to Buddy Hicks. Byrd was shaken, unsure if he would be allowed to return to his job.

Clete moved slowly, his right arm secured in a sling, and his shirt was bloody and missing a sleeve. "John Wayne used to get shot in the arm all the time. He made it look painless."

"Clete, what the devil are you doing here? You should be home," Crosby said.

Clete dropped into one of the chairs by the table. "I had to come by and thank everyone," Clete said. "I thought for a minute we wouldn't make it. The marshals said the building was closed."

Byrd tapped Crosby on the arm. "My boss wants to talk to you."

Byrd could hear Hicks ask, "Do we have any problems on your end? I assume you heard everything Danny said?"

Crosby cleared his throat. "If the government over there is willing to admit they let our people be set up, then we'll address any fallout from their rescue. It's as simple as that."

"What about the two men who attacked your people?" Hicks asked.

"We had a DPS airplane with a special zoom lens fly over the area, looking from the US side within thirty minutes of the shootings. There were no bodies and no sign of any law enforcement investigation at Rojo's airport. I took the extra step of calling the Inspector General for the Policía Federal Preventiva. He told me his people had learned of the assassination attempt and had escorted the Texas officers to safety. That is the official story, as far as the Mexican Government is concerned."

"And if they make an issue, does the State of Georgia need to be prepared to defend our people?" Hicks asked.

"Again, per the governor, there is no way the Texas Rangers would allow anyone other than a ranger to execute any rescue. By direct order of the governor, DEA Agent Arlow Turner and GBI Agent Daniel Byrd were appointed Special Texas Rangers for the purpose of supporting special ranger operations. The governor made the appointment retroactive."

Byrd could hear Hicks's chuckle. "I like the way you do business. Any other issues I need to be aware of?"

"We don't have an issue unless it's a problem to offer Agent Byrd a full-time job as a Texas Ranger."

Byrd heard Hicks ask, "Do you have anything to trade. I can probably make you a deal?"

Crosby laughed. "Are you in a hurry to get these two back?"

"Not if you need them."

Crosby looked over and made eye contact with Addy Riley. "I'd like for them to stay long enough to see Investigator Adeline Riley receive an appointment as a Texas Ranger."

Addy looked shocked. "I'm not on the promotion list."

Crosby smiled. "Under extraordinary circumstances, the governor can still appoint rangers to the service."

Byrd heard Hicks say, "By all means. Send them back when their work out there is done."

Crosby said, "Thanks, Director. You've got some good people working for you."

Crosby closed the phone and looked at the faces around

the table. "Is there anything else we need to handle before I go home and fix a tall drink?"

Montana stood beside Clete. "Why don't we just make it one big celebration?" Montana asked.

Clete struggled to his feet. "I'm all for that. Let's find a place we can all get a drink."

"Actually, I was thinking while everyone is here, let's get married," Montana said.

Clete sat down hard.

Byrd shook Clete's left hand and laughed. "Congratulations."

FRIDAY, MAY 27, 2005
9:35 A.M.
EL PASO, TEXAS

Byrd passed Arlow a patch to cover the bullet hole on the skin of the Aero Commander. The two men had spent the last hour examining the control cables. Arlow had meticulously examined each cable and wire as Byrd held a flashlight for him. Arlow did most of the work as Byrd supplied moral support.

"How much trouble do you think we're in?" Byrd asked.

Arlow shrugged and stopped sanding the patch he had just placed. "I think Dagget will keep his mouth shut. He doesn't gain anything except some little bit of satisfaction by trying to jam us up."

Byrd wasn't convinced. "He seems petty enough for that to be enough."

Arlow turned back to the patch. "That's not how the

company works. They'll do all they can to pretend none of this happened. As long as we go along with their narrative, we'll never hear another word about it. The CIA was never here."

Byrd sighed. "I sure hope you're right."

Arlow turned and grinned. "Me, too."

MONDAY, MAY 30, 2005
3:05 P.M.
EL PASO, TEXAS

Addy Riley stood at attention in front of Major Stetson Crosby. She looked small next to the six-foot-seven ranger. She had taken the oath and Crosby handed her husband the official cinco peso badge. The shiny badge, hand stamped from a Mexican silver coin, was a symbol of the rangers' heritage. Addy's husband pinned it to her chest as the witnesses applauded.

Crosby stepped to the side of the room and took a call on his cellular phone. After several minutes, he rejoined the group.

Judge Obregon Ortega stepped up and prepared to perform the wedding ceremony. Crosby motioned for Byrd to join him.

Byrd stepped over beside the major. "That was Douglas Hogan with the US Attorney's office."

Byrd didn't like the look on Crosby's face. "Uh huh," Byrd said.

"Omar Warren and Adam Benjamin have been released from custody by the marshals. Seems someone from Washington showed up at the lockup with a writ."

Byrd's jaw dropped. "Where are they now?"

"Marshals say they tracked them to a flight to Cambodia," Crosby said. "Cambodia doesn't have an extradition agreement with the US, by the way."

Byrd looked around the room. Montana looked radiant in a simple white dress, and Clete was smiling from ear to ear. Addy polished her new silver star with her sleeve as she, Rae, and the other men laughed.

Jamie was watching Byrd and Crosby. Byrd could see on her face she sensed something was wrong.

Byrd walked over to Jamie. "Omar and Adam walked."

"What?"

"If I had to guess, our friend Dagget got a writ and they were released."

The two GBI agents watched the wedding party assemble. Jamie leaned over and whispered in Byrd's ear, "Can you believe that?"

Byrd nodded. "Sadly, I can."

Jamie shook her head. Then she whispered in Byrd's ear. "I may buy drinks tonight. And don't you tell Doc!"

Byrd smiled. "Scout's honor."

MONDAY, MAY 30, 2005
7:10 P.M.
EL PASO, TEXAS

Byrd and Jamie Abernathy sat at a table in the corner of the motel bar. There wasn't much to say. They had sent the newlyweds off and congratulated Addy, then they got a cab back to their motel. They were booked on a flight on Tuesday.

"Do you think there is any chance we can get the Warren crew back to face charges?" Jamie asked.

Byrd shook his head. "That's above my paygrade. I sure do hope so. But they probably have passports in some other name, or even a dozen more names. I doubt we got them all in Bowens Mill. Who knows?"

Jamie stared at her drink. "So, nobody goes to jail for all this mess? That just isn't right."

Byrd slumped in his seat and took another sip of the vodka and tonic while Jamie sat back in her chair and examined him over the top of her drink.

Jamie finally asked, "Are you okay with all this? You haven't said much about what happened in Mexico."

Byrd hung his head. He kept his eyes low as he said, "I'm okay. I did what had to be done. But taking a life isn't easy. No matter what the circumstances are, you can't help but wonder about the impact of what you did."

He looked her in the eye, then Byrd sighed deeply. "I wonder if those gunmen had children or people who depended on them. And I wonder if killing may come too easy one day."

"I understand. But you shouldn't eat yourself up. Those men were trying to kill Addy and Clete. As you said, you did what had to be done."

Byrd stared at his drink. "One minute someone is alive, with hopes and dreams. The next, everything is gone. Even bad people must have dreams. It takes a toll when you realize you snuffed that out."

Jamie slumped back in her chair. "I see what you mean. But they chose the path they were on, not you."

Byrd shrugged in response. Jamie seemed to sense that talking might help him.

"What were you thinking when you and Arlow went

into Mexico? Did you consider that you could end up in a Mexican prison?" Jamie asked.

Byrd thought the question over. "I was mostly reacting. When we made all those plans the other night, I never for a minute thought everything would go sideways. We were so sure of a kidnap attempt at the border."

Jamie nodded. "I see that, but I'm talking about what *you* did. You ran up on that shooting by yourself, you could have asked Arlow to come with you. Why didn't you do that?"

Byrd shook his head. He shook the ice in the drink and took a last sip. "Arlow wanted to come," he said. "But I was more worried about getting stuck in Mexico alive than getting killed there. I knew he was our only way out."

"So, you just ran up there alone? Danny, you could have been killed. You get that, don't you?"

Byrd looked around the empty room, trying to avoid her eyes. "It's kind of crazy, but I wasn't ever really scared. My heart was thumping to beat the band, sure, but I never felt that panicked feeling."

"Are you trying to tell me you're some kind of fearless warrior?" She said it with a smile.

Byrd stared at his drink. "Hell no. I'm scared of snakes and heights. I'm scared of women and commitment. I'm scared of fucking up an investigation or getting another agent hurt. I guess I'm scared of everything."

Jamie smiled, trying to lighten the mood. "All good traits, I figure."

Byrd wouldn't meet her gaze. "I guess I figure I'd want somebody to come running if I needed help. Hell, it was kinda nice to be the cavalry for a change."

Jamie shook her head. "Danny Byrd, the one-man rescue mission. You know that's why the bosses get mad at you. You dive in headfirst without gauging the consequences. You had to see that the rescue mission might not have ended well."

Byrd ran both hands through his hair. He picked up his drink and swirled the ice cubes for a moment. "We're in the state where the motto is 'Remember the Alamo.' Those defenders at the Alamo died for a cause they believed in." Byrd looked up and met her eyes. "Isn't there anything you'd be willing to die for?"

Jamie thought it over. "You took a damned big risk. I hear Mexican prisons are hellholes."

Byrd smiled. "If people hadn't taken risks when World War II broke out, we'd be speaking Japanese."

"More likely German on our side of the country," Jamie pointed out. "But I guess there are things any cop needs to be willing to die for." Jamie held up her drink. "These margaritas are to die for. I think I might get drunk tonight."

Byrd smiled, wryly. "It's overrated. But sometimes you just need to do it." Byrd turned the glass up and drained the last of the alcohol. "I'm ready to get back up in the North Georgia mountains and work a couple of killings with Doc."

Jamie nodded in agreement as she finished her drink.

The bartender approaching them got Byrd's attention. He sat up and watched the man's hands as he stood by the table. Byrd put his own hand over his drink and shook his head.

Jamie pointed to her drink. "I'll have one more."

"I'll get that right away," he said and then he turned to Byrd. "Would you be Mr. Byrd?" the bartender asked.

Byrd glanced up, curious. "I am."

"The front desk has a phone call for you," the bartender said.

Byrd ambled to the desk and the clerk passed him a phone. "Byrd," he said.

"Danny?" Tina Blackwell's voice came over the line.

"Hey, Tina," Byrd said. "We'll be back tomorrow. The Director approved us to stay."

Tina ignored what he said. "Danny, Doc is in the hospital."

"What?" Byrd thought he had misunderstood.

Tina sighed. "He was getting dressed this morning and had a heart attack. They got him to the ER and did everything they could, but it's touch and go."

Byrd slumped against the front desk. "Is he going to make it?"

"Sorry, Danny, the doctors can't say. I know you two are close."

Byrd couldn't think of a reply. "Okay. We'll be back tomorrow afternoon."

He handed the phone back to the desk clerk. He dreaded telling Jamie and hoped his eyes wouldn't well up again.

Byrd wiped his eyes and walked stiffly toward the bar.

EPILOGUE

MAY 26, 2023
CANTON, GEORGIA

Byrd followed the hearse in his truck, the concealed blue lights flashing rhythmically in tribute, through the city streets and onto the interstate. He could see the line of police cars, sheriff's cars, and trooper cars, their blue lights flashing, stretching toward the horizon. He knew Chuck Page would have been impressed. Byrd thought it was the least the profession could do for someone who had to endure the burden of a law enforcement life.

The procession, with law enforcement officers from all over the area, was a show of respect for Page and what he represented. Byrd had seen far too many of these processions winding through other cities as cops were laid to rest.

Ralph Page, Chuck's youngest brother, sat on the seat beside him. "I don't believe I've ever seen so many cop cars," Ralph said.

"We do funerals right. Every cop knows that he'll end up being the guest of honor one of these days, hopefully after a long retirement. So, we celebrate the lives of those who go first." Byrd glanced over at Ralph. "You wouldn't believe the number of officers who turn out for a line-of-duty death. Those are the most impressive."

Ralph watched in silence as the motorcade slowly made its way toward the memorial park.

Byrd passed men standing outside their cars, ordinary citizens with hats over their hearts, honoring the life of a person they had never met. Average folks who respected life and took a moment out of their day to show it.

Deputies on motorcycles blocked the last turn as the long line of cars filed into the cemetery. The marked police cars had to double and triple park to get off the main road.

Byrd helped Ralph Page out of the truck and the two walked toward the tent erected over the gravesite. Officers in dress uniforms streamed to the grave. The officials created two lines for the family and friends to walk between as people neared the tent.

"Was you ever married?" Ralph asked as only an elderly man can get by with.

Byrd shrugged. "I guess I just worked too much."

"Do you wish you'd gone another way? Chuck always regretted his family being tied to his job. Him having to run out in the middle of the night, and her not knowing when he'd come back. Missing the kids' ball games and such."

Byrd stopped and stood for a moment. "Ralph, I could lie and say I never married for exactly those reasons. I've seen other men whose families suffered for this thankless job."

Ralph looked Byrd up and down. "The good Lord puts us here for a reason," Ralph said with conviction. "I'm sure your life has had purpose."

Byrd smiled. "You know what my prayer is every night?"

"Nope. What?"

Byrd looked around at the crowd gathering around the tent. "I pray every night that whatever it is that I was put on earth to do, I hope I didn't do it today."

Ralph laughed, nodding, his gray hair shining in the

sun. He turned and left Byrd to ponder as he found a seat under the funeral home tent.

Byrd stood a moment, looking around. He was in no hurry to watch the casket lowered into the ground.

He reached into his left pocket and felt the challenge coin that was always there. It was his habit to keep only his car keys in his righthand pocket, in case he needed to make a quick getaway. The left front pocket kept everything else, coins, folding money, and credit cards.

He thought back to a trip to Texas in 2016. He had met Montana and Clete for dinner the last night of a conference. Clete gave him the challenge coin made to commemorate his promotion to Major in the Texas Rangers. The front bore the legendary rangers badge. Without looking, he remembered the moto inscribed on the back: "Say what you mean, mean what you say, and cover the ground you stand on."

The slogan was a variation of the concept of honor above self. And the idea that people should stand for something.

Byrd looked to the sky, saying a quick prayer for Chuck Page and for the lawmen who had gone before him.

He ended up standing near the back of the burial tent. Everyone listened to the preacher give a short sermon. Most of the mourners were surprised when the police officer in a kilt played "Amazing Grace" on the bagpipes.

As Byrd and Ralph headed back to the car, Byrd said, "I'm tired of going to funerals. I was at one just two days ago."

Ralph nodded. "The older you get, the more you go to. Wait until you're my age."

Byrd stopped and smiled. "Sometimes you go just to make sure they're dead."

"Is that the only reason you'll come to my funeral?" Ralph asked, laughing.

Byrd shook his head. "No, but I *had* to go to the funeral I mentioned. The family was from up this way, and I had known the deceased. The GBI wanted someone there. We found out the day before the funeral that she died of a fentanyl overdose."

Ralph gave a questioning look.

"Lots of counterfeit pain pills on the street are loaded with fentanyl. Just a speck of fentanyl can be deadly," Byrd explained.

"Street drugs? A junkie?" Ralph asked.

"Judge," Byrd said.

"Wow!"

Byrd corrected himself, "Actually, she was a Justice of the Supreme Court of Georgia. Justice Linda Pelfrey." Byrd smiled.

"Was she someone you worked with?" Ralph asked.

"She's someone. I met her during some wild times." Byrd watched his Page for a reaction. "I guess it's hard to imagine a pill addict sitting on the Supreme Court," Byrd said.

Ralph shrugged. "I'm eighty-five years old. I've been to two county fairs and a goat roping. I've seen things just as crazy, I bet."

Byrd opened the door of his truck for Ralph. "I'm not taking that bet."

ACKNOWLEDGMENTS

My life wouldn't be what it is without the support of my family and friends.

My wife, Grace, has endured the life of a cop's wife. She made sure the kids got to school or to a sporting event when I got called away to a murder or a drug deal. She was a loving mother to our children, and now "Gigi" to our grandchildren. We met on a blind date during the days when smuggling airplanes seemed to fill the skies. Then I had to cancel the next three dates in a row to run off to South Georgia and chase down smugglers. She must've seen something there, but I still haven't figured out what.

I must also recognize the Texas contingent: Zack, Erika, Addy, Rae, and Stetson for their faith in me; and Shelia, Mark, Ashley, and Alexis for their sage counsel.

The biggest thanks go to Emma, who worked with me, corrected me, and encouraged me. Emma has been, and will be, my sounding board, my editor-in-chief, and most importantly, my daughter.

To say that I love each of those individuals listed above would be an understatement!

I must thank my first readers, who found the little mistakes and inconsistencies, or were kind enough to tell me that what I wrote just didn't make sense. In particular, a shoutout to Jess Hampton and Mark Hodge for being willing to take on that responsibility. Jess, a retired electrical engineer, read the drafts I sent him with an eye for detail. Mark, a former naval aviator, kept the airplanes on course and communicating with the ground controllers in the right language.

I am indebted to Sheriff Lane Akin, of Wise County, Texas, a former Texas Trooper, DPS Narcotics Investigator, and Texas Ranger, for some details I had trouble figuring out. And thanks to Fanny Butler for giving me guidance on Spanish. As always, mistakes about the Texas Department of Public Safety, the rangers, the troopers, any of the details about aviation, Spanish language, or anything else, are all on me.

I have had the pleasure of meeting, talking with, and being encouraged by so many people that it becomes hard to list everyone. Thanks to the friends at the Book Exchange. The Book Exchange is a small, non-national chain bookstore in Kennesaw, Georgia. If you are in the area and have a chance to check them out, please do.

I might not have lived to write this tale of modern-day adventurers without the partnership and help of DEA Agents Wayne H. Smith and Ludlow C. Adams; United States Customs Patrol Officers CW Moore, Norm Bergstrom and Brad Luca; from the GBI, Special Agent in Charge Mike Eason, Deputy Director Kent Wilson, Inspector Harry Coursey, Special Agent Mike Mason, Special Agent in Charge William 'Billy' Shepherd, Special Agent Charles "Chuck" Severs, Special Agent Daniel "Danny" Drake, Special Agent Victor "Victor Recardo" Rethman, Special Agent Tim Millians, Special Agent John Willis, Special Agent David Hartsfield, Special Agent in Charge Greg Owen, Special Agent Rick F. Jordan, Special Agent in Charge John A. Cagle, Special Agent Dan Gardiner (RIP), Special Agent Jim Burch, Special Agent in Charge Kathy Rigdon (RIP), Special Agent Frank Ellerby (RIP), and Special Agent Mike Dull. These men and women were beside me when the airplanes landed or the boats came ashore. There were others, but I walked the swamp, slept on the ground, and followed cars around the southeastern US with this crew.

For more information, some of which is true, about the wild and wooly days of drug smuggling in Georgia, I refer you to a book called *Waffle House Diaries* by my good friend Wayne H. Smith.

I couldn't have made this book work without telling and retelling the stories this adventure is based on to my friends still in law enforcement. A shoutout to Ken, Jamie A. and Jamie G., Buster, Tommy, Jay, Lindsay, Fanny, Frank, and the other Ken. And especially to Walter. I've watched each of these men and women as their law enforcement careers have flourished.

And last but not least, thanks to the staff at BookLogix who helped guide me through the process of getting my stories in print.

ABOUT THE AUTHOR

Phillip W. Price began his law enforcement career in late 1974. On January 8, 1978, Price was appointed to the Georgia Bureau of Investigation (GBI) as a Special Agent. Price served in various capacities with the GBI, from working in extreme South Georgia swamplands to the North Georgia mountains. SAC Price retired on October 31, 2006, with twenty-nine years of criminal investigative experience.

In 2010, Price was hired to lead the Cherokee Multi-Agency Narcotics Squad (CMANS), a drug task force in Canton, Georgia. Price re-retired on December 17, 2021.

Price has an associate in arts degree from Reinhardt University, a bachelor of science degree from North Georgia University, and a master's in public administration from Columbus State University.

He lives in Canton, Georgia.